BOSS CROKER

Padraic O'Farrell is the author of *The
Burning of Brinsley MacNamara* (1990),
The Blacksmith of Ballinalee (1993), *Who's
Who in the Irish War of Independence and
Civil War 1916-23* (1997), and a Michael
Collins novel, *Rebel Heart* (2000), which
won critical acclaim. He has also written
two historical plays and a musical based
on the Great War. He lives in Mullingar,
County Westmeath.

To Tim and Maxine

and to the memory of their beloved niece, Catherine Mullane, whose talents in music and other artistic disciplines brought joy to many. Even in her courageous fight to hold on to her young life, she retained her sparkling wit and good humour that inspired those dear to her and helped alleviate their distress at her sad parting.

BOSS CROKER

PADRAIC O'FARRELL

SITRIC BOOKS

First published 2003 by
SITRIC BOOKS
62–63 Sitric Road, Arbour Hill,
Dublin 7, Ireland
www.sitric.com

A CIP record for this title is available from
The British Library.

1 3 5 7 9 10 8 6 4 2

ISBN 1 903305 11 X (hbk)
ISBN 1 903305 10 1 (pbk)

Set by Susan Waine in 11pt on 13pt Dante
Printed by ßetaprint, Clonshaugh, Dublin

PREFATORY NOTE

Boss Croker is a novel. Its characters are based on personalities and events from the life and times of Richard Boss Croker (see Chronology and Illustrations at the back). The author uses carefully researched details from Croker's career as a framework for his story. While many of the characters existed, they did not necessarily react to factual incidents in the way described.

BOSS CROKER

PROLOGUE

'I SEE YOUR MAN Sam Beckett is writing about Boss Croker's Gallops.'

'Ah, will you ever forget him? The poor auld Boss. Lord, but the court case was a sight! All the childer tryin' to get him from lavin' everything to the wife.'

'The second wife. A whippersnapper of a young one not half his age. An Indian, if you don't mind! Maybe the childer was right.'

'Ah, now!'

'Francie saw his ghost again last night.'

'Boss Croker's? Where?'

'Above at the graveyard. Hovering between his own grave and Honor Bright's.'

'The murdered prostitute?'

'Yes.'

'Jaysus! That's the third time he was seen.'

'All dressed up in his stripy frock-coat, waistcoat, gold chain and silver goatee; dapper as ever in his bowler.'

'Go away!'

'Sure as bedamned! They should never have moved him from the big house. He was restin' easy there.'

'Francie was woeful close to him as a gosoon.'

'Who knows how close?'

Like seeded dandelion in a storm, the story spread among the customers in the Gallops Bar. Heads bent closer over creamy pints of stout, and voices moulded and garnished the account until it featured Francie sitting on a headstone at Kilgobbin Cemetery, smoking one of the Boss's cigars and talking to him. All about the dead man's carry-on in American politics and in English and Irish horse-racing.

'Francie said he was starting to rave about his regret for some terrible thing he did during his life. Oh, Francie and himself were getting on famous until Honor Bright, the whore, came along and said to the pair of them, "Get away to Hell out of that; I'm expecting a client and that's the only horizontal slab that's any way comfortable."'

'He built the Mussolini for to lie in peace in Glencairn and he should never have been stirred.'

'Mausoleum, you thick!'

'Arthur Griffith, Oliver St John Gogarty and Michael Collins carried the coffin.'

'Collins wasn't there. It was Alfie Byrne – the Lord Mayor.'

'I'm telling you, Collins was there.'

'And I'm telling you he was no such thing.'

'Francie says he was a gentleman to work for.'

'Indeed and he was. Paid the highest wages, with a nice bonus at Christmas. Maybe a big cigar, too.'

'There was no auld bullshit about him.'

'Not like some we know!'

'You never said a truer word.'

'He was never the same after the court case.'

'Ah, that was woeful. Family squabbles over money does terrible things.'

'The Boss's second wife stayed on seven years after Croker dying. Francie says she used to sit on the Mussolini talking to The Boss and that she claimed he told her to leave all her property to Timothy Hall.'

'To Tammany Hall, you clown! It's a big place in New York.'

'Oh! Anyway, she didn't do that. She gave Glencairn over to relatives and went back to the States.'

'It got horrid run down.'

'Until our landlord here bought it, fair play to him.'

'With money spent by us! Francie says he only paid £8000 for it and that he got that much for the gallops alone, from Joe McGrath.'

'A great horse-trainer, McGrath.'

'None better. Do you know something?'

'What?'

'I heard that the British are going to buy Glencairn.'

'For what, in the name of Jaysus?'

'For their Ambassador's residence.'

'Go away!'

'So Francie says. And he should know.'

'Oh, indeed and he should.'

'I suppose. But, back to Boss Croker –'

ONE

YOU WELSTEADS wouldn't fight if your enemies were at your mothers' knickers.'

Blue in the nose and red in the eye, Major Croker's cousin from Ballingarde in Limerick was embarrassing the wedding guests with his slurred drunkenness. He was telling everyone within range about his ancestor, Sir Eyre Coote.

'My goddamn forefather, Sir Eyre Coote, was a respected general and Commander in Chief of the British forces in East India. The chap assisted Robert Clive to break French rule. Then, as Baron Clive of Plash ... Plassey, he became India's f ... first governor to boot. To boot the lousy Sheek ... Sikhs from the Punjab! Ho! But lift a glass in this Quartertown home of Major Henry Croker and let us toast the grallant goom ... gallant groom, his shon Eyre. But not shon and heir, ho, ho!' The cousin slapped Eyre Coote Croker on the back.

Frances Welstead, the bride, blushed.

'Shocking!' her aunt, sitting next to the boasting Croker, hissed.

'No, ma'am, I didn't shay "shtocking", I shaid "knickers". The Crokers always get to the b ... bottom of things. We ad ... admit to being a roistering, gambling, horse-loving Limerick clan, given to joining the a ... army, drinking and chasing women. And Eyre is one of the b ...best. A hard man for the women since he was out of short trousers, by Jove. Frances will have more than her hands f ... full.' His coarse guffaw left no doubt as to what he meant. 'But at least the Welsteads are Presbyterians, like ourselves and, l ... like us, have been in Ireland for over two hun ... hundred years.'

'The Welsteads own wide acres in Ballywalter and Shandangan in West Cork, and are a lot more refined,' the bride's aunt whispered her companion. 'The groom is penniless from living too frolicsome a life. As for their army service, didn't we all hear the Muskerry saying:

Croker, Crewys and Copplestone
When the Conqueror came, were all at home.'

When Major Henry stood to speak he admitted that Eyre Coote was his favourite son.

'As a young lad he took on a gang of anti-landlord Whiteboys who burned the house, hay and oats of one of our tenants,' he said. 'At eighteen, he out-rode me at the Duhallow Hunt and he ended the day by trailing the fox's brush behind and galloping his horse through the door of the local she-been, leaping over a keg of ale and drawing rein only when the animal's head was almost touching the terrified innkeeper's behind the counter.'

The Major's eldest son, John Dillon Croker, was jealous.

————

A glance at the gilt dial of the grandfather clock ended John Dillon Croker's reverie. The heir to the late Major's mansion opened the drawing-room door of Quartertown House and called to his wife Elizabeth, 'The carriage is waiting.'

'Oh! So soon?' Elizabeth puckered a fair eyebrow and left down her embroidery ring.

'Yes, we should go immediately. It's fifty miles to Balliva and we want to be there before dark.' Impatiently, John slapped a carriage whip against his high leather boot before adding, 'Frances would pick November to give birth!'

'Women alone do not choose the dates, darling!'

'Christ, hasn't she given my wastrel brother seven children already? And what has he done? Lost his commission as a captain in the army and squandered his wife's fortune trying to live like a country squire in the West Cork countryside. My poor, foolish father bought Balliva for him but he has not the slightest idea about farming.'

'He's good with horses,' Elizabeth ventured.

'Not to mention fillies!'

'Now John, it was kind of him to invite us over.'

'Kind! All he wants is the chance to badger me for money.'

'And poor Frances nearing her time too! You are hard on him, John.'

John admired his wife's graceful walk down the steps and across the pebbles. He was pleased that he could afford to dress Elizabeth so elegantly, but would have preferred if she were wearing her fine crimson gown for something better. He hated visiting Eyre and Frances.

Awaiting their arrival at Balliva, Eyre Coote Croker's staff were sitting around the great oak table in the kitchen. Malachi Hurley, the farm steward, had come in from the fields and was having something to eat.

'The ground is as cold as a stepmother's glance; we're wasting our time tilling it,' Malachi was grumbling. After buttering a thick slice of sodabread, he poured himself another mug of tea and began tucking into the plate of cold bacon that his ten-year-old daughter Nellie had laid before him. Perched on a stool beside him, the little girl was studying tea-leaves in the cups that had come down from the library. Her lisping prognostications were amusing the staff. All but Sarah Donnelly, who was upstairs helping the midwife in the Mistress's bedroom.

'The child will grow up to be a man of great power and – Father, it's going to be a boy,' Nellie shouted excitedly. 'And he will cross the sea twice. Janey Mack, he won't know if he's comin' or goin'!' Nellie turned the cup to the light.

'There's somethin' else there that's a bit puzzlin'. I'm not sure I like the look of it.' Malachi smiled at his daughter telling the cups, just like her late mother had taught her.

'Whisht! Did you hear that?' Nellie called to the others. 'It's the guinea-fowl. Oh, Father!' Great tears filled the child's eyes as she ran to Malachi and threw her arms around his shoulders. 'Father! Oh, Father!'

'There now, child. Sure it's only an auld *piseóg*.'

But as Malachi was consoling his daughter, he looked sternly over her shoulder at Sarah Donnelly rushing in, smiling.

'It's a boy and they're going to call him Richard!'

The other girls rose and gathered around Sarah.

'Had she a hard time?'

'What weight is the babby?'

'We never heard it cryin'; did the midwife not slap its arse?'

'Oh, and the poor Mistress wanted another girl.'

'But hasn't she Harriet, Eliza and Mary?'

'She probably don't want another like them other pups.'

'Ah, I like Master Henry. I'm not too fond of George or young John, though.'

'Do you know he was the second John? Another John died.'

Sarah laughed. 'The Master didn't care, anyways. He likes girls. Hadn't he a *cailín* from the Winking Widow of Rathbarry.'

This brought whoops from the others and they danced around, tossing cloths, dusters and besoms in the air and catching them. Up and down the stone flags they went then, like Slattery's Mounted Foot marching in a line to the scullery; every one of them knowing that a child had been baptized privately in the Protestant church of Mallow four months before and was given the name Mary Anne, after its mother.

Nellie Hurley did not join in the merriment. She closed her eyes and felt the salt tears drop onto her perspiring face, making it even hotter. She snugged into her father's shoulder and whispered in his ear.

'When the guinea-fowl cry after a boy baby comes, it means he will kill or be killed before his time.'

'Sshh! There now, alanna,' Malachi whispered softly. 'Don't you be frettin'. All auld nonsense, that's what that is.'

Yet Malachi wondered. His own mother had told him how guinea-fowl had cried all night at the birth of a distant relative of Eyre's; Edward Croker, had been murdered at Raleighstown in the County Limerick the previous month. The Master had kept the news from Frances, because of her confinement.

A footstep on the stairs sent the women scattering in all directions around the big kitchen, attending to real or imaginary chores. Malachi Hurley stood and dusted crumbs from his mouth while his daughter whipped the plate from before him and ran with it to the scullery. The others followed and slammed the door behind them.

Malachi retrieved his high-crowned, sweat-blackened hat from beneath his *súgán* stool and started shuffling slowly towards the back door. He would have preferred if the Master did not catch him in the kitchen at such an early hour of the evening. Yet a land steward, even of a miserable estate, should not display undue haste, because one of the women would surely be peeping through the keyhole and would gossip in the village later. She would brand him a coward, and his peers would hold him up to ridicule. He had his hand on the latch of the door when the Master entered.

'Ah, Hurley! Just in time!'

'In time sir? In time for what?'

'For the celebration, of course. And another Croker boy child. Sarah! Where's Sarah?'

Sarah Donnelly opened the door of the scullery a little. When she slipped out and closed it again, she was trying to suppress a smile. Eyre took a key from his waistcoat pocket and tossed it towards her. She missed, and went scurrying under the table to retrieve it. The hem of her dress caught and Malachi Hurley frowned as his Master leered at the exposed flesh of her legs.

'Whiskey from the cellar. Port wine and mead too. Drink your fill to the new son of Balliva. I got a glimpse of the little fellow. A fine, noble brow but he has the round visage of the Welsteads, I fear. I will drink with you until the midwife allows me to visit Mrs Croker. She had a difficult time, I'm told.

Broad at the shoulders, the little bull calf. Sit down, Hurley. Where are the other women?'

'In the scullery.'

'And a new boy in the manor! Call them out, man.'

Malachi stood and moved to do his Master's bidding. He knocked on the door and could hear the women inside trying to stifle giggles. He could distinguish every voice. All but Nellie's. She would still be fretting about the guinea-fowl, he thought.

'Come girls! The Master wants us all to celebrate.' Malachi opened the door and one simpering servant pushed Nellie out into the kitchen. She stood, a shy mite, wringing her skirt and looking up at a giant, not knowing what to do. Sarah Donnelly's tramping up the stairs from the cellar broke the awkward silence. Bottles were jingling in time to her panting breath.

'Well done, Sarah. One more trip and you'll have enough to get us started! Some tankards and glasses, Ellen, isn't it? Eh, little one?' He tickled Nellie under the chin. She scampered away, bare feet flipping on flags, glad of something to do. Climbing onto a stool, she took a glass from the shelf she could reach, then clambered down and laid it on the floor. She continued doing this until she had four glasses and two tankards. Then she reached up again, grabbed a towel from a nail and began polishing them. Eyre was already uncorking a whiskey bottle.

'Quickly! A glass, girl!' He whipped one from Nellie's hand, decanted a generous measure, and gulped some back.

'Here, Hurley! Oh, hang the formality. Here, Malachi! Malachi, by Jove. Ancient Irish High King, wasn't it? A bumper of malt, my royal-blooded man!'

Malachi smiled at the way he pronounced his name – 'Maul Youki!'

'Thank you, sir. I'll wait for the ale if you don't mind.'

'Ale for a male, Malachi? When there's whiskey available? You are a foolish man.'

'Foolish in one way, sir, but wise in another, maybe.'

Eyre was in no mood for philosophizing. Already he had poured a second measure. This time he added a little water.

'Must be temperate until I meet my wife,' he smirked.

'Now ladies, charge your glasses with port wine and drink to the health of Richard Welstead Croker.' Feeling foolish, the women stood in a bunch at the end of the long, scrubbed table.

'Oh, how silly of me. Let me uncork the wine.' Eyre went to work and three loud pops demonstrated the speed at which he was able to use the corkscrew. A gossamer of vapour rose from every bottle as he clutched one and began pouring lavishly. 'Come on, take a glass.'

Malachi Hurley took the jug of ale that another woman had brought from the pantry. He was pouring it slowly into a tilted tankard and watching it form a smooth, white head when Eyre raised his glass and called:

'Let us drink! I give you baby Richard Welstead Croker.'

Sarah Donnelly sniggered and sipped. Nellie placed the glass to her lips but did not. The older women gulped.

'No, no! This is a toast. You must repeat the name to which I drink. So, you all answer my call by repeating, "Baby Richard Welstead Croker". Now! Again!'

This time, they observed the ritual. All except Nellie.

After four drinks, Eyre began picking his steps carefully across the kitchen, waving his arms about and shouting orders.

'Prepare food, lamb, fish, quail. I shot some quail today. Let us have a feast. My brother will be arriving from Quartertown with his wife. Prepare a room and look after them if they arrive before I come from paying a short visit to my Fran ... Fran ... to my wife.'

He was still mumbling as he ascended the stairs and Sarah Donnelly ran to close the door after him. Strapping her back to it then, with legs and arms spread-eagled, she laughed coarsely and the others took it up.

'Drink! Drink to Richard Welstead Croker,' one called, splashing more wine into her glass as she imitated the Master.

'Oh, how silly of me, let me uncork the wine,' another screeched, tossing back a glassful.

'Fran ... Fran ... to my wife,' Sarah Donnelly spluttered again as she replenished her glass. 'And he calling for lamb and the divil knows what. Doesn't he know there's not what would feed a cricket in the larder. A plate of prawkeen and a few heels of griddle bread,' she rubbed her ample stomach. 'Twould be like giving a daisy to a bull for breakfast to put that on the table for the five of us, let alone that John fellow and his stuck-up wife. I hate when they come.'

Malachi smiled as he began scraping the dottle from his clay pipe. He puffed through the stem twice and observed wryly, 'It matters not to a Croker if there's no food in the house – as long as there's wine in his cellar. Yes?'

'True! They'd drink the quarter sessions and go back for the courthouse!' Sarah staggered across the flags, pretending to be tipsy. She knelt in front of the huge sheep-dog that lay by the fire. 'Hey, Shep! Shep, you cur, wake up and shpeak to your bhetters.'

Shep stood and was eye to eye with Sarah, who said, ' I've a hangover the size of Carrauntuohil, so I have, Shep, an' do you know whah?' Then louder, exaggerating her concern, 'I'll tell you whah, Shep. You can bite me arse with your fangs; you can tear the rags off me back with your paws, buh

Shep! For the love of Jaysus, don't bark.' The others laughed and poured some more and called on Sarah to dance.

'Dance! Me dance? And the state I'm in?'

'Yerra, we know you're only lettin' on. Come on!'

The fun was beginning. Malachi's pipe and the carbon parings from its bowl went flying as the girls quickly pulled the table to one side of the kitchen to make room for a set dance. There was an air of great gaiety. It continued until the guests from Quartertown arrived. The servants served them and the Master with a meal of sorts in the cold dining-room. Then Eyre Coote brought John to the drawing-room while Elizabeth chatted with Frances in her bedroom. After the washing-up, the older girls went home. They knew the Master would return to the kitchen as soon as his guests retired for the night and that it would be wise to be out of his way.

Late that night, when little Nellie was asleep in Hurley's cabin, Malachi was sitting alone on his stool by the corner of the hearth. Drawing long and slowly on his pipe, he brooded on his position as steward at Balliva.

'He won't last, so he won't,' he muttered to the soot in the chimney place before spitting into the *griosach*. Malachi studied the black smudge it made, before fading in a frass of ash. He knew enough about dark spots in the Croker family background to worry. He know also that Eyre was one of the few Crokers who had left the military service involuntarily; his behaviour would not have been tolerated in any society, not even in the Crown Forces.

Malachi's lips began drawing rapidly, protesting at finding only air. Cursing the pipe's emptiness, he leaned back and prised a knob of tobacco and a worn knife from the Rosary hole. When he had hacked off a few slices into his palm he started grinding with the ball of his fist, teasing with his fingers and poking the new charge into the black bowl. Then he took a glowing coal in a black tongs, raised it carefully and sucked the new tobacco to life.

He thought about his late wife and her dying request that he should look after Nellie. 'Keep her innocent as long as you can,' she had begged. 'Don't be having her around Balliva when there's animals being serviced or cows calving. She'll get to know about these things in God's good time.'

But how will she learn? Malachi was agonizing. With no mother to guide and instruct her when 'God's good time' came. And he couldn't tell her. No father could mention things like that to his daughter.

He sighed, rooted in his waistcoat pocket for his Rosary, dropped on his knees and prayed to the Blessed Mother to ask God to guide him to do the right thing. Then he stood, turned down the wick in the old brass lamp, placed his hand behind its globe and puffed to extinguish it. With the dying light of the fire, he picked out the route to his bedroom.

TWO

Eyre Coote Croker strolled out the front door of his home and through the orchard to its right. He looked down on a stretch of clear blue sea towards which the low hills of his own land funnelled. After skirting a hillock he came to the bend in the drive where he always paused to look back and admire the cut-stone barns and outhouses he had built, the walled garden he had cultivated. They framed Balliva House, with its five elegant windows on the upper storey and four below, all embracing a stout central porch. To the left, the gentle ridge of Greenacres. O'Donovan's and Hurley's smallholdings led the eye towards the dancing waves of Dunnycove Bay. The bracing air and the magnificent scene nearly always lifted his spirits. Not today, however. Eyre had much on his mind: legal matters about which he knew little. He strode ahead determinedly, not even noticing young Peter O'Donovan in the paddock by the drive. Nellie was with him, trying to teach little Richard, now five years old, how to milk a cow. The lad was ducking his head and lisping abuse at the animal for flicking its tail into his face. Peter and Nellie had been minding Richard since infancy and the three had become great pals. Nellie tried calming the cow with a blessing, as was the way with country folk.

'Slán agus Día leat!'

Richard's small hands were unable to coax milk from the udder. Nellie encouraged him.

'Stand on the stool, Richard.'

'It'll topple over,' Peter warned.

'No, it won't.' Nellie was lifting the boy onto the stool and standing him between the cow's legs.

'Now get a good grip on his tits and squeeze,' Peter was advising but Nellie had more initiative. She was coaxing Richard to finger the teats along with her and imagine that he was doing the milking. Milking over, Peter and

Nellie took a hand each and swung Richard as they all were making their way back for the farmyard. Peter took care of the milk pail with his other hand. The youngest Croker felt secure grasping milky fingers. And happy. He could not remember far back but his most warming recollections were of Nellie's and Peter's kindness.

Malachi Hurley was driving the chestnut horse, Macha. The name came from Liath Macha, foaled at the same moment that Fionn Mac Cumhaill was born and later his steed. The sturdy animal was finding it easy pulling a four-wheeled cart up the drive. It contained two large churns full of water that he had taken from the Well of the Thistles, named because it lay in the corner of neglected bottoms near Ardfield. A track that had developed through years of use cut like a grey strap through a proliferation of high, purple-topped thistles. Malachi hailed a *meitheal* of neighbours who had gathered and were discussing local topics, especially the potato failure, while they sliced through the prickly weeds with scythes. The silver innards of the fallen stems shone. They would remain like that for a few weeks until a new and vigorous growth raised them again and they became untidy black relics.

Malachi had tied sacks across the tops of the churns but the roadway was rutted and water slopped through, dripping its trail in the dust behind. He tipped the peak of his cap at his Master passing by. Eyre twirled his silver-topped cane before pointing it at Malachi.

'See that the sick heifer in the haggard gets a gallon, Hurley.'

'Yes, sir.' Malachi resented the instruction, issued as if he did not know his job. Eyre had said it only to impress his authority on the *meitheal*. By the time Malachi was passing, Peter, Nellie and Richard had crossed the fence to the drive.

'Whoa there!'

Macha halted and began grazing from the grass beside the drive. Malachi took the pail of milk, allowing Peter to lift Richard into the cart and leap up beside him. Nellie sat on the shaft and steadied herself by holding on to Macha's harness.

'Hup!'

The children chatted to Malachi for the remainder of the journey. After reaching the yard, Richard tugged Peter's hand and brought him into the orchard to see if the bird he called 'Robbie' was there. It was. Tugging a worm from under an apple tree. And Richard told Peter that Balliva was the best place in the whole world and that he and Nellie were his best friends forever.

Meanwhile, Eyre had reached the end of the drive and was passing through the ornate gate-piers and onto the high road from Clonakilty. On the final bend of the road, he left the shelter of the rising hills and arrived at the Red Strand. It was like reaching another climate. From his home, it had appeared calm and blue. Now, he had to steady himself and hold down his wide-brimmed hat as the wind tossed the sea against the rocky coastline, sending towering sheets of excited spray into the air.

Eyre began walking along the pebbled shore, trying to figure out the legal complexities of selling Balliva. His solicitor, George Gregg, had been unclear. All this talk about indentures and first part and second part was confusing. At times Eyre could not tell if he were selling to Hough Smith Barry of Foaty or James Roche Dean of Innishannon. But then, it probably did not matter all that much who bought – as long as he got the fifty pounds offered in sovereigns. That would purchase passage for himself, the girls and Frances to America and leave just a little to help them all get settled.

He hoped his older sons, Henry, John and George, would be welcomed at Quartertown. Later, he might coax his tight-fisted brother to buy tickets and send them out too. Or perhaps he might earn enough to do it himself and save being under a compliment to the skinflint. But what about Richard? He was not yet six, after all, and Frances would want to bring him, he felt sure.

The boy would be broken-hearted leaving Balliva and his robin and Nellie, not to mention Peter O'Donovan. Peter was only a couple of years older but he had become better than a brother to the lad. Friends were often more loyal than relations, Eyre thought, and had to admit that his own family loyalty was often suspect. Yes, Richard would fret about Peter, most likely. And Nellie.

'I'll have to begin hardening up the lad soon,' Eyre muttered to a yellow ragwort, a *buachalán buí* he promptly beheaded with his cane. 'Still, I shouldn't have kicked him that night! He probably thinks I hate him.'

Eyre understood the risks involved in moving to America. The poor Catholics in the parish had become used to going. Especially since the potato blight had arrived, depriving them of their staple diet. They even held American wakes before a departure, where they all got drunk and drowned their sorrow at parting. Why were they always able to get drink and not food? They must have been like the Crokers, he quipped to himself, before becoming serious again.

The stigma of failure hung over those members of the broad Protestant family who decided to emigrate. They were supposed to have the establishment firmly behind them. So having to abandon a good farm of sixty-eight acres would be taken as a sign of incompetence and of ineptitude. Like his Catholic neighbours, he had relied too much on the potato crop. His livestock had been his salvation for a while, but now that had dwindled and only a few animals remained. Although he feared that in America they would be treated just like all the other Irish immigrants, there seemed to be nothing else for him to do.

Telling Frances would be the most difficult part. While the rapture of their early years of marriage had dissipated, mainly due to his philandering habits, he still felt some love for her. She loved him too, he thought. And Balliva House! It would break both their hearts to leave it. They had become accustomed to its large rooms that could be kept warm from good fires of timber from the estate. They loved West Cork, with its wild promontories and secluded beaches. In better days, when they had five horses, they had enjoyed riding together along the sand-hills to Dirk Bay or Dunowen Castle.

Mourning the loss of these good times, Eyre cursed the legacy of Croker intemperance he'd embraced with such exuberance. Now they were almost as destitute as their Catholic neighbours. Of an original staff of twelve, only Sarah Donnelly and Malachi Hurley remained, and they would have to be dismissed soon. Packing everything up and going to America just like the Catholic peasants would be shattering – unless!

'Unless!' He shouted it to the tall rushes by the track. 'Unless, unless!'

His psyche had been dulled since his discharge from the army for bad conduct, but his craving for soldiering nurtured dreams. America might represent a fresh chance to follow in the footsteps of his ancestors. As he had done before for a short while: marching, hardening the body, inspecting his troops on the barrack square. And the mad capers! Listening to older officers' tales of military derring-do or humorous escapades.

In the New World, the Irish had spearheaded the drive against colonial frontiers in pre-Revolution days. They had pushed out to the edge of the wilderness in Pennsylvania, Maine and Maryland and down the Great Valley to the Carolina Piedmont. Four signatories of the Declaration of Independence had been Irish: Thornton, Smith, Taylor and Ruttledge. So Eyre's Irish background might be his entrée to a life he still hankered after. It could, of course, take some time, but after getting Frances and whatever children they brought settled, he would concentrate on making useful contacts and then he might be able to find a way of securing a commission in an Irish regiment.

The idea rocked the gloom and put zest into his step. The more he thought about it, the more exhilarated he became. When he reached the lane above the shore, he deliberately dashed into the sea-spray splashing across it in great foamy sheets. It washed his hat away and he chased it, laughing at the chill of surf dripping inside his clothes. He grabbed its brim and tugged it down on his head again, squelching more water from his hair.

There would be yet another advantage in going to America. After the meagre threshing of the harvest he'd had too much to drink and had lured a young woman from Ardfield into the haybarn. Her father was making accusations that were not without foundation. The man was becoming more threatening.

But little Richard? Bringing him would present all sorts of difficulties.

Unless?

Unless, indeed!

Would Malachi Hurley allow Nellie to come as the little lad's nursemaid? For some material gain in these hard times he might. Nellie as Richard's nursemaid? He and Frances could make sure Nellie kept her place as an employee. And they could find her some other employment as soon as they did not need her for Richard any more. Richard would grow up to meet more sophisticated women and, being a Croker, would forget about Nellie. And Nellie was growing into a delightful young woman. Very delightful!

Eyre dashed into the surf again.

'America mightn't be such a bad place at all,' he shouted at a swooping gull.

THREE

'POOR RICHARD'S FIFTH BIRTHDAY and only scraps to eat.'

Nellie Hurley's long black curls bounced against red cheeks that were glistening with perspiration. She'd been stoking the fire that roared in the wide-open hearth. With a slim hand that belied the rough work to which it was accustomed, she drew back her hair, revealing eyes almost as dark. One stubborn wisp refused her fingers and danced over her finely shaped nose. Nellie puckered her lower lip to blow it back, left down the cup and returned to the fire. She leaned over it to settle the iron kettle on the crane. Firm breasts strained at her calico dress. Her father noticed and sighed. Nellie was so tall and well developed! She reminded him of his wife, Mary.

'Yesterday was your mother's sixth anniversary, Nellie.'

'I know, Father. Wasn't she lucky to escape this hardship?'

'Galloping consumption! God, it made her a frightening imitation of the woman I married.'

'Ah, try not to be fretting, Father. This Famine will turn us all into skeletons if we don't get a good potato crop soon. You should have seen the women and children I met on the road to Clonakilty yesterday! Like *sceacha* in winter they were.'

'On their way to the workhouse, I suppose.'

'They say the fever is all over Carbery.'

'This god-forsaken farm is finished anyway. Do you know, Nellie, I think you'd be better off away out of here altogether?'

Malachi studied his daughter's reaction closely. The question was prompted by something the Master had hinted at, something which would have horrified his late wife. He too would have dismissed the idea, if it were not for the Famine. He didn't want Nellie having to go to a soup-kitchen. Or worse. If he were right about the Master's hint, it would be a great chance for Nellie. But going with a Croker! With Eyre Coote Croker!

'Christ!'

'What's wrong, Father?'

'Ah, nothing.'

Now Nellie was standing back, allowing the flickering flames to highlight every aspect of her face, her neck, body and legs. Malachi reached for his mug and slowly brought it to his lips.

If the Crokers left Balliva he might get a job with the new owner. But there would be nothing for Nellie; of that he was convinced. The liberal reforms introduced through the efforts of Daniel O' Connell had brought about more movement of workers. Some were arriving in Cork and other Munster counties from distant parts of Ireland. In the south, most Protestant landlords had been prospering since the 1798 Rebellion, unlike those in Leinster, the West and the North, where that struggle was greatest. From there emerged the wandering workers, *spailpíní*, who still sought employment wherever they could find it. Large landowners were taking advantage of the situation, offering meagre wages.

The depleted staff at Balliva considered themselves lucky to be still employed. But Malachi knew this would not last much longer. He sympathized with Eyre's plight. It must have been difficult to endure being a hard-up Presbyterian. A poor Catholic had plenty of sympathy and the offer of helping hands. If a farmer of another religion fell down on his luck, he could expect only scorn from his own and delight from Papists at his predicament. Roman Catholic Christianity did not stretch to helping a dissenting neighbour.

Malachi recalled the last time Eyre had been in the kitchen. Six months ago, surely. Sarah Donnelly had scalded her upper thigh when she'd dropped a pot of steaming pigs' mash. Nellie had run to fetch the Master.

'Go to the haggard and collect some goose dung,' Eyre had shouted, rushing from the library with some camomile. When Nellie had arrived with the evil-smelling substance, he mixed them together and applied them to the burn. Malachi had noticed Eyre's attention to Sarah's seared flesh, and the long time he had taken rubbing on the compound. He remembered how he had then sworn to himself that if Eyre took any liberties with his daughter, Malachi would tear him limb from limb with his bare hands. Then there was the talk about his bastard child in Rathbarry. And here he was contemplating Eyre's hinted proposal!

Malachi tried to balance all this worry against his trust in the Mistress. He felt she knew her husband's failings as well as anybody else and would be particularly vigilant towards Nellie, of whom she was very fond.

In the haggard next morning, Sarah Donnelly was feeding the last two hens with food leftovers she had collected from sweeping the kitchen floor.

'Tioch! Tioch! Tioch! Oh, how are you Malachi? Have you a bad head from celebrating Richard's birthday with buttermilk?'

'Hello Sarah.'

'There's somethin' I've been meaning to talk to you about, Malachi,' Sarah said and twiddled her finger in the basin.

'Yes, Sarah?'

'It's hard to put into words, but I think you should know, Malachi. I was sounding her out and discovered that even though your Nellie has been in Balliva House for two births, she has no idea of how they came about.'

'I know. She thinks they come from the fairies or from under a head of cabbage or something.'

'But wouldn't you want to tell her, Malachi? She is a fine girl for her age and the men about here are hoors for the handle.' Sarah winked and added, 'Especially one we know well.'

'Her poor mother wanted me to keep her innocent, Sarah. I even kept her from seeing the cows calving and the pigs farrowing.'

'Well, God rest your wife and it's none of my business, Malachi, but I think it's wrong to have Nellie that way. And dangerous.'

The Master calling for help from a stable put an end to the conversation. Sarah went scurrying back to the hens shouting, 'Oh Jaysus!' instead of 'Tioch! Tioch!' Malachi headed for the stable. Eyre Coote Croker was gently squeezing the flesh above the seeping sore on Macha's leg. He looked up at Malachi.

'A bad dose of farcy. Place a poultice of dried mud from the bottom of Lough Crannóg around the swelling. Fast him for twenty-four hours and pour the contents of this bottle into him. It'll make him sick, but have no sympathy. Saddle him up and I'll gallop him across the Hungry Ridge until he defecates. Then, after a few days on grass, he will be as right as rain.'

Eyre handed over a physic containing a glass of turpentine and a gill of linseed oil. He smiled as Malachi took the bottle and led Macha from the stable. Prescribing medicine for animals always pleased him.

'If you go, the neighbours will miss your cures, Master. They say they're as good as they'd get from Biddy Early, the wise woman from Clare.'

'I tried most of the treatments when serving with the horse artillery, Malachi. I became a type of unofficial veterinarian physician in my regiment. More luck than medical skill, I can assure you, but the experience helped.'

'If Murtagh didn't cure you, that fellow's dose doesn't have a ghost of a chance,' Malachi muttered to Macha. When Eyre was opening the gate of the haggard he called back: 'That matter I mentioned to you about Nellie, Malachi. I may be in a position to have a discussion with you soon.'

Malachi shuddered.

Eyre's treatment worked for Macha, but the concoctions he had prescribed for the rest of the livestock did not. Over the following weeks Malachi buried three sows, a calf and the remaining two hens. On neighbouring farms, many more animals suffered from a dreadful disease that nobody could diagnose. It had the appearance of farcy, but was far more debilitating and awful. Ribs pressed paper-thin flesh into tapered ridges until the animals' sides looked like button accordions. Dogs staggered around farmyards, tongues swollen by seeping sores and heads bowed from dry growths that hung from their snouts. Huge strips of rotting flesh fell from the thighs of beasts and birds. They lay in barns, in sties and in fields, bellowing or squawking in pain.

A month later, labourers' families living in cottages around Balliva began crying in agony too: from the pain of typhus or hunger. Their desolate wails carried across the still evenings like keeners at a wake, as women with gaunt white faces tottered weakly to the stench-laden potato fields and sprinkled Holy Water. Many prayed loudly for their Lord to rescue them from their ordeal by obliterating the filthy blight and by killing the lice that was spreading the typhus. A few implored Jesus Christ to take them from their ghastly plight altogether.

There were no cries of anguish from the victims who contracted cholera. Severe dehydration weakened them and suppressed their urine and their saliva. Their vomiting and chronic diarrhoea, neglected for days – even weeks – made the stench of their homes overpowering.

The Famine was growing worse and new babies kept arriving as intercourse offered a respite from wretchedness, and the Roman Catholic Church stipulated it be practised for procreation only. Not even the virulent fevers prevented a population explosion. Midwives were struggling to coax occupants of hovels to practise hygiene during the birth process, but few could muster the strength to comply.

Eyre never had the patience or industry necessary to run a small farm. Now, in difficult times and with his tentative plans to emigrate, things were no different. He was still hatching impractical schemes while lacking the perseverance to see them through.

Heretofore, Frances had overlooked these deficiencies because Eyre's wit and imprudence made him a refreshing contrast to his more staid peers. She had even forgiven him her many pregnancies. But now he had dissipated her fortune as well as any farm income that had accrued, with no regard for the family's tomorrow. She was in fear of what might be in store for them if they remained in Balliva. John Dillon Croker might take charge of John, George and Henry and her uncle in Ballywalter might pay to send them to a boarding-school. If the worst came to the worst and they were left to fend for themselves, they could probably survive. They were strong and able and spent many evenings fishing the sea at Muckruss Head, catching enough to prevent them from starving. The girls were showing signs of great beauty and pleasant temperament and would, hopefully, get good husbands some day. Richard's welfare concerned her, however. He could easily succumb to typhus in this blighted land.

Frances worried and wondered why none of her Protestant neighbours were in the same plight. Even those with fewer acres than Eyre. Some were so untouched by the Famine that they were setting up soup-kitchens in their haggards and homes. Zealous about their religion, they were constantly doling out sustenance for souls while they proselytized unashamedly. Was that why they seemed to thrive, perhaps?

Bad as Eyre was, she could never see him going to those extremes. He would never accept aid in return for beslobbering the establishment. Or the Church. Yet, while things at Balliva were bad, with animals perishing and crops failing, the family members were, so far and thankfully, quite healthy. Frances wondered if they should sell the farm and leave. She spoke to Eyre about it when he returned from the miller of Timoleague.

'Two bushels, that's all the oatmeal he would give me; and a few pecks of seed barley.'

'Perhaps he had no more. The government is buying up a lot. For their relief schemes.'

'My God, Frances. You are naïve. Those so-called relief schemes are rackets. They are impounding all the grain to look after their own supporters' bellies.'

'And are we not supporters? You were in the army! In what better way could you support your government?'

'All in the past, Frances. These days, loyalty to the State is represented in cash, woman. Golden guineas come before valour – not that I displayed much of it. But we'll survive.'

'How will we survive, Eyre?'

The Master of Balliva noticed the steely undertone. Not at all like Frances, whom he had often considered to be somewhat unintelligent and frivolous.

'On fresh air, perhaps?'

Sarcastic too, by Jove.

There was a rising blush to her cheeks when Frances continued. She had never spoken to her husband quite like this before. But the image of a small boy with square shoulders and an impish smile commandeered her mind's eye, approving her accusatory tone.

'What about Richard's future? Isn't it about time we considered that. Not to mention the rest of the family and ourselves. You and I.'

She did not seem to have any control over her words. It was as if everything she was uttering surged from somewhere deep in her soul.

'There are families being wiped out all around us. Malachi Hurley's cousin lost eight children last week. They were carried on a cart to a common burial in the sands near Owenahincha. They say the sea will find them and deliver what remains of their flesh to the sharks. Are we going to await a similar fate and sit back in the meantime and do nothing? Are we, Eyre? *You* may, but if you think I will, you are wrong.'

'What will you have me do?' Croker was posing the question so meekly that it was almost reverential. After some delay, he whispered an added 'Frances?' Almost as if he had experienced some urge to worship this woman. The unexpected gentleness deflated her, and for a moment Frances wanted to forget her urgent mission and go to his arms as she used to do many years before. Instead, she recovered her poise, looked him squarely in the eye and demanded in a monotone, 'Tomorrow you see the solicitor about selling Balliva. We are going to emigrate. To the New World.'

To her disbelief and utter amazement, her husband said, 'I have already been to the solicitor. But the only offer I can get is fifty pounds.'

Frances was dumbstruck but, recovering quickly, she rushed to her husband and kissed him on the cheek. She had no wish to emigrate but anything would be better than the hell through which they were living. What's more, the matter had been settled without even an argument!

'I love you so much, you rascal. Why did you not tell me?'

'Because I thought you would be furious at the idea.'

'Oh Eyre!' This time Frances kissed his mouth.

FOUR

T HE BARE UPSTAIRS ROOM in Balliva House echoed Richard's cough. The faded picture of a bearded man grinned up at him from yellowing newspaper. Black lines defined gaps between floor-boards beneath. They sliced off the top of the man's head for sneering at a little boy's misery. He had not thought he would miss his brothers so much, and he had cried for a long while after they left with his uncle and aunt the day before.

'They will learn how to ride horses properly,' his father had mumbled. But something was telling Richard they had not left just for that. Wonder what was so special about this America place that they had to go to? Bet it wouldn't be half as good as Balliva.

From under the skirting, a scrap of linoleum put out its tongue, a reminder of the items that were taken up and sold at the auction of household goods. For Richard it now became an outline of the beach around Balliva. A pink flower had only half of a petal and two inches of green stem. Could someone so young cut himself off from his father and mother and sisters, already in the long-cart outside? Quicks of peeling blue wash rose from the mottled mildew below the wainscot. Often, in bed at night, he had counted them. At least, he thought so. He could count to eight.

'Good at sums for his age', his father had said.

When he pulled the shutter from its hiding-place, a spider ran across the sill and Richard recoiled. Only for a second. He could not leave without his secret box. On tiptoe he reached up and got it from the space where the shutter had rotted. Black, webbed dust tumbled and made him sneeze.

So loud in the emptiness! Echoing like his memories.

His small hand rummaged in serge and deposited the box deep in his breeches pocket. He would hate the new suit as long as he had to wear it, and that was always for a five-year-old.

'Richard! It's time.' Frances's voice sounded unconcerned. Loud too, resounding through emptiness. His own voice slid around the lump in his throat and cracked.

'Coming, Mother.'

A last look at his lost private world. The robin he had so often studied from the window picked the wrong moment to perch on its sash. It swivelled its little head sideways as if disapproving of the vacant room. Tiny red feathers brushed against the glass, revealing grey-white under-down. There was no great heaving or snuffling when Richard's tears started, nor when they coursed quietly down his face past his reddened cheeks.

Red, under-down of grey.

A robin, and a young boy with a shattered dream.

They were all on the long-cart when his father pulled the door for the last time. The sound seemed to visit all the rooms and come back out through the windows. Why were tears so hot, Richard wondered.

Crunching down the avenue, they took a left turn for Clonakilty. Little Peter O'Donovan, thin and gaunt, stood on the bank of the field where they had kicked around an inflated pig's bladder so often. His best friend was now twisting the hem of his tattered jacket, mud on his face, not really knowing what to do. Mother had said the O'Donovans had hardly any food to eat. Why did they not bring Peter to this great place across the sea, if that was so? Then the two of them could get a whole lot of pigs' bladders and tie them together and float back to the Red Strand on them. Peter gave a small wave and ran away. Richard bit his lip, trying not to cry again. Malachi Hurley noticed and allowed him to take the reins.

Malachi was silent, thankful that the Crokers were leaving him Macha and the long-cart in return for bringing them to Cove. The last cow too, together with its grazing until the new owner stocked the land. That was good. But Nellie going with them! How had he ever consented to Frances's pleas? Or accepted her guarantees about his daughter's welfare? America was offering her an opportunity he could never afford, but was she not far too young, too beautiful and innocent to be going to a strange country with nobody of her own to protect her? Was he not betraying his dead wife by letting Nellie go? Or should he have betrayed her earlier – by telling his daughter all she should know about her own body, as Sarah Donnelly had advised? But, Christ, how could a father discuss that sort of business with his daughter?

He had asked her to tell the priest she was going, in the hope the man of the cloth would pass on some advice.

He feared the Master. Terribly. Everyone in the parish knew how Eyre Coote Croker had had his way with a number of women. Still, the Mistress promised faithfully to take good care of Nellie and he trusted the Welsteads.

As the cart trundled along and Malachi began praying to his dead wife Mary to ask God and his Holy Mother to take care of their daughter.

Frances was wondering about Nellie too. And about Eyre. All the way from Clonakilty to Bandon. After that she became concerned about her daughters and Richard.

Nellie sat still, keeping her eyes on the road ahead and brooding.

She was in a state of shock over what had happened the evening before, what Eyre had done to her. After the evening meal he had said he would drink the cellar dry before he left Balliva. When her father was out attending to the cattle the Master had brought her to the library and had done a terrible thing to her. Drunk and slobbering over her and … oh, the thought of it nearly made her sick. It was over in minutes that seemed hours.

Eyre was considering the indignity of it all. Emigrating out of poverty and near-starvation. Just like the peasants. Travelling to Cove on a long-cart with his family, his labourer and Nellie, all packed together, holding on to pieces of luggage. If his brother in Quartertown had any decency, he'd have come over and brought them in his carriage. And Nellie? He was thinking he should have waited until they were in America. Confounded claret! But if she hasn't told Malachi before this, it should be all right.

'We're in Inishannon, where the fleas ate the excise man,' Malachi joked, drawing the cart into the roadside and letting Macha graze.

Harriet, Mary and Eliza went into a field with Frances. Nellie waited across the road until they returned, then went in herself. They all told Richard they were going to pick mushrooms but he knew better. Hadn't Peter O'Donovan told him girls had to sit down doing their Number One and that they wouldn't shoot it over the churchyard wall in a million years? He felt very important standing by the pier of the gate doing it beside his father, impressive with his sideburns and stovepipe hat and swallow-tailed coat. Why did Malachi have to go to the wall on the other side of the road, he wondered.

'I done my Number One with Father,' he boasted to the girls when they came back.

'We saw Mother's knickers when we did ours,' they retaliated.

'I thought youze were picking mushrooms?'

'You, Richard. It's *You*', Harriet corrected him.

'It's not me. I smell nothing. What would be wrong with making a bang anyway?'

'You better not do it on the ship,' Mary laughed and nudged Eliza.

'Are we going on a ship?' For the first time that day, Richard felt consoled.

'Did Father not tell you?'

'Tell me what?'

'That we're all going to America because the food in Ireland is nearly all gone.'

'Of course he told me. But he didn't say we'd be going on a ship. Gosh! A real ship?'

'How did you think we would get to America, then?'

'In the long-cart, I suppose.' Richard had not given the problem much thought.

'You're silly,' Eliza said as Frances called, 'Come on everybody. Something to eat.'

She gave them some griddle bread she had baked for the journey and told them to pass around two whiskey bottles filled with milk.

'Make sure to wipe the rim with your sleeve before you give it to the next person,' she warned. She offered a small medicine bottle-full to Malachi, saying, 'You can share that with Nellie.'

'Why have Malachi and Nellie a bottle all for themselves?' Richard asked.

'Be quiet, Richard,' Eyre ordered.

Richard pouted and deliberately spilled some milk on Eliza's dress. She slapped his thigh and it smarted. But he did not cry or tell on her. He remained silent for a long time, pondering the injustice of Malachi and Nellie not having to pass around their bottle among six, or wait for a second slug until it came around again. Life just wasn't fair, so it wasn't.

Passing through Cork city, Richard could not believe his eyes. The houses were so high and there were so many of them. And the shops! The girls joined in the expressions of amazement. All but Nellie, Malachi noticed.

'The number of carriages!'

'And all the people!'

'Wait till you see America.' Harriet was being superior again.

There were as many people on the road when they approached Cove. Gaunt, grey women and children. Richard could see bones through the skin of a boy no older than himself. No bigger either.

Except for his stomach.

Like the pig's bladder Peter and himself kicked. But so much bigger!

The unfortunates' eyes were dilated, stuck onto paper faces. Green spit running from their mouths. And there was a terrible smell that was getting worse. He saw Malachi and his father sniff and look hard at each other.

'Jaysus, they're grazing. Like cattle, Master.' Malachi could not prevent himself from speaking before being addressed. Unheard-of for an employee of the gentry.

'Some of them must have walked miles. The Galway ships are all full and they're coming from as far away as Roscommon and Leitrim, I heard. But the smell, Malachi. Isn't it –'

Eyre's reply went unheeded. Nellie was crouching, pressing her face into her lap. Frances rummaged in her pocket for what remained of her smelling salts. Richard's three sisters screamed and clung to each other as they rounded a bend and were jolted into horror at the sight ahead.

For a second, Richard thought it was a high bank by the roadside. Then he realized that it was a pile of corpses. Bodies of men, women and children. No! Not bodies. Bags of human limbs. Not like the bloated carcasses he and Peter O'Donovan had often seen whenever an animal died on a farm in the neighbourhood. The same colour, though. Brownish yellow. Decaying. Pieces of rags and sacking that had covered them now were disintegrated and lay twined through arms, legs and –

Frances reached for him and tried to bury his head in her breast, but he wanted to keep looking. He'd often wondered about the bumps on women, but never had a notion that they had nothing where men did their Number One. No wonder they couldn't get it over a wall. He turned to Nellie, who smelt nice, but the stench from the pile was too strong and he began to feel sick. A policeman was supervising some men with spades who were digging a huge hole beside the pile. Malachi tried to get Macha to canter, but he was too tired after the long journey. It took another half-hour to reach Cove, with nobody uttering a word about the horror they had witnessed and that they knew would stay with them forever.

They went directly to the ticket office. In one line, under a sheltering canopy, well-dressed men rapped silver-topped canes on hatches, demanding attention. Their womenfolk, stylish in cloaks and capes, stood nearby, beside fine leather trunks with protective cane ribs. They spoke in the haughty accents Richard had heard guests using whenever he visited his uncle and aunt in Quartertown.

The majority were in another line – most of the men wearing black waistcoats over white knitted *geansaithe.* Their breeches were of coarse, unrefined wool. Women standing alongside wore linen blouses or homespun jackets and red petticoats. Clamouring and pushing, a few were laughing but most were crying. It was an unruly mob, all packing the footpath outside a tin shed. In its doorway, an agent stood, waving a fistful of tickets. Although the men were haggling about the fare, they knew by the smug smile on the agent's face that his price would never come down.

Eyre thanked Malachi Hurley, shook his hand and said goodbye. Displaying more than a little distaste he then joined the mob at the tin shed. His family stood back, allowing Malachi to take leave of his daughter with as much privacy as was possible under the circumstances. He drew Nellie to the back of the shed, opened his collar and drew out a gospel. Its brown cord was threadbare. His wife had worn it during every confinement. God forbid that my child should need it until she marries, he thought as he began hanging it on Nellie's neck. She spoke for the first time since leaving Balliva, her words fumbling through a welling grief.

'How is it I never seen it before, Father?'

''Twas your mother's and I never took it off my own neck since the day she died.'

'Oh Father!' She threw herself to him, not knowing if she should tell him what had happened the previous evening.

'It's really for childbirth, but it protects against other evils too,' Malachi whispered. Then he looked deep into his daughter's eyes and appealed.

'Now, child. I want you to promise me you will go to Mass and Communion regular. Confession too. And say your prayers every night and morning like your poor Mother – God be good to her – taught you.'

'I will, Father. I promise.'

'Then bless you, daughter.'

They embraced quickly. He ran back, only taking time to wave briefly to the Crokers. Then he pulled himself up on the cart and flicked the reins. And drove out of his daughter's life, knowing the moment would haunt him forever.

Nellie crouched at the back of the shed, bent in grief and weeping bitterly: great, heaving cries borrowed from curlews and gannets. Tears stretched the gospel's words as she read:

'In The Name of God and of The Blessed Virgin, Amen. This Gospel will be found an infallible preservation against the fatality of child-bed and it is earnestly recommended to all women with child to carry it. And also, no gun, pistol, sword, or any other offensive weapon, can hurt or otherwise injure the person who has this paper in his possession.'

Sure what would I want that for, she thought. Childbirth? Why would anyone need a gospel for getting a baby from the fairies? Was Sarah Donnelly hinting at something? Wonder could she ask the Mistress.

She looked at the gospel again and whispered to it, 'Father should have given this to little Richard. Because of the guinea-fowl.'

She read the words again. Then looked up. Because the road they had come was winding, Malachi was almost facing her again but he did not realize it. His head was bowed, but she could see him wiping his eyes with the back of his hand.

FIVE

RICHARD HATED being on board the *Henry Clay*. He had got violently sick for the tenth time since leaving Cove. Frances had insisted on bringing him to the doctor. It was the thirtieth day of their voyage to America. The doctor gave him some medicine – horrible white stuff – and told his mother not to allow him food for six hours. Richard was feeling miserable. He was missing Nellie.

Little did he know that she had entered the doctor's cabin, moments after he had left. Now she was looking across the doctor's shoulder, studying the contents of his cabinet. Brown glass jars of castor oil, salts, laudanum. Hartshorn too. She shivered, remembering how its ammonia made her eyes water last time she used it. That was in Balliva, the day before Master Richard was born. The midwife had made her throw a few drops into the water before washing the clothes for the waiting crib. Born? She thought of something Sarah Donnelly had said the morning they had left for Cove and was now beginning to wonder if the fairies hid babies under heads of cabbage at all. Sarah was laughing and hinting about married men and women doing funny things, but, sure, you could not believe a word out of Sarah's mouth. Sarah had said that a man … God, had it anything to do with what the Master had done the evening before they left?

What did a midwife do anyway? Why was there one with the Mistress in the bedroom that evening? Confusion was forming a cloudy whirlwind in her mind until she began thinking of Richard again. How was the little boy behaving himself in the upper deck? The third day out from Cove, she had seen him. He looked small and lost and she wanted to hug him. Forgetting her place, she had started to run up the companion-way. A gruff sailor had caught her and thrown her back.

'Don't you see the line on the third step, you slut? You do not cross it. Ever!'

35

The doctor had completed his examination. He wrapped the worn tubes of his stethoscope around its rusted ear-piece and scowled. 'It is not sea-sickness you have, young lady. You are pregnant!'

'Is that bad, Doctor?'

'Christ! Another uneducated Irish wench,' he pronounced coldly. 'You are going to have a baby, woman.'

'Jesus, Mary and Joseph, how could that be? I'm not married!'

The fleeting suggestion of a smile crinkled the doctor's grey face.

'How many days out are we? Thirty? It may or may not have been conceived on board this hell-ship then. Either way, I hope the father is sailing with you.'

'Father? What do you mean *father*? I told you I'm not married.'

'That's why I hope he is on the ship. We must arrange for the captain to marry you. You may not be accepted by the immigration authorities in this condition, unless accompanied by the father of the child in your womb.'

'What's a womb, Doctor?' Nellie's eyes were full of tears. The doctor slapped his hand on the table. Once, twice. The third time it was a closed fist that hammered. Nellie was frightened.

'You are all the same. You know well how to go fornicating around the hedges and ditches. Like wild boars and vixens and badgers, pleasuring yourselves. And yet you nearly drown yourselves in holy wells and holy water, say your prayers and go to Mass. Over and over again in your Rosary you chatter away about the fruit of the womb. But you haven't the remotest idea of what it means. Or of your responsibility to the human race or to the child you might bring into the world through your lustful pursuits.'

'My wha', Doctor?'

'Lustful pursuits!'

'Yes, Doctor.' Nellie wondered had the doctor been drinking and why she had never heard that babies were brought into the world through a place with such a strange name.

'Do you know what being pregnant means, Nellie?' The doctor was trying to be patient.

'It means there will be a baby. But there's no cabbage garden on a ship so it can't happen until we land.' Nellie brightened up a little at her deduction.

'Nellie!' The doctor shouted, but quickly brought himself under control and called her name again. More gently this time.

'Nellie!'

'Yes, Doctor?'

'Nellie! Being pregnant means that there is a baby inside in your womb. In your stomach, to make it simpler. It will grow in there for some months and then will be born.'

'But how will it get from my stomach to the garden?'

'It will not get from your stomach to the garden, Nellie. It will drop from between your legs, head first.'

'Jesus!'

'No. Just an ordinary baby.' The doctor was pleased with his quip, even though Nellie hadn't the foggiest notion what he was talking about. She was too terrorized by what she was hearing.

'Sure a babby could get kilt that way, Doctor!'

The doctor dismissed his patient. In sheer frustration he made a dive to the medicine cabinet, pushed some jars of potions aside and pulled out a brandy flask.

'Merciful Jesus,' he swore, before he put it to his lips.

Nellie returned to the passengers' fireplace. It was set in the centre of the deck and steerage passengers of good behaviour were allowed to use it during the day. A large canvas suspended from the after-mast kept the miserable creatures from the gaze of those travelling in a better class. Their section of the deck could be reached by a narrow companion-way but another sailor was guarding that to prevent any trespass.

Nellie moved in a daze. Five men playing pitch-and-toss made way for her. A group of women praying over their beads eyed her suspiciously. They had spotted how her sickness came in the mornings. They had noticed her craving for blackberries too.

'Yerra there'll be a bush full of them over the next wave,' one of them had joked the first time Nellie told her. Now she hardly noticed the women. Her eyes were staring at the ash clinging to the bricks that lined the large timber fire-case. Its shape reminded her of the settee in Eyre Coote Croker's library.

The evening before she left Balliva.

Where he had laid her down and hurt her.

In the place where the doctor said the baby would come from.

What Sarah Donnelly had called a 'grunt' or something.

Only Croker had called it a different name. A woman's name that she could not remember.

She should have told her father.

And stayed back home with him.

A cinder dropped through the iron bars in front of the fire.

'It will be hot and red,' the doctor had said. A woman was making stirabout in a small skillet. It balanced on a few coals that she had raked on to the flag before the fire. *Leac na tine* they had called that stone in the cabins around Balliva. Reserved for the Master of the household when there would be dancing. Only at home, there would be a hollow ash pit beneath it, giving the footwork a fine resonance.

Another woman was baking bread on a griddle. Nellie had tried to eat some of it the previous day: two hard crusts holding uncooked dough and plenty of fresh air, because of the scarcity of meal. She smelt fish and looked enviously at the man who was holding a herring on a toasting fork above the flames. Two sailors on the deck nearby were watching everything. With legs stretched straight before them, they were mending a sail. Instead of a thimble, each had a piece of metal strapped by a thong to the ball of his thumb. Nellie wondered why they did not sit like tailors, with their legs folded beneath their buttocks. The smell of salt-damp canvas mixed with the tang of tar that another man was painting on a sheet. Nellie had been told that sailors called ropes by that name and was pleased that she remembered.

One passenger grabbed a small boy and dabbed some of the tar on his face. He took a rusty knife from his pocket and pretended to shave the lad. The little boy began crying and his father struck the man with his knife handle. A free-for-all broke out, men hitting and kicking, women screaming and children crying. The noise and the smells became too much. Nellie's stomach heaved and she felt as if it was turning over and over. She remembered what the doctor had said and was afraid the baby would fall out. So she ran to a mast of the ship and clung to it until the fight was over.

'Have some of my lobscouse!' A tall youth with fine features stood holding out a tin plate of stewed meat, vegetable and ship's biscuit. Oval beads of grease were floating on the thin gravy, changing shape each time the plate tilted. Nellie gulped back the resurgent nausea and tried to smile her gratitude, but failed. The lad's wide blue eyes showed hurt and when he bent his head, long locks of fair hair curtained a flushed, handsome face. Nellie wished to apologize but knew if she tried to speak she would be sick. She wanted him to remain, but was afraid of vomiting. He began shuffling away, but Nellie caught his ragged sleeve and managed to blubber.

'I'll be alright in a minute.'

He beamed the biggest smile Nellie had ever seen and she knew immediately that she could live with this man by her side forever. She wished the sickness would go away so that she could talk to him. With a nod of his head he indicated the pile of sacking under the life-boat. She followed him and noticed his long, clean hands that invited her to sit. He tugged at the knees of his heavy serge breeches and knelt beside her, looking at her and smiling.

'I'm Tim. Tim O'Mahoney. I've been watching you since we left Cove.'

Nellie thought him the most handsome creature she'd ever seen. He reminded her of a fellow in a picture she had noticed in a book about Greece that her father normally kept locked in an old trunk. Malachi had left it out one day and she had peeped at its illustrations. Only the fellow in the picture had no clothes on him. Nellie blushed at the memory.

'I hope you're not too shy to tell me your name.'

'Indeed and I'm not. It's Nellie Hurley.'

'If you're a Hurley, you must be from Cork!'

'I am. And where are you from yourself?'

'Tipperary.'

'The Stone Throwers!' Nellie laughed, feeling better. Tim sat down beside her.

'Were you ever there? In Tipperary?'

'I was never outside our own barony until the day I went to Cove.'

'Were things bad in Cork? The hunger, I mean?'

'Not too bad for us. The Master's sister-in-law sent over the odd sack of oatmeal from Quartertown. Unbeknownst to her husband who's a mean old get.'

'Who was your Master?'

'Not was. Is. He's on the upper deck.'

Tim scowled. 'Never fear he is.'

'He's not very wealthy, if that's what you mean. He had to quit the country too. He started the voyage down here with us but the Protestant chaplain arranged for him to go up. He and his wife brought me to look after the youngest when we reach America. The missus is lovely. A real refined sort of woman. And I'm mad about the *garsún*. Little Richard. He's a dote. But a tough nut betimes.'

'And could your Master not have brought you to the swanky deck and let you look after the lad during the voyage? You'd be well fed and comfortable up there.'

'He tried to. But the chaplain said he could only arrange privileges for his own flock.'

'To be sure, he did,' Tim whispered. Then he added a little bitterly, 'Strange to see the gentry having to emigrate.'

'He drank everything he had. Then had to sell the farm.'

'What's his name? Your Master's.'

'Croker. Eyre Coote Croker.'

'Few enough with a handle like that are hungry. Not like their Catholic neighbours.'

He realized, from the expression on her face, that he had upset her and changed the subject quickly. 'Can we be friends for the rest of the voyage? I could get you some extra food and things.' Then he laughed and added, 'Not lobscouse! Do you still suffer from the sea-sickness? After three days out it had no effect on me at all.'

Nellie rubbed her hand across a sack and found a piece of straw sticking out. She pulled it away and fingered it. It twirled and tweaked Tim's nose.

'There's too many people watching here; come away down to the stern behind that big capstan. You go first and I'll follow. That way we might avoid the gossiping.'

For a moment, Nellie thought about Sarah Donnelly's warnings and about what the doctor had told her, and on her way down the deck wondered why she was fearing no danger from this man. While waiting at the stern, watching the spindrift circle and froth, she was excited. Then she felt Tim's strong hands around her waist and his face next to hers. To the port side, a breeze whipped one wave-tip into an eddy and they both watched it coursing towards the backwash and becoming part of its torrent. Like their emotions. The breeze became wind, flecking droplets of foam onto Nellie's long hair. When Tim's fingers lifted a tress that was dangling in front of her eyelashes, they were gentle. Nellie had always regarded men as tough, coarse creatures who could treat their livestock and dogs better than their womenfolk. This Tim O'Mahoney was different.

Sails were flapping. A sudden gust rocked and rattled spars and recalled for Nellie the horror of the settee in Balliva. Tim noticed her sudden hesitation and took her face in both hands.

The ship lurched, pressing their bodies closer.

And Tim O'Mahoney kissed Nellie Hurley.

And the young servant of Balliva felt like a queen.

'Nellie Hurley?' The gruff voice was calling to the group they had left.

Nellie looked from behind the capstan and saw the sailor who'd thrown her on the deck earlier.

'Yes?' She moved towards the caller as she answered.

'You're wanted on the upper deck. A passenger has got the Captain's permission and you're to come immediately. Get your things.'

'But –' Nellie looked back towards the stern. Tim was approaching.

'I said get your belongings; if you have any.'

'Now listen here –' Tim stopped speaking when the sailor drew a truncheon from his belt and coldly glared at him.

'You told me earlier that I couldn't cross the white line on the companion-way,' Nellie protested. She did not want to go. Not now.

The need that she could not understand fully flared inside her. She would not mind going up. It was a chance to see Richard again. But she would prefer to sleep below, with her equals.

Where she would be near Tim O'Mahoney.

'I said, get your belongings.' The sailor tapped his palm with the truncheon. She went to where her few possessions were stacked and gathered them into a bag.

'Who wants me? How long will I be up there?' Nellie was asking foolish questions only to get some time to think. The sailor grabbed her by the shoulder and pushed her ahead. She stumbled and fell.

Tim bellowed, 'Don't treat the girl like that, you cur.'

The sailor blew a whistle. Four more tars seemed to emerge from nowhere. They held Tim roughly as the sailor led Nellie away.

'Nellie!' Tim called after her, but only caught a fleeting glance of her distressed face before she disappeared above.

The sailor brought her to a type of small scullery and instructed her roughly.

'Go in there and scrub yourself all over. I'll come back for you in about an hour.'

He pushed her inside and Nellie heard him locking the door behind her. There was a tub, some soap and a bucket of cold water. She stripped and began washing and when she was done and dressed again she stood shivering for what seemed an age. Then the key rattled in the lock and, grinning grotesquely, the sailor took her hand and dragged her along behind him. They came to a cabin and the sailor knocked. Eyre answered the door. He was leering.

Like he was in the library of Balliva.

'Delighted to see you, Nellie.'

'Will I hold on to these for her, sir?' The sailor was indicating Nellie's parcel of belongings.

'For the moment anyway.' Eyre was dismissive.

They were inside now and Nellie, in spite of her distress, was admiring the shiny mahogany timber panelling and the gleaming brasses in the cabin. Rich embroidery adorned antimacassars on chair-backs – rare birds, all blue and slender-beaked with glaring red eyes, stared back at her. A dress that she had seen many times on the Mistress hung on a hook behind a rack of the Master's suits. Clothes belonging to the Croker girls too. There was a bottle of wine on a small bureau that was fixed to the side of the cabin.

And there were two glasses.

'Where's little Richard?' Nellie asked, when she had regained her composure.

'Oh, it's only a touch of the colic, I'm quite sure. But the ship's medical people want him and the women in an isolation cabin for a few days in case he develops anything worse. Just a precaution.'

'Oh, the poor *garsún*; let me go to him.' There was concern in Nellie's eyes.

'Oh, there's no need for that, Nellie.' Eyre filled the glasses with dark ruby wine. The significance of the two glasses suddenly seized her.

'But didn't you send for me to look after Master Richard?'

'Don't ask questions, Nellie. Enjoy the comfort while you can. Here. In the cabin the chaplain so kindly arranged for me. You … *we* could enjoy many pleasures tonight, Nellie.'

'You're not going to go near my … my … You're not going to pull my clothes up again, sir? Ah please don't, sir. You hurt me the last time.' Eyre raised his eyebrows and grinned at her simplicity.

'This time I will be more gentle, Nellie. I promise.' He offered her a glass.

'I don't drink.'

'You drank the night Richard was born. I saw you.'

'I didn't, sir. I only let on.'

'Well then, we will dispense with the wine.'

He sipped from his own glass before leaving it on the table, then took off his jacket and hung it over his wife's dress. Stripping silver arm-bands from his shirt sleeves, he began removing cuff-links. Nellie was terrified. The ship lurched and frightened her more. The Master stumbled towards her.

'You're not undressing, Nellie? It will not hurt if you take all your clothes off and stretch on the bunk. It will be more comfortable than the settee in Balliva. I assure you.'

'But I'm –'

'I know you're afraid, Nellie. But really, there's no need to be. Last time was a trifle hurried. Too many people likely to come into the library. Here, we will be all alone. You will like it.'

Nellie wondered desperately how to protect herself. Another heave, and she felt the ship must have been almost on its side.

Pretend to do a deal? Yes, that's what Malachi had told her. 'If ever you're in a jam, take time to think what to do.' She knew what she would do if she was still on the bottom deck. Shout for Tim O'Mahoney, that's what. The thought of Tim made her more determined than ever to find some way out. That short while with him was the first time in her life she had felt there was something good about her own body. It was not like the clergy had told her at all; anything as wonderful as Tim's kiss could not be wrong. Somehow, if he had suggested undressing and doing what Croker had done in Balliva, she did not think she would have minded.

'Here! Let me help you.' Eyre was in his underclothes. He moved across the cabin. Nellie ran behind a card-table, lifted it and held it in front of her.

'Surely you should show more gratitude to me for taking you away from the dreaded Famine?' Eyre was sneering.

'Did you really think it was vital that you should come to America with us to take care of Richard?' Now he was smirking.

'I enjoyed that short encounter in Balliva. You're very, very young, but in-experience and innocence has its own charm. You and I could have a … an arrangement of some type. That would make things better. More civilized. A way of earning your keep, so to speak.'

'No, sir. I won't let you near my grunt.' Nellie thought that would shock him. He would never expect her to know the right word for the place. She was surprised when he only laughed.

'You are a comical lassie. Put down the table now Nellie, like a good girl.'

'No sir.'

'I would advise you to be reasonable, Nellie.' There was no laugh this time. Only chill determination.

Play for time, Nellie told herself.

But how?

By telling …?

Yes!

Yes! That might shock him into stopping.

'Nellie!' He took a table leg and began tugging.

'I'm pregnant. And the babby is goin' to drop between my legs if you come near me.'

It worked! She knew by his features when he released the table leg.

Then, she saw him redden. His face first. Then his neck. Even his shoulders.

Staring.

A little frightened?

Then rage, that might have been genuine, or –

Both of them tottered as the cabin tilted and a book slid along the table and fell to the floor.

'So, you pretend to your betters that you don't know the first thing about fornication and yet you become pregnant by some coarse peasant. What sort of a servant is that for a gentleman to have?' As he ranted, Eyre whipped the table from her. When he grasped her roughly by her throat, she watched the pulse in his own contort like a bagged weasel. Her face drained of colour as he pressed his thumbs into her neck; infuriated that the pleasures he had been planning could be marred by Nellie's confinement and disrupted by her nursing an infant.

Her closeness calmed his temper dramatically, however, and his hold was relaxing as he began pressing his bare chest to her heaving bosom and thrusting his thighs against hers. Her struggling only added to his anticipation of conquest. Physically overcoming her refusal would offer additional relish.

As he was guiding her to the bunk, Nellie knew time was running out. His slobbering kisses were on her neck, on her shoulders, and he was tearing the dress from her. It hurt when a bone of her bodice caught her right nipple. Then he was devouring, biting, and she screamed out with pain and with disgust.

Convinced of his powers of seduction, Eyre took this to be a release of passion and he became more savage. He moved a hand to draw down his combinations.

Two mighty lurches threw him against the cabin wall and back in the opposite direction. Nellie fell to the floor.

Eyre was not sure if he was experiencing a powerful sexual phenomenon or if Nellie was the strongest woman in the world. He shot from the bunk and careered across the cabin, hitting his head against the upturned card-table before spinning towards the drinks cabinet. A bottle of brandy fell, and port splashed from the decanter onto his face.

For what seemed like an eternity, great forces kept buffeting them about the cabin. Nellie thought of little Richard's young body tossing about in the storm. She remembered the guinea-fowl at his birth. The cry that meant he would kill or be killed before his time. Was it to be so soon?

Then she thought of Tim O'Mahoney. Oh, if she were only with him, she would not be so terrified. When she discovered herself lying on her back against the cabin wall, Nellie realized that the ship must be almost balancing on its stern.

A sudden drop to the horizontal then, and the leg of the card-table rammed into her stomach. If what the doctor had told her was accurate, she thought, the baby would surely drop from her now. Several times she grabbed something – the bottom of the bunk, the drawer of the drinking cabinet – but the force of the sudden movements always heaved her away. Eyre managed to catch his breeches and jacket and pull them on. He tried to open the cabin door but the ship kept pitching and knocking him back along the floor.

There was a loud thud overhead, followed by the sound of splintering timber as a cabin wall shattered and water came gushing through a porthole. The door opened with a crash. The sailor who had brought Nellie to the cabin just had time to shout 'Abandon ship' before a torrent of foaming water swept him through the demolished wall. It engulfed Nellie and Eyre and hurled them along the deck outside.

Nellie was the first to see young Richard. He was clinging to a mast, the rain and the sea lashing against him. She ran to him and held him tight.

'Oh Nellie! Nellie!' He wept into her soaking bodice. They heard Frances screaming, pinned beneath a spar, as a sailor and the Croker girls were lifting it to free her. Eyre slapped up against them as the ship righted itself for a moment. Between the five of them, they managed to release Frances.

The sailor ushered the Crokers and Nellie towards a lifeboat. It had only one oar and its seats were broken. They huddled inside and Richard stammered to Nellie through chattering teeth, 'Sure you won't leave me ever again, Nellie?'

'I won't Richard. Ever!' And she squeezed him.

Just then the first mate came along and ordered their rescuer out of the small craft. The sailor obeyed and stepped down to the deck. The first mate called him to lower the boat. Before it hit the water an enormous wave broke against its bow, and when it jack-knifed, Nellie was flung out.

'Nellie! Oh, Nellie!' Richard screamed at the sight of her swirling around and away. He jumped up and had one foot on the edge, ready to jump into the dark waters to be with Nellie. Frances grabbed him just in time. She took him to her breast and hugged his heaving, sobbing body.

The boat went spinning like a top across the waves, while the first mate kept battling with the single oar, gradually bringing the craft under control.

The waves were becoming less violent, convincing Richard that Nellie Hurley had calmed them. Good, kind Nellie! Now his mother was shaking with fear. He held her tighter and told her he would mind her. This comforted her; somehow she believed that he would.

If they ever reached land.

'You'd be better off organizing a few men for fishing instead of arguing,' the sailors had said when they released Tim. Within minutes, thirty men were casting out lines and catching mackerel, using pieces of string and thread holding pins bent into hooks. Bait was no problem; hungry mackerel would devour anything. Enthusiastic anglers kept tossing every catch towards the womenfolk at the fire, who quickly gutted the fish, rammed them on toasting forks, pokers, bits of wire or anything they could find, to begin grilling.

Tim caught the most: five, ten, twenty of the silver creatures in as many minutes. Even the sailor who had struck him admired his skill.

The women cooked fast and Tim joined his companions eating their fill of the only good meal they had had since leaving Cove. He cut a handsome figure, lying with his shirt front open, blond hair curling on his chest. His even, white teeth were flashing in the firelight and young women were casting admiring glances towards him, but taking care not to let their mothers or guardians notice. Night was settling and a pinkish glow began sprawling in layers across the northern sky. From all directions, fiery meteors shot across the glowing canopy, zigzagging their amber trails like some exotic flies at play. The group around the fire stopped what they were doing to behold the phenomenon.

'The Northern Lights! A bad omen,' one old man predicted.

'See the "Rory Bory Alice" on a full bag and you'll retch wih' fear before morn,' cackled an old crone, before turning her back on the sight and peering into the fire. A dark frown rutted into her grey forehead. She closed her eyes and her lips began quivering in prayer. Then she spat in the embers and, in a subdued crooning, she uttered her final 'In the name of the Father and of the Son and of the Holy Ghost, Amen.'

It seemed as if the skies took up her moan, because darkness began to blot out the Aurora Borealis and the whine of a rising wind accompanied a sudden creaking of timbers, flexing of halyard and flapping of sail. The rough sailor's countenance darkened with anxiety. He began running along the deck, speeding towards the companion-way and climbing four steps at a time. Before he continued on to the captain's cabin, he leaned across a rail spitting down an order, 'Quench that fire.'

The women complained that they would be cold during the night, but an old seafarer who had been tearing flesh from a fish with his fingernail said, 'Do as you are bid. There's evil in them portents and the sky at sunset was heavy at the butt.' He looked earnestly at Tim O'Mahoney and said, 'Get yonder shovel and start chucking every bit of *griosach* overboard.' Tim had heard his father talk about sudden storms off Mizen and how the first thing sailors always did was quench the fire in the wheel-house.

He seized the shovel and, ignoring the complaints of the women, began taking the red coals from the grate and carrying them to the gunwale to toss them over. As they sizzled on the water, their glow allowed Tim a quick look at the murky swell. He felt fear, dashed back to the fire and began shovelling harder than ever.

The ocean needed no coals to outline its ferocity now. Leaping in black treachery, waves like backs of giant whales heaved and built up to a fierce anger. As Tim moved across the deck with another shovelful, a gigantic breaker crashed against the port side, its impact flinging a young woman across the deck. Her shoulders crashed against Tim's ankles, sending him slithering along the slope against a lifeboat. This tossed the burning coals into a coil of tarred rope which burst into flame. Tim was winded from the impact. A pain shot through his ribs, but he had to try to quench the fire. The last of the embers in the grate scattered across the deck. Some bounced into sea water in puffs of filthy ash. More rolled along a stretch of deck in front of the fireplace that the frying of the mackerel had coated in grease and fish oil. Boards began burning.

Another wave broke and Tim used the shovel to try scooping some water onto the burning rope. As he did, the deck fire began spreading. Women screamed and the bodies of those ill with the fever slid around everywhere as another wave crashed over them.

Flames outlined the raging water all round. First a wall of it, then a castle reaching to the sky. Each one bigger than before. Great clouds of steam arose as water quenched burning wood and Tim thought everything might be brought under control. Members of the crew raced around the deck, beginning to take one action, but immediately seeing something more urgent to tackle. All of them were shouting to passengers to hold on to the ship's ropes, her masts, anything.

Some responded, but most of them were too weak after the long journey, all of it except the past few minutes endured in a state of great hunger.

Tim tried to help the women and children, but the storm was still gathering momentum, whipping sails from masts as if they were pieces of bog-cotton. The creaking of beams added to the terror as the ship tossed and reared against waves towering like mountains before her bows. Tim saw three men in the wheel-house labouring to control the helm that kept wrenching itself from their grasps, spinning left and right at the whim of nature's awesome power. What he saw next made him stare in disbelief. In a crash of splintering wood, the main mast of the ship rose right up from the deck. Torn sails helped the storm to twirl it around like a twig in a stream's eddy. It soared into the air, before crashing down onto the wheel-house. The captain's head rolled from the debris, its tongue protruding. Tim saw a great spout of water rise through the hole from which the mast had been torn. Then he was struggling in a sea alongside spars and beams, metal and rope, trunks and buckets. The ship was disintegrating.

He saw a lifeboat being tossed about close by; a sailor and six passengers its only occupants. Surely it could have taken more. He tried to grasp its edge but the sailor smashed an oar down on his knuckles. Then the boat was hurled out of sight and another wave crashed over him. There was an explosion, a pall of black smoke and more flames. What remained of the ship became a fiery lattice that lit up the waters intermittently as the swell allowed. All around, Tim saw terrified faces. Gasping, grasping, grappling. There were surprisingly few screams. Wet faces emerged from under water, mouths gulping, eyes red and dilated. Particularly hers.

Nellie's!

'Christ, Nellie! Nellie!'

Tim lunged to catch her searching hand as a torrent whipped her past. Their fingers touched.

And their eyes.

Terror in hers.

Then suddenly she was over his head looking down at him – held aloft by an enormous wall of water.

Churning.

Tangled hair; still rich and wonderful.

Spinning.

Clothes almost gone. Long, shapely limbs.

But for Tim, there had not been time to learn just how young she was.

Their eyes met again. For the briefest moment. Then her body washed across the seething foam and out of his sight. In his desperation, Tim almost missed the rope thrown to him by the rough sailor. The man was squatting on the side of a lifeboat with only a few survivors on board. He was trying to guide it with a piece of plank. Tim looked around for the women and children, but could see none. He was alone in the water at that spot. He slid gratefully in and lay exhausted in the flooded stern.

SIX

THE STORM SUBSIDED as quickly as it had started. Nellie Hurley regained consciousness at about the same time. She heard the sound of wood knocking gently against wood: pieces of flotsam bobbing against something?

Against what?

Could it be?

Against the sides of a boat?

Voices!

She wanted to open her eyes but something cautioned her.

Something, or someone?

Her late mother?

Her father?

Tim O'Mahoney?

Of one thing she was certain: she was not among anybody she knew.

The fishing-boat's skipper was disgruntled. He had missed a night's catch because of the rescue. More, he'd hoped from the moment he picked her from the water that Nellie Hurley might recover consciousness and show her gratitude for being saved.

It had been a long time since he had seen such a perfect young body. The sleazy wenches he was used to pleasuring in quayside brothels were coarse and embittered, their skin hard and pock-marked. When he had hauled Nellie in earlier, her soft white flesh was visible through tatters of wet clothes and her skirt was coiling around her neck. While he had been thumping her stomach to make her cough up the sea-water, his eyes burned lustfully into her half-exposed breasts.

He was still gaping at them now and the crew looking on were grinning at how he chewed his saliva-wet lips.

'Skipper will demand his fare tonight,' one sneered.

49

'First Class cabin. Bottom berth,' another added.

'Shut up and fetch warm blankets from the engine room.' He was stern at first but then added, chuckling, 'You can't race a brig that has shipped half the Atlantic Ocean. Too much fore 'n aft sail on gaff and boom.' He grinned and there was a general guffaw.

Nellie heard, but was too weak to register any response. Thoughts began tumbling through her head.

Frances and the girls. God love them!

Little Richard.

And poor Tim.

Tim O'Mahoney being engulfed by that gigantic wave; the meeting of eyes and fingers before he was swept away from her. It was so cruel. She bit her lip to stop herself from crying.

'Her mouth moved!' Nellie heard, and realized with terror that they had noticed.

'Wishful thinking.'

'No. I tell you it did. Wait now!'

'If you want them lips on yours tonight, you'd better hustle up the rum, skipper!'

'I'll waste no rum on her. She'll come to in time and I'll … Ho, ho! I'll take a run over her pedigree, I will. Ho, ho!'

'You'll enter her on the ship's log, eh skipper?'

Coarse laughs.

Nellie almost grimaced, but remembered.

'Why wait for her to come round, skipper? It sure would be different to have it with a knocked-out woman.'

'Wha? Gee! Bed an unconscious dame, what?'

Nellie stiffened. All this talk must be about the thing Eyre Coote Croker did in Balliva. It had to be.

The pause lengthened unbearably.

'Aw heck, no.'

She hoped her relief did not give anything away.

The crew carried her to a makeshift berth of old sails and fishing nets. Wooden floats hurt her back. She needed to settle herself more comfortably and hold her nose, as the smell of their catch was overpowering. She'd spent almost a day unconscious, lashed to a section of the wheel-house, tossing about the sullen sea. A gallant old passenger from Galway had made her safe but was himself swept off the raft before the trawler came by. Now her stomach heaved again and she feared she might vomit and give her protective game away. The nausea passed, however, and exhaustion brought sleep.

To her delight, the babble of early-morning quayside commerce awoke her. The crew was unloading the catch and the voices of stevedores along-side were engaging them in banter.

'Where did you catch the mermaid?'

'Nice tail fin on that one in the net!'

'I suppose you used your harpoon, skipper!'

The catch was almost unloaded when Nellie stood up.

'Where am I?' she asked.

'New York, lady. Want me to show you around?' One of the crew tipped his cap as he spoke. He looked like someone she might trust, but Nellie thought it wiser to try finding her own way. She refused politely.

'Thanks, but I'll be alright.' She began to pick her way across the slippery deck, dodging crates of fish, nets, barrels and other paraphernalia.

'Which of you is the captain?' she asked.

There was a loud laugh and the crewman who had offered help pointed to a tall, bushy-bearded man.

Nellie walked up to the man and thanked him for rescuing her and for bringing her safely to the harbour.

'I have no money to repay you, sir, but if you tell me where you live, I will pay for my passage as soon as I earn some.'

The skipper thought for a moment. He was trying to figure out how he would meet Nellie and receive another kind of payment: something he would far prefer to money. But he could not invite her to his home. His wife knew his ways and watched every caller.

'Ah, forget it, lady,' he said as he took her hand and led her to the wharf. The fisherman who had offered her guidance, threw a blanket around her shoulders and walked alongside her as she set off along cobbles that seemed to stretch miles ahead like a black honeycomb, vast and shiny. She barely heard his whisper through the rattle of wooden wheels and the shouts of merchants and fisherfolk.

'This is a tough city, lady. Especially for the Irish. Our skipper won't pay to get you registered as an immigrant, so you'd better stay out of harm's way and keep clear of the police. If you get into trouble, I live in that small stone house over yonder beside the chandler's. Butch Maguire's the name. Better talk to an Irishman if you have problems. *Bí cúramach! Slán!*'

'*Slán!* And I will be careful, Mr Maguire.'

Butch's words of Irish gave Nellie confidence. If this man had used them on the boat, she might not have been so dismissive. It was good to know that someone from Ireland was available, if she failed to make out on her own. Not knowing where she was going, she followed the tempting smell of freshly cooked cakes and breads. This led her to a large sidewalk store. It had long tables of cakes, fruit and vegetables. A man was making fudge and she accepted the helping he offered on a spoon. About to leave and continue her exploration of the city, she noticed the man studying her carefully. Then he smiled, stopped stirring and asked, 'You're very young. Do you think you could do this?'

'Well, eh, I suppose so. It doesn't look as hard as snagging turnips.'

'I'm on the lookout for a good girl. I need to spend more time at my other stalls. Where do you live?'

'Eh! I'm afraid I have nowhere to live yet. I have just landed. I was ship-wrecked.'

'You weren't on board the *Henry Clay*, were you?'

'Yes. I have just come ashore. A fishing ship rescued me.'

'Aw, heck. Jeeze, I wondered about the blanket. Hey Rosa!' From the far end of a store a dark-skinned woman appeared. She was the fattest young woman Nellie had ever seen, but she had the biggest smile.

'Rosa, this here lassie was on the *Henry Clay*.'

To Nellie he said, 'Everybody's talkin' about the tragedy. At least a hundred lost, they are sayin'.'

The woman linked Nellie's arm and took her away to a small kitchen at the back of a cash desk. It had a black stove with a kettle even bigger than the one that used to hang on the crane in Balliva. Rosa explained that she was an Italian and that the Italians did not particularly like the Irish. Then she laughed.

'But I married one. How young was he what gave you *bambino*?'

Nellie just stared, puzzled.

'*Bambino*! What you say? Baby. Yes, baby. Who put it there?'

Nellie blushed, although only partly understanding.

'How did you know Mrs …?'

'I told you "Rosa". Call me Rosa. Woman must not see bump on belly to know. Not Italian woman who have twin *bambini* at twenty that live two years only. Typhus fever from this filthy town.'

'Oh! I am sorry.'

'When?' Rosa sounded stern. Or concerned?

'A … a few months, I think,' she stammered.

'*Mamma mia*. I think! You not know for sure?'

'It's alright … Rosa. I do not wish to be a burden. Your husband has offered me work stirring that lovely brown stuff.'

'Sure, he did. Make sure he pay you in money, honey. And you watch he not stir your own fudge.'

Nellie did not know if Rosa was joking or serious. She detected some great sadness in the woman. Kindness too.

'Stirring fudge be harder than it looks. You not do it until *bambino* comes.

We have rooms for some of our ... eh ... staff. You can stay in one and I will deliver *bambino*. Until then, you only do light housework. Dust furniture, prepare evening meal – *pollo e peperoncino* for me and corned beef for Jack McHugh. Never changes.'

Nellie had no idea what the first dish was but was willing to learn.

'So he is Irish, your husband?'

'Jack McHugh? Irish as St Patrick.'

'That's the second Irish person I've met since I landed. Is New York full of us?'

'They beginning to land by the hundred. Some good people but many – ooooh!' Rosa shook her head in disapproval and held up two pudgy, clenched fists. 'They fight so much when they drink.'

Nellie laughed. She was warming to Rosa, yet was sensing some nervousness in her demeanour. Was she trying to decide if she could trust Nellie enough to tell her some secret? She was glancing around so often, as if fearing Jack's return. Nellie was clever enough to realize that, no matter how compassionate a woman Rosa was, she was taking on a considerable inconvenience by giving shelter to a pregnant woman. A foreigner at that.

'I get you some coffee.' Rosa fussed and struggled with the big kettle, pouring a thick, black brew from it into a mug. She gave it to Nellie and said, 'I go to store for short time. I be back and will show where you sleep.'

Nellie was glad of the time alone. So much had happened in a short period and she feared drifting into a situation from which she would later find it difficult to escape. Still, she had little choice at the moment. She thought of Tim O'Mahoney and wished he were with her. He would know what to do. She was about to start praying for his soul when something convinced her that he was alive. An absolute conviction that would stay with her and keep her comforted. How wonderful if their meeting happened in this new city, far away from the prying Irish eyes in Balliva or on a ship's deck!

There was whitening on the lower panes of the kitchen door, but she could see the faces outside. Rosa was deep in conversation with Jack. She was doing most of the talking; gesticulating flamboyantly and frequently while Jack kept his eyes lowered. Nellie could not hear what they were saying but it was obviously a serious exchange. Eventually, Jack looked up and answered. At the same time he nodded his head in agreement. Back he went to his kneading table and Rosa returned to the kitchen.

'Come! Follow me.' She led the way from the kitchen, through the back door and across a yard. Along a narrow alley then, between four- and five-storey tenements. The cobbles were filthy, with goats and dogs tied by short, frayed ropes to walls whose plaster was crumbling.

'A cent apiece,' called one man who was doling out pints of stale beer from a keg. Another, one of a group playing cards, stretched back his tankard without looking and got a refill.

Women lay stretched out in the sun beside the beer-vendor. Nellie had to step over one whose face was a blob of suppurating skin.

'*Ubriaco*! Drunk to world,' said Rosa, throwing her eyes upwards. Nellie's followed, studying the decayed state of one building. Its shingles were split and rotten and the roof sagged about four feet. It would admit rain like a colander, she thought. Her heart sank when Rosa stopped opposite it. It was the moment she decided to give herself a false surname. She would never allow her child to be known as a Hurley until she was free of this horrible situation. Until then, she would use another name. She decided on O'Connell, after Ireland's great 'Liberator', Daniel O'Connell, about whose death in Genoa she had heard before they left Cove.

An organ-grinder of Rosa's colour was trying to pull his instrument up a flight of steps. His monkey was prattling and leaping ahead.

'He must be male *scimmia*, Mario! Lazy *bastardo* should be helping you!' Rosa gave a high-pitched laugh at her own joke and the monkey seemed to imitate her. Rosa explained that the man was the *padrone di casa*, the owner of the tenement. But he dealt with any *paesani* or rural clients through Rosa.

'I understand you problems better,' she said. 'You pay me seventy cents each week from wages and I pass on to him. He like it that way. You pay for break things, too, for firewood and kerosene, but I give you meals,' Rosa prattled on as they climbed. The rickety stairs were without banisters. The sound of their footfall suggested there was timber beneath the accumulation of trodden dirt that sealed feathers, animal hairs and matchsticks into a thick, grey-black coating. Nellie was dismayed to find that she was to be on the top floor. She remembered the sagging roof, yet was not prepared for what she saw when she entered. A black, pot-bellied stove with a broken fire-door stood by the end wall as filthy soot and smoke marks traced its flue line to the ceiling, through which she could see sunlight. Pieces of plaster – damp-pink, sandwiched between dun – stuck to drooping sheets of lath, some of them below head-height. There was a large straw shakedown in one corner, a broken chair in the other. A few items of chipped crockery lay scattered on the floor beside a steel bucket. A three-legged chair propped against another wall was a snowscape of candle-grease. One short stub and wick protruded from its centrepiece of dead matches.

'It not much, but better than cellars of Houston Street,' Rosa sighed. 'There men, women and *bambini* of each families live, sleep, eat and shit in same large room. You be here with only one other woman, Fay Clark. Can be tough at times but she's okay.'

Nellie was horrified. She had never slept in the same room as a stranger before. Even on the ship she had remained on deck, huddling beneath whatever bit of shelter she could find, rather than share accommodation below.

'You not work today; too late. But come to kitchen at half past seven sharp in morning and I show you what to do.' Rosa looked hard at Nellie before leaving. As Nellie heard her clump down the stairs, she moved over to the window. It was filthy and was open a few inches on top.

She rubbed soot and dust from one pane of glass and looked down on a small square below. Some men in check trousers and brown frock-coats were mauling women that they held pressed against walls.

'Watching our fine, clean-living politicians enjoy themselves?' It was Jack. Nellie, turned from the window, startled.

'Eh! Would you like to sit?' Nellie did not really want Jack to stay, but thought she should behave politely. He watched her closely, took the broken chair by its back and, without taking his eyes off her, he pulled it to a spot a few inches from where she was standing. He sat and began tapping his left thumb against his thigh. All the while he continued to stare, until Nellie became uneasy. She looked back out the window. The tops of some of the women's dresses were pulled down and the men were handling their breasts.

'What do you intend doing with the kid?'

'You mean – '

'When it's born. What will you do with it?'

Nellie remembered again what the ship's doctor had told her. About the illegality of her situation. And she remembered what Rosa had said.

'I haven't thought about it yet. Plenty of time.'

'We can have it looked after for you. Won't cost you anything extra.'

'Oh, no thanks. I would prefer –'

'Only thing is, you'll never see it again.'

'That wouldn't do at all.' Nellie could not understand the casual way Jack was talking.

'It might be best. That's what the others will be doing.'

'The others?'

'The tenement occupants. All of them ready to pop. They work for me too. I pay them a little, of course, but they are happy to have a roof over their heads.'

'A *roof* ?' Nellie could not resist the remark, but she knew immediately that she should not have made it.

'The *padrone* can find plenty of tenants for the place if you think it is not good enough. He only obliges me by taking my women … my staff.' Nellie noticed the leer as he spoke the last word in grandiose fashion. She felt fear frosting up her spine. Jack was not behaving at all like he had done in the store. Then he had seemed quite friendly, even caring.

'Rosa is a very good midwife. You were lucky to happen upon us today. This is a bad city, Miss ...?'

'Nellie O'Connell,' she lied.

'As I said, this is a bad city, but you are in good hands with us.'

There was a long pause, during which Jack's eyes roamed all over Nellie's body.

'Was your husband lost in the shipwreck?'

Nellie knew his eyes were watching every reaction, every gesture as she tried to decide what answer to give. She knew that if she told a lie, he would notice. Yet she could not bring herself to admit to being unmarried.

'I know! In Ireland it is a terrible thing, but bastard children are ten a dime here in New York.'

'Don't use that word, please.'

'And how am I to describe an illegitimate child?'

'In Ireland, we call it a *leanbh na ngrádh*. You should know that.'

Jack sneered, 'If it is a love-child! Rosa is not so sure.'

Nellie was having difficulty figuring out what Jack meant. He could not know about Eyre Coote Croker's behaviour in the library of Balliva, if that was what brought on the child.

She tried to remember if she had let anything slip when talking to Rosa. No, of course she had not. All the same, Jack seemed to know something. His grin was beginning to test her temper. Being so dependant on the McHughs at present, she realized that she must be patient. She would try to humour Jack and find out exactly what was going on in the place.

'If I did want to part with the baby, what kind of people would take it?'

'Rich.'

'How rich?'

'Very. New York has many very wealthy people.'

'Do you know many of them?'

'Plenty. Some of them down there in the courtyard have money to burn. The child would have opportunities that you could never give it.'

'Would I know the foster parents?'

'No!'

'Would these people be without children of their own?'

'Of course.'

Nellie caught the flicker of his tongue behind the stubbly cheek skin and knew he was lying. She was on the right track, and knowing that would have made the situation exciting if it were not so serious. Pressing him further at this stage would make Jack realize she was suspicious, so she ended the conversation.

'I'll think about it and let you know.'

Jack leaped from his chair, obviously pleased. He left the room. In spite of her plight, Nellie was satisfied that she was learning how to sense evil and to be cautious about trusting people. Her father would be proud of her. Tim O'Mahoney too. She returned to the window. The square was deserted.

'Hope I can disappear from here as fast,' she heard herself whispering.

SEVEN

STEPPING FROM the rescue vessel after berthing at the Battery, Eyre Coote Croker felt foolish in the ill-fitting suit he'd been given. He and Frances began looking around for someone who might advise them on a place to stay. Their daughters were sitting exhausted on the wharf and Richard was clinging to his mother's skirt and crying. He was cold and miserable. Worse, he had lost his secret box and Nellie Hurley. He squeezed his eyes shut at the thought of his last terrifying sight of her.

Some of the other passengers were falling into the arms of waiting relatives and the boy thought only of how warm they must feel, cuddled together like that. When he clutched at his mother's leg hoping for similar heat, his cloche hat toppled off and she chastised him.

'Pick that up and put it on. Then stand up straight and be a man.'

Richard obeyed angrily. He tugged his high-buttoned worsted jacket close to his waist, securing it with crossed hands that were purple from the cold. Seeing them, he thought his knuckles looked like the damsons that grew in shining patches on the hedges back in Balliva. He recalled the comfortable kitchen, and the strange and wonderful sensation he had experienced whenever Nellie Hurley hugged him. Her embraces were so different to his mother's.

Tight.

Loving.

And there was always a strange haunting scent. Not altogether a pleasant perfume, but something more mysterious and therefore intriguing for a small boy. The opposite to the stink of this new land he had been told so much about. All lies, he thought.

Frances noticed his misery and relented.

'We'll find somewhere to stay, won't we, Eyre?'

He nodded, yet looked around helplessly. He wanted to investigate the city but was nervous of leaving his wife and children just then. The high-hatted reprobates in wide flapping breeches who were lurking by the wharf looked evil.

Rain was beginning to fall and he ushered the women and Richard across flagstones slimy from fish-scales and entrails left by the gutters and packers. Nails protruded from pieces of broken boxes, reflecting spots of weak light from the gas lamps. They picked their steps carefully.

'You folks no place to stay?' A deep voice boomed from beneath an upturned cart that had strips of sacking wrapped around it. Through the loose weave, Richard could discern the outline of a dark face in candlelight. The accent was strange and the boy became scared.

'There another cart round that there corner. Why don' you use it?' Frances and Richard felt like running away, but Eyre and the girls thought it might be a good idea to take shelter until the morning.

'Alright then, how much?'

'How much? Jeeze, you don' think ah'm into cart charter or somepun? How much? Well, Jeeze, that be good one. I'll be damned. How much!'

There was a loud chuckle and then, as if the effort of talking had been too much, the man just toppled over and continued his tittering, punctuated by an occasional, 'How much – Jeeze!'

The Crokers could still hear him when they found the cart around the corner and clambered under it. Father, mother and son left their meagre belongings on one side, Harriet, Eliza and Mary on the other. They undressed and spread garments for lying upon, then snuggled under their coats. They used the few pieces of luggage they had managed to rescue from the *Henry Clay* as pillows. Fearful and miserable, Richard lay watching rain dripping through the cart and splashing on the hard ground inches from his face. In the distance, he could hear sounds of revelry. Bands were playing and guns booming.

'Is there a war?'

Eyre turned on his side and said, 'Go to sleep, boy. It is the Fourth of July. Americans are celebrating their Declaration of Independence from King George, made ten years ago today.'

Richard wondered why his father always used such big words. They sounded good but meant nothing. As he lay awake, he thought again of Nellie Hurley. She had been so kind to him, and now she was gone. Where, he wondered. Down under the dark waves? Swallowed up by a shark; her eyes picked out by a sea-bird first?

He shivered and crept farther under his mother's cloak. Sleep came slowly and, when it did, only in the interrupted snatches that troubled dreams allowed.

When he awoke fully next morning, his father was missing. Richard peeped through a hole in the covering. A bright sun shone on scores of men and women who all seemed to be in a great hurry. He could hear his sisters outside, chattering excitedly about all the bustle and activity. He joined them and cautioned them not to disturb his sleeping mother.

Carters kept shouting at flower-sellers and fishermen ambling home-ward after a night at sea. A Fulton steamboat was docking and discharging passengers who'd travelled down the Hudson River from Albany. The girls marvelled at the high fashion of the women and men stepping into horse-drawn carriages before sweeping out of the square towards the city. On the corner of South Street, merchants in long coats and nankeens stood chatting with bankers wearing silk hats, bows and swallow-tailed coats. A jolly-looking young woman sat under a bright, striped canvas shelter selling bowls of turtle soup and oysters. As far as they could see, piers jutted out and masts from myriad vessels wove a wickerwork against the bright morning sky. Their cargo was piled high and auctioneers kept yelling offers on behalf of merchant importers.

Richard and the girls wandered about, delighted with the commotion and excitement. When they returned, their mother and father were kneeling inside the cart-shelter. Frances was sobbing.

'But it is so far away, Eyre! And we don't know if he will keep you in work when and if we get there.'

'But it seems that new industries are starting up every day there and that the opportunities are great. And in any event, they tell me the Irish are out of favour in this city. A young man called William Marcy Tweed is trying to ingratiate himself with an institution called Tammany Hall.'

'Tammany Hall?'

'The headquarters of some political power group for the Democratic Party. The people I spoke to say he hopes eventually to run Tammany Hall, take control of City Hall and the Hall of Justice in New York, and make vast sums of money as a result. His gangs make it unsafe for the Irish to live here, let alone get work.'

Eyre noticed Richard listening and summoned him. He crawled in and squatted beside his father.

'We're moving inland, Richard. I got up early and went to the Trans-portation Depot. I've received temporary employment in Ohio, well over 600 miles away. We'll get free passage, because I have contracted to work as a veterinary adviser in the company's headquarters in Cincinnati.'

Richard wished again that his father would not use such big words. Standing up, he bumped his head off the cart floor above.

'Ow! It's all your fault,' he said to his mother.

'How is it all my fault, Richard?'

'You keep ordering me to stand a wreck.'

Frances managed a weak smile, but her face creased in worry again as she tried to comprehend the enormity of what might lie ahead. A near-penniless couple with a young family in a strange and huge continent, full of all races and creeds; a land of plenty, it was said, but not very welcoming towards Irish immigrants. She had no time to ponder further, because Eyre pushed a round travel case into her hand and nudged her in the back.

'We must go. We catch a steamer from a jetty just a few yards away.' He turned to Richard.

They crouched as they left the shelter of the cart and called the girls. When they all rounded the corner, their benefactor of the previous night was stripped to the waist and shaving with a cut-throat razor and water from a steel bucket slung to one shaft of his cart. The girls giggled.

'Mornin' folks! Had good shut-eye?'

'Fine, thank you very much,' Frances answered but looked away when the man turned around. Harriet kept staring until her mother coughed a protest. Richard stood rooted. He'd never seen such dark skin. Not even on Malachi Hurley, who often stripped at hay-making time when the summer days had made his muscular body look like well-tanned leather.

His mother pushed him along, but Richard was still looking back at the remarkable image, even when they reached the half-rotten boarded sidewalk that Eyre indicated they should follow.

Eyre had lied about the distance. They walked for what seemed like miles. Richard did not mind. More and more he became interested in the sights, all so new to him. He had never known there was such a thing as a wooden house. Yet here were blue and grey and green residences with old men sitting on verandahs smoking long pipes and peering at him through fine-mesh net. He asked his father and learned that the device was a protection against mosquitoes. The first shop they came upon was like nothing he had ever seen, even when passing through Cork city. It was just a long timber roof perched on poles. Vegetables of all sorts stood on long tables. Stacked on huge racks were mountains of hot, steaming bread, buns and cakes of every description. Their magnificent aromas tortured his hungry stomach. At a table in the centre, a man dressed in white, wearing a tall cloth hat, worked as if his life depended upon it. He perspired so much that a scarf around his neck was drenched. With what looked like a huge wooden shovel, he was stirring a thick brown substance, kneading and moulding until it became hard. Noticing Richard staring in awe, the man flicked the corner of his shovel and sent a smudge of the fudge slapping into the boy's face. Reacting quickly, Richard's finger transferred it to his mouth. The man winked as Richard allowed the glorious substance to linger on his tongue, before guiding it in a slow trickle around the roof of his mouth and swallowing. It had all happened so quickly that Eyre and Frances did not notice. Richard decided not to tell them. This would be a big secret between himself and this new country that had begun to appear less hostile to him already.

They were tired when they reached the ticket-booth near the jetty. Eyre spoke to a man with the biggest moustache Richard had ever seen; it was at least two inches longer than the one Peter O'Donovan's father used to keep dipping into the buttermilk when he drank. It curled up towards a flat, black, peaked cap as the man squinted through a brass grille. Richard peeped over the ledge on which his father was leaning. The man took up a rubber tube with a brass ring at its mouth, and spoke into it. Beyond a glass partition that had patterned paper on its lower panes, he could hear another voice. It was too muffled to convey any meaning, but, without a word, the man took five small pieces of card and handed them to Eyre.

'What about the lad?'

'Doesn't need one. Think I don't know my business, fella?' The abruptness unnerved Frances, who feared Eyre might retaliate, as he would have done back home. He remained calm and she wondered if he was changing for the better. The notion relaxed her for a few moments, but when they were seated in the steamer, she became apprehensive again. Richard did too.

They sat on forms fixed along the sides of a long, enclosed compartment. In the centre were children, dogs, luggage, hens, chickens, vegetables and a foul-smelling pig, caked with mud. The other passengers stared at the Crokers. Despite their ordeal at sea and beneath the cart, their clothes appeared stylish among the rags that almost everyone else was wearing.

'Very grand. Shouldn't you be travelling First Class?' Richard had never seen anything like the woman who was taunting his mother with the hard, menacing words. The paint on his wooden horse at home was never as red as the daub on each of her cheeks. Large lips glowed even brighter and Richard could see tiny particles of whatever substance they were painted with on the woman's chin. Her hair seemed blacker than the tail of the Balliva horse and just as coarse. It had curls falling all over the place, but they seemed to be crinkly and rough – not at all like the shiny, soft texture of Nellie Hurley's. His mother had told him once that the songbirds in the hedgerows around Balliva often snatched loose hairs from Nellie's comb for making their nests soft and comfortable. Not even a rough cormorant would steal that woman's hair for its nest, he decided.

The coarse woman's voice kept rasping cynical asides but he was not hearing. Not until he heard his father say, 'Now listen here you, young woman. One more word out of you and I'll –'

Richard saw it first. A knife flashed from somewhere in the pile of flesh, fowl, people and vegetables. Its point thumped into the timber beside his father's ear and its handle quivered. At the same time, a lad of about eleven picked an egg from a basket and smashed it into his mother's face. Richard saw and did not hesitate. He leaped on top of the offender and began pummelling him with his fists. He could hear his mother screaming at him to stop. His father's voice boomed about going for the skipper. Friends of the egg-thrower were pulling at Richard's breeches and jacket. He heard buttons snap and go rattling across the floor. A boot rammed into his crotch and he yelped with pain. The Croker girls ran to help but two harridans caught them and flung them across the compartment. As Richard's hands dropped to parry another kick, his opponent seized his chance. Jumping to his feet, he aimed his boot right into Richard's face. Richard heard his father call, 'You cur!' and other words that gelled and became an incoherent, fading whine ending in blackness.

When he recovered, his mother was standing over him. He kept his eyes on her face as recollections of the steamer and the fight stole back through fuzziness. She looked so much older than when he had last taken time to study her features. Older, but more pleasant, somehow. Her hand was caressing his cheek gently and her bottom lip seemed to be trembling ever so slightly. He had never noticed how beautiful her eyes were before. Then, as if it had been there all the time but out of focus, his father's face! A large bandage across the brow. Richard noticed that there was no sound of an engine, no cry of gulls. Yet the walls and the furnishings were as old and as ramshackle as the compartment where he had been fighting.

'Where am I?'

'In our new home, Richard.' Frances tried to be brave. 'We have travelled by river, lake, canal and by train, but you were unconscious throughout. Oh, thank God you're all right!' There was a crack in her voice.

'We're in the company veterinary officer's residence.' Was there pride or resignation in his father's?

That first glimpse of their hovel in the City of Seven Hills would remain with Richard for a long time, yet he soon grew to like the place. His mother brought him to the Hanna Finn Coffee Shop on Front Street where he heard the Irish-American proprietress argue women's rights with Augustus Obermeyer, the German-American owner of livery stables. While his father worked, Richard learned the rudiments of baseball from neighbours' children. The game was quite like the cricket he remembered watching Canon

Henshaw supervising on Saturdays at the Vicarage, when Ardfield played Clonakilty.

Taking his family on a steamer up the Ohio River. Eyre told them about the city, pointing out its many factories, all stretching back from the port.

'They manufacture chemicals, engine parts and tools,' he explained, but Richard was more impressed than his sisters. This pleased Eyre and he promised, 'I'll take you to where I work, son, and show you the wonders of engineering that skilled men are beginning to achieve.'

'Oh, I would like that,' Richard said enthusiastically, before dashing over to the side of the steamer to watch two swans fighting on the river bank. Her son's interest pleased Frances, but she was quite shocked when Richard began urging a large cob to attack more savagely.

'Eyre, will you stop the boy. This is a pleasure trip and the passengers are staring.' Eyre did not have to. The steamer was slipping around a bend and the company was relaxing and listening to its skipper explaining, through a megaphone, how the river had been formed from the confluence of the Allegheny and Monongahela at Pittsburgh, Pennsylvania. Captain Richard Wade all dressed up in a crimson frock-coat with black cuffs, was gesticulating dramatically.

'The old girl wanders west to join the great Mississippi at Cairo, Illinois, folks, and a series of locks and dams makes it navigable for its entire length. A French explorer, Robert Cavelier, Sieur de La Salle discovered her in 1669 and seized both herself and the Mississippi for the French. The French are fond of the ladies, madam!'

There was a polite titter when he addressed his aside to a dowager, overdressed in tiered skirt and crinoline and wrapped in a deep-fringed cashmere shawl. She withered him with a haughty glance and he resumed.

'The Ohio passed to British control in 1763 and to the United States in 1783.'

Then Wade told how Tammany had formed the channel of the river. Some male passengers grinned, until the man said, 'Not the Democratic organization, folks, although their august New York institution, Tammany Hall, is called after the same Redskin. Legend claims that a great Indian hunter and warrior chief called Tammany lived in the land west of the Allegheny Mountains in Pennsylvania.'

'We saw the range when we travelled to Cincinnati,' Eyre whispered.

'I was looking at other things most of the time, Father. When I was dreaming!' Richard laughed. Eyre patted his head and his son was pleased. The commentary continued.

'He defeated the Evil Spirit in battle and, by way of revenge, the Spirit made plants spew poison, causing a great plague. Tammany burned all the vegetation and then the Evil Spirit sent rattlesnakes, but just like St Patrick in Ireland, the Indian warrior danced on their heads and killed them all. The Evil Spirit tried a herd of mammoths then – great hairy elephant-like creatures. Again Tammany thwarted him by digging pits and impaling them on stakes that he planted within. So the very angry Spirit caused a mighty earthquake, with thunder, lightning and an enormous deluge. During the downpour, he built a dam near Detroit. This blocked the water and formed the Great Lakes. Tammany's tribe would have been drowned had their leader not scooped out a huge channel to let most of the waters flow away. Today, my friends, you are cruising on that very river.'

Richard had spotted an open door above the engine house and was peering into its black, oily innards. The movement of cogs, spindles, belts and fans intrigued him. A sailor noticed Richard smiling at him and laughed and aimed his grease-gun. A spurt of thick yellow slime shot past the boy's ear and landed on the bonnet of the sedate dowager. The sailor pressed a dirty finger to his mouth, cautioning Richard to say nothing. Young Croker sauntered back to sit beside his mother.

The man with the megaphone was droning on. 'You know, folks, until the opening of the New York State Barge Canal twenty-three years ago, this here stream was the principal route to the West.'

Uninterested in the evolution of river traffic, Richard looked back at the engine house. He fell to wondering why he got on so well with important people like fudge-mixers and sailors, when he found it difficult to tolerate the children in the block where he lived.

True to his word, the following week Eyre took Richard to visit his place of work. The boy admired the long line of horses being led out to be hitched to carriages. A morning sun was polishing their coats, pink wisps shimmering through neatly trimmed manes and tails. Fearlessly, he ran under the belly of one and gave his father a start by stroking the bare flesh above the animal's thigh. The horse shuddered, but lowered its head and gazed contentedly at the small boy.

'I thought you came to see the engines!' Eyre took Richard's hand and pulled him away. The lad followed but kept looking back.

'I did. But I like the horses too.'

When Eyre opened up a large wooden door and the smell of oil emerged, Richard peered in with awe. A gigantic cut-away of a rail locomotive occupied most of the building. A mound of coal glowed in a firebox. Steam was hissing and half of a huge piston eased fore and aft in a similarly cut-away metal chamber. Young apprentices were gathered around and a man wearing a smart black suit, high collar and cravat was explaining steam power to them. Richard stopped behind the group, in time to hear the man ask, 'Now what happens when that mighty piston moves back and forth?' The group remained silent.

'Come on now. You're three weeks here and you should know.'

Still no answer, so Richard ventured. 'Them crankshaft yokes on the pistons transfers the back and forth power into a rotary motion to turn the wheels, so they do.' It was a parroting of something Eyre had told him previously, but Eyre was as surprised as the instructor at his son's impeccable explanation.

'My goodness, there's a smart lad. A kid, able to tell you lot what you should have on the tip of your tongue. Well done, fella!'

As he paid the compliment, the instructor smiled at Richard, yet the boy and his father thought the man looked a little peeved that his own charges had been shown up by a young outsider.

Eyre took Richard away and showed him lathes fashioning parts. 'Very soon, machines will replace horses,' he predicted, 'and Herr Obermeyer will be leading the field when that happens. That's why he's conducting all this research.' The shine of raw steel fascinated young Richard. He handled filings pared off by lathes, noticing how they clung together. He turned cogs, stroked wheels, and felt the power surging from everything he touched.

One evening he was walking home with his father when Eyre said, 'I'm afraid that's your last visit to the works, my son.' Richard was horrified. Was he always going to be taken away from places and people he liked?

'Leaving? But we've only been in Cincinatti a few weeks. Oh, Father!'

'I'm sorry, Richard. My boss has promoted me into his New York depot. It is for the best. At any rate, it is time you went to school. Your mother and I were postponing sending you because we knew our stay here would be temporary. You will like it in New York, I know you will.'

'New York! Oh, Father! That horrible place! We will be sleeping under a horse-cart again and we will be cold and wet and miserable like we were before. No, Father, please!'

They were at their own doorstep when Eyre took Richard's shoulders in his large hands and looked his son in the eye. 'Your mother is not in good health here, Richard. And it is not a good place for your sisters either. With what I will be earning in New York, I will be able to care for your mother better, should she need any medical attention. She will be away from the smoke and the smell of chemicals and oil fumes. Please try to understand and not make her feel guilty about moving. Don't let me down. Promise?'

'I promise, so.' But Richard's heart sank while he mumbled the reply.

EIGHT

EVERY DAY in her new surroundings, Nellie was growing wiser about the ways of city folk. Jack began visiting her at least once every week. With great persistence and not a little menace, he spun woeful predictions about what would happen to her and to the baby, if she did not hand it over immediately after it was born.

She was thinking about this one night, pacing up and down in her room. For no particular reason she went to the window and looked down into the courtyard. Rosa was sitting alone on an old box. Probably taking a rest from her chores, Nellie thought. Light coming from a window opposite was shining on her face. Perspiration varnished a woebegone expression that was sculpted in grey, making her look much older than her years. Clinging tears magnified her large eyes. Nellie would have loved to rush down and ask her questions about the birth but could not. She looked so unhappy, too overburdened with cares to take on Nellie's.

Could she ask her room-mate Fay? No. She felt she did not know her well enough yet. All this was making her afraid. She wanted to be back in Balliva with its easy, uncomplicated way of life.

What if Jack was really evil? If he did not get his way by making Nellie give up her child, might he not force Rosa to do something during the birth that would harm the baby? On her first day in the store, Nellie had got the impression that Rosa controlled Jack; in fact, on this issue, the opposite seemed to be the case. Was it that, although she disapproved of what Jack was arranging, she was afraid to go against him? As a mother, she would understand how difficult giving away a new-born baby would be for Nellie.

Far away from family or close friends, Nellie began to panic. She would have to confide in someone. But who? God, how she wished she could be with Tim O'Mahoney!

Footsteps on the stairs. Irregular and unsteady.

'Oh, Sacred Heart of Jesus, help me. Don't let it be Jack. Oh, please, God.' Nellie jumped into her bed and pulled the clothes up to her nose. Her eyes were watching the doorknob and they were full of terror. The knob turned.

'Fay! God, you frightened me.' She did not say that, while relieved it was not Jack, she was still apprehensive. Because she could hardly believe the transformation in Fay.

She was wearing a short, pink satin frock, all sequinned with tassels on the hem. Dark, diamond-meshed stockings. Black velvet straps around the ankles secured red shoes that had a glass ornament on each toe. Fay's long, blonde hair was shining. Thick powder coated her face and her lips were almost comically red in contrast. Like one of the clowns she had once seen in a circus at Clonakilty.

Fay was holding the door for balance. She tugged off one shoe and flung it into a corner. Then the other.

'You know what he's after, of course?'

'Who, Fay?'

'Who? Who do you think? That Broadway Joe, Jack Slippy Ass McHugh, of ... of ... of course.'

'Eh, I think I'm beginning to get wise to him, but I'm not sure, Fay.'

'You might as well know it. He wants to ... to ... to sell your kid to some ... some rich, childless family. Did you not see him talking to that over-dressed d ... d ... dandy in the store today?'

Nellie gasped. She had noticed the stranger.

'He was si ... sizing you up good and proper when Jack was leading him out.'

'Lord, did you see the lovely carriage he got into? All gold and big comfortable red seats and four sleek, black horses wearing plumes.'

'Plumes! Plumes my ass, Nellie. Would you like a feather in your ass, Nellie?'

Nellie felt like laughing at Fay's drunkenness. But she thought it might help her get some more information about her situation. 'Drink talks,' her father used to say.

'Rosa is beginning to act strangely too, Fay.'

'In what way?'

'Well, every time I come across her in the store or in the kitchen, she makes some excuse and leaves. And she was so chatty before!'

'Rosa is one very dis ... disturbed lady, Nellie. I'll swing for that Irish cor ... cornthresher of a husband she has. He treats her like – Oh sorry, love, I forgot. You're Irish too. But you're not like him. So be careful.'

'Of what, Fay?'

'Listen to me, kid. That store down there ain't nothin' but a f ... f ... but a front for McHugh's more lucrat ... lucrat ... shady moneymaking dealings. Listen! You need to know this. You're only a kid and you've come from the li'l ole Emerald Isle, a good holy country, to live in New York's filthiest whore-house.'

'A what, Fay?'

'Whore-house, kid. Not know what a knockin' shop is?'

'No, Fay.'

'Jeeze!' Fay was startled at such naivety. Feeling pity for Nellie's dilemma and envy for her innocence, she began to explain.

'Know that row of cubicles that lead from the back of the store?'

'Well, I know where it is but Rosa warned me to keep away from that area until after my child is born.'

'Good Rosa. A good woman, Nellie. I'll tell you about them there cubicles. They –'

'Rosa also told me not to deal directly with any of the shoppers.'

Fay laughed.

'Rosa was so right. You never notice the cli ... cli ... clientele in that store, Nellie? Most of them are masher politicians, firemen, police and lawyers. Men, Fay! Your furry ole Irish head never clicked that men don't do no shoppin' for vegetables? Oh, sure, they ask for "somethin' to go with a parsnip pie" or "a slice of curly kale" but them no-good bums never puts nothin' into cookin' pots. No, man. They puts their own darn carrots into our burnt out skillets.'

Fay laughed coarsely. Nellie did not understand. All this talk about vegetables! Unless ... Maybe she was beginning to put two and two together.

Fay raised the hem of her dress. A silver flagon of gin was hooked to a frilly black and red garter. She tugged at it, took a slug and offered it to Nellie.

'Have a shot, baby. You're goin' to need it when I tell you about them cubicles.'

'No, thanks.'

'Go on, take some! Gasoline for grinds.'

After teetering to her feet she began rasping out an up-tempo tune and attempted to dance sensuously:

> Ka, cha, bum doo, de dee dah doo
> Ka coochie, coochie, coochie coo
> Da dump; da dump da dooooooo ...

Her song kept skidding into coarse chuckles as she staggered. Then Fay flopped onto her pallet and some gin spilled on her dress. As she pulled its skirt up to dab it, Nellie admired her fancy red French knickers with their black-lace frills, matching her garter.

'Nellie, go home to Ireland. You're too nice a soul for this poxy city.'

Nellie wished she could.

'Listen to me kid. Sit over here.' Fay patted the straw pallet beside where she was lying. Nellie did not move.

'Afraid to make yourself comfy?'

Fearing she may have hurt Fay's feelings, Nellie sat. For all of five minutes she kept her eyes to the wall, scarcely believing what she was hearing.

'Let me tell you a bit about Fay Clark, Nellie. I was a dancer in a dime museum. Three shows a night on a small stage in the gambling area and sharing a large dressing-room with a group of hookers who operated from dingy rooms on the top storey.'

'Hookers?'

'Prostitutes, kid.' Nellie knew what they were. Rosa had told her.

'I began going out with a customer. One of the dice-throwers. Boy, but didn't he chuck me a six and a three.' Fay shook her head at her awkward joke. There was no reaction from Nellie.

'Six and three, Nellie! Nine, Nellie. Nine months makes what, Nellie? Jeeze, Nellie, you'll have to learn real fast. You gotta', kid, honest!'

Then, more seriously, 'He was a bit actor in a Broadway show. The rat was playing in *King Charming*. He used sing a song that went:

> *A wife like this I could not live a day with;*
> *She's one to run away from, not run away with …*

'King Charming, I ask you, Nellie. King Chawming! King Critter he was. And boy, did he run away like hell from me. Never did any no-good hog ever skedaddle as fast as he did when he heard I had a pumpkin in the bayou.'

There was a long pause. Fay sat up and drank more. Then, with her knees drawn up and her arms hugging them, she began rocking slowly on the pallet. One large tear was rolling across her eyelid. Nellie saw her own tiny image in it before it changed course and began clearing a small channel through heavy face-powder. Fay rubbed it away quickly with one hand, then continued rocking. Her voice was cracked and pathetic.

'I loved the bastard, but he wronged me so much, Nellie.' Nellie was still staring ahead and initial pity for Fay began lurching into intense fear for what she herself might be facing.

Fay told how, when she became too big to dance, the owner of the joint shoved her upstairs to prostitute herself.

'Right up to a month before the kid was born, Nellie. Drunken clients were di ... directed to my cubicle; them who wouldn't notice my belly or who wanted something different. And I was back in that hell-hole two weeks after I gave birth. Weak, miserable and feeling filthy.'

'Where's your baby?' It was almost inaudible. Nellie continued looking, not seeing, and her whisper alone betrayed her emotion. Fay's bottom lip cosseted its partner and her eyes dulled with pain when she replied.

'It only survived a week. It was lucky.'

Nellie closed her eyes. Her soul and body died for an instant. Fay placed her right hand on her room-mate's shoulder. Although uttered in her drunken state, slurred and erratic, accompanied by burps, her message had stabbed at Nellie's heart.

'Nellie, you should leave this house. A sweet kid like you shouldna have to end up in The Sleeve.'

'What's The Sleeve, Fay?'

'I was about to tell you a few minutes ago and our con ... conversation wandered. That's what we call that line of knockin' corners Rosa didn't let you go into. The cubicles at the back of the store. We gave it the name because it's always full of goddamn bare flesh. Even if Rosa does let you – she might send you in to clean up – don't go there at night, kiddo or you might see somethin' that'll make the hair stand on your head. And on other places too.'

Fay swallowed hard and laughed. Not as raucously this time. But she stopped suddenly.

'Oh, sorry, Nellie. I'm sorry. I shouldna said that and you such a sweet kid.'

'It's alright, Fay.' Nellie had only a vague idea of why Fay was thinking she could be offended.

'I'll let you in on a secret, Nellie. Rosa has taken a shine to you and I think someone might be prompting her to do just that. She is trying to stop Jack sending you to The Sleeve when your kid is born. But I don't think she will succeed. That mean bastard will earn every penny he can from you.'

Nellie's mind was in turmoil, but she did not know how to ask for all the answers that might help to calm it.

'Christ, we'll have to find some way to get you out of here. And your kid, when it pops. But I have to tell you that it is a bad time to be homeless and Irish in New York. Bad, bad time, Nellie. Tam ... Tam ... Tammany Hall does not care for the Irish, I'm afraid. Them's the crowd that run the show in this city. But politics ain't no talk for women, eh, Nellie?'

Fay swept an unsteady arm and bent her wagging head to look along it. 'This kip, The Sleeve, is bad, but is the goddamn Plaza compared to the slums in Five Points and Oak Street. As for Dover or Water Street and the alleys leading to the East River where most of the Micks hang out! Jee-sus! Nobody will employ the Irish and few enough will give them lodgings, even in cellars. You could put your kid into the city home on Randall's Island and hope it isn't given for adop … adoption before you find another place to live. It would be a slim chance. But then, how would you slip away to do it without Jack McHugh knowing? The muttonhead watches us all the time. Like a buzzard. And all over the ward, he has pimps and informers in bars and brothels and every goddamn place. Jack is a repeater for the Tammany Hall lot – that means that, come election time, he votes oftener than he shits – and he is in cahoots with the police and the welfare authorities and anybody that matters in this hell-hole town.'

Nellie felt desolate. She thought about the kitchen in Balliva and the fun and support she used to have from the staff and from Mrs Croker. Even from Eyre, until he had hurt her. That night! God, the thought of it! And, as far as she could gather, Fay was telling her the same thing was going on all the time in The Sleeve. If only she were a child again, back playing with Peter O'Donovan and Richard Croker.

Thinking of Richard reminded her of the guinea-fowl's cry and of the tea-leaves. Worse, it made her realize how impossible it would be for her to part with her own baby. If she had been so attached to Richard, how much more would she dote over an infant from her own body. Even if, from what she had learned all too suddenly, Eyre Coote Croker was its father.

Fay was watching Nellie's large eyes fill with tears. She moved closer and hugged her. Her breath reeked of gin, yet Nellie found the warmth of the embrace comforting and lovely and nobody ever needed solace so much. She cried as she had done so often since the shipwreck.

The stench of Fay's drinking assailed Nellie's nostrils, mixed with a more heady concoction of cheap perfume, powder and the odour of an excited body. Fay's hand was moving to her right breast and her rural upbringing left Nellie unaware that she was experiencing the beginning of an erotic encounter. She felt her nipple harden and instinctively thrust it forward for Fay to fondle more. She threw her head back and felt Fay's teeth gently bite her neck. Two tears dropped on Fay's hair and Nellie smiled weakly at the way they glistened, before scurrying to trickle around her ear.

Now Fay's hands were caressing her swollen stomach and Nellie thought how gentle and lovely and thoughtful this was. A thumb traced the outline of her sunken navel.

Over and over.

Slowly.

Around and around.

So gently.

Like gossamer.

And Nellie thought of the sea's slanted whirlpool of human bodies that included Tim O'Mahoney's. Fay's thumb was circling inside and the sea abated. Fluffing frissons were flicking through Nellie's relaxed stomach and fondling her baby. She felt it move for the first time and, in her excitement at the sensation, pressed her body to Fay's. Fay responded by dropping both her hands to hoist Nellie's skirts and chemise and roughly pull her knickers down. All gentleness gone now. With fingers spread to embrace Nellie's inner thighs, Fay was kneading and easing, pushing hard, then gently teasing, tormenting a young girl into a passion she never knew existed.

There was only one other body in the sea of Nellie's imagination now.

Tim O'Mahoney's. His body in the swirling foam of an ocean: water all around him, water that was now washing her baby and dropping from his hands.

Fingers that touched in the ocean.

Fingers drawing closer and closer to her most secluded place.

Fay's gasps were his. Fay's tongue, her passionate plunges were Tim's and Nellie responded with fire. She writhed, straining her body against Fay's. Then Fay opened her bodice and Nellie threw herself into its folds; kissing, biting, licking the warm flesh of Fay's large breasts. Opening her mouth as wide as she could, she poised over Fay and then descended. Fay's nipple slid readily between Nellie's lips as the young female who had learned nothing of physical desire from Church or parents, sucked and shaped flesh to fill more and more of her mouth. If Fay's hands stopped for a moment, Nellie seized them and led them back. These wonderful, incredible, new sensations drove her to a frenzy, and she screamed out.

Shrieks of hurt, but ecstatic.

Then her hands were doing the same things to Fay. A maelstrom of limbs and flesh and groans and delighted gasps.

Nellie stretched her arms and her legs and invited her Tim to do things she had never dreamed of.

And then the sea washed smoothly over her shore and she lay exhausted on the damp sand.

Neither woman said anything. It seemed ages before Fay gently lifted her hand, kissed it and then moved across the room to the ewer.

Nellie looked at her undergarments tossed around the pallet in little carefree heaps and did not remember removing them. She did not feel shocked or ashamed; she just stood and pulled them back on one by one.

Dazed.

Confused.

But strangely happy after her lesson on the meaning of womanhood in this bewildering, bizarre classroom.

Still terribly perplexed, she felt that at least she was beginning to hack a way through a wilderness of ignorance about her body.

Fay offered her a mug of water.

'Jeeze you sure sobered me up, kid. Where'd ya learn to raid the mint like that?'

'Nothing like that ever … I … gosh, I don't know what to say.'

'Say nothin', baby. But I tell you one thing for sure. You're not goin' into no whore-house, 'cause if you did, believe me, none of us hornrousers would have a customer left. Every butt sucker from here to Balitimore'd be sniffin' around your doss.'

Nellie blushed. More and more, she was beginning to understand what Fay's gibberish meant. She drank all the water before glancing over the rim of the mug.

Fay smiled. 'Yeah! You're some kid! Some goddamn kid. I can see how you got your accommodation booked!'

'My?'

'Your larder full! Your goddamn kid! Jeeze! What am I goin' to do with you?'

'I'm stupid, Fay. Sorry!'

'Stupid nothin'. You're a sweet kid. But with your gut-kickin' body, it's gonna be real hard to keep you a sweet kid.'

Nellie then realized that what she had done might have been wrong. The clergy in Balliva and Clonakilty had forever been warning young women in confession to stay away from men. Hell fire would rain down on any young woman who offended against holy purity, they had warned. Their mission in life had seemed to be the fulfilment of the Church's contract for keeping West Cork supplied with this commodity. She never knew what holy purity was, but the easiest way to get to heaven was to keep away from men, so the clergy said.

One confessor had been different. He used to ask her embarrassing questions about what underclothes she wore.

'I must ask these questions to make sure you do not offend against holy purity,' he had explained. He had also encouraged her to name parts of her body that she would not mention even to her mother. Once, she thought he came close to the grille to look down the front of her bodice. She had told her mother about it. Her mother told her not to be sacrilegious. Yet her father advised her one day not to go to confession to that priest any more.

'But he's on every second month and I have to go once a month,' Nellie had argued.

74

'You'll do without confession when he's on duty.' Nellie had never seen Malachi so cross and so adamant about anything. Later, the priest left the parish and locals said he was gone 'to get his parsnip snagged'. She never knew what vegetables had to do with the priesthood! Or with the things of which Fay spoke.

The remainder of the clergy and the few nuns she had known always frightened the life out of her with stories about men and how evil they were and the harm they would do to a woman. They had never explained anything, and if Nellie asked a question they just told her she was a brazen hussy. Now something had happened to her pregnant body in the company of a woman. She was not sure what, but she did not think she would need to tell it in confession. No religious had ever mentioned company keeping with women being sinful. So it must be alright. Still, she would have to confess to her bad thoughts about Tim O' Mahoney and how could she do that without mentioning what had occurred with Fay?

Important as confession was, she had other things on her mind just then. Fay drank no more that evening and, as she sobered up, she explained more and more about Jack's prostitution racket using unmarried mothers and the 'baby farm' that he had near Patterson, New Jersey.

'If they can't sell an infant privately to some rich person, they despatch it to be wet-nursed by other down-on-their-luck women. Such children remain on the market but, if they are not sold off by the time they get to the age of puberty, girls and boys alike are moved back to New York; to a joint in Baxter Street where they become young prostitutes.'

'Sorry, Fay. Am I right in thinking puberty is when ... when –'

'When the red river runs, kid. When you have your aunt, call it what you will.'

'OK, I know, Fay. And I now know about hookers or prostitutes. But you said boys too. Boys?'

'Yes, Nellie. Some men prefer to mess around with good-looking boys. Or other male adults. They are called homosexuals, and plenty of other names.'

'God!'

The two women kept talking for hours. Nellie found it easy to ask Fay awkward questions. And she learned more about her body and about life that evening than she could ever have done from anyone else.

She was less innocent when she fell asleep on her pallet that night but better prepared for the life that was stretching out before her in this city of the New World.

'You have strong west Cork thighs. It will be an easy delivery.'

In spite of all that Fay had told her, Jack's words shocked Nellie. She still thought it was not right that a man should be saying such a thing to a woman. Indeed, he should not be in the kitchen at all during a time like this. She wished Rosa would tell him to leave. It would be bad enough having to take off her clothes and let Rosa rub her and maybe reach inside her, as she had explained.

Not touching her the way Fay had done. That was nice. A long time ago now, and it had never happened again. But Nellie remembered. And when she did, her fantasy that it was Tim O'Mahoney made the thought pleasurable.

She looked around the kitchen. The big kettle was still black with crusted soot. Rosa had never allowed her to touch it. Everything else was bright and clean after her long days scouring pots, sweeping the floor and flicking cobwebs and smuts from walls and windows. Even the table for preparing food was looking as well as the one in Balliva that Sarah Donnelly had always kept so spotless. The mortice of one long board had separated a little and Nellie had been poking along it for an hour with a knitting-needle. From the hard, grey grime, she had unearthed a hair clip, bits of walnut shell, apple pips and a nail. Now she was glad she had been so painstaking, because Rosa had suggested that the table would be a better place for child delivery than a bed.

'How often now?' She wished Rosa would not keep reminding her about the pains. It was bad enough when they came, grappling at her insides and tearing them down.

'The last one was about five minutes ago.'

'Plenty of time. I go fetch some towels.' Rosa waddled out and Jack came to the stove and opened it. He held a shovelful of coal.

'Don't raise smuts, please, Jack. We must keep the kitchen clean. For the baby.'

'The only thing Jack would raise with you is your skirt, honey.' Nellie flinched at the coarseness and at the foul yellow teeth he bared. She felt a jab of pain, but ignored it.

Because he was coming over to her.

Standing behind her chair.

Hovering above her face.

Another pain. Already? Rosa had said there would be long intervals at first and that they would gradually decrease to about …

'Oh!' What in heaven's name was keeping Rosa? The last stab was only seconds ago.

'You know, Rosa is fat and looks strong. But if your little Irish runt is awkward about leaving the trough, it might need a man's hands.' Nellie almost screamed. Such a foul thing to say!

What was he laughing at? She loathed seeing his horrible coated tongue when he did.

Filthy hands. Fingernails dirt-packed like the split in the table.

Couldn't let them near a baby. Must hold on until Rosa came back.

'Open up those filly's flanks, honey. I could loosen up the delivery chute, maybe.'

Revulsion blazed within her, and she was about to berate him, when her stomach heaved. It was as if a carriage wheel without rims was spinning inside her, its bared metal spokes lacerating her flesh.

Then she screamed. A horrible, agonizing wail.

'Up on the table. Here! Let me help.' Jack was bending over her and was slipping one arm under her knees, the other around her shoulders.

'No! Not you! Never!' The words were wrapped in the continuing screech. Her fists rose to hammer at his face but had not the strength to reach it. All the effort, all the turmoil was below. She felt the hard wood beneath her.

'I said, *not you*! With your filthy hands and coarse tongue.'

'I won't be using my tongue, so shut your mouth. I'll help you with the important opening.'

'You cur! Where's Rosa?'

A speck on the ceiling? How did I miss that?

'Take it easy, you bitch.'

'Where's ROSA? Shit, Rosa! Where have you got yourself to?'

What's that I said? Shit? Oh, I'm getting as bad as him. Well I'll say it again. To him.

'You shit!'

A furnace inside.

White, blue, green flames. Red-hot metal twisting through brimstone.

Hard table. Hard raft. Lashed to the raft. Fingers held out to Tim O'Mahoney.

'Oh, Tim, Tim!'

Lashing fury.

Bad Eyre Coote Croker!

Lurching ship.

Thumping, crashing. Ogling skipper!

Turmoil.

Metal blades.

Tearing tissue. Cutting. Destroying?

'Don't. No! Away from me!'

'Good thighs!' Good for Fay. Wet for Fay.

Drenched for Tim.

Speck on the ceiling now a smudge. Spreading, grey to black. Grime in the split beneath her. The rest of the table spotless.

'Jesus, I'm drenched, you bitch. If it wasn't valuable, I'd let it die inside you.'

What did he say? 'If it wasn't valuable'? What could that mean? What Fay was talking about? Baby farm?

'Don't sell my baaaaaby!' The last word hurtled through the kitchen to echo in the alley beyond. Then became strangled by groans.

Rosa was on her way back from the tenement where the organ-grinder kept a small shop. She was mumbling complaints:

'No damn towels. Only sheets. Had to buy goddamn sheet to tear up. Such waste! Jack, mean *stronzo*, will kill me. *Mamma mia*! Nellie's scream!'

Now the complete ceiling was black and was falling on to her in a menacing pall.

Dark, waving blanket.

Evenly dropping.

Down.

The way the ship's doctor said.

Enveloping.

Completely.

She was still unconscious when Jack carried her across the alley to the room and laid her on her pallet. Fay held her hand. Rosa kept an eye on the infant in the orange box. And told Jack to leave.

When Nellie opened her eyes, Fay took the boy and placed him gently at his mother's breast.

During an argument later that night, Jack beat Rosa with the wooden fudge shovel. She was taking Nellie's side about keeping the baby. Again.

'Jeeze, I have an offer of good money, you stupid Italian heifer,' he shouted, but as he was admonishing her, Rosa was becoming more resolute and stubborn. Jack could not understand this. She had never interceded on behalf of one of the girls before. Sometimes she had been as mercenary as himself.

'Nellie is different to others. If we kind to her she will repay us. You'll see.'

'I'll see you in the Earl of Hell's pantry, you fool. Anyway, you have no right to interfere. You weren't even at the delivery.'

'Boy know that all his life. You make knots like a chandler – reefs.'

Next evening, Fay made Nellie some beef soup. She sat up in the pallet and peeped in at her baby.

'I'll call him Brian, Fay. After Ireland's great king killed at a battle in Clontarf, near Dublin, in 1014. Will you be his godmother?'

'What the heck is that?'

'His sponsor. You'll have to promise to look after his soul if anything happens me.'

'Gee suss! Fay Clark looking after anyone's soul? That's like a coyote minding a field mouse but if you wanna, kid, I'll move heaven for you.'

'Rosa has arranged it already. It will be in a small oratory off St Patrick's Cathedral; the baby of an unmarried mother cannot receive baptism in the main basilica.'

Nellie wished Tim O'Mahoney could have been there to stand for the child. She knew he would be big enough to ignore the circumstances of its conception. Conception. Rosa had told her that word. A nice word. If it could happen with Tim O'Mahoney. But with Eyre Coote Croker! She shuddered.

'You cold, honey? Here, let me put a blanket around you.' When she did, Fay kissed her gently on the cheek, then looked into her eyes.

'I love you, kid.'

Nellie felt no fear. Somehow she knew that Fay would never repeat what had happened that evening. Unless she asked her, and that was hardly likely. As soon as she was well she would search this city for Tim O'Mahoney. And if she found him and he wanted to, she would behave with him just like she had done with Fay.

'And to blazes with the priests!'

Fay was at the table and looked around.

'What's that you said?'

'Nothing, Fay. I was just thinking out loud.'

'Gee, I thought the godmother had to set fire to them with candles or something!'

As soon as she was steady on her feet, Nellie asked Rosa to take care of the child for an afternoon.

'Sure, Nellie. I love holding *bambini* and playing with them. You go and have good time.'

'Will Jack mind?'

'No mind Jack. He depends on me for baking. I take care of him. And of the *bambino*.' She laid stress on the word *bambino* and Nellie knew she would not let Jack do anything with her son.

There was a spring in her step while she was walking down to the wharf. She called into one, two, ten offices of shipping lines. She questioned sailors and fishermen, even disembarking passengers. Most of them looked at her in astonishment when she asked.

'Have you seen a handsome young man with a Tipperary accent by the name of Tim O'Mahoney? Tall, lovely blue eyes and the finest features you ever saw. He was on the *Henry Clay* shipwreck but I know he's alive.'

A friendly harbour pilot told her he had heard rumours about a few people off the *Henry Clay* being picked up by a cattle boat plying to Quebec. Because they were from Ireland, they were quarantined on Grosse Ile, on the Saint Lawrence River. There they contracted fever and died. Nellie tossed her head and said, 'Tim O'Mahoney could not have been one of them. He and I are destined to meet again. I know it.'

Yet, she was deflated when she returned.

'You get no news about your *uomo*? Your man?'

'No news, Rosa. Oh, thanks for minding my little boy.' Nellie took the baby and was kissing his head. She stopped and looked at the older woman.

'How did you know what I was doing, Rosa?'

'Oh, harbour have ears, Nellie. And news travel fast along water. You never hear that?' She laughed and then creaked herself out of her chair. 'You have cup of coffee? Or tea?'

'No thanks, Rosa. Shouldn't I be feeding Brian?'

'Brian?'

'The baby. That's what I am going to call him.'

'Brian. That nice name. But feed him here. I watch and tell how do it right.'

'But Jack might come in.'

'So? You think he never see *seno* before? When he not see them in the flesh he see them in his mind. All the time.'

'*Seno*?'

'Oh, what you call it? Oh! Eh, breast. Yes, that be it. Breast.'

Nellie was hesitant, but Rosa's experienced and kindly face convinced her. She pulled open her dress and allowed Brian to find her nipple.

'Naw! Soften with fingers and squeeze drop first.' Nellie was glad of the advice when she discovered how easily Brian fed and how much more pleasurable was the sensation for herself than when she had fed him before.

'You will come to the christening, Rosa, won't you?'

'Galloping gorrillas not keep me away.'

There was a long pause. And a silence save for soft, satisfied sucking. Nellie was thinking that Tim would, somehow, meet the boy some day and would be a good stepfather. She had checked her own tea-leaves so often and they had said as much. Rosa's cackle halted her dreaming.

'Jack not bad *uomo*; only treats women roughly.' She was hinting to Nellie that her husband might make a good enough godfather, Nellie knew. She had said it before. But Nellie refused to have him anywhere near her child on his important day. Yet she had to have someone. All of a sudden she remembered the Irishman who had promised her help the day she landed.

Yes, of course!

Butch!

Butch Maguire.

'Rosa, I hate asking you again so soon, but would you change and dress Brian and let me run out for another few minutes?'

'But I must –'

'Please, Rosa?'

'Oh, alright. But you not be long time. Jack not like see me still sitting when he come back.'

Nellie ran and ran. As fast as she could. The little stone house near the chandler's looked neater than she had remembered it. There were window-boxes with wisps of fern and pansies. Just like an Irish cottage, she thought. Butch answered the door and remembered.

'Ah! The lassie that nearly got drowned and just escaped worse. *Conas tá tú, mo chailín deas?*'

'*Tá mé go maith* – in fact, I'm very well, and thanks for asking. I am the mother of a wee boy that is about to receive baptism and needs a godfather.'

'And?'

'I was hoping –'

'You want Butch Maguire to –'

'To stand for the child. You told me to call on you if I needed help.'

'I did. But I thought I'd be called upon to fight an Italian or kick a Red Indian for you. Maybe even redeem your locket from pawn. But godfather to your son! Jaysus, look at the cut of me Miss eh ...'

'Nellie. Nellie O'Connell. And the cut of you is fine. Any young Irish boy would be proud to have you as his sponsor. You have the look of a man would look after the soul of Cuchullain himself.'

'There's blarney for you. But listen Mi ... Nellie. What day is the christening?'

'Saturday.'

'Jaysus, Nellie I –'

'Eleven in the morning.'

'Ah, Jaysus twice, Nellie. I'm supposed to be going fishing at half eleven.'

'You'll be finished by then. Sure you only have to say the Creed.'

'Four times Jaysus, Nellie; I couldn't remember a word of the "I believe" if you paid me. Oh, jumpin' catfish. No! Honest to God, Nellie. I can't do it. I have no decent clothes and – the "I believe"! Do you know I wasn't in a church for ten years, woman.'

'Oh, God bless us and save us! But you gave me your promise, Butch. It will come back to you in bad luck if you break it.'

'And so will my piss if I do it against the wind. Oh, sorry, Nellie.' But Nellie was laughing, and her happy face was leaving him helpless.

'Come on Butch. I believe in God –'

'The Father Almighty, maker – of all the curse o' God clowns!'

'Maker of Heaven and Earth, come on Butch. And in –'

'Jesus Christ!'

'Yes, Butch. That's it. And in Jesus Christ His only son, Our –'

'Lord!'

'Try, Butch. Like a good man. Please! Was conceived by –'

'Conceived by – The fellow who rents me the house! That's it. He's the man for you. He'll act as sponsor – as long as there's a jar or two in it for him afterwards.'

But Nellie's eyes were pleading through her smiles and he did not stand a chance.

Without realizing it, Butch was walking back with Nellie, wafted along by her personality, despite protestations. Every time his own words chimed with those of the prayer, she began laughing, dazzling him with her beauty.

'Suffered under – my skipper –'

'The third day He arose – but what about Jack McHugh? Wouldn't he do it?'

'What do you know about Jack McHugh?'

'You work there, don't you?'

'How do you know that?'

Butch hesitated and scratched his hair. 'I hear about nearly everything that happens around these parts.'

'I asked, how do you know, Butch?'

Now she was standing defiantly before him on the sidewalk and her parted legs were stretching the fabric of her dress into their shapely outline. She was also wondering if what she was hearing had anything to do with Rosa knowing of her earlier quest.

He was shifting, kicking the dust with the toe of one boot, glancing at her. She noticed the redness where his beard was thinning on his upper jaw. He was blushing! She demanded again.

'Butch?'

'Oh, very well. If you must know, I followed you that day. At a distance. I was worried for you. Jaysus, you were so young. And innocent. This city could have gobbled you up and spat you out. I wasn't too happy when I saw you go to Jack McHugh's, but I thought you'd be all right staying there for awhile. Meantime, I –'

'You?'

'Ah damnit, I plucked up courage after a couple of days and called to see Rosa. Asked her to look after you.'

'Oh, Butch!' Tears were moistening Nellie's eyes but she tried hiding them by looking away. Now she really knew why Rosa's attitude had changed. But why would she do it for Butch? Was there something between them? Could he have paid her in some way for looking after her. But why would he do that? One guess played hide-and-seek with another until they were in a tangle and she thought it better to postpone trying to tease them out until after the christening.

Butch would not enter Jack McHugh's but promised to meet her at the church on Saturday. Nellie agreed to bring along her late mother's prayer book, the only thing saved from the shipwreck because it had been in her buttoned pocket.

'You can read the Apostle's Creed from it, Butch. And I swear to God you will be in time for your fishing.'

'I don't know if –'

'You can leave right after the priest drowns the little mite.' She laughed again and Butch was sorry that he had to go fishing at all on Saturday.

— ⁓ —

The morning was bright and sun lit the gently swaying branches of the tall trees beside the cathedral's side-door. Inside, the officiating clergyman was brusque and impolite. Nellie thought he looked suspiciously at Butch. As if he knew something about him that displeased. In a short homily, he left them in no doubt that he disapproved of women bringing children into the world out of wedlock. He was unhappy that Nellie had no papers to confirm her names. Then she told him the story of the shipwreck and he entered the given name in the cathedral register – Brian O'Connell. Nellie silently prayed God's forgiveness for the lie.

Butch had no trouble reading the Creed. On the steps outside after the ceremony, Nellie gave him a thank-you peck on the cheek and he blushed.

'By Jaysus, I'd better catch a few good fish today.' He was laughing as he left and Nellie caught him winking at Rosa.

The two women insisted on treating Nellie to lunch. They drank too much wine and pressed her to have some as well, but she refused. She had to feed Brian in a toilet and this upset her. The celebration continued until nightfall and she told Rosa she needed to feed her baby again and get him to bed. Rosa understood but asked her to bring home the bottle of wine.

'We pay for it, but Fay have too much. I humour her and get her home as soon as I can. I collect bottle in morning. *Si?*'

After thanking them profusely and saying she would return the compliment some day, Nellie left.

The short journey back to the alley shocked her. Drunken old men sitting on the sidewalk reached out to her as she passed. Some of their obscene remarks she understood; others meant nothing. She screamed when one slid a gnarled hand under her skirt. A younger man fell in step behind her. She could hear his heavy footfall but did not dare look back. At a jewellery store she stopped, pretending to be interested in its display. He halted too and perused wares in the adjacent window. The store lights helped her to see that he was tall, heavily built, with an enormous stomach and a chest that heaved to a cacophony of asthmatic wheezes. From Rosa's directions, she could tell she was near the turn, yet she was afraid to continue. It could be unwise to let him discover where she was living. Brian was stirring and beginning to whimper. Soon, he would need sustenance. The man heard.

Oh, Christ! He was coming over to her.

Panting.

Saliva on his chin.

Perspiration on her nape.

Suddenly, on her throat too.

A foolish grin.

'Bay … bay … baybee!' Nellie swung aside when he spoke and attempted to poke Brian's face with a twisted finger.

'Bay… bee… nice.' He persisted and she continued swerving.

'Give me bay… bee.' He grabbed her left arm, forcing it from beneath Brian. A struggle, and the bottle of wine fell.

'Baybeee! Blood! Aw, no!' His hands shot to his face. He spat and foamed and ran in circles between the store and the sidewalk. Arms waving all the time, until suddenly he dropped to his knees and began crying bitterly and hammering the pavement with his fists. Nellie's heart went out to him but she saw her opportunity and ran. She did not stop or look back until she reached the corner of the block. It would be wise to check before she turned into the alley. He might be following quietly.

He was still there. The glow from the window picking up the saliva on his chin, his lapels; lighting his face and chest only, because he was kneeling down, revolving his head and smiling nothings.

When she got to her room and was feeding Brian, Nellie prayed to the Blessed Virgin to ask God to protect her son from the city's dangers.

NINE

I F RICHARD HAD BEEN taken aback by his first look at their Cincinnati home, he was doubly perturbed when the family arrived in New York and his father and mother took him to a shanty town not far from Fourth Avenue.

A small man squatted in a hogshead and old people were asleep in packing-cases and under heaps of dirty sacks. Others nibbled butternuts, chestnuts and hickory nuts.

'Eyre, look at that poor creature tearing at that half-rotten head of cabbage. Ugh!' Frances winced.

'Never mind him. Tread carefully over those women.'

Prone bodies of drunken women were lying on the cobbles. Richard gingerly sidled past one's discarded knickers before hopping across the legs of another, naked to the waist. The scene reminded him of the road to Cove.

Gullies were piled with garbage, even human excrement. On they walked, past bar-rooms, gambling dens, rickety haberdashery and food stalls.

By the time they reached the small Mulberry Street dwelling that the firm had arranged for them, Frances was feeling ill.

Her illness lasted for days; days that Richard spent roaming the block trying to become accustomed to its squalor. Opposite their home was a four-storey tenement. To Richard's young ears, this represented the tower of Babel that the Ardfield vicar had spoken about at service one Sunday. In accents of assorted countries, men and women with greasy, matted hair and wearing tattered clothes kept hurling what he presumed were obscenities from rust-railed balconies. Everybody seemed to be arguing with those above, below and on either side.

'You're a no-good booger.'

'My honey-pot is the sweetest in the block.'

'Jeeze, look at that kid!'

A boy no older than himself was swinging like a monkey, from one balcony to the next. His mother was shouting after him, 'Fall, son, and get some peace from this god-forsaken hell on earth.'

The only saving grace for Richard was the large number of horses roaming freely. Neglect had turned up the hooves of some like Dutch clogs, but others were well-nurtured animals that had strayed from better neighbourhoods. Richard loved helping his father round them up and he looked forward to riding them to their new owners' homes whenever Eyre made a sale.

One morning, Richard came across a woman in Baxter Street who was milking a goat.

'Where are you from, kid?'

'From Ireland, ma'am.'

'There are plenty of lousy Irish in this city. When it was New Amsterdam, it was a respectable place to live.'

Then she squirted a drop of milk from the goat's teat in his direction and shouted, 'Now, be off home with yourself and tell your mother you saw a real Manhattan goat. This goat's ancestor was brought here in 1633 from Virginia, a gift from the State's governor to his counterpart in New Amsterdam.'

When he returned to Mulberry Street that evening, he asked Frances, 'Mother, what's a State governor?'

'He's the man in charge of each state in the country, son.'

'And why should he have a counterpane in New Amsterdam?'

Frances was puzzled. 'I really don't know, Richard.'

'Mother, will we ever see Nellie Hurley again?'

'I'm afraid I don't know that either, love.'

He liked when she said 'love'.

By the time Richard went to school the family had moved to a better house. It was on Twenty-eighth Street. That was not far from the school on the corner of Madison Avenue and Twenty-sixth. Richard liked the one teacher, but hated lessons. There was a long, flat box of white seashore sand on the floor. The teacher traced out words and figures in this, trying to interest children who were more keen on running, jumping, riding horses, sticking hot chestnuts up under goats' tails or watching dogs give each other jaunts around the streets.

A tall man, he wielded a hickory-stick that was shiny from slapping boys' backsides or hands. Richard often added to its lustre. Yet, when it met his flesh, the lad gritted his teeth and seldom cried. At these times he remembered his mother telling him to stand up and be a man.

After school, he and the other boys spread like locusts along the sidewalks and wharves. One evening, Richard attended a horse auction in the Bowery.

'A dime for you if you ride that horse up and down the cobbles, lad.' A well-dressed man lifted him on to the back of a chestnut and handed the reins to him.

'Hup, there!' Richard flicked the reins and trotted the beast as instructed. He loved the rise and fall on the horse's back and the air streaming past his face.

'I wish I could gallop away to somewhere nice that would be full of horses to ride and engines to repair,' he whispered into the horse's mane.

He was sorry when the man told him to stop. He slid off the horse's back without help and was very proud when the man asked him if the horse was easy to handle.

'Grand, sir. Sure even yourself could manage him, old as you are.'

Richard meant no insult but the man whipped his hand from under his cape and cuffed his ear.

'What about my dime, sir?'

'I'll give you over to the police if you give any more impudence,' the man said. But he paid him.

Over the following weeks, Richard earned more money doing the same thing for prospective purchasers wishing to test animals' temperaments. He could earn as much for throwing off a line for a departing boat or polishing a brass lantern on a berthed tug. Six cents was the going rate for fetching a pail of beer from a tap-room and hanging it on a long pole to reach a thirsty sailor confined to his ship.

Sometimes, a friendly stoker on a steamboat allowed him into his fire room to warm his hands. Richard loved exploring with his friends, investigating the floodwaters of the East River or the broad fields of Upper Manhattan. He was always the organizer, thinking quickly if they got into trouble and leading them out of it unscathed. Being small, he was tough, winning fights against boys twice his age and height.

Because his mother insisted, he stuck to his hated school. He even became a Late Monitor, perhaps because he was a good scrapper and could deal with troublemakers. On his first day in his new role he arrived all spruced up in his best Sunday suit.

'You are well attired, young Croker,' the teacher said. 'All ready for your new job as Late Monitor. That's good. Now, one duty of a Late Monitor involves search and recover excursions when boys play truant. We've a few offenders this morning: Barrett, Schultz, Russamano and Bobby Browne.'

'You take Browne, Richard,' the other monitors said almost in unison.

Browne was a sour, surly brawling son of an Irishman, and the greatest bully in the school. When the teacher heard that Richard had the job of apprehending him he whispered, 'Leave Bobby alone if he refuses to come voluntarily. He is bigger and stronger than you; just ask him to accompany you back. If he refuses, so be it. I'll inform his parents and they'll punish him.'

Undaunted, Richard set off in the rain to seek out the errant scholar, slightly aggrieved that the teacher had considered him no match for Bobby Browne.

I'll show him who is tougher, he thought, as he crossed the street to Thompson's Tavern on Madison Square. It was only a short journey, but Richard's good suit was soaking wet when he entered the saloon to find Bobby playing dominoes with an older man.

'I'm the new Late Monitor,' Richard said by way of introduction.

'And I'm the Lord Jesus Christ. Hallelujah Hobnail,' Bobby sneered, not even looking up from the table.

Richard pulled himself to his full height.

'It is my duty to ask you to come back to your class in school.'

'It is my duty to tell you to go jump in the Hudson.'

'I'm serious. It's wrote up on the notice board. Everyone seen it this morning before the bell rang. So I'm warning you, Bobby. You better come with me.'

'Jeeze! I'm terrified. Shittin' my breeches, I am. Get away out of that; you rat-guzzler. You wouldn't beat snow off a rope.'

Richard caught Bobby by the lapels and dragged him from the stool. Bobby swung at him and connected. Richard fell against a table. Six beer tankards scattered around the floor of the saloon. The men who had paid for them shouted, 'Well holy hogwash!'

The bartender called, 'Hey you street arabs. No fightin' in here.' One in each hand, he caught the lads by their scruffs and landed them on the pavement. Bobby seized the chance to kick Richard's shins. The pain stung and he was barely able to stagger to his feet and face the truant who was now flailing in all directions. He was pounding Richard's eyes, ears and stomach. When an uppercut landed on Richard's nose, he saw, through a red splash, that his good suit was daubed with a mixture of blood and slime.

Caring nothing for the larger boy's crushing blows, he waded in again and again, taking two or three punches for every one he landed. Richard's were the more telling.

'We'll call it a draw,' Bobby said. Richard did not answer.

One, two, three swings, each one finding its target.

Four, five, six. Exhilaration because his puffed ears were hearing Bobby agree to come back to school and resume his place in class. Richard stood behind the vanquished foe and frog-marched him along.

When the pair entered the schoolhouse, the other boys looked up, not believing their eyes. Richard's new suit was in tatters, but he was swaggering through rows of desks like a victorious general; a brave, if dishevelled legionnaire delivering his prisoner. The teacher caned Bobby Browne.

Later, the teacher walked down through the benches, hickory stick at high post behind his back. Leaning down to Richard, he whispered, 'I thought I told you not to attempt an arrest? Your mother will have my life.'

He was wrong. When she heard what had happened, Frances did not even chastise her son for the torn clothes. She just smiled and, after stripping him, began bathing his cuts and bruises gently. Then iodine she applied hurt Richard far more than Bobby's fists and boots had done.

Next morning, Bobby was the first boy in school. Richard was second.

＊＊

Despite Frances's ill health, the Croker family grew over the following years. Four young American children were born and Henry, George and John came over to New York when Uncle John Dillon Croker stopped paying for their schooling at Wilson's Hospital in the Irish midlands.

'He was good to pay their passage, Eyre,' Frances ventured.

'It saves him the expense of further rearing and education,' Eyre grumbled. 'They cannot all live here. I have rented a house close by for them. We'll put Harriet in charge.'

'Yes, Harriet has good sense,' Frances agreed.

'The rest can begin working and looking after themselves.'

Only Richard remained with Eyre and Frances. He was pleased about that. He disliked his brothers and although he cared for his sisters, he thought their interests in music and sewing and painting silly. Far better to be wrestling and fist-fighting with lads than bothering with those sissy pastimes.

Richard moved to Lafayette Olney Grammar School on East Twenty-seventh Street, but worked in the evenings as a mechanic in the machine shop attached to Harlem Railroad. There, he helped build locomotives. His interest in mechanical gadgets grew and when the works closed in the evenings, he often spent many extra hours turning parts on lathes and experimenting with gadgets. He was working to his own specifications on a particular railway engine.

In the nearby districts of Third Avenue and Twenty-third Street, gangs held sway. Eyre told him about them.

'The main opposing factions are the Bowery Boys and the Dead Rabbits.'

'That's a queer name, Father.'

'Yes. At an early meeting of theirs, someone flung a dead rabbit into the room.

'Radical Democrats, opposed to the extension of slavery to free territory, are called Barnburners. This came about when a critic said they were like farmers who got rats out of their grain by burning their barns.'

Richard wanted to ask what a Radical Democrat was but Eyre was in full flight: 'Hunkers, on the other hand, did nothing about slavery; many of them were comfortable office-holders. Then there are Wideawakes, Plug Uglies, Roach Guards, Softshells, Hardshells and others. Often vicious and powerful.'

'Your Harlem Railroad Company has perpetual and exclusive use of Fourth Avenue. Its workers invariably join the Fourth Avenue Tunnel Gang which targets hackmen and teamsters in the Railway Company's freight depot. They'll probably ask you to join.'

'And should I, Father?'

'It's up to yourself, lad, but being a Croker, you probably will.'

Richard joined next day.

'Damnit! A one and a two!'

'Craps out!' crowed Bobby, holding out his hand for the last of Richard's money.

I've nothing to bring home to Mother, Richard thought. I'd better go down to the wharf and make a few bucks before tonight.

He passed through Fulton Fish Market, dodging through its rows of giant scales thrusting their scoops out at him like whales' tongues while vendors were weighing the day's catch. Stevedores were supervising the loading and unloading of wagons from a Liverpool packet, and Maiden Lane and Canton & California brigs and schooners were lying alongside. One had a carved naked woman for its prow and Richard noticed how her bare wooden breasts shone. He sat on a windlass wondering why, until he noticed every sailor and fisherman that passed by, gently stroking them.

Farther on, a clipper of the Black Ball Line had just docked. Its timbers creaked and its thick-ribbed berthing hawser was complaining to the windlass on which Richard perched. Porters from the hotels that backed on to the harbour appeared as if from nowhere, their pillbox hats tilted jauntily over their brows. Richard admired the rows of bright buttons that ran from neck to waist and wondered why they were all so thin when they worked in catering establishments. The passengers began coming down the gangway and their predators homed in. Bustle and *badinage* then, while they got down to loading trunks, valises and portmanteaux onto handcarts. Rattling on cobbles, clearing a path for the owners. All busy. Beggars and pimps were offering ladies cheap accommodation and inviting men to 'sample some away-from-home comforts'.

When most of the uniformed porters had left, Richard noticed a girl in need of help. Golden ringlets fell almost to her waist and she had flushed cheeks and ruby lips. In particular, Richard admired her long graceful neck and tiny waist. She reminded him of a china doll his mother always kept on her bedside locker. Although he had seen hundreds of stylish women disembarking from ships, none was more striking than this girl. Shyly, he slid down and shuffled towards her to offer advice. He reached her at the same time as a tough runner for a lodging house in Baxter Street.

The harbour people called this fellow Slasher and he was notorious. He wore a dirty tall hat with no crest and only half a rim. Filthy lining protruded through tears in his greasy coat. The girl looked terrified as he grinned. Black stumps of teeth made his breath smell like garbage.

He squinted and croaked, 'I'll bring you to a good clean house where you can stay as long as you like for an English florin a night. Run by a good woman like yourself, my lady. The Blue Duck's the name of the establishment.'

Richard was horrified. He had heard about the Blue Duck. It was not a boarding house; not even one of the good-class taverns that rented rooms. His father had told him about it only a few days before – when he was explaining about the dangers of picking up diseases from bad women. Eyre had described it as a den of vice and corruption frequented by the lowest form of human life.

He began waving to the girl and shaking his head, warning her not to accept. She noticed. A respectable-looking gentleman in a long cloak saw too. Then Richard found himself worrying about finding alternative accommodation for the young lady. All the porters and runners from decent houses had left the wharf, well satisfied with the gratuities given by their wealthy charges. They would not come back until another ship docked. He wondered if he should ask the stranger, who was strolling up and down the quay, keeping them all under observation. No! He would ask his sister Harriet to shelter her until she found a suitable place to stay.

His planning was interrupted by Slasher who, noticing that something was attracting the young lady's attention, suddenly whipped his head around and caught Richard making signals to her. He went to hit him, but Richard ducked and swung his right fist. It only caught Slasher on the shoulder but it was enough to send him reeling into a row of beer-casks. A loose hoop on one opened a deep wound over his eye. At that moment, a police officer arrived on the scene. Seizing his chance, Slasher moaned and wailed, 'That young guttersnipe tried to kill me, officer. Throw him in a cell until I discuss the matter with my lawyer.'

Richard thought Slasher was playing a game. He doubted if any lawyer would countenance defending such a low criminal. Not so the police officer, who grabbed Richard by the arm, dragged him along the cobbles saying, 'You're coming to the station with me, you young hoodlum.'

'Just a moment, officer,' the strange gentleman interrupted. 'I observed everything that happened, sir, and I can assure you that the chap whom you hold is completely in the right. You should at least hear his side of the story.'

'But he tried to murder me,' Slasher screamed, running up to the officer and whispering, so that the stranger could not hear. 'If you don't lock him up, you'll only need those pewter buttons for shooting crap.'

'Oh, is that so?' said the police officer, grabbing Slasher with the other hand, 'A night in the jug will massage that gob of yours.'

As he moved off with Slasher in one hand and Richard in the other, he said to the stranger, 'You might be better off keeping your mouth for cooling your clam chowder.'

The lilting Irish accent reminded Richard of Malachi Hurley and he thought of Nellie again and wondered if she had survived the shipwreck.

'Let that gentleman go.'

A huge, red-faced man in heavy tweeds and a shining top hat appeared and spat the order, while he jabbed a thumb towards Slasher.

'He's under arrest for a breach of the peace,' the officer snarled.

'If he is, you'll be tending goats out in Harlem tomorrow. Do you know who I am?'

'I don't care if you're the son of an Irish Famine victim.'

'I'm Mike Walsh of Tammany Hall.' Richard saw the officer pale. He heard Slasher's whispered barb too: 'Ever hear of the Spartan Association, officer?'

While Slasher laughed, Richard remembered hearing his father say something about the gang of fellow Irishmen who acted as thug bodyguards for Walsh. He made a mental note to question Eyre some more.

'Sorry, Mr Walsh, you ought to have told me at the jump.' The officer released Slasher.

'Okay, pal, you're new in this stroll. You'll learn.'

The stranger could not believe what he was seeing. An English immigrant of two years' standing, he considered himself law-abiding. Although his head told him it might be unwise, he felt in honour bound to interfere.

'Excuse me, officer. Are you going to allow this gentleman to dictate to you?'

Walsh moved menacingly towards the man and growled through clenched teeth, 'Stow it, you old English codger. Maybe you still haven't learned that more graves have been dug with the tongue than with the shovel. Now, my advice to you is to start slipping away down to Fifth Avenue where your kind belongs. It would be a sight, mind you, if the Gang got to know you too well and thought you could do with a wash in the river some night.' He turned to the officer and added, 'Take that lad in. I'll be down later to look him over.'

Starting to leave then, Walsh noticed the girl who stood petrified at what she'd witnessed. He raised his hat and smiled to her before nodding to the officer. 'Bring her along for the ride too. Come on you!'

When they went strolling off, Slasher was smirking at Richard.

The officer took the girl by the hand, saying, 'It might be for the best; Mr Walsh will find you some place decent to stay. You'll see.'

He noticed Richard smiling at the girl and added, 'Your eyes are stuck on her like a barnacle on a boat bottom. Get a move on out of that.'

The three headed off, but the stranger fell in behind, remonstrating about justice and fair play. He was still complaining when they entered the precinct headquarters. A burly station captain looked up from the newspaper that he was reading and growled, 'Screw out of here, Nelson.'

'I'll have my say. I'm a taxpayer of this country. I will have justice.'

'Then you'll have it with mud on your face,' said the captain, signalling to two officers who were stuffing thick hunks of beef bread into their mouths. Without a word, they leaped forward, grabbed the gentleman and tossed him into the gutter outside. His flying body just missed Mike Walsh, who was entering. The station captain grinned.

'He will have justice, Mr Walsh. Gee, we oughta send that to the Joe Miller Joke Book. What's it to be, Mr Walsh?'

'Nice clean beds for the lad and the lady – separate diggers! I'll check the business and let the judge know before morning.'

As he was about to leave, the arresting officer said, 'But Mr Walsh, it was only a mess up on the wharf; there's nothing in the book that says they should be detained.'

'What?' Walsh walked menacingly around the officer. 'Now you are not as new on the stroll as you were twenty minutes ago, officer. Surely you know the lad smashed poor Slasher with an iron bar and that this young lady is his accomplice; an accessory after the fact, so to speak.'

The officer looked in astonishment at the captain, who nodded towards the door and ordered, 'Back to your beat.'

Walsh accompanied the officer to the sidewalk, his face almost resting on the man's shoulder as he warned, 'I told you before that you have too much lip out of you. If you don't think more and gab less, you won't be a cop long enough to wear the shine off your boots.'

Richard was lodged in one cell, the girl in another. The stranger went back to the wharf and asked a group of waifs if any of them had seen what happened. One said he did and also that he knew Richard. The man offered the boy ten cents to lead him to Richard's home. Eliza and Harriet were there, visiting Frances. Eyre was out drinking. Harriet went to the station to plead for the boy's release, but without success.

Next morning, a turnkey brought Richard in some cold porridge and a crust of bread. He advised him to plead guilty to whatever charge was made against him.

'Will they release me if I do?'

'Aye, they will. To Blackwell's Reformatory. It will be a ten-dollar fine and two weeks on the Island, but if you protest innocence and Slasher has to be brought to give evidence, he will swear you half killed him and you'll get eight months. Now hurry up and brush off those crumbs and march upstairs to the pen.'

'The penitentiary? Before I'm even tried?'

'The pen is the dock, lad. But you can forget about a trial in this precinct.'

A police officer arrived and hustled Richard up three long flights of stairs, leaving him out of breath when he entered a narrow room that reeked of humanity. Relatives and friends of the day's accused squeezed together as much for support as for comfort. Their tattered clothes were muddy, just like their faces and hands. At the end of the room, a few officials stood in front of a raised dais, chatting to police officers. His escort led Richard to a small dock from where he could see his father and Harriet on the inside of a row. They were sitting erect and looked awkward and embarrassed.

A clerk called the court to rise as the magistrate entered. He was short and fat, his frayed and shiny black gown speckled with dandruff. He took his seat and glowered at Richard, whose heart sank. A clerk called for the first witness. It was Slasher.

'You are the complainant?' the magistrate peered over wire-rimmed glasses.

'No sir. I'm Slasher.'

There was laughter but the justice chopped it off with a curt command.

'You say you were assaulted by this youth called Croker?'

'Yes, your honour.'

'Tell your story.'

Cockily, almost in a confidential manner, Slasher began.

'Well, your honour, I was going for a stroll by the harbour, minding my own business, when a young lady asked me where she could find a place to

94

stay. I was giving her directions when this blackguard here hit me over the eye with a bar. A mebby-iron, I think it was. The girl began shouting encouragement, sir. "Hit him harder. Kill him." So the defendant beat me some more around the body until I fell. He kicked me in the face and in the ribs while I was in the gutter –'

'Lies! All lies!' Richard recognized the voice, booming from the body of the courtroom, of the gentleman who'd protested at his arrest earlier.

'How dare anybody interrupt a witness's evidence,' the magistrate was fuming. 'Stand up, whoever said that.'

'I demand justice. This boy must be heard by a jury. That witness was attempting to lure the girl to a house of ill repute.'

'The Blue Duck ain't no house of … of … of whatever that old codger says,' Slasher shouted.

'You seem to be inviting a charge of contempt for this court. Who are you?' the magistrate demanded.

'A taxpayer, sir, and that captain of police sitting before you threw me from the station when I protested the boy's innocence. I will have him brought before his superiors.'

Richard saw the captain grinning and heard him say to a colleague, 'That's what they all threaten.'

'Is the Blue Duck a place of good repute, captain?' the magistrate asked.

'Well, it ain't no Astor Hotel, but nobody expects fancy livin' in Water Street.'

'Is it not a hostel for criminals?'

'Shucks, your Honour, criminals must live somewhere when they're not in the jug.'

A titter around the courtroom expired when the door burst open. Mike Walsh strode down the aisle and halted before the bench. The magistrate stood and gave a slight bow, before resuming his seat and speaking mildly.

'You wish to say something, Mr Walsh?'

'This is preposterous,' the gentleman shouted.

'It's worse. It's shit awful,' Slasher said.

'You again, old sport!' Walsh laughed at the Englishman before continuing, 'If you would only be quiet I will settle this as easy as throwin' dice.' Then he turned to the bench and said, 'This is a pimple on an elephant's rump, Your Honour. Slasher made a mistake. Let the boy go.'

Slasher gaped 'But –'

'Shut up, Slasher,' Walsh hissed.

'And the girl, Mr Walsh? She is to appear on a charge of abetting a crime.'

'She committed no crime. I've checked.' He bent and whispered to the magistrate, 'She's one of the Frasers. Her ship docked early and her folks weren't there to meet her. Normally I'd be pleased to have one up on old man Fraser, but there's no point in lookin' for trouble.'

Slasher stood in the witness box, agitated, and complained, 'But what about my poor eye?'

Walsh rubbed the tough's hair and growled, 'Don't be leavin' your peeper around where it can get walked upon by a whippersnapper of an Irish kid.'

'What is the magistrate doing in this court?' protested the gentleman.

'Shut the heck up you or you'll be in the dock,' Walsh shouted back.

'No hog o' hell is goin' to bust up my eye –' Slasher was about to continue his tirade but Walsh leaned on the box and thundered, 'One more peep out of you and I'll have a boat waitin' to bring you on a vacation to the Island for at least two months. You'll remember how I arranged your last trip.'

'Okay, Mr W.'

'The charges against the kids are withdrawn, magistrate.'

'Sure, Mr Walsh. The magistrate sighed with relief and added, 'I suppose it's no costs charged?'

'You're gettin' bright. I like clever judges.'

Walsh came over to Richard and whispered, 'Hunt me up next week. Any cop will tell you where to find me. Any smart cop, that is. I haven't heard a yelp out of you since all this began, no more than if you was a Boston terrier. I could use a guy that can keep his trap shut and kick like a Kerry mule.'

Another case began and Richard ran to the door where his father and Harriet were waiting. Harriet hugged him and Eyre ruffled his hair. He told him never to get into a fight with boys at the harbour again and to go to Mr Walsh as instructed. Stepping from the courtroom, free and delighted, Richard realized that he'd discovered a way to power. Better, he was pleased at how, during the court proceedings, he had found himself more concerned about the girl's welfare than his own. Best of all, he saw her just then.

A stern woman was holding her hand, but she escaped and ran over to Richard. 'Thank you so much for all you've done,' she said.

'No … trouble. A p … pleasure,' Richard stammered, embarrassed as the girl kissed him on the cheek. And because his father was laughing.

'Come along now,' the stern woman ordered. 'We have to take care of you until we contact your parents.' The woman from the police department, strutted off with an important air. The girl sneaked a peep back and waved at Richard. He wondered why he felt a lump in his throat.

TEN

JACK MCHUGH WAS at the end of his tether. He'd given in to Rosa's insistence that Nellie's duties be confined to cleaning and serving vegetables in the store. But Brian was now what age? Four years old or so? A strong young fellow too. And smart. Damnit he was getting fond of the kid. Nonetheless, it was time Nellie began making some real money. He tackled Rosa about it and they were arguing in the kitchen just as Nellie, holding Brian's hand, was about to enter to scrub the floor. She stopped abruptly when she heard raised voices inside.

'Nellie meet clients. She speak well. Can chat up. She also keep Sleeve tidy. Not like Fay and others, Nellie so very neat. Not like many *Irlandese* either. *Donna delle pulizie.* Very, very clean. It be good for business.'

'Clean! A lot our clients care about cleanliness! That kid has a body that we could charge treble for. Men would come from East Jesus for her. You don't let me sell her baby and now her bird's nest is not to be on the market either. What has got into you, woman?'

He noticed the door ajar, kicked it shut and began abusing Rosa. Nellie did not hear precise words, only incoherent shouting, sounds of chairs and tables falling too, before Jack came charging through the door. Before it slammed again, Nellie got a glimpse of Rosa inside. Shaking her head in despair, she was standing staring at a picture of the Virgin, and crying bitterly, with splayed fingers lying across her lips and cheeks and two pudgy thumbs tucking up her chin.

Furious, and red-faced, with his left fist clenched in anger, Jack reached for a coat that hung behind the fudge slab. Because it did not come away properly, he almost ripped the hook from the wall.

'Blast you,' he shouted at Nellie, 'with your hand on your ha'penny and your fingers on your Rosary beads.' He strode out into the night.

Nellie heard Rosa's wail. Worrying that Jack had injured her, she wanted to help, but knew if she entered when Rosa was in such a state, it would embarrass her. What would be best? There was a scrape in the lime-wash that covered the glass in the door. Peeping through it, she saw Rosa flopping into a seat and dabbing her eyes with her pinafore. Her voice was barely audible.

'Mamma mia, where will it all end? I will soon be too weak to resist any more.' She held both hands over her right breast, as if in agony. Red-ink crescents had replaced fingernails bitten away from constant anxiety. Nellie knew that Jack had struck his wife. It had happened before. So often, Rosa's bloodied face and black eyes had offered adequate testimony. Nearly always it was on Saturdays. Jack continued to practise the Irish custom of over-drinking on Friday nights.

It never ceased to surprise Nellie that Rosa interceded so vigorously on her behalf. Especially at the risk of a beating. After all, she was an Irish immigrant about whom Italians generally cared little. Furthermore, Rosa had not appeared to be very taken by her when they first met, although they had since become friends. Was it because of Butch Maguire's request? Whatever the reason, she was thankful, and she wanted Rosa to confide in her and to trust her.

She wanted to tell her, too, how the Hurleys were renowned for their loyalty; how her uncle had once walked twenty miles, through snow-drifts six feet high, to attend the funeral of an acquaintance who had helped him strike a bargain at a horse fair in Ballinasloe. Her father was particularly loyal. Many times, Malachi had been offered higher wages than Eyre Coote Croker was paying him in Balliva, but a Hurley had worked that farm years before the Crokers purchased it, and so he would keep on the family tradition. For a moment, she thought how her father would frown at her calling Brian by another surname. But that would end as soon as they were both free of this den of vice.

God, if my father knew I was working and rearing a child in a place like this, Nellie thought as Rosa became quieter. She peeped through the scrape again. Rosa was dozing in her chair and a tear was squirming its escape from a fold in her eyelid. Nellie signalled to Brian to remain quiet, turned off the light and led the child back to their room. Brian began playing with a wooden fire-engine Fay had bought him, while his mother told Fay what had happened and listened to her response.

'Jack is a no-good tumbleweed. He is so crooked, if he cried the tears would run down the back of his dirty neck. Him and Rosa get on well for long periods an' he palavers her and calls her his little hummin' bird. Then, she makes some blunder that costs him a dime or two an' he kicks the shit out of her.'

The sound of dogs fighting came from the courtyard. Fay walked to the window, rubbed away a few inches of grime and looked out. Her bottom lip curled and, with intense pressure, flattened the upper one. Then it dropped and front teeth bit into it. As if she did not know Nellie was there, she grated her curse:

'That he may finish up with dogs tearing off his scrawny testicles.'

With eyes closed, Fay was remembering her obnoxious first evening in The Sleeve. When Jack McHugh had insisted that he had to assess her worth himself in order to enter a price for her in his books. Whatever rating he had decided, he himself had not been worth much for a good three weeks afterwards. When he had tried to force himself upon her, she had whipped her knee up.

Nellie noticed Fay smiling. She liked when Fay smiled.

'Will you keep an eye on Brian for a few minutes, please?' She knew how much Fay liked minding him.

'Sure will.'

'Thanks.'

Nellie left them, crossed the courtyard and headed for the store.

There were about five dogs in the fight now but she steered clear of them. She breezed into the kitchen, pretending to Rosa that she wanted a loan of some sugar, but the Italian woman sensed something. She pulled a wicker chair up to the stove and invited her to sit and have a cup of coffee. Then she grinned and corrected herself.

'I forget again. You Irish so much love the tea. Tea is only for weak people. Strong coffee so much better.'

She made tea in a pot. Her own coffee dribbled, thick and tarry, from the large black kettle. Rosa sat into her own chair; a creaking bentwood rocker whose springs were rusted. Tufts of dirty hair sprouted from tattered upholstery on its arms, where a thousand circular mug-stains mingled on a timber protrusion. She took a mouthful and rested her mug.

Nellie was sipping nervously, not really knowing how to begin.

'You want ... for to talk, Nellie. I sorry. You must go into Sleeve tonight. Jack insist.'

'Oh, Rosa!'

'Not as *prostituta*, Nellie. I swear. You meet people. Be nice. Like you always are.'

'Thanks, Rosa.'

'But you wish talk about something else.'

It was not a question. Nor a demand. Her tone, and a pause after the first two words gave Nellie an undertaking of absolute understanding, just as surely as if Rosa had offered a signed statement of confidentiality. Instead of encouraging Nellie, however, this worried her. Rosa would be willing to help Nellie with a problem of her own, she felt sure. Her nature guaranteed as much. She might not wholeheartedly welcome Nellie's intrusion into her own affairs, however. Back in Ireland, Nellie knew, a 'do-gooder' was often despised. 'Always check that there's bread under the butter,' they would say of one. So she was faltering as she began:

'I ... you ... Well, I just thought you might like to have a chat with ... You have been good to me and I ... You ... I, you know, would ... that is, I –'

'You like for to listen to my problems with Jack.' The matter-of-fact, continental lack of shame was refreshing, but it caught Nellie unawares. In Ireland, it was almost an accepted ritual, to 'beat around the bush' before launching into a delicate or awkward topic.

'Not ... eh ... not unless it would help, Rosa.'

'Talking always is good. If talk is to *amica*. You *amica* ... How you say? Pal?'

'Pal. Friend. You have certainly been my friend. Although ...'

'Yes?'

Nellie decided to be just as frank. 'Well to tell you the truth, Rosa, I was afraid of my life of you when I came first. Now, however, I think you may not think as badly of me.'

'No woman likes to see beautiful princess arrive on her premises. Makes her feel ... how you say ... not ... not ... not ... oh, sounds like footwear?'

'Not sure?'

'*Si. Si.* Not sure of herself.'

'I was feeling like anything but a beautiful princess after the shipwreck, Rosa,' Nellie laughed. 'A Silkie, more like.'

'Why you speak about fabric?'

Nellie laughed again. 'Sorry, Rosa. The legends at home talk about the Silkies. Families who were bewitched and turned into seals. If ever they came out of the sea, they took on the form of humans again.'

'Ah! So you O'Connells be Silk ... ees, yes?' Nellie noticed, not for the first time, when Rosa smiled, her face brightened, lines of care disappeared and she was beautiful. As if reading her mind, Rosa took another slow sip from her mug before allowing its brim to nudge her chin and echo her crooning whisper, 'I too was called *principessa* once.'

There was a long silence. Rosa was first to break it. When she did, Nellie was stunned.

'How often Fay bother you?'

'What do you mean, Rosa?' Nellie was blushing.

'You know what I mean. How many times Fay be like lover with you?'

Nellie found a loose thread on her chair-cover. She began tugging it and examining it. She answered slowly.

'Only once. When I came here first. But I was willing, Rosa. I knew so little –'

'Sure! Sure! Rosa know.'

'But how, Rosa? How do you know?'

'I know by way I see Fay looking at you, Nellie. Her eyes tell story. Just like yours tell me when you come here. Tell man had way with you.'

While Nellie was recalling Jack sneering and hinting that Rosa suspected this, Rosa was stroking her arm comfortingly.

'Nellie, Fay is lovely person. It so easy to fall to her – how you say – charms? Poor Fay. I should have give warning to you, but I not think it happening so soon. So, when I know Fay take you, I get so sorry for you. And so mad with Rosa for not be telling you of danger all this time.'

'Danger, Rosa?'

'Yes. Not just danger to soul. To body too. Maybe even to *bambino*.'

'How do you mean, Rosa?' There was panic in Nellie's query.

And there, in front of a blackened stove, Nellie Hurley learned about degredation and disease and what could happen to unwary young women. Told in words that no Irish woman would dream of using: honest, down-to-earth statements, some of which she had to have explained. As they were sinking into her young mind like ploughshares, they were turning soft, gentle green fields of wild-flowers on pasture into dark, earthy tracts, all maggot-ridden and stony. By the time Rosa had finished explaining, it was trampled into slime. But she thanked Rosa for helping her understand.

'I change towards you, Nellie, when I knew you were no longer a princess. At least, not an innocent princess. And because I knew you needed me.'

Rosa did not mention Butch Maguire's request. Nellie smiled at this before she remembered what she had come for.

'But Rosa! Oh, Rosa, I am so selfish! We haven't spoken a word about your problems. About you and Jack.'

'You saw me through door when Jack beat me? Yes, I thought you might.'

'Is there anything I can do to help, Rosa? To give something back. Tell me if there is. Please!' Nellie reached over and took Rosa's hands.

Hands like red-ridged lisle.

From hardship.

Yet they were tender hands that had gently coaxed bodies into childbirth and confidently delivered those new lives into a world of sooty stoves.

'You may have already done something good for me, Nellie. Come, we clean the store.'

There was a demand in the suggestion. Not to ask any more questions.

Rosa hoped that the man who had come into her life just to ask her to look after Nellie might be her salvation. Eventually.

Nellie fell into a routine as a receptionist for clients: taking their coats, seating them and chatting to them until their women were ready. Some were self-assured but a number of fellows, there for the first time, were nervous or embarrassed. These she always put at their ease with her friendly manner. Jack McHugh was beginning to accept that the girl he had held such hopes for since the first day she'd wandered into his store would never be one of his women for sale. He had to agree with Rosa that her presence in the reception area took away some of the seediness of the place. Rosa was even able to coax Jack into giving Nellie the use of a room where herself and Brian could have some sort of family life.

Fay too, was clear about the nature of their relationship. She had long resigned herself to the fact that Nellie would remain a good friend but never anything more than that.

Nellie's Irish sense of fun was becoming sharper as she grew familiar with New York street-life. Fay helped by taking care of Brian on mornings when Nellie cleaned up The Sleeve, and on occasional free afternoons when she combed the harbour area, enquiring, searching, ever hopeful of finding Tim O'Mahoney. She enlisted the aid of Butch Maguire and he began plying sailors and dockers with drinks in search of information. Nobody recalled any man answering Nellie's description, but several people remembered the *Henry Clay* disaster and mentioned a surviving family sleeping rough near one of the wharves overnight. Under an old cart that a hobo had pointed out to them. There were reports that they'd gone inland to Cincinnati.

All of the descriptions suggested it was the Croker family and she would have given anything to meet Richard again. She'd adored the child and liked Frances too. Then she thought of Eyre and decided she could never face him. And she vowed once again never to become involved with anyone other than Tim.

Her self-imposed celibacy, in anticipation of a dream, was not proving too difficult because, in spite of learning more about the tough new world, she kept practising her religion and observing her Church's code of conduct. An old superstition lingered too.

Somehow, she kept believing that she would be the instrument through which Richard Croker would be saved from the curse of the guinea-fowl. If he still lived. Even if he were in Cincinnati.

Fay and Rosa advised her not to be living out her twenties in pursuit of a dream, without a mate. Whenever they did, she'd just smile and say, 'It's no dream. It will happen.'

'In Italy we say, bird in hand worth two in *albero*, but, *Mamma mia*, you do not even have tree. Go and enjoy yourself,' Rosa urged.

Fay asked, 'What about Butch Maguire?'

'No, not Butch,' Rosa clipped her short. Nellie was wondering why, and thinking of a lovely reason.

'He has visited the store five times in the past month,' Fay was saying. 'He'll sure be able to see where he's goin' if you partner him. He's eatin' more carrots than a buck rabbit.'

Nellie blushed. 'He's only passing on information about the family I set out from Ireland with.'

'Who you say they were?' Rosa was changing the subject.

'Crokers.'

'Goddamn bull-frogs.' Fay was rubbing her quicks with a pumice stone.

'Strange name. Not like Irish name.' Rosa seemed to be puzzled about something.

'They're Presbyterians.'

'Oh, Jeeze! Eyes close together, legs wide apart.' Fay sent Rosa into convulsions of laughter, through which she managed to quip, 'They say even their carriage lamps be set only inches apart.' Then she was suddenly serious again.

'Croker? Croker!'

'Yes, Rosa, what is it?' Nellie was alert. Pleading.

'Naw! It must not be so.'

'Mustn't be what, Rosa? Oh, Rosa!'

'Just a think. Ah my *dimenticanza*. How you say? I not remember?'

'Please, Rosa. Try to remember. Oh, please.'

'It will come to her, baby. In time. Some night she's on the roof, it will slip back into her head. You'll see.' Fay had noticed Nellie's distress.

'Name I read on paper Jack leave lying around? Cannot be sure. I will tell you if I theenk.'

ELEVEN

RICHARD SAW HER again the following week.

He was out walking with his father – their usual stroll before breakfast. Eyre liked glancing through a newspaper while he was eating and the newsboys never delivered to his area. Elizabeth Fraser was all dressed up in a fur-collared coat and white fluffy muff, and an expensively dressed woman, tall and delicate of face, accompanied her. Eyre lifted his hat to Mrs Fraser. She smiled back with her lips, but not with her eyes. Richard winked at the girl, then blushed. Eyre told him that Mr Fraser was one of the wealthiest men in New York.

'A bit of a silk-stocking dandy. Made his money from buying and selling property and invested his profits well. They are the type they call "savages in silk", a wealthy circle who, when not gossiping about some recent scandal, limit their topics of conversation to golf, treasure-hunts, polo, paper-chases and balls in mansions.'

'They sound boring, Father.'

'Correct, son. Their literature is bank books; they invent family pedigrees and hold garden parties – even for dogs. Monkeys attend their evening soirées in posh drawing-rooms!'

Richard was listening attentively but could not agree with Eyre's outright condemnation of these people. The phrase about bank book literature, in particular, appealed to him.

'The Frasers are the "dime looking down on a nickel" type, who quarrel if they don't get due precedence at recitals, operatic evenings, art exhibitions or on the golf course – where they expect other players to let them play through. Pleasure is their trade; idleness their occupation, son. That and watching their stocks increase in value. The Frasers and their ilk are a race bruised from wealth and the sores are becoming cancerous.'

Richard was surprised at Eyre's passion when he spoke so. Especially since much of what he was saying did not offend Richard in the least. What was wrong with sitting back and watching stocks increase in value?

'What's Mrs Fraser like, Father?'

'She's a harmless enough creature, but foolish in her way too. Very interested in the Roman Catholic Church and hosts ladies' lunches and afternoon tea parties to make money for charity.'

'Maybe we should go to one,' Richard joked.

'It will be some time before you can mix with such class, Richard; but it will happen,' he predicted. 'And when you do, be careful, son, because they will smile and be polite to you even when they are pulling knives from the pockets of their frock-coats. But I tell you, if you ever get the chance to tell one of them what I have just told you, take it. If not for your father's sake, then for the sake of the downtrodden Irish that the Frasers would spit on.'

Richard was not sure if his father's words were intended to put him off considering Miss Fraser as a friend. Had he noticed his wish to meet her again? He had always thought women could not compete with men as companions – except Nellie Hurley. Nellie was such fun! He was only a child then, of course. No, Elizabeth attracted him in other ways: in ways that promised excitement.

Recalling their earlier involvement with the police and Mike Walsh, Richard sensed the existence of some powerful machine behind municipal affairs. The huge buildings beginning to rise all along the Hudson River seemed to be monuments to it and, if he was to go through life in this city, he knew it would be foolhardy not to be a cog in it.

'Father, tell me again about this Spartan Association,' he asked abruptly as soon as they were sitting down at breakfast. Eyre was grave when he began answering:

'It's a group of young thugs of the labouring class from the Sixth and Fourteenth wards on the East Side. They obey Mr Walsh's commands. Mostly, they attend ward meetings and forcibly remove those who oppose Walsh. Then they go on to dominate the proceedings. They disrupt election conventions. Every time Walsh takes control of the platform, they lead a claque, laughing and applauding his sarcasm and satire. Some people call them "shoulder hitters", because of the way they intimidate opponents by jostling them in a crowd. Walsh formed the association in an attempt to build a firm political base for himself at Tammany Hall.'

'You talked about that before, Father. Where the hell is it? Or what goes on there?'

'You know that ugly old brick building east of Irving Place. On Fourteenth Street?'

'Can't say I do.'

'You know Sharkey's Place? And the Rialto Theatre?'

'Aye.'

'Well, there's a small lodging house near there. I think it's called the Central Family Hotel. Tammany Hall is right beside it.'

'It's a queer name, Tammany Hall.'

'Do you recall the captain of the Ohio River steamer telling us about the great Indian Chief called Tammany? You were only a boy then.'

'Only bits of it. I think I was more keen on looking into the boat's engine. Wasn't there some stupid yarn about Tammany creating the Ohio River?'

'Yes. Some say Tammany was a saint and people in Philadelphia celebrate a St Tammany's Day on 1 May. But it's from Tammany Hall that the Democratic Party's powerful political machine operates. They call their steering-group "The Wigwam" and their leaders "Sachems" so the Indian theme is maintained.'

'But what do they do, Father?'

'A good question, son. A good question, indeed. They claim to champion the poor. They get jobs for some; they provide homes for others – but always in the knowledge that those assisted will be available to carry out certain roughhouse tactics on Tammany's behalf. They have close ties with the police, fire and municipal departments. Some people say they are heading towards controlling the city completely some day.'

'And Mr Walsh is in Tammany Hall?'

'He is, Richard. The Irish were not very popular there and Walsh's rise to power was resisted. Recently, however, they nominated him for the assembly, so we could be hearing a lot more of the Irish in city politics from now on.'

Richard found his father's words fascinating. Coupled with his court experience, they were reinforcing his desire to be part of a movement that could influence things, that could make him somebody important, somebody powerful, somebody who could order that things be done and have his wishes obeyed – just like Mr Walsh. His Balliva birth might become a valuable asset and wouldn't it be great to have the Irish running the city? He was becoming excited by what he was learning.

Breakfast over, Richard helped with the washing-up. He always did that before leaving for school in the mornings. He wanted to do whatever he could to assist his mother, who was becoming frighteningly thin and delicate.

'I done the crockery, Mother,' he called, drying his hands.

'Did, Richard. *Did!* Your grammar is atrocious.'

Richard knew and did not care. He wanted to speak in the same way as his colleagues at work, who called him 'Dick' and brooked no hint of airs and graces. Besides, he knew Mr Walsh would not think much of fancy language or accents. If the Irish were becoming a force in politics, then Richard wanted to talk like them and act like them; after all, being a Presbyterian did not make him any less Irish, did it?

Taking his school satchel from the hook behind the door, he kissed Frances and bid her and Eyre goodbye. They wondered why he used the back door. They found out later, when the teacher at Lafayette sent around a pupil to enquire about his absence. Richard had never played truant before. After searching the house and garden, they found his satchel hidden in a shed.

Richard was taking action in pursuit of his ambition.

'Son of a varmint! His Spartan Association curs are the scourges of this ward.' The surly police officer was giving directions on where to find Mike Walsh. When Richard thanked him, he added, 'If he agrees to see you, which I doubt, don't tell him what I said about his muck birds.'

'What more do you know about him, officer?' Richard was not sure if it was wise to ask but it would be useful to know what lay ahead.

'At first he seems a good old soul, all friendly, if a little blunt. But he is as cunning and secret as a mole. He made money through politics and spent some of it on the poor. But he was no Robin Hood; he remembered every favour and would call for repayment at some stage. Woe betide them that refused.'

'Has he many enemies, officer?'

'He has, but he has a knack of crushing them. He'll stop at nothing when he wants to weed out any sign of rebellion among his clique.'

Richard thanked the officer and hurried to his destination. It was mid-morning and the sun was shining brightly. Stooping first to brush dust from his trouser-legs, he entered. A tall bartender with a greased moustache and white apron was polishing a glass. He looked sullenly at Richard before jerking his thumb towards the waiting area. Richard went over and sat. The bartender came over and murmured:

'Mr Walsh has a few rules, son. You sit here until the client that's with him leaves. Then it's your turn. Unless someone more important arrives.'

Richard was becoming nervous, being just a few yards from the man who could be the lighthouse on the first headland in this dark and dangerous sea of politics.

Walsh was sitting in a secluded corner, surrounded by boxes of documents, chatting to somebody. He was acting more like a customer than a proprietor. He called for a drink for his client and paid for it. Three times. He took only coffee himself. He looked shrewd, forceful, courageous and enterprising.

Suddenly Walsh began laughing loudly and shouting to the client he was interviewing, a man known to Walsh and his associates as Jackie the Mule. Jack McHugh.

'Well, you son of a sea cook!' Walsh was gleefully thumping the table with a large fist, but he was also sizing up the young man across the room, whom he had invited to call at noon. He was pleased to see Richard arriving at half past eleven. Yet he appeared to be lost in conversation with his client. The politician's dark hair was split in the middle and sleeked to the side with pomade. The face seemed friendly but, even across the dimly lit bar-room, Richard was able to detect green, penetrating eyes. They emphasized that this was a man who should not be trifled with.

When the client left and Walsh nodded to Richard, he felt important going over and taking the extended hand.

'Richard Croker, if I remember, from the courthouse. Was that your first time before a magistrate?'

'Yes, sir.'

'Forget the sir. Have you had much schooling?'

'Only a little, Mr Walsh. At Lafayette Olney.'

'That's enough. Books can get between a man's knees and trip him up.'

Walsh pointed to a group of customers at another table and said, 'Better know people than pages of print. Them's my library. I can learn and benefit more from them that's in shoe-leather than by studyin' what's between leather covers.'

'Them's wise words, Mr Walsh,' Richard was pleased to answer in similar dialect.

Walsh enquired little about his family or home. He seemed to know as much as he needed, and called him Dick. Probably checked him out at the Railroad Company, where he went by that name.

'No matter who kneads the dough, Dick, lad, it's the loaf that matters. And in the heel of the hunt, money makes the horse gallop, whether it has shoes or not. Come on.'

Walsh stood and shouted across the bar to the others who were waiting:

'Back tomorrow, guys; I gotta go now.'

'But Mr Wal –'

'I said tomorrow, cheesepuss!' A guffaw and Walsh took a long nap-coat from a hook behind him, then strode to the counter. The bartender handed him a stovepipe silk hat and silver-topped stick. He placed the stick across Richard's back and ushered him out.

'Must get you a job, lad,' he said, breaking into a brisk walk.

Richard told him that he'd employment at the machine shop of Harlem Railroad.

'What do they pay ya?'

'Three bucks a week, but I can earn more at the wharf in the evenings.'

They had arrived at a greengrocer shop that had boxes of meal, barrels of fruit and crates of vegetables on the pavement outside. The Jewish proprietor welcomed them.

'Very nice you to visit me, Mister Valsh. And how is your young friend?'

'He's well. But will be better for the job you'll give him driving your wagons.'

'Sorry, sorry.'

'Give him five bucks a week and three good meals a day.'

'Can't Mister Valsh. I like to but no.'

'I will buy him new duds, if that's what's worrying you.'

'Even if dressed like President, I cannot. Like I saying, no vacancies, Mister Valsh.'

Walsh took his gold watch from his pocket and glanced at it. His manner changed dramatically. Grabbing the greengrocer by the arm and pushing him into a corner between baskets of cabbages and corn, he began bellowing: 'Look here, Holy Moses! Half the sidewalk is taken up with your produce. That's illegal. You feed your horses on the street. Illegal too. And what do you sell in that back room over the furnace? Liquor, that's what.'

'Ssshhh! Mister Valsh. People pass by. Might hear.'

'The police pass by and they don't hear, Moses Kohn. Nor do they see, my friend. And you know damn well why that is. Yet you waste my time spouting out excuses. No vacancies! Well, make one. Fast! I know that three of your staff is not from my ward. For your impudence you will pay the boy six dollars a week.'

'Ah, Mist –'

'Seven!'

'Yes, yes, yes, Mister Valsh. Of course, Mister Valsh. I vas just trying to think what horse I vud allot to your nice young friend.'

Walsh told the Jew that Richard would report for work the following morning. As soon as he was out of earshot, his affected tantrum disappeared and he chuckled.

'Think what horse he vud allot, my backside! Let that be a lesson for you, Dick. Get them indebted to you and the farther on the wrong side of the police the better.'

He led Richard into a drapery store whose manager began adopting the same servile attitude as Moses Kohn and venturing complaints. Ignoring the excuses, Walsh tossed a ten-dollar bill on the counter.

'Dress this lad in your store's best tweeds. Give him top class shoes and a cane. You realize, of course, that the Fire Chief is aware of your premises not complying with regulations? And, by the way, them skips in the ladies' underwear store contain no French knickers and the excise officers know as much.'

Twenty minutes later Richard left the store in clothes that would indeed pass muster by a President. He was also wiser to the ways of Tammany Hall; wiser, and wanting to experience more of its power. He thanked Mike Walsh, who replied, 'That's all right, Dick. I owe you somethin' for gettin' you locked up. Now we're quits and let us keep it that way.'

He held out a hand and Richard clasped it and shook. As they passed by Moses Kohn's premises on the way back to Walsh's bar, Richard noticed that another stall had been erected on the sidewalk!

When he arrived home in his new clothes, his mother and father were so impressed that they forgot to chastise him for playing truant. But they were not at all pleased when he said he would be leaving school.

Next day, Richard began working for Mr Kohn. When he got to know him, he found him likeable enough. Moses began confiding in him, outlining the stranglehold being maintained on the business community in the ward by Tammany Hall.

'Okay! Vee get something from them, Dick, but by gosh, vee must to pay dearly for everything.'

Richard found the work boring, but remembered what Mike Walsh had said about learning through knowing and studying people. So he endured the dull routine of collecting and delivering vegetables. A number of lonely housewives attempted to lure him into their homes on various pretexts. His rugged features had some magnetic appeal. One appeared at her door to take his delivery on a cold, frosty morning in January. She wore the flimsiest of negligées.

'It is so cold outside. Can I make you some hot chocolate?' she invited in a voice as smooth as what she was offering.

'Sorry, Ma'am, I'm late with my deliveries.'

'Then come again. I can wait for your deliveries.'

Richard did not. He told Moses to get someone else to visit the dame. Moses tried, but all the staff knew her tricks. So Moses had to go himself. When he came back, he said to Richard, 'She asked me vas my kosher long, Richard. I said "No" and she said she vould stick to the Irish men. What she mean, Richard?'

Richard was smiling. He had learned more than mechanics in the railroad yard.

Business was quiet and Moses often moaned about the difficulty of making ends meet. Richard suggested a plan that had been forming in his mind for some time. 'Why don't you supplement your income from the produce by servicing the machinery of the suppliers?'

'But how, Richard? I not have the money.'

'Get it from the plant manufacturers. Their works are miles away and they'd be glad to have a service depot locally. They'd save on transportation costs if someone in the city done the job. You might even branch into servicing for more than the greengrocer trade. People are inventing all sorts of contraptions, and most of them need a mechanic now and then.'

'But I know nothing about machinery, Richard.'

'I do, Moses.'

A month later a delighted Moses was able to tell Mr Walsh that he would be taking on another horse-driver from his ward. Richard was happily making engines for hoists, sorting and grading machines. He still did part-time work at Harlem Railroad too, and colleagues marvelled at how quickly he could shape hot iron on an anvil, using two forty-five-pound lump hammers, one in each hand. Night after night he continued, working on a particular locomotive he had designed himself. It was to be a modification of George and Robert Stevenson's 'Rocket' system, which had twenty-five tubes of water crossing the firebox to create steam.

Richard's had an extra three and a refined exhaust system. The tilt of the thrust piston was more acute, too, and its water container stood inside the locomotive casing, not on a separate wagon. When he finally bolted the long stack to the giant round body, Richard called his friends John and Florence Scannell and Big Tim Sullivan to help him stoke the engine and to be his crew for a trial run along a siding used for the purpose. As the three worked feverishly to get up steam, Richard strapped a mast bearing a brand new Star-Spangled Banner to the stack.

'First one of its kind used in Harlem; it has the thirty-third star for the State of Oregon on its canton,' he boasted. Then he went to his locker to remove a box that had been there for more than a month. Excitedly he began emptying its contents on the footplate – red, blue and white streamers. Scrambling all over the engine, he tied them to flanges, escape valves, and to every available hook, eye, rivet and chain until hardly any metal was visible. The fire was glowing as he dashed back to the locker and returned wearing the tallest hat his friends had ever seen. It was fashioned from a sheet of light tin that he had burnished in the workshop. From its brim dropped a tassel that was at least five feet long, made from strips of coloured paper, mixed with scraps of silk and satin – remnants that Moses Kohn's wife had given him from her dressmaking room at the back of the store. Richard's excitement was matched only by his apprehension, as he stood erect in the cab manipulating the handle projecting from the driver's wheel. Feeling resistance, he called to his friends.

'Open the sweat door!' yelled Richard. This was a high, heavy, wood-beamed monstrosity that almost filled one wall of the workshop. It was so called because of the perspiration of anxiety shed whenever a new engine was moving through it for an initial trial run.

As his three men were struggling with its bolts, Richard called, 'Be ready to le'p on when I pass through.'

The door was opening slowly. It was dark outside, save for some gaslight spilling over a high wall to the right of the siding, shielding it from the street. Richard pulled a lever and the engine's own lamp shot a single, wide beam through the door and probed the blackness beyond.

Another lever.

Another held breath.

Nothing happened.

Richard tugged again.

No movement.

In frustration he whirled the wheel. There was a metallic jar as it reached the end of its play and whipped back, striking Richard sharply on the elbow.

'Thunderin' shit!' he bellowed, leaping from the locomotive and sending his carnival hat rattling across the floor. Crouching in agony, he turned his back to nurse the injury in folded arms.

'Get back! Quick!' There was urgency in John's scream.

'Dick! For chrissake!' Panic in Thomas's, as Richard looked around to see his locomotive's wheels turning ever so slowly to the thrust of its long shaft. There was a clawing cough and a black pall belched from the stack to mushroom against the ceiling. Richard sprang. No pain in his elbow now as the lump came leaping from his belly, disintegrating and shooting pellets of exhilaration.

'Yeeeh Hooooo! I done it! Up, boys, up!'

'Hurrah!' They replied in chorus and leaped onto the footplate to join him.

Through the workshop door, finding speed.

Puffing.

Chugging.

Pumping blood through adventurous young bodies. Streamers flying, flag fluttering, tossing shadows through iron tenement stairs on the left of the track. Responding to shouts from windows hurriedly opened, Richard released steam and the engine blew a hoarse, self-congratulatory whistle.

An elderly prostitute threw up a sash and displayed her upper body, holding a breast in each hand and shouting, 'When you get more steam up, young soap locks, you can come whup your pistons on an ole railroad lass.'

As the engine snorted indignation before re-entering the workshop, Richard was smiling at a young lady standing by the greasy tool bench. She was gazing admiringly at him.

'Well done, Richard.' Her approval was better than a state baseball trophy. A smut drifted from the stack of the engine, now welcoming sleep. It floated on to her nose. Both her glove and her cheek became smudged when she tried to brush it away. The blemish gave her a tomboyish look even more attractive than her refined countenance. Richard thought he was in love with Miss Fraser. And wondered how or why she had come.

The day after, Richard did some swimming and running before going to work out in the gymnasium.

'You're a good scrapper and wrestler,' his coach told him, 'but you'll have to sweat more, train more. Now get punching that bag harder and strain to make every muscle in your body hard and strong.'

Head down, Richard was pummelling away when the leader of a rival Gas House Gang by the name of Oweney Geoghegan passed by.

'You never built no locomotive yourself! Another lie to give yourself a big name.'

Richard stopped punching.

'You callin' me a liar, Geoghegan?'

'What did it sound like, platterpuss?'

'Care to step into the ring?'

'With a whippersnapper like you? I'd make mincemeat of you.'

'Come on in and try.'

'Go on, Oweney, and destroy him,' another of Geoghegan's gang urged.

'You asked for it, river rat.'

The coach noticed what was happening and came over.

'You guys gonna spar?'

'Yep,' Geoghegan answered.

'You want to, young Croker?'

'Sure, coach.'

'OK. Let's do this properly.' The coach arranged referee, seconds and timekeeper. Richard and Geoghegan were in their respective corners when the referee examined their gloves and discovered that Geoghegan had a horseshoe inside one. He removed it, warning Geoghegan never to do such a thing again.

After a couple of rounds, Richard was winning. Suddenly Geoghegan shouted to the referee, 'Look! He has a brass pin in the palm of his glove.'

Richard dropped his guard and opened his hand to prove his innocence. Geoghegan waded in and hit him with a haymaker. Richard fell, almost knocked out.

The referee disqualified Geoghegan. Richard, furious and wanting to teach his opponent a lesson, pleaded with him to allow the fight to continue, but the man was adamant.

The referee was a member of the Volunteer Fire Service. When they left the ring he said to Richard, 'We could do with men like you. Care to join?'

Richard remembered Mike Walsh advising him to do so if he got the chance. Many Tammany Hall memberships evolved from the Service.

Richard told the referee he would join if he did him one favour.

'What's that?'

'Tell me where Oweney Geoghegan's gang hangs out.'

'Mike Haggerty's sporting house in Thirty-fifth Street.'

Next day Richard told Florence Scannell and a few of the gang to scour the ward and to tell him if they saw Oweney Geoghegan. When they spotted him entering the sporting house, they hurried back and reported.

'Come on. It's the Gas House Gang's headquarters.'

They joined him eagerly in a race to the premises. When they burst through its doors, they were faced with at least twenty toughs who immediately rushed them, hurling chairs and tables in all directions. Richard flung a spittoon at Geoghegan opening a wound over his left eye. An Irishman called Patrick Kelly attacked and Richard locked his head under his arm. After the encounter, Kelly's right ear was missing. There was a piece of flesh between Richard's front teeth. Moments later he pinned Oweney Geoghegan to the counter, grabbing his fringe and lashing him with a chair-leg. Terrified, Geoghegan left his hair in Richard's fist. It was the only way to escape.

By that time they heard police in the street outside, both gangs hurried to leave. Some got stuck in the door, punching and kicking their way out.

Later, Florence Scannell told Mike Walsh that Croker was responsible for biting Kelly's ear and for hammering Geoghegan. Mike sent for Richard and sat him down in his saloon.

'I like a guy who can look after himself with his fists, Dick, my boy. And I like a guy who doesn't allow whiskey to fool him or steal his head. Such a guy will go far in politics – a good game that can be brought to pay out as well as a bank.'

Then Walsh told Richard all about 'repeaters' at polling stations; people who, through various ruses, voted a number of times for their preferred candidate, or the one who looked after them best. He expounded on other ruses, rackets and rigmaroles too.

'You will soon see for yourself, because there's an election coming up, Dicky Boy.' In the meantime, Richard became leader of the Tunnel Gang and a member of Tammany Hall. He began meeting Elizabeth Fraser more often, too. And he became a voluntary junior fireman.

TWELVE

During the years that followed, Rosa continued helping and protecting Nellie as best she could. Nellie repaid her by teaching her better English and watching Jack's movements, his drinking and his tempers. She seemed to be around every time he felt like venting his spleen on his wife.

As Brian grew up, Jack began treating him almost as the son he never had, taking him with him on the cart when making deliveries and teaching him how to fight and how to defend himself. He insisted that Brian attend school, and even saw to it that the lad studied at home each night. People were calling New York the largest Irish city in the world. With Brian's height and strength, under Jack's tutorage, he was learning how to survive. He acted and appeared far older than his sixteen years and knew the city and its ways better that some men twice his age.

Jack introduced Brian to many of the powerful politicians and city fathers who visited The Sleeve, educating him in the ways of the world, while introducing him to some of the lowest dens of vice in New York. 'To make him aware,' as he explained to Nellie: 'If a dog knows the cat scratches, he'll be careful.'

At Jack's behest, Brian joined the Democratic Party. 'The only future for the Irish in this city is to pack bunches of them into the organization,' he said.

'Any one of them in particular I should watch out for?' Brian asked.

'For the moment, get to know a fellow called Mike Walsh. He's another Irishman who came to New York as a child. Walsh sticks to an old saying, "Any dead fish can swim with the stream, but it takes a real live one to swim against the current." He's a lithographer and publishes his own newspaper.'

'What was it called?'

'The Subterranean.'

That evening, Brian read a copy of the publication in the local library.

From it, he established Walsh's political philosophy. In a leader Walsh pointed out all that was wrong with Tammany Hall:

> I know perfectly well, and no man who knows anything about the matter will dare question the truth of the statement, that the delegates to nominating committees in Tammany are not chosen by the electors in each ward, but generally by a few unprincipled blackguards, usually office holders or office seekers, who meet in the back room of some low groggery, where they place upon a ticket for the support of their fellow citizens a number of wretches of their own moral calibre, whose characters and consciences have been so long buried that they have become putrid.

Brian wondered did the low groggery referred to belong to Jack McHugh. He told Jack about his research. McHugh laughed and said, 'A fish will swim against the current until he sees bait going the other way. Oh, Walsh is a tough, but shrewd, nut. As a lad, he deliberately slept on park benches, believing it would harden him physically. Now he is a very powerful man in New York. Even though he's Irish, Tammany Hall was afraid of him and this forced its Sachems to vote him onto its Assembly.'

'Oh, there's gangs on the streets, Brian, but there's tough nuts in politics too. I saw one fellow chewing up a live rat to show his savagery.'

'They seem to have plenty of money, Jack.'

'They have all sorts of rackets. A worker at James H. Keyser's foundry told me that when iron chimney-pots on the roof of City Hall were condemned as unsafe, Keyser took them off, got them painted black and re-fitted them instead of supplying the new ones that was ordered.'

'Things are that bad?'

'That bad! People who never put a foot inside City Hall are on its payroll. The stationery bill for the Mayor's office is two and a half million bucks.'

'Ah, go to blazes! Sure you'd buy enough pens and paper for the whole country with that.'

'Not if you hand out blankets, saddles, and other sorts of goods to members of the staff.'

'Is nobody trying to stop this?'

'Stop it! Some chance. Would you believe even I have to pay back-handers to keep them out of my hair?' Jack shrugged.

Brian knew the reason, but said nothing. He had a few free hours, so he went and joined some other young men with whom he often pasted up election posters and delivered mail for Tammany Hall. Then he went to his part-time work. He sometimes drove a doctor's carriage but mostly he assisted in his surgery and kept some of his books. There was a large crowd in the waiting room when a young man limped in. Brian told him to take a seat at the end of the line, but the man told him he had a bad wound in his thigh. He hopped close to Brian and whispered:

'I saw you in Tammany Hall collecting posters for Mike Walsh. I work for him too. The Plug Uglies got me at it and stabbed me in the thigh.'

'Come this way.' Those waiting glared as Brian led the patient into a small corridor. 'You're right, I work for Tammany. I'll get you in next by the doctor's side door.' He held out his hand.

'Brian O'Connell's the name. Irish!'

'Dick Croker. Irish too, although it doesn't sound it.'

'Your voice does.'

They shook hands and at that moment, the door of the doctor's surgery opened. Brian ushered Richard in. The doctor stitched the wound and told Richard that it was nothing to worry about as long as he kept it clean. The stitches would have to be removed in two weeks.

'Thanks for that,' Richard said to Brian when he was showing him out.

'No trouble at all. Glad to help a Tammany man. We might meet again sometime.'

'I'd like that, begod.'

'Are you free tonight?'

'Yeah. Sure!'

'The stoop at Tammany. Six o'clock?'

'Fine.'

They met and walked and talked, Brian touching on everything Jack McHugh had said and on what he had read in *The Subterranean*. From accompanying the doctor on his rounds and from Jack's guidance, Brian was able to show Richard places in the city he had never dreamed could exist: upper-class mansions and decrepit alleys. He pointed out a nest of hobos sheltering in an approach to a sewer.

'They live along the service-path of the sewer. Hundreds. They crawl onto the streets before daybreak and return to their rat-holes after nightfall.'

'Poor bastards,' Richard mumbled as Brian began explaining strange words to him.

'A leatherhead is a stupid person, so those who don't like the police often call them that.'

They passed a barker standing outside an eating house who was calling out a long rigmarole:

> *Biledamancapersors.*
> *Rosebeefrogsegoosemuttonantaters.*
> *Biledamancabbagevegebles*
> *Walkinantakeaseatsirs.*

'You can guess what most of those dishes are,' Brian said, 'but do you know what "slaughter in the pan" is?'

'Beefsteak?'

'Right! I bet you can't tell me what "red mike wit a bunch o' violets" is?'

'Mike Walsh and a few virgins,' Richard laughed. Brian too.

'A real Irish one, would you believe. Corned beef and cabbage. And "drop one on the brown" is hash with a poached egg, but in the Bowery they call hash "mystery".'

'Bejaysus, I won't be hungry in this town anyways,' Richard said.

Richard liked Brian's sense of humour who, in turn, appreciated Richard's blunt, outspoken manner.

'You're a bit older nor me, I'd say?' Richard asked.

'What age would you say I am, Richard?'

'Most of the Tammany lads calls me Dick.'

'OK, Dick. What age?'

'About twenty-four.'

'Seventeen.'

'Ah buzz off!'

'Honestly.'

'Begod, we'll have to keep an eye on you in Tammany Hall. You could go places.'

'No. I'd rather be a henchman for someone else. "The tallest nettles hide the nicest flowers," my mother says. She's Irish too.'

'Oh! From what part?'

'County Cork.'

'Well, that's a good one. That's where I'm from too. But I left it as a kid. A lovely little spot called Balliva. I was fierce fond of a girl that used to mind me there. She was great fun. I can still see her lovely face and I always thought she had a lovely smell off her.'

'Well, you would never think you had so much romance in you!'

'I haven't. Well, not much anyway.'

When they parted later that night, Richard was convinced he had met a loyal ally. Brian felt some strange sensation. It seemed to suggest that he had almost a duty to protect Richard, perhaps for many years. He was still thinking about that when in bed in the corner of his mother's small room at McHugh's. But before falling asleep he had decided to ask the doctor if he could work extra hours in lieu of renting the unused bedroom above the surgery.

The doctor was a generous man who had, at times, lent him his carriage to run personal errands. Next morning, Brian explained his position to the doctor and asked about the room. The doctor agreed. But he did not ask for any extra work.

'The place will be safer with someone sleeping in it at night,' he said. 'Why don't you take the carriage at lunchtime and bring your mother for a drive while you tell her. It will be sorrowful news for her.'

Nellie was very proud when he arrived outside The Sleeve and led her to the carriage. Brian drove her around a few streets and into a new park that was being developed in the city centre.

When he told her, the clop of the horse's hooves was the only sound for a few moments. Then she put her arm around him and said, 'I will miss you, Brian. But I was beginning to get concerned myself. It's not right for us to be sleeping in the same room, now that you're a young man.'

'Thanks, Mother.'

'As long as you mind yourself, son,' she said and kissed him gently on the forehead.

Horses' hooves again. And Nellie in a long-cart with Malachi driving. A guinea-fowl in the park shrubs. The debris from the park development a pile of rotting bodies.

'Mother!'

'Yes, Brian.'

'Did you love my father very much?'

Nellie was taken by surprise. 'We were … The shipwreck separated us so soon.'

'The shipwreck. Of course. We never really talked about him, though.' Another silence.

Nellie was relieved by Brian's next remark.

'Is it not time, maybe, for you to … to walk out with someone else? You've been faithful to him so long. I'm certain that's what he would want.'

Nellie was pleased with her own cleverness when she said, 'I really hope to find a good step-father for you some day, Brian. Honestly, I do. But I have to be sure he's a good, kind person.'

'You deserve nothing less, Mother.' Then he changed the subject.

'What part of County Cork did you come from, Mother?'

'A lovely little spot called Balliva. Why?'

'Ah, nothing. Just wondered.'

Richard was learning fast from Brian. He made Frances furious one day when he jokingly told her the house was like a 'slap-bang'. He used some of the terms he had learned to Elizabeth Fraser too, just to torment her.

'Good to see you, my little patterer.'

'What on earth is a patterer?'

'Ah, what everybody knows is hardly worth knowing, girl. Here, take my arm.'

Elizabeth did not have her parents' permission to accompany him to Phineas Barnum's American Museum on Prince Street. Nor to wear the green dress, fringed with lace and bows that they'd bought for her in Lord and Taylor. A tiny boat-shaped hat of similar material tilted forward from her well-groomed chignon. Richard lifted his brown derby to her and gaped while he led her up the steps from street level to the first Grand Hall.

Inside one of the showman's dark display rooms, she shuddered at the sight of a 200-year-old mummy. In another, she was enthralled by the artefacts of American Indian culture.

'All that stuff was in a museum that was in Tammany Hall before the present crowd of redskins got hold of it!' Richard told her.

While they were passing into another room, he enlarged on the story of Tammany that he part-recalled from his river trip on the Ohio as a boy.

'Cripes, look at this little fellow. He's like a leprechaun.'

'Can't you read the notice? It's Tom Thumb.'

The antics of General Tom amused both of them. Strutting about like a lord, twirling his cane at cardboard animals and flirting with a selection of pretty dolls, he cut a comic figure. He passed a few risqué remarks at ladies in the audience, including Elizabeth, and they blushed.

'Come on, Elizabeth! The Hall of Mirrors might be better.'

Richard's grotesque shape there made Elizabeth laugh, but her own elongated image on the opposite wall was frightening.

'That's what I'll look like when I'm an old woman,' she said.

'You'll never age. I will keep you young forever. Honest!'

In the theatre that the showman had recently opened, Elizabeth was wildly enthusiastic about The Colleen Bawn by Dion Boucicault. She followed every twist in the story with interest.

'You Irish are a funny race,' she said during the interval, as they were sipping a soft drink together. 'You use ten words when four would suffice.'

'That's because we love listening to ourselves prating. A chat never done anybody no harm, so it didn't.'

Elizabeth had a habit of frowning slightly when he used bad grammar, but the ridges always smoothed back quickly to a broad smile.

As the play reached its happy conclusion, everybody began cheering. Hands in the air, Elizabeth was clapping loudest. Her face sparkled and Richard was delighted at her enjoyment, thrilled to be the escort of such a beauty. When she finished applauding, she looked at Richard, leaned her head on his shoulder and asked him if he would dive into the Hudson to save her, as Miles had dived into the lakes to save Eily in the play.

'I would lep into Niagara Falls for you,' he replied, and meant it. He took her hand and squeezed it. She pressed closer to him and he was just about to kiss her when the house lights came on. They both blushed and laughed. A long winding corridor led from the auditorium to the foyer and they dallied there to embrace briefly. They were arm in arm when they stepped into the street.

Nothing romantic or sweet was happening there.

Masses of people were gathering, all of them shouting at a row of police confronting them. Some yelled, 'The draft law is only for the under-privileged.' Others were waving large pieces of torn cardboard cartons. Badly scrawled messages accused: 'The Rich can Buy their Way Out,' and 'You Don't Have to Fight if you Have $300.'

'Quick! This way!' Richard steered Elizabeth away from the crowd and hurried her along. His voice was jerky while he explained:

'For the past two days, mobs from the slums are protesting against the draft because wealthy people can dodge it by paying $300. After making shit of … sorry! After smashing windows and looting, they burned buildings, maimed and even murdered people.'

'Good Lord!'

'I am Irish and you are too well-dressed,' Richard warned as they went scurrying along the sidewalk.

'Is this the same as what has been happening in Baltimore and Philadelphia, Richard? I heard Dad discussing it with Momma.'

'The very same. And the poor old Irish are coming off worst in the street battles everywhere.'

'Oh, I'd say they're well able to stand up for themselves.'

'God, I'm sorry. I shouldn't have brought you here. They did not move this far up Manhattan before, Liz.'

When she saw a tall man throwing a kick at a police officer, Elizabeth began trembling. She became furious, however, when about a dozen of the officer's colleagues stormed in, raining down truncheons on the offender's head. Blood spurted from his face as he tore himself away, howling in pain.

Richard was trying to move her along hastily but as they passed the Provost Marshal's District Office, huge flames mushroomed from its upper-storey windows. Part of the crowd broke away and began rushing towards them. Richard pulled Elizabeth close to a bank building nearby. To protect her, he covered her body with his and placed his hands against the wall above her head. Racing men pounded into him, but he took the buffeting and stood his ground. More and more degenerates were piling into the street. Some looked as if they were starving. Others were fat and frothing at the mouth. All were hurling profanities and insults.

'Let the draft blow up the asses of the wealthy!'

'Damn to hell the Tammany Hall muckrakers!'

'Shouldn't you tell them not to blame Tammany, Richard?' Elizabeth asked naively.

Richard thought better of enlightening her by explaining that there were indeed too many muckrakers in the institution. Furthermore, he was recalling a piece of Irish advice Brian O'Connell had given him.

'Never take the bull by the horns if his tail is pointing to the gap in the hedge, Liz. No! I have to mind you. Maybe we could go into that hotel there.'

'You're not afraid to stand up for what you think is right, surely?'

'I'm not. But I don't want you coming to no harm. Them fellows could knock you over and trample on you.'

The mob continued its rampage, waving cudgels, oars and slash-hooks. A few swung grappling irons, hammers and jemmies, all the time chanting:

> *Don't you be daft*
> *Don't face the draft.*
> *Pay the thieving bastards*
> *And sit back on your ass.*

Some looked dope-sodden, their eyes glassy.

They continued roaring out their grievances. A giant of a man with long black hair flowing down his back was smashing windows with a barge pole. As he passed, he thumped it savagely into Richard's ribs. Richard wanted to chase him, but was fearful for Elizabeth's safety now. Her parents might never allow her into the city again. If they knew she was in the company of a young man during this rioting, they would be frantic and might never allow her into the city again.

The crowd swelled and to protect her more, he pressed himself closer to her. The sweet smell of her breath and the warmth of her body were distracting him from what was going on around.

He kissed Elizabeth gently on the cheek, but she turned slowly and offered her mouth. Richard feared this might draw attention, but someone shouted that police horses were coming and the main body of rioters began moving away quickly.

Their shouts were fading into the distance, but other thunderings sent reverberations surging through Richard's young blood. Elizabeth's response astonished him. He'd regarded her as a refined and demure young lady but now she was responding to his kisses in a passionate frenzy. She opened her mouth and received his tongue. Neither of them had ever done this. It seemed the most natural thing in the world. And it was driving them wild.

'Let's go somewhere else. The police could see us here. It wouldn't do if they reported us to your father and mother. They –'

Richard's advice was silenced by Elizabeth's lips; hungry, demanding and uncontrolled. Her face was glowing in the reflection of smoke-edged flags of flame unfurling from a warehouse opposite. Her breasts were heaving and her long white neck stretching, inviting his mouth to begin a new exploration. More flames, orange and angry, leapt in the air. The young, learning lovers kept fuelling their own blaze. Elizabeth's hat was awry, hanging over her left ear. Richard smiled.

Fire-tender bells called time, however. Men were leaping from running boards and drawing hoses in all directions. There was a hydrant beside the blissful couple and they had to move away.

As Elizabeth was settling her hat, she suggested returning to her own home, but he had no wish to confront her parents yet. It would be some time before they would consider him a suitable escort for their daughter.

'What the hell are you doing here? Are you mad?' Brian Hurley looked down from the driving seat of a carriage. 'Jump in quick,' he called. 'There's another mob gathering in Forty-first.'

Richard helped Elizabeth inside and as Brian was urging the horse into a canter, opened the communicating door and looked down.

'Well, haven't I the handsome couple below?'

'Elizabeth Fraser. This is Brian O'Connell.' Richard performed the introduction and thought how strange it was, Brian's arriving to his rescue when he was in so difficult a situation. The carriage swerved as Brian tried to avoid a boy running away from the police. Elizabeth fell across Richard's lap. She made no attempt to rise so he bent and kissed her. Hard.

'That blooming hat!' She threw it on the seat and arched to receive his embrace. She took his face in her hands and was kneading his temples with her thumbs while looking longingly into his eyes. He saw her swallowing, then running her tongue-tip around her lips; and all the time her grey eyes were reaching in beyond his, her breasts rising and falling, in slow, deep motion at first, then quickening. His breaths kept time as their bodies came together. Then the carriage rocked to their abandoned kissing, biting and the running of fingers through hair.

There was a tapping on the communicating door. Brian grinned down at them. 'Sorry for interrupting, but we're clear of the trouble. I'm supposed to be driving this thing to collect my employer, so where'll I drop you?'

Elizabeth did not want to go home, but Richard thought they'd better.

'Your parents will hear about the riots and will be worried,' he said.

'But when will I see you again? Oh, Richard!'

'Oh, Richard!' Brian laughed. 'Dick isn't good enough for a gentleman.'

'I'll give you your instructions in a moment, horseman,' Richard sprang up and closed the flap. 'And you can call me Dick if you damn well want to. What's your address, Elizabeth?'

'Waverly.'

'We'll leave you at the corner of Fifth.'

Then louder, so that Brian would hear, 'Corner of Fifth and Waverly!'

Brian knocked his whip butt on the door and they began cantering.

Richard was holding her pins and clips while she settled her hair and hat, telling her for the fifth time that she was the most beautiful girl in New York.

'When can we meet again, Elizabeth?'

'Anytime. But someplace that we can be alone,' she implored.

Richard worried a little about this, but did not let it show. Her father Samuel Fraser was a powerful man in the city and Richard did not want to 'dirty his bib'. Furthermore, he wondered how long more he could force himself to bear Elizabeth's passionate embraces without becoming more intimate with her. The good sense in his head was no match for his emotions.

'Meet me at the Harlem Railroad workshop at six o'clock any Thursday or Friday. I'm working there on a bigger and better locomotive.'

'That will pull us in a golden coach to heaven's gate,' she laughed.

'This time I promise you won't get smuts on your pretty face.'

He helped her on to the sidewalk and she kissed his cheek. Richard began blushing, because Brian was looking. For a while he kept admiring her slim body as it walked away. Then he clambered up beside his friend.

'Hey! There's only supposed to be one riding up here. A leatherhead will take me in.'

'Not in this ward, he won't.'

'God, you're beginning to sound like a Sachem. Lucky I came along when I did or you might be a scalped one.'

'Yeah! Thanks.'

They rode along for a while, down along the outskirts of a park, with Richard enjoying the view. New buildings seemed to be sprouting up everywhere. They passed a structure that already had eleven storeys in place. He marvelled at the way builders balanced themselves on girders being swung into place by a crane, and at a mason walking nonchalantly along a narrow wall more than two hundred feet above street level.

The horse then lurched into a brisk canter, almost breaking into a gallop. Its collar and traces were flapping and its tail and mane trailing. Brian winked at a woman who gaped in consternation at their speed. She flounced away in contempt. Richard was glad when Brian delivered him to his own house. He was later than usual and his father met him at the door. He looked drawn and upset.

'It's Mother, Richard. She took a turn today. I was trying to contact you everywhere. I tried the store, the railroad depot, and Tammany.'

'Where is she? In her room?'

'Yes. But –'

Taking three steps at a time, Richard bounded up the stairs. The bedroom door was open and he was shocked at what he saw. Only a few hours before she had seemed reasonably healthy and cheerful; now her dark hair and eyebrows were all he could notice. Her face was almost the colour of the bed linen. Wasted. She was struggling to take a deep breath and there was a grinding of air battling through mucus.

'Mother! Mother! What the hell happened?' There was no reply. Not even a flicker of recognition.

'No! No!' Richard fell to his knees beside the bed and held her hand. It was cold, but not stiff. As he listened to his father's heavy footsteps approaching, he prayed to God not to take his mother from him. The floorboards creaked as Eyre entered. Seeing his son sob uncontrollably, he moved to the bed and placed a hand on Richard's shoulder, squeezing gently.

'A massive heart attack. If it does not recur, she will live, the doctor said. But she may be paralyzed. She was dragging the black and brass bed from the wall in the spare room to sweep under it. Always tidying up.'

Richard felt his father's hand trembling. Then it moved from his shoulder and Eyre Coote Croker hugged his son and,although Richard had always yearned for such affection, he wished it had not happened at such a moment. Then father and son were feeling embarrassed and Richard moved away.

'Have you told Eliza? Or sent word to Quartertown?'

'Eliza was here. She has gone to buy a few groceries and things. She will be back presently.'

'A pity Harriet went back to Ireland. Father, we will have to get a servant. I will pay some of her wages.'

'We will get one, Richard. But I will pay her myself. I wish I had employed one long ago.'

Eyre was more abrupt than he had been for a long time. Was it a father's pride? Resentment at an offer of help from a son?

Even though he'd borrow what he could from his brother or his wife or her family, there was an innate Irish resistance to accepting material help from sons or daughters.

Richard had many more opportunities to ponder his relationship with Eyre over the following weeks. They talked together often now.

'You know, Richard, I long to become an officer in an Irish regiment. None of my attempts to secure a commission has been successful.'

Richard made a mental note of this and wondered if Mike Walsh might be able to arrange one.

'I have a few wishes myself, Father. I'm getting horrid fond of that Fraser lassie, but I'm a bit windy about her family.'

'I told you a long time ago to tread carefully there, Richard. But in the long run, a man's relationship with a woman is no affair of his father's.'

Richard dropped the subject, because he was old enough now to realize that his father was not faithful to his wife and was frequenting some of the brothels that Brian O'Connell claimed could make a man plenty of money in this city, if he controlled one. It could bring power too, because leading politicians were using them and they paid well by giving favours in return for discretion.

Frances had another minor attack but the doctor kept assuring them that it did little harm and that the threat of paralysis had all but passed. She would have to take it easy for a long time to come, however: absolutely no manual work and a strict fat-free diet. Eyre had engaged one servant but had to sack her when she took to drinking his cognac. Another stayed in the house only a day.

'I just come off a ship from Ireland,' she had cried, 'and sure I didn't know the Crokers were the wrong collision when I took the job. I couldn't work for Press be Tearins. Anyone that does will deceive and have a babby out of fetlock and it'll have the evil-eye and if it's a gosoon, an' when it grows up it could shake the hand of a seventh son of a seventh son, and his hand will wither, so it will. An' that's because the Press be Tearins are all hairy ticks.'

Eyre found it hard to keep a straight face when he paid her a day's wages and let her go.

The third maid was very beautiful. Tall and shapely, she had large hazel eyes and long flowing red hair. She stayed a week.

'She got a better job elsewhere and left without giving notice. How inconsiderate!' Eyre complained to Richard.

'Desperate altogether,' Richard replied, not revealing his doubts.

Eliza came to help during the day but at night, when Frances was in bed, Richard and his father would sit in the kitchen discussing the threat of civil war, or arguing for and against slavery. Dressed neatly in their best suits, as was their domestic habit, they loved discussing politics. Eyre liked sipping a bourbon or two, Richard preferring Vichy water. Tammany Hall was a constant theme in their discussions.

'Given a strong leader, the Irish could be a dominant force there,' Eyre kept insisting and Richard agreed. He had been of that opinion for some time, and he was convinced he could be the one, if he played his cards right.

The conversations became personal at times, each man probing the other to confirm or dispel suspicions or theories they might have held. Richard again reflected on his father's early clashes with his mother, especially during his drinking bouts. It was one of the reasons Richard drank Vichy water.

Another topic was the apparent anomaly in Richard's love of small children, when his favourite canine was the bulldog.

'I often saw you drop something vitally important to go and play with a kid.'

'Aye. I love childer.'

'Yet, you admire those horrible bulldogs.'

'Ugly animals, but horrid loyal, Father. Friends should be like bulldogs.'

'Dribbling all over you?'

'A friend should stay by your side through thick and thin, and if he has to fight for you, he should be able to win. If a bulldog was a man, he'd be a powerful pal entirely.'

'How philosophical! There are plenty of bulldogs in Tammany Hall so,' Eyre laughed.

'Aye, but a few of them should be neutered,' Dick answered. 'And I can tell you, a bulldog doesn't get drunk either. If there's anything I hate more than a two-faced bum, it's a drunken two-faced bum.'

'Hey, easy on, son. I get sloshed an odd time.'

'Yeah. But you're not a bum. At least I don't think you are.' And he fastened his eyes on his father's until Eyre looked away.

One piece of advice passed on by Eyre during those discussions was based on words he'd heard many years before from Malachi Hurley.

'Know when the river is in flood, and don't try to ford it.'

Richard remembered, and was developing an uncanny knack of assessing a proposed plan of action, whether at work, at boxing, swimming, in athletics, at rat-baiting or at horse racing.

Most of all, in politics.

He trusted colleagues, believing that nine out of every ten earned that trust and that their appreciation would overcome any difficulties caused by the one rotten apple in the barrel. Not only that, but if the one who did Richard wrong came to him and admitted it, he forgave immediately.

Mike Walsh was neither a rotten apple nor a bulldog either. So for another few years Richard continued carrying out his wishes. At the same time, he was studying the lie of the Tammany land so as to be prepared when Walsh's fortunes began to wane. Tammany would experience a flood of dirty water in the meantime and Richard would have to stay away from the ford. But he would be selecting a steed that would eventually cross through – and bring him on his back.

He would have to choose wisely, because there was another prize he wanted in the future. Despite his initial reluctance, he had decided to marry Elizabeth Fraser. He was confident that he had already won her heart, but the man whose consent he needed before making their union permanent was an enemy of the current Sachems in Tammany Hall; a man who despised many facets of the organization itself. Samuel Fraser would take persuading that Dick Croker was a fit match for his daughter.

THIRTEEN

RICHARD HAD ASSURED Elizabeth that she'd enjoy the sport to which Brian had introduced him; that it was something she would never have seen before.

'You'll like it better if you give me a few bucks to bet for you,' he said, before adding a favourite saying of Brian's: 'There's no use in shouting at a fair when you have nothing to sell!'

Elizabeth was not so sure. Her father had always warned her not to lend money to anyone, but Richard was so excited. Eyes dancing with enthusiasm, he put his arm around her and gave her a squeeze. She rummaged in her purse and handed Richard some loose banknotes. He kissed them and said, 'That you may be as lucky as you're pretty.' The remark thrilled her, even though she knew all about Irish 'blarney'. Her father had warned her about that too.

When Richard led her through a maze of ill-kept lanes, however, she was began to feel apprehensive. But being with the man she loved – this unpredictable and outgoing Irishman – was so exhilarating that she overcame her inhibitions. Only for a short while, however. They returned to upset her when he led her into a dark passage. Elizabeth could hear loud voices ahead. About twenty men were pushing and shoving to get into what appeared to be a run-down saloon. When Richard approached, some doffed their stovepipe hats to him, others muttered, 'Afternoon, Mister Croker.' They made way for him and Richard led her through a door, up a steep stairs and on to a balcony packed with people of all colours and classes. Most were men in frock-coats and bowler hats, with gold watch chains slung from their waistcoat pockets and jewelled pins stuck in their silk cravats. Many of them wore loud check breeches.

All were looking down on a small square below that had a low woodframed pit in its corner. This was about five feet deep, oblong and lined with zinc. It contained fine white sand. A door opened on to the square. It led to a tavern, she assumed, because she could hear chatter from inside. The thinnest man she had ever seen emerged. His dress was comical – a sort of blue soldier's uniform. He peered down the alley as if checking that the coast was clear. Satisfied, he skipped a few paces to another, lower door. When he unlocked it and entered, Elizabeth heard dogs yelping.

The man came out, leading a wheaten fox-terrier, on a rope. He kicked back others that yapped at his feet. Returning to the tavern door, he called inside and immediately a group of men poured out. They were in various states of inebriation. Behind them came a tall, foppish man leading another fox-terrier. This one had a sleek, black coat and sported a fancy leather collar decorated with brass studs. A man strode dramatically into the centre of the pit. He carried a large white box. When he opened it, a black ruffle of rats scuttled from it. There must have been a hundred of the creatures and, even at such a distance Elizabeth recoiled.

When the thin owner held his dog between his legs in the pit, the brute was trembling with fear. Its dilated eyes protruded and a yelp shattered and became a craven moan. The man kicked the brute into the middle of the rats, which immediately started attacking. With bared teeth, the dog tried chopping at them but they outnumbered him. Rats were lacerating his ears, tail and paws.

'That's enough. They're blooded,' the man with the black dog shouted. 'Your bets, gentlemen!'

'You'll be alright here for a while.' Richard did not wait for an answer. He dashed back the way they had come and, in a few moments, she saw him crossing the yard below and handing over the money she had given him to the man who had called out. She was furious at his leaving her there among so many odd-looking strangers. More so, when they began pushing and jostling her to get a better view of what was going on below. She clutched at her hat to keep them from knocking it off, but the button of someone's coat tail caught her long skirt and tore it. A small area of her shapely upper leg appeared and a young counterjumper who was standing back from the rush leered. She had seen this fellow working in one of the fine stores she had visited with her mother.

That he may lose every dime he has, she thought while flouncing away along the balcony to put as much distance as possible between them. Her fury with Richard was growing. If he were a gentleman like her father he would never dream of bringing her to a dreadful place like this to watch a despicable and cruel pastime – she could not regard it as a sport.

She'd risked her parents' disapproval by coming out alone with Richard, an Irishman and a Democrat, the party of 'Rum, Romanism and Rebellion' according to Republicans. That disapproval would turn to wrath if ever her father found out that she'd watched rat-baiting. Tennis and polo were his sports.

There was disorder down below too, she could see. Richard joined others who forced their way forward as a man rescued the wheaten dog and brought him back to the kennel. In one minute Elizabeth witnessed more banknotes being handed over in stakes than she had seen in her whole life. She saw quite a few hats being doffed to Richard too, before the thin man in the uniform returned to call.

'Enumerators ready?'

'Aye.' 'Here.' Two men replied, then added, 'One hundred rats confirmed.'

'Timekeeper?'

'*Presente!*'

'Bloody Italian minutes, we'll never get finished before the police come,' a joker quipped.

'Referee, take over.' The uniformed man seemed glad to have finished his chore. He ran back into the bar.

'Hope the Mayor doesn't know his henchman is refereeing a rat-bait,' said a jolly-looking stout man who approached the ringside. He began counting.

'Ten, nine, eight, seven –' The black fox-terrier knew what was happening. He had been through the ritual several times. As each digit was called, he raised his forepaws and spread their claws, while keeping up an eager whine and straining at the lead. After the referee called, 'One', he shouted 'Drop!' and the dog was tossed in among the rats. Immediately, he snapped at two and they squealed shrilly, dropped, drew up their legs and expired. He bit again and another died. One after another they went down as the dog, his head held low and swivelling like a predatory serpent, kept snatching. He seemed to ignore the fact that the beasts were swarming over his back and hide. Their fangs were sinking into his neck, his thighs and his head. One scrawny black rat tore the poor brute's eyelid off. Yet the animal seemed to feel nothing. He just concentrated on one rodent at a time; disposed of it, then turned his attention to another. Occasionally, he shook himself and tossed clusters of rats in all directions. Elizabeth almost cheered when a brace of them landed among the spectators and three terrified men tried to rush through the tavern door together and got stuck. The howls! Another squat individual ran screaming down the alley with a rat's teeth firmly implanted in his penis. Someone shouted, 'That poor rat won't have much of a snack off Isaac!'

Elizabeth looked on for more than a half-hour. Most of the rats were dead by then. The dog was looking the worse for wear too. The sight disgusted her, because as more rodents were dying, those all around her were roaring exhortations. The cheers of the gathering below were getting louder too. But Richard Croker was loudest of all.

Two men left the balcony suddenly, almost knocking her over. Another nodded his sympathy, remarking, 'Two of our fine, clean-living politicians enjoying themselves? One hundred rats in twelve minutes; that's the record the two-legged ones want to beat. Those in the silks. Look down now!'

When she did, the crowd was piling through the door. Richard was almost knocking others over in his hurry. The thin man was back shovelling up dead rats into a dirty sack.

The people on the balcony began dispersing and Elizabeth became worried at the possibility of being left alone. When a group of four remained, she became uncomfortable because the counterjumper who'd spotted her torn skirt was grinning impudently at her. There was quietness now and she was becoming alarmed, wondering would she be able to find her way back home alone before darkness fell. The counterjumper was probably hoping that she might accept an offer to escort her, she was thinking. It might be the sensible thing to do, but she would never gratify someone so ungentlemanly. Loud shouts from the bowels of the tenement distracted her.

'Elizabeth! Elizabeth!' Richard was gasping when he staggered onto the balcony and threw his arms around her. 'Here, my lassie! Here! Your money back and more. Lots more.' And he stuffed a pile of banknotes into her hand and as many more into his own pocket. Then he grabbed her and swung her around, the intense annoyance she felt since he left the balcony, along with her vows to reprimand him, were already becoming lost in his exhilaration.

Over a meal in a restaurant later she emphasized her disappointment at not being treated like a lady. But she could only laugh when he defended his actions: 'Sure, the queen bee always has to be provided for.'

Afterwards they took a carriage ride to Upper Manhattan where Brian had brought Richard the previous Sunday. It had lanes and woods and Elizabeth appreciated its serenity after her experience earlier. They held hands, but he was thinking how he might use his winnings to gamble on an upcoming cock-fight at Kit Burn's Sportsman's Hall in Walter Street. He hardly heard a word of what Elizabeth was saying about her mother's charitable work and how she loved helping her with it. Until she interrupted.

'Please talk to me, Richard!'

'All night, if you want. As long as it's about engines and horses.'

'Not really subjects for a lady.'

'Love, then. Here, give us an auld kiss.'

She did. And then was furious with herself. Especially because, although their interests were miles apart, she was unable to resist the rugged charm of this young man. He could quell any bad feeling she had for him with a phrase or a gesture. Even a coarse one.

They sat on a bank covered in oak leaves. It sloped to a small stream and Elizabeth allowed its water to go rippling through her hand. She thought about her strict upbringing and how her Church discouraged what it called 'keeping company'. She was doing this now, and enjoying it. Richard suddenly kissed her. For a long time. Delight and pleasure began playing and skipping through a thousand winding catacombs far inside her. He kissed her again and this time she responded, although she knew she should not.

After the kiss, she allowed her fingers to slide beneath the brownish water, saw her palm cup and capture. She was playfully allowing it to drip onto Richard's neck, to glisten and scurry and trickle around his ear. Then, in mock anger, he grabbed her wrists and pinned them to the mossy bank. He looked down at her breasts, marvelling at how erect they were. He felt the warmth of her body against his. And its haunting fragrance. A chaffinch sang overhead and a beech branch, beyond the stream, mottled the sunshine that seemed to seek out Elizabeth's soft skin. And he began to wonder was he as tough an Irishman as he considered himself.

'Begod, we seem to be best when nature is wild.' He smiled.

'Let's see can we prove that,' Elizabeth answered, sounding bolder than she felt but wondering what new delight they would be exploring on their bed of leaves.

Sea, city and a million hardships had no place in a Manhattan glade that evening when Richard Croker and Elizabeth Fraser explored their youthful pleasures. Not in lust – Elizabeth knew full abandon could come only within marriage, and Richard realized this and struggled to respect it. But it was blissfully enjoyable.

They waited and dozed in each other's arms, she wrapped in sweet enchantment, he a little surprised that he was allowing desire to dominate when he should be taking satisfaction in the amount of money he had won. Idly, he picked a fern and drew it across Elizabeth's brow, lightly brushing it around her temple and finding her delicate neck. It discovered a tiny ladybird trespassing and flicked it away. Before they left the place that evening, they knew that they had fallen in love. Elizabeth was pleased. Richard was berating himself. The Frasers were wealthy and influential and could be a distinct asset to a man's advancement in New York; but he was worried in case love should make him sentimental. Or, more seriously, that it might encroach on the time he knew he needed to give to Mike Walsh to ensure his own advancement in Tammany Hall.

FOURTEEN

WHILE SHE WAS WATCHING Brian develop into a strong and handsome young adult, Nellie never forgot Tim O'Mahoney, wondering each morning if the new day might bring news of him. Although disconcerted by her early experience with Fay, she cherished it for making her aware of what life with Tim could be like. That anticipation kept her spirit alive.

At least once a month she visited the shipping offices, looking for traces of either Tim or the Crokers. Although it looked as if they had all been lost, she remained confident. She had to meet them. Now that Brian had left The Sleeve, she would have to follow suit, so that both of them could use the name Hurley again. Although glad he was free of the place, Nellie was lonely when Brian left. Fay noticed, and arranged a party to cheer her up.

'Don't we all need to let off a bit of steam,' she had laughed, adding, 'Is there any fella' you'd like to bring?'

'There is. But I don't know where he is,' Nellie had answered with some melancholy.

'Sometimes I think it's about time you had a man, and other times I feel you are better off. They're all bums and bastards,' Fay said.

Yet, when Brian had asked later if he could bring a friend, Fay answered, 'Ah, heck, no, Brian. There'll be too many women here as it is.'

'It's not a woman, Fay.'

'Oh, Jeeze. Then bring him along, pal. And a few more.' She sounded her copper-based laugh.

Now the guests were gathering in a large room above a saloon. Gaudy cardboard harps and shamrocks hung from the ceiling. Nellie arrived, wearing a plain black organdie dress. Her pallor added a subtle elegance to her beauty that tendrils of long and short ringlets, trailing across her bared shoulders, accentuated. She shuddered on remembering the christening party and her terrifying walk home, then prayed silently for the poor imbecile who had accosted her.

'Thanks for going to so much trouble, Fay.'

'The only trouble I had was squeezing into this dress. But your son helped me.' Fay winked at Brian, who was kissing Nellie.

'Don't mind her, Mother. It was Jack McHugh who prized her in.'

'Aye! With his jemmy!' Fay laughed coarsely.

In the tight-fitting, gold dress, Fay looked a real hooker, but for Nellie she radiated the kindness of one stout heart that had suffered for another. Fay picked up a tray loaded with small plates of poppy seed bagels and goat's cheese. She took her place at the entrance to the room, greeting everybody with a big warm smile, saying, 'Here, try my poppy with a shmear.'

Even Jack, but he answered coarsely, 'What if I like your poppy with no smear?'

Fay was not going to let him away with that.

'That's the way it would always be for you, you no-good skunk.'

Butch arrived, dressed in a green jacket and bow tie. He gave Nellie a present all wrapped up in tinsel. A black handbag laced with strands of silver.

'But why the present, Butch?'

'Because this party is for you,' Fay explained.

'But why?'

'Because you're such a fine lady. Now shut up and enjoy yourself.'

Nellie was touched. She took Fay's face in her hands and kissed her gratitude. She kissed Butch too.

'Thanks for the bag, Butch. It will go beautifully with this shawl Brian bought me.'

He blushed and his finger kept coaxing a bagel crumb to the rim of his plate. Then he noticed Rosa in the crowd and began waving. She was smiling back secrets.

They ate off trestle tables neatly covered with green cloths. 'Happy Days' was done out on gold paper pinned to them. There were piles of cold swordfish, hake and even lobster that Butch Maguire had collected from fishing friends.

Jack McHugh supplied the vegetables.

'For free!' Fay enthused. 'Jeeze I'm goin' to enjoy them. Getting' sump'n off McHugh for nowt! Christ!'

Rosa served the minestrone soup, macaroni pie and *zabaglione* that she had prepared. Back-brushed and shining, her strong, jet black hair plaited in a thick coil was held in place by a large rosewood comb. Her new blue dress had a deep, scalloped neckline. She bent low when she served Butch and he blushed at the closeness of female flesh.

'Christ, you are too much of a beauty for that racoon in a bear-trap.' Fay winked at Rosa and slapped Jack on the back. When he laughed, she added, 'I thought you only used your teeth for catchin' deserters from rat-pits.'

'If that was so, there'd be bits of your gristle between them,' Jack retorted.

Brian had brought two fiddlers, a concertina player and a button accordion player, and they were tuning up. He was hoping to join in with them as the night wore on, because a few Irish friends had been teaching him how to play the *bodhrán*.

'I'll hit it a few thumps when you're too drunk to notice if my drumming is wrong,' he told Fay.

'You started playin' yesterday so,' Fay answered. 'Anyway, nothing could be wrong with the timing of a son of Nellie O'Connell. A great kid! Jeeze, I'm still callin' her a kid!' Then, casually, 'Who else is comin'?'

'My pal, Dick. Dick Croker.'

'Didn't I hear your mother …? Ah, no. Maybe I'm wrong. Anyway, I'm too bloody tipsy to think.'

'You were good to let me bring him. You'll like him. Plain, honest – maybe a bit rugged but his heart is in the right place. Thanks, Fay.'

'If he's rugged, I might be doin' the thankin'. I like hard men.' She rasped the words, 'Hope he arrives soon or there'll be nothing left. This crowd would eat the hind leg of a mangy racoon.'

'I told him not to come until late. It's a sort of surprise for Mother. Croker is from her home place.'

'In Ireland?'

'Yes.'

'Oh, now I remember. She did say something about it. To Rosa.'

'Says he has been looking forward to meeting her for ages, Fay. To find out exactly where us O'Connells lived. He never heard of a family of that name from his mother or father and he only remembers a few families himself. There goes the music. Come on and dance.'

'Dance with your mother, you scut.'

'She's already on the floor. Look!'

'With Jack.'

'Jackie the Mule.'

'Where did you hear that? He'll kill you if he hears you using that name.'

'Nobody in Tammany calls him anything else. But come on!'

Brian whisked Fay onto the floor and they faced another couple for 'The Siege of Ennis'. Nellie had taught him the old Irish dance well. Hand properly held across his chest, he took Fay's. Poised on his toes, he awaited the downbeat that would signal the beginning of the set. Then, incredibly light-footed for such a tall young man, he began moving forward and back.

Once.

Twice.

And again.

As a musician shouted '*Slios céim*', Brian was already gliding his partner to the side with a breeze of agile steps. His movement seemed effortless.

Up through the couples.

Little said.

Concentrating.

Until they faced Jack and Nellie.

'I have the most beautiful mother in the whole world.'

'Pay attention to your steps, young fella', she's my partner.'

'Jeeze, will you look at McHugh! Never saw him in a suit before. It bulges. Your flanks is hoppin' like two ferrets in a bag.'

'What about your own, Fay? They're not exactly tidy.'

Hands up.

Pass under.

Face another couple.

Brian knew Jack's slight had hurt Fay. He saw the tiny tear before she shook her head to flick it onto his shirt. A very small, oval-shaped, damp patch emerged and he remembered his mother telling him Fay always wore the Miraculous Medal of Our Lady. There should be medals to Mary Magdalene, he thought.

The musicians were speeding up the tempo.

Wild swinging.

Brian was holding his head high as a heron inspecting the morning.

Faster.

Heels, toes tapping harder.

Long legs lifting until they were parallel to the floor.

Again.

Five times.

Higher every time.

Fay dropped out. Exhausted. Others followed. Accordion, fiddle and *bodhrán* diversified to a fast hornpipe, encouraging the remaining individuals to display their skills.

Jack McHugh lasted longer than Brian thought he would.

Now the musicians were signalling. Grinning at each other.

'The next modulation will get him.'

Clattering of boot studs and heel tips.

'It didn't, bejaysus.'

Nor the following three. But as the fiddle bow began moulting and the accordion player perspired, the man hammered Brian's *bodhrán* until the bone was furring its goatskin. Jackie the Mule gave his last kick and pushed his way to the counter.

'Having a good time, Mother?'

She was smiling when he faced her.

'You were good to get the shawl for me. It's beautiful.'

'Like you.'

'Thanks, my darling son.'

'Now, Mother?'

They reached back into centuries as they closed their eyes and let the primal chords clutch their souls. Mother and son danced; stepping high and fast and proudly for themselves and for generations gone. And Nellie Hurley wanted to be dancing for Tim O'Mahoney.

But tonight she would dance for her son.

'You're the best mother in the whole wide world,' Brian told Nellie when he stepped past her, as the ancient ritual demanded. He kissed her lightly on the cheek. Her heart commandeered the *bodhrán* beat and decreed that she must cry.

Dancing on and on, her tears received no welcome. Intense high-stepping was atomizing them and flinging them to nothings.

Aon, dó, trí. Aon, dó, trí. Now it was Malachi calling, 'One, two, three' in a language, grand, Gaelic and gallant – the only tongue with which to whisper words of love, its speakers always claimed. Nellie was watching him on his creepy stool in a small whitewashed cabin overlooking a blue cove. The sea swelled suddenly and she was feeling the beating of wind and rain on the stern of the *Henry Clay*. When she opened her eyes to worship Brian, her shoes began battering birth pangs into a bare board table with a slit cleaned of its grease.

A fiddle's inflection was urging the accordionist to renewed gusto. The *bodhrán* player was standing, the more to emphasize his throbbing demand. Nellie Hurley danced to the moon and back by the galaxies with verve, but also with grace and dignity.

When they finished, the crowd applauded and closed in on them. Brian embraced his mother and kissed her.

'You're as grand as Queen Maeve of Connaught, Mother, and I love you.'

Butch Maguire requested the next dance and she asked for a drink of water first. Brian rooted in his waistcoat pocket for a fob watch, wondering why Dick Croker was late. It was fifteen minutes after the arranged time.

After Nellie's dance with Butch, Brian brought her to the section of the counter opposite the entrance door, where she would get a good look at Croker. Would she recognize him? Fay joined them. Tipsy. She introduced a story about a prostitute soliciting in Baxter Street.

'This dame approached a guy and he took one look at her and passed her by, saying, "Beat it, Hookie. I'd get crabs off you." The hooker shouted after him, "What the hell do you want for a buck? Prawn bisque?"'

Brian smiled in embarrassment. He could enjoy that sort of story in the company of Dick Croker or other men, but not in front of his mother.

The party was becoming tired. After the excitement of Brian and Nellie, and their sensational exhibition, the following dances were tame. When the musicians stopped for some refreshments, guests began thanking Fay, telling Nellie she deserved the evening out, and leaving.

Brian was despondent. Only Fay could have known why, and she was drinking too much to remember. She and Rosa were sitting on either side of Nellie, drink loosening their thoughts. Rosa placed her hand on Nellie's arm and said, 'Nellie, you too nice not to have man.'

'And you should be taking a drink too,' Fay added.

'That young man you have on mind. It time you forget.'

'Indeed it is. All these years waiting for someone you only met for a few minutes on a ship. Crazy!'

'And you were only child. I hope you not mind us talking so, Nellie.'

'Not at all, Rosa. I know what you say is probably sensible, but I just don't want to leave go of the memory.'

'He's probably a skunk. Like all men.'

'Then why should I bother with any of them, Fay?' Nellie laughed.

'Fay! There be lots of good men. You know it. Take Brian there, he's –'

'I'll take him any time Nellie gives him.' Fay laughed and slapped Nellie's thigh. 'Jesus, keep him away from the likes of me, Nellie. Seriously, though, would you not just try going out with someone once and see would that make you forget?'

'But maybe I don't want to forget, Fay.'

'Wouldn't mind, but you're a passionate dame. I know it. Remember?'

'Enough, Fay!' Rosa's reprimand rode on a darkening glance. Fay gulped down most of her tankard of beer. Too quickly. She belched.

'S ... sorry!'

Nellie reassured Rosa. 'Don't worry, Rosa. Let her talk away. We have avoided the subject for too many years.'

Fay thumped her empty tankard on the table.

'I have been with wo ...women and men, Rosa knows that. Every ... body knows it. And I can honestly say about that one incident with you, Nellie, that you were the ... the hottest bit of –'

'Fay!'

'Honestly, Rosa. It's alright. Let her talk. I don't mind at all.'

'Christ, look at all those ... them ... those fine fellows from Five Points that are sw ... sw ... swaggering around in f ...fancy uniforms. All answering Pres ... President Lincoln's call and m ...marching off to war. Wouldn't Nellie put f ...fire in any of their bellies and make them fight all the better?' Fay staggered to her feet and tried to salute. But she had had too much to drink and flopped back into her seat.

'Maybe I'll try to seduce one of them when they all come marching home, Fay.' Nellie nudged Rosa. Rosa winked.

'And Fay handle ten more at same time!'

Fay twisted her head and glared mockingly at Rosa. Then the three women laughed heartily and held hands.

'Christ, if Pres ... Pres ... If Linc ... If they they sent a few strong women like us to Illinois, we'd settle the whole cussed war in days, eh girls?'

Most of the guests had left. The caretaker of the premises began sweeping the floor. A paper shamrock got entangled in the strings of a cardboard harp. Nellie watched their progress ahead of the brush until dust covered them up. Maybe Fay and Rosa were right!

'What the hell became of him?' Brian asked Fay, not expecting an answer. She was incapable of delivering one.

Butch helped Rosa haul Jack to his feet to bring him home.

Only Brian and Nellie left the saloon sober. Each had a shoulder under one of Fay's arms and they were dragging her along. She was trying to sing a song from an old musical called *Tammany; or The Indian Chief*. Although her words emerged slurred and faltering, she managed it reasonably well:

> *Fury swells my aching soul*
> *Boils and maddens in my veins*
> *Fierce contending passions roll*
> *Where Manana's image reigns.*

FIFTEEN

SOUTH CAROLINA and six other states had seceded from the Union, forming a Confederacy. On 12 April 1861 they fired on an isolated garrison at Fort Sumter. When the President called for volunteers, four more states joined the Confederacy. Serious military operations had begun in June and despite the Union's advantage in government control and manpower, the conflict had now dragged into its third year.

'It's as bad as Ireland. The agricultural, slave-owning South resenting the North's free, city-dwelling wage-earners!'

Eyre Coote Croker made the remark without looking up from the newspaper. Frances paid little attention. She was having trouble turning the flower design on her crochet work. Since her heart attack, her fingers had become stiff. Still, she thanked God for a quick recovery and for having such kind and considerate children. Richard had seldom left her bedside while she was ill; when he did, it was mainly to run errands for her. She worried that he must have missed some important meetings on her account. Eliza was a great help too, but it was unfair to be relying on her to look after the house.

'You have dismissed three maids now, Eyre.'

'One more unreliable than the next.' Eyre lowered his newspaper. 'Irish servant girls, they expect the earth, but work as little as they can. And they are so slovenly!'

'I thought the third girl was very efficient. Accomplished. Beautiful, too.' Frances did not say what she was thinking. 'Speaking of Irish girls, Eyre, Richard asked me a few times if I remembered a family called O'Connell around Ardfield. I cannot place them. Can you?'

'O'Connell? No! Why is he asking you that?'

'Oh, just some fellow he has befriended. One of that Tammany Hall crowd. Told him his mother came from around Ardfield.'

'But his father might have been from anywhere. I must ask him what her maiden name was. When my mind is not on this Civil War.'

Since Richard's involvement with Mike Walsh and Tammany Hall, Eyre had become a staunch American patriot. At least, that is what he believed. A year after the war had begun, he became a hastily promoted Lieutenant in the New York 88th Regiment, something he had been hoping for quietly since he had splashed through the surf at the Red Strand in Balliva all those years ago.

'All the Crokers were good fighters; Richard should think of joining too,' he had urged Frances, but she would not hear of it.

'He is only a child,' she chided.

'Don't let him hear you say that, woman. Twenty-two and worldly wise, he is.' Richard came into the room while his father was still expounding.

'Richard should join William D. Kennedy's Tammany Regiment. It'd help his future.'

'I can't, Father. I'm not initiated yet. Only true Braves can join the regiment.'

'Oh! Are you here? You might be drafted into some other unit so.'

'My God! Could he?' Frances paled.

'Not at all, Mother. Mike Walsh needs me too much. He is sending my father instead!' Richard winked at Eyre, who did not realize the full implication of what his son had said. At Richard's request, Walsh had helped Eyre to receive the commission he had craved. Walsh had paid the $300 needed to keep Richard from being drafted too.

Richard was pouring himself a glass of milk. 'Besides, politics does be the same as war, except that nobody gets kilt. At least, not many.'

Now that Frances was fairly well again, Richard was immersing himself in the affairs of Tammany Hall with renewed vigour. An ambition to become a Sachem was consuming him, to the exclusion of every other consideration except his mother's health, Brian O'Connell's friendship and Elizabeth Fraser's love.

Since the outbreak of war, Eyre had spent almost three years at his regiment's city headquarters, but now he was awaiting despatch to Pennsylvania where he would join an ad hoc reserve regiment in support of General George C. Meade. The objective was to prevent General Robert E. Lee's troops from crossing the Potomac.

Frances had mixed feelings about her husband's departure for the war. Since their arrival in America, their marriage had gradually deteriorated. She was quite sure that he was unfaithful, but never accused him. Although Eyre was kind to her during her many illnesses, he spent most of his evenings in saloons or sporting clubs, arriving home late and drunk, demanding conjugal rights. Despite her illness, she had given birth to their tenth child the previous month and was making a crochet bonnet for her. Often, she wondered if they'd have remained happy had they not become reasonably well-to-do. When times were tough and they had to work hard together to earn a living, their companionship seemed to matter more.

Eyre's army wage was reasonable and, during frequent days off duty, he still did some veterinary and farrier's work in the wagon yards around Brooklyn and the harbour.

Richard was contributing to the home, too, some weeks quite handsomely. Whenever he gave her an unexpected bonus she'd question him as to how he earned it. Always, he would just grin and say, 'What you don't know won't worry you, Mother.'

But it did.

Often.

'Damn! I dropped a stitch.' Richard came over and patted the back of her head.

'Are you picking up the soldiers' language from Father?' he laughed.

Eyre grinned knowingly. 'You might pick up more than soldiers' language if you keep frequenting those sporting houses, my son. You'll soon be going to Kit Burn's Rat Pit.'

Richard knew what he meant. The establishment at 273 Water Street sold vegetables and confectionery but was also a brothel. Jackie the Mule ran it and it was better known as The Sleeve. He often intended visiting it, to investigate allegations that the Mule forced fallen women to prostitute themselves in return for accommodation. Brian O'Connell's mother had a job as receptionist there.

Frances missed the implication in Eyre's taunt, so the moment passed with Eyre returning to his paper and Richard regaling his mother with stories about the railroad, Moses Kohn's vegetable store and his now-thriving machinery business.

'I done a great deal with the a merchant from Stratford today.'

'Did, Richard! *Did!*' Frances was becoming tired of correcting his grammar. Her reprimand did not dampen her son's enthusiasm.

'This fellow supplies chickens from Connecticut to Kohn's store and others. He does be always ullagoning about the cost of servicing his wagons. So I arranged with Moses to start loaning him a wagon to deliver to the other stores while I repaired his own. That way, Moses gets paid for the wagon-hire, I get paid for the servicing and the merchant comes out better.'

'How, Richard?'

'Because we can undercut the other machinery yards. And I get a little sweetener from Moses too.'

'Sweetener?'

'A few bucks extra. For getting cheaper chicks for his store.'

'You are getting very wise to the ways of the world, Richard.' Frances was proud of her son, but anxious too. He prattled on.

'Mike Walsh advised me to form a Young Men's Club. He told me I could use a room over his saloon for meetings.'

'I hear there's a dumb waiter there for sending up drinks and tobacco,' Eyre grinned.

'Neither of which interests me, Father; barring the odd cigar.' Richard did not reveal what did appeal to him: Walsh's advice to enrol two hundred respectable young men who would organize excursions on the river. Saloon and store keepers, office holders, breweries and transport companies would use them for staff outings.

'Balls, fêtes and theatrical entertainments can make plenty of cash too, Dick,' he had said. 'Up the bills for bands, lighting and costumes and other paraphernalia. Down the tally on tickets sold. There's more than one way of skinnin' a cat, boy.' Richard smiled when his father echoed Walsh's final piece of advice.

'See to it that you become its President and Treasurer.'

Except that Walsh had added, 'A good cook always licks his fingers.'

'What's the name of the club?' Frances asked.

'The Green Teepee Association, Mother.'

'Everybody will think it a reservation of Irish Red Indians,' Eyre laughed.

'Led by a Clonakilty Brave!'

Frances liked Richard's repartee.

'Which reminds me; do you know who this O'Connell woman from Ardfield married?' Eyre asked. 'Your mother can't remember any O'Connell family there, either. Nor in any of the parishes around it in our time.'

'I must find out more about her. In fact, I was supposed to visit her and forgot all about it.'

'Considerate, like your father.' Frances was being playfully sarcastic.

That was the last evening the three were together for some time. On 14 November General-in-Chief H.W. Halleck sent a message to Major General Ambrose E. Burnside, who commanded the army of the Potomac:

> 'The President has just assented to your plan. He thinks it will succeed if you move rapidly; otherwise not.'

Eyre responded like his forefathers would have done and was full of pride as he went away to fight. The long journey reminded him of his trip to Cincinnati when he first arrived in America. He recalled the anxiety, then, over Richard's accident in the steamer, but also those happy days when

Frances was more exciting and adventurous. For the first time in his life, he realized the great affection he had for Richard. He had never been ostentatious about it, but it was there. Firm and fertile. If he were to analyse his real reason for going to war, he would probably discover that it had more to do with his son's political career than he cared to admit.

He arrived into a military stalemate. The army's advance had ended as soon as it reached the ice-edged Rappahannock tributary that blocked its way into Fredricksburg.

There were no pontoon bridges to take them across.

Days went by.

One week.

Two. Three.

His men, immigrant Irish from the slums of New York, drank like their grandfathers did in 1798. Around their campfires at night, they danced the Carmagnole with local lasses and sang 'Scalteen Forever'. When the bridges arrived and were in place, they marched across them into the home town of George Washington. General Robert E. Lee's North Virginian Army awaited them on the hills to the west.

As part of the Irish Brigade, they attacked on 13 December. Cannon pounded their ranks from above. Hundreds died or lost limbs in the advance across the plain under the flag of green. Eyre felt a tradition of cavalier leadership course through his veins as the call came, 'Give it to them, boys.' Then, in the bloodiest days of the war between the States, the blue-uniformed Presbyterian farmer from Clonakilty learned that there is no glamour in combat; no chivalry; no inspiration. War is brutal, inglorious and foul. He witnessed young men performing deeds of bravery. Some succeeded in dangerous missions, others were cut to bits. He recorded their names, with the intention of having them recommended for citations or medals.

Eyre fought bravely too. And survived. Just about. He was never again the man who had left Frances and Richard in such high spirits. His ambition had been excited by eager waves near Balliva so long ago. Its realization was drowned in blood.

When the conflict ended, he returned to the city. A shattered wreck, he sought solace with Frances. Unwell and disturbed by his condition, she was unable to respond.

'Please come with me to a saloon where survivors of my platoon will be gathering,' he asked Richard. There was desperation in the plea that Richard could not ignore.

'Of course, Father.' Feigned enthusiasm concealed his reluctance.

As they reached the saloon, Eyre placed a hand on Richard's arm.

'Wait!' he said. 'Listen to that!'

Through a dirty glass door, Richard could see a uniformed soldier standing on the counter. The man was singing loudly, in broken phrases and with wild, embracing gesticulations to his audience:

> Come all you warriors and renowned nobles,
> Give ear unto my warlike theme,
> And I'll relate how brave Eyre Coote Croker
> Lately aroused from his sleepy dream.

There was a whoop from the others and Richard could not decide if it was in derision or praise of his father. Eyre knew. Better than anybody. No, he had not done anything gallant or meritorious during the campaign. He thought of Richard's political future and of how it might be affected if satires on an unsoldierly father should begin circulating. And he felt ashamed that his son should hear the lampoon.

Eyre remembered when he was very young, hearing the son of the land steward in Quartertown singing the original song, while grooming a horse. The boy had stopped on hearing Eyre approach. After asking him why he did not continue, the lad had replied that his father warned him never to sing it in front of a Croker because they were all soldiers of the King. Later, he had recalled the song and had asked Malachi Hurley about it. It was a ballad about Ireland's 1798 Rebellion and Father Murphy, its Wexford leader.

'Lays of Irish gallantry, Richard.' Was Eyre being sarcastic? Richard wondered.

Beyond the smeared glass, far from his native green fields of Cork, the singer was amending the lyrics to suit his adopted country's Civil War:

> Sure Julius Caesar nor Alexander
> Nor brave King Arthur ever equalled him
> For armies formidable he did oppose them,
> Though with just a musket, he did begin.

Another raucous roar and men began wrapping comradely arms about each other's shoulders. The singer was tottering towards the edge of the counter but a wild propulsion of arms was helping to restore balance. As his audience kept shouting at him to continue, he bent slowly from the waist, trying to focus his eyes on a tankard of beer a few feet from where he was standing. Each time his hands came close to it, someone would push it farther away.

'Not until you shing the shong.'

'F... F ... F ... Father Murphy of B ... B... Boolavogue never f ... f ... f ... fought no f ... f ... f ... fight like the one we f ... f ... f ... fought at F ... F ... F ... Fredricks ... at F ... F ... F ... you know yourselves, lads.'

'Sing up or shut up!'

'*Erin go Breagh!*'

The performer heeded the heady exhortations and postponed the quest for beer. Despite his condition, he managed to stand to attention as he continued, pausing to substitute placenames every time it became necessary:

> *The … New York cavalry he did unhorse them,*
> *Their first lieutenant he cut him down,*
> *With broken ranks, and with shattered columns,*
> *They soon returned to … Fredricksburg town,*
> *On the hill above it he displayed his valour,*
> *Where a hundred Corkmen lay on the plain*
> *And at the battle, his sword he wielded*
> *And I hope to see him once more again.*

At the mention of Corkmen, the saloon erupted into a delighted uproar. Men shouted names of little known localities, their home villages and townlands. Defiantly, seriously; as if, being exiles and soldiers, they were entrusted with an important task of registration, of establishing that the places from which they hailed had played some part in a foreign campaign.

'Glanbanoo!'

'Gortnadhoughter!'

'Sillahertane!'

Feeling seriously challenged, men from other parts of Ireland were adding their voices.

'Kilclonfert!'

'Loughaclerybeg!'

'Poulathlugga!'

'Donadea!'

'Ballinafid!'

'Order, lads, order. One voice. Give the singer a chance!'

'Give him ether!'

Factions offered faltering bars of other songs. A lone Blackpool Royalist was intoning 'De Groves of De Pool', a tribute to a notorious unit who used pitch-capping and half-hanging in quelling the Rising:

> *Now de war, dearest Nancy is ended,*
> *And de peace is come over from France;*
> *So our gallant Cork City Militia*
> *Back again to headquarters advance.*
> *No longer a beating dose rebels –'*

That was all he sang. Four others grabbed him, raised him above their heads, ran him horizontally through the swing door and landed him in the gutter beside Eyre and Richard.

Representatives of all counties, united in support of the eviction of a traitor, called for a resumption of 'Father Murphy'. This time the singer added no local flavour. With closed eyes and feelings that transcended epochs and oceans, he shunned levity. One by one each man fell silent, as the lamentation of a beloved land demanded their attention.

> With drums a-beating the town did echo,
> And acclamations came from door to door,
> On the Windmill Hill we pitched our tents,
> And we drank like heroes, but paid no score.
> On Carraig Rua for some time we waited,
> And next to Gorey we did repair,
> At Tubberneering we thought no harm,
> The bloody army, it was waiting there.

The men's rapture at the song, and their fervent acclaim when it ended, shocked Eyre into realizing just how tough a struggle Richard was facing in Tammany Hall. Although Presbyterians, the Crokers had not been as supportive of the British Crown in Ireland as many others of similar persuasion. Yet Eyre knew he had more in common with the ejected stranger than he had with his celebrating soldiers within. This would remain his secret, however. He was concerned that Richard's career might suffer, simply because he had been born a Presbyterian descendant of gentry. He would need to be as passionate about the Old Sod as those beyond the smudged glass.

What if Richard did not remain a Presbyterian? That was something he might start working on. Perhaps Miss Fraser might bring more than her father's wealth to Richard!

Richard helped up the ejected singer who'd dared to praise the Cork Militia. Eyre couldn't remember seeing the man in his platoon during the battle.

'Come on, soldier. Join me and my son in some other saloon.'

Richard was concerned. 'Do you not think we should find where this soldier lives? I'll pay for a carriage and have him brought home.'

'No, I insist. The three of us will celebrate together.'

They went to a bar in Fulton Market. Richard sipped water and watched Eyre and the soldier becoming tipsy, but not drunk. In the maudlin way of men home from war, Eyre was retracing his life, particularly its progress since landing in America.

'Wonder what became of Nellie Hurley? Do you remember her, son?'

'I do, Father. And I think of her often.'

'We'll go home, Richard.'

'Yes, Father.'

Richard passed a banknote to the bartender.

'Get a carriage to take this poor soldier home,' he said, patting the drunken man on the back. Aroused, he attempted to resume his song:

> De noggins of sweet Tommy Walker
> We lifted according to rule,
> And wetted our necks wid de native
> Dat is brewed in the groves of de Pool.
> When the reg'ment went into de Common –

'Now, sir. No singing please. Out you go now.' For the second time that night, the soldier found himself on the sidewalk. The bartender spat on the five dollar bill Richard had given him and tucked it into his waistcoat pocket.

Eyre and Richard were retracing the route they had walked that first dawn. They passed the store where the man had been wrestling with the fudge. It now had a glass frontage. Cupping his eyes with his hands, Eyre peered through. The store looked neater than he remembered. The long kneading table was still there, scrubbed clean, awaiting another day of knuckling and twisting and shaping. Smarting in the frosty air, his eyes misted and his footsteps seemed to beat a slow dirge as he moved away.

On an impulse he returned. This time Jack McHugh was standing outside. Eyre ignored him as he went to the window and peered through again. Jack's breath stank of garlic as he came close to leer and whisper.

'You won't get to see much looking through there. Only cakes and vegetables. A buck will let you see all – and more. Nice woman would let you see behind her parsley.'

'Come on, Father.' Richard knew that his father frequented brothels, but he also knew that Jackie the Mule's place could be dangerous. Brian had told him things that made the hair stand on his head.

Jack McHugh was still marketing his empire. 'We have a hooker called Fay, who can make a man forget his troubles in all sorts of unusual ways.'

But Richard succeeded in dragging his father away.

Poor woman, he thought. Being advertised like a flitch of bacon.

SIXTEEN

OTENGEN, THE INSTRUCTOR at the gymnasium where Richard trained regularly, was rated second to Yankee Sullivan among the city's boxers. He'd noticed Richard's potential, but considered that he was becoming a little arrogant about his skill and needed a lesson. So he suggested a sparring match. When Richard agreed and was tying up his gloves, Otengen said, 'I will not be sparing you so don't you spare me.'

Richard felt his stomach churning as he saw seconds, with buckets and sponges, starting to take their places in each corner. Then, a referee, a stranger to the gym, was slipping between the ropes and glaring down at him. At a thumb-jerk, the fighters entered. Richard realized that his mentor, a good four inches taller and with a considerable reach advantage, meant business.

When the two were facing each other, men working out on punchbags, shadow-boxing around the gym, stopped what they were doing. They had heard that Otengen had been threatening to teach 'that big-headed Irish bum' a lesson. One or two of the older men might have agreed, but the majority crowding around the ringside were rooting for Richard.

During the first round each man was sizing the other up. Richard tried once or twice for an opening for his best punch, a right hook, but Otengen's guard was secure. Glowering at Richard through beady eyes, the instructor tossed a probing left to the head. Richard brushed it aside with his right, leaving Otengen to come in under with a telling punch to the ribs. Richard grunted in agony and his opponent followed with a flurry of crisp, effective blows. One caught Richard on the jaw and he went down.

On a count of seven the bell sounded and Richard's seconds dragged him to his stool. There they worked on him feverishly and he came to as the sharp clang of the bell announcing the second round exploded in his dulled brain.

Otengen was wading in, planting sharp jabs. One landed on Richard's nose which began spouting blood. He thought of Nellie Hurley, and of how she had told him on a fair day in Clonakilty not to be afraid of a menacing mule that had been blocking their path. Why did he always think of Nellie when he was in trouble? Then he remembered his mother ordering him to stand erect and be a man.

Playing around, giving his fuzzy brain time to recover, he eventually focused and led with a left. But again his opponent floored him and the bell saved him.

Richard fared a little better in the third and fourth rounds. He remained standing! His arms were tired, however, and he was weakening from the punishment Otengen was delivering to his midriff. A lump raised by the first knock-down blow was swelling against the lobe of his ear. His opponent's gloves were drenched in Richard's blood. But through the round Richard had noticed him becoming more careless with his guard.

Deciding his pupil should be delivered the *coup de grâce*, Otengen whipped back his left hand to deliver a swing. Faster and more powerful than a kick from that Clonakilty mule, Richard forced through his right. He heard his fingers crack, but felt no pain.

Because Otengen was toppling, and his eyes were glazing over.

Because a maelstrom of new, invigorating strength was urging Richard on.

One, two, three straight jabs, each found its target with a punishing thud. Then a right cross, using every ounce of strength from every muscle in his frame. Otengen almost floated horizontally before crashing to the canvas. The referee counted sullenly. The seconds, both Otengen's and Richard's, went to the instructor's aid. A single, hesitant, handclap came from the back of the gym. One, six, a dozen followed before well-wishers began cheering wildly and yelling approval.

'Chrissake, you have got to become a prize-fighter.' The owner of the gym was excited.

'I'll get you all the money you want,' a two-bit promoter scouting for talent promised.

Richard barely heard.

The Harlem Railroad was holding its annual picnic in Jones's Wood the week after Richard's fight with Otengen. Richard had been so proud when Elizabeth consented to be his partner. She was dressed in a tight-bodiced, crimson dress and wore a hat of the same colour that had a short veil. To Richard, her white parasol was as an angel's halo.

Almost four hundred staff and employees had turned up. Children romped and paddled in an artificial pond, oblivious to the half-hearted warnings of chatting parents and friends. Young men strutted in their Sunday best. One tried concealing his shyness by laughing far too generously at a friend's joke. Another marvelled at a colleague's claim of conquest with the loveliest young employee in the company. She, and other ladies in their finery, were promenading primly along tree-lined gravel paths or lying in the sun on the lush-grassed turf. Barrel organs played. Tricksters invited bets and the supervisor of a coconut shy promised prizes of stuffed bears and goldfish. Elizabeth tried her hand but failed to win anything.

An able organizer, Richard had directed many of the tasks in preparing the venue. He was sitting astride a strong branch of a tree, fitting ropes for a child's swing. Elizabeth helped set a table below and smiled to herself when a young woman told Richard that his thighs were as thick as the tree's trunk. Elizabeth began unpacking from a company hamper: cold meats of all sorts, fowl, breads, jams and cakes. She reminded Richard of Nellie Hurley. As he had often done before, he began thinking of how much he had loved his nursemaid and of his horror at seeing the cruel sea sweeping her away from him when the *Henry Clay* had sunk. An arrival in the field jerked him out of his reverie.

'Oh-oh! Watch out, Elizabeth!'

'Why? Oh, I see what you mean.'

Elizabeth had spotted the bareheaded drunk tottering towards her. A big man, almost seven feet tall, he had broad shoulders and a purple bull neck. His hair was grey-brown, unkempt and dirty. Clothes trailed loosely from his gangly frame, all grease-buffed, worn and tattered. Pimples marked his puttied red nose. One spectacular pustule perched on the widest part over the left nostril. People wondered where he had got the booze so early.

'It's Dick Lynch, a prizefighter from a third-rate booth in the Bowery.'

'That appendage on his nose. It's so ugly looking.'

'It got him a nickname. Vesuvius! He's a bloody scourge in Moses Kohn's. Always falling across vegetable stalls, crushing tomatoes to a pulp and scattering cabbages and things onto the street and sidewalks.'

'But where did he get drink so early in the day?'

'That fellow would find war-water in the desert. Watch out, Elizabeth!'

Vesuvius lurched into a table, bringing it to the ground. Cream and icing from cakes spattered in all directions.

Richard was already sliding down one of the ropes. He caught the thug amidships with his two feet. Vesuvius gasped like one of the company's engines releasing steam. He fell beside a handcart that was idle after transporting the hampers. Richard parcelled him up, trussed his arms and legs like a turkey awaiting sale, tossed him onto the cart as if the big man were a bag of feathers, wheeled his load to the gate of Jones's Wood and beyond, before dumping Vesuvius into a disused stone-quarry.

When he returned, Elizabeth kissed his cheek. As the picnic continued, Elizabeth found she was enjoying herself. She was not used to mixing with plain folk and was finding them far better company than those whom her parents forced her to join on excursions and at parties.

⎯ ⎯

During the days that followed, the Plug Uglies used the picnic incident to belittle the leader of the Tunnel Gang. Eventually, one came to Richard at Moses Kohn's store and challenged: 'Vesuvius had drink on him and you took advantage of this. His pride is hurt and you must fight him clean when he is sober.'

The taunting continued until Richard could put up with it no longer. He did not want to fight someone unfit and past his best, but Moses was complaining about the arguments taking place inside and outside his premises.

'Okay! We'll meet again at Jones's Wood tomorrow at three,' Richard told his tormentor, who retorted, 'And by four, you'll be a pulpy mess like them there tomatoes.'

Richard turned up at Jones's Wood. Vesuvius did not. Nor did he ever appear in a prizefight booth again.

The incident reinforced Richard's standing among his peers, and when he entered Tammany Hall for his initiation ceremony, he was full of confidence. While walking up its granite steps, he stopped to admire its red brickwork and its five rows of elegant windows above an entrance porch crowned by a verandah. It was 1868 and The Wigwam was sparkling at the prospect of accepting its newest recruit. Torchlight from ten huge sconces flickered across its facade. Richard knew what was expected of him. He had studied the history of the Tammany Society.

Initially it had been a brotherhood of men from all walks of life. Some were humble, others wealthy – professionals, tradesmen and artisans of all political and social persuasions. It had then evolved into a benevolent, fraternal organization. Its first Grand Sachem, William Mooney, was an upholsterer and paperhanger.

It had had two previous homes, both on Broad Street. The later one, occupied from 1790 to 1798, had boasted a museum. The society relished parading every year on the anniversary of its foundation, 12 May. Further parades took place on the Fourth of July, on George Washington's birthday, 22 February, and on the anniversary of the departure of British forces from

New York in 1783, known as Evacuation Day. That was 25 November. The society conceded patron status to Christopher Columbus in 1792 and thereafter celebrated the annual Columbus Day.

What he saw when he was walking into the vestibule challenged Richard's common sense so much that he feared he would laugh out loud. Two lines of grown men were standing on the great staircase. All were wearing traditional American Indian garb and war paint. Because their skullcaps were flesh-coloured, they looked bald. A few, carrying bows, had quivers of arrows slung across their backs. Others raised tomahawks in salute. When he began approaching, they uttered a loud whoop in unison before effecting smart left and right turns. Then, in single file, they solemnly started marching upstairs.

All but one, who remained standing at the bottom step. It was his proposer, Mike Walsh, and he was beckoning Richard forward.

Richard's eyes rose to the Initiation Sachem on the top landing. The 'braves' began muttering incantations and he tried to suppress a smile as he advanced.

In the meeting room above were rows of high-backed redwood benches reaching to a dais. Placed centrally on this was a red, green and yellow striped wigwam. It was at least ten feet tall. All around it, Sachems crouched on low stools. Richard noticed Slippery Dick Connolly and Peter Barr Sweeney. The Initiating Sachem stood at the flap of a teepee. He was a member of the New York Board of Supervisors who was organizing gangs to gain control of the city, the infamous William Marcy Tweed.

The man was a craggy giant who looked as if he was hewn from granite. Shoulders, head, hands, nose and chin were enormous. More red-brown hair clung to his face than to his head. It was tidier there too. Although imposing, Tweed seemed to be casual about what was happening. This belied stories Richard had heard about his crudeness and bullying tactics among roughnecks in political back alleys. But he remembered Nellie Hurley once warning him, 'Even a tin knocker will shine on a dirty door.'

There was no humour in Tweed's penetrating blue eyes when they closed on Richard's. It was one of the few times in his life that Richard trembled with fear. Yet were it not for his sinister aura he would surely have been unable to remain serious throughout what followed.

Two porters began locking the doors of the Long Room. While this was happening, Walsh whispered to Richard: 'They do this since a guy named Fernando Wood used to disrupt meetings. He tried to take control of Tammany but Tweed summoned veterans from Cincinnati, Boston and Philadelphia to vote him down. A reporter wrote, "There were old Injuns, young Injuns, lame Injuns and blind Injuns, wounded Injuns and whole Injuns".'

Richard spotted his rival, Oweney Geoghegan, sitting in a bench near the dais. The leader of the Gas House Gang was scowling, and Richard recalled reading the rest of the newspaper article: 'Injuns with gold-headed canes and Injuns with red shirts on, whiskey Injuns and Injuns who came in carriages, Injuns with political aspirations and Injuns with no aspirations, except eternal. In short, Injuns of all varieties turned out and congregated within the bounds of The Wigwam.'

'There's a quare assortment of Injuns here tonight, too,' he whispered to Walsh. He did not answer but nudged Richard to start walking, slowly at first, as he had been briefed, then gaining momentum until he was in a lively trot. When he reached the dais, Tweed stood and ushered him into The Wigwam.

It was hot inside. The musty smell of canvas, too long in storage, became the stink of brown powder, puffed from a coshapooka he had kicked around the barnyard in Balliva. That early memory of Ireland lingered as his initiator placed a band of gold braid around his head and directed him to kneel. Tweed picked up a long, single feather and placed it inside the band. Then he took Richard's hand and led him from The Wigwam and around it three times. Reaching into a long trunk and taking out a tomahawk, Tweed stood waving it over the assembly before handing it to Richard. Then he snatched it back and tapped him three times on the head with its blunt side. There was a loud cheer as Tweed began shaking the hand of Tammany's freshest brave, welcoming him to The Wigwam.

Two panelled partitions slid apart behind the rows of seats. There was a mighty whoop and all began crushing through to a long bar. A number of minor chiefs began plying Richard with drink. Others were treating him too, and by midnight he was gloriously drunk for the first and only time in his life. After some coaxing, he started singing, unsteadily and out of tune, a song that Nellie Hurley had taught him.

> I was born in Mallow in the County of Cork
> Thirty-six hundred miles from gay New York.
> My father never gave a good goddamn
> Because he was a good old Irishman.

Drunk as he was, he was noting remarks about the 'dirty Irish creeping into Tammany too fast'. But he was encouraged by the number showing approval and calling for another and longer song of the Old Land. He obliged:

> A short time ago a gentleman called Doherty
> Was elected to the Senate by a very big majority.
> He became so elated that he sought out Denis Cassidy

Who owns two big saloons of a very large capacity.
Says he to Mr Denis, 'Please send out to a brewer
For fifteen hundred kegs of beer, and give them to the poor;
Then send out to a butcher stall, acquire a hundred tons of meat
And say it's for an Irishman so you'll be back for a repeat.'

'You sing like a castrated weasel!' There was no mistaking the menacing rasp of Oweney Geoghegan. He was drunk. He tried to throw a punch at Richard but lost his balance and tumbled. There was a crack as his head hit a bench leg, knocking him unconscious. Nobody bothered to move him. Men kept stepping over him on their way to the bar and spilling beer on his feathers when they were returning. After an hour he recovered briefly, stood, leered, got sick and fell again. This time four Sachems dragged him into a closet and locked the door on him.

Time was passing, with the room becoming a mass of heaving, heated bodies. Cigar and cigarette smoke were fouling the air. Red-faced men were laughing or sneering or grimacing in anger, while debating bargains bungled, deals delivered or the quality of Bowery brothels. When Mike Walsh brought his new initiate home, Big Splitting Head Croker vowed never to drink heavily again.

The following morning Walsh took Richard to see John Kelly, a Sachem of The Wigwam hotly tipped to be its next chief. When word went around that this meeting had taken place Richard began experiencing a new respect from his friends. Even from some enemies.

He met Elizabeth that evening and told her that in no time at all he would be a big name in New York.

She said, 'I always knew you would.'

'Thanks for the confidence.'

'In fact, I think you will be good at everything you try.'

'What might that mean, now, girleen?' Richard thought that her sparkling eyes and cheeky smile were answering.

At Walsh's behest Richard began hand-picking a coterie of the toughest and most ruthless of the Tunnel Gang. Gathering them together one evening, he issued each with a whistle, some dried peas and steel ball-bearings.

'Now, we'll keep putting these into the whistles until each one has the same sound. That way, we will always be able to call each other when we are in trouble. Now, one apiece.'

They each eased in a pea and a ball-bearing.

'OK, then. Blow!'

'Jeeze, that's like a kitten in a jampot.'

'OK. Three peas and two ball-bearings.'

They blew again.

'Like a long-tailed cat in a room full of rocking chairs. One more ball bearing.'

This time, the whistles were screeches from wounded hawks.

'Great! Every blast the same. That'll do.'

'What will we call ourselves, Dick?'

'The Tin Whistlers. And bejaysus, when we get our dander up and our enemies hears our signal in the night, they will start locking their windows and bolting doors.'

'Christ aye, Dick, and the drug stores will get ready their iodine, bandages and lint.'

The gang's moment of truth arrived quickly. An election campaign was in full swing and two days before voting day Richard received a call from Mike Walsh. He went to the saloon and sat waiting. Walsh was not in his usual place. The bartender disappeared for a while, then returned and told Richard to follow, adding, 'You are honoured; not many enter the eyrie.'

The room was large, with expensively covered red leather chairs on polished walnut floors and heavy green velvet curtains complementing three walls painted in rich burgundy. Hanging tapestries displayed prairie coyotes, waterfalls and long-haired buffalo. A gigantic mural of Indians on a reservation covered the fourth wall. On a rostrum in front of this, Walsh was lounging behind a huge oak desk, covered in green leather. He pointed to a chair. When Richard sat, he felt dwarfed, but made a mental note of the effectiveness of the layout in cowing an interviewee.

'I brought you here because I like what I seen since we met,' Walsh began.

'You are still keeping your mouth shut about things that matter. And you are getting even better with the fists.' He stared at Richard for a moment before continuing, 'John Kelly agrees with me. Congratulations.'

Richard was glowing with pride, but Walsh cut the experience short.

'But now your first real test is about to begin.'

Richard wondered what was in store. He had wanted the approval of Tammany so much and the nod from Kelly was of immense importance. But he also realized that Mike Walsh would demand something significant, something that he might fail to deliver. He began to feel apprehensive. It showed.

'You'll be well able for it, kid.' Walsh was reassuring. 'You and your Tin Whistle Gang!' Richard was shocked. He thought its name was known only within the gang itself. Walsh laughed.

'Don't look so surprised, Dick. Tammany Hall has eyes and ears everywhere. I want the use of you and your boys on Election Day.'

Richard was relieved. He now felt excitement welling. Establishing his very own clique within a gang and hearing a Sachem of Tammany Hall requesting its services! That was enormously gratifying.

'On Election Day, polling ends at 6 p.m. Thirty minutes before that, at half-past five precisely, mind you ...' Pointing a pencil at Richard and peering along it to underline his need of punctuality, he continued, 'At half-past five, I want you and your Tin Whistlers to start wading into the polling booths and forcing all workers, repeaters, ticket-sellers and ticker-tapers of the opposition out. Then you'll chase them into the next ward and prevent their return until the ballot boxes are taken away after 6 p.m. Clear?'

'But –'

'But what?' Walsh was steely now.

'How will we know the opposition?'

'By their badges, duff-head.'

Richard was blushing and cursing his stupidity. He recovered quickly, because he knew he was virtually on trial for Tammany. With as much officiousness and confidence as he could muster, he asked, 'How much force?'

'As much as is needed. But we would all be better pleased if nobody was hurt too much. Blood gets on the papers and can become messy.'

Normally, a gang leaving its own ward invited attack, and police protection did not exist. Even if police officers were patrolling, they would look the other way rather than start interfering with a gang fight. On Election Day, however, ward invasion was considered an acceptable risk. Like many others struggling for more power within Tammany Hall, Mike Walsh realized that his candidate for alderman had to win at all costs. If he did not, then his own days of influence would be numbered.

'The first rule in politics is to think for yourself and about yourself. Every Irishman knows that from the cradle, lad. That's why I quit the Old Sod. Got out before the British government deported me.'

'You ran from a Queen, then, but now you kow-tow to another Boss – at Tammany. Why?' Richard asked timidly.

'Good question. I like kids to ask questions. But I didn't run from the Queen; I ran from her laws. To succeed, every organization must have a Boss. President Buchanan's a Boss. The Pope's a Boss. Moses Kohn down at your store is a Boss. Ireland would have been a free country decades ago if she had a native Boss. You do your job for the Boss even if you hate him like shit; that way, you may become Boss yourself. Tammany is dealing you a hand, Dick pal. Take it. And on Election Day play the hand and trump any dirt-rotten bastard that stands in Tammany's way.'

Richard relished the impact of the word 'Boss'. Walsh was fidgeting more than usual when Richard asked, 'Are you afeard your man will be bet?'

'Let me tell you somethin', Dick,' Walsh answered, 'the candidate is not a good one, I'll admit. The Sachems picked him knowin' just that. But they selected him not to make him win, but to make me lose, me being in charge of the election, like. But he won't lose. Not a chance – if you do your work right. Now go away and tell that to your Tin Whistlers and let me see them play to Mike Walsh's hornpipe.'

On the afternoon of Election Day, Richard rounded up the best of his coterie and brought them to the ward polling booth. The City Hall clock was striking the half-hour when they arrived. Polling was taking place briskly at a converted truck that normally served as a local fuel-merchant's office. It stood among piles of lumber and coal and its door was open. The polling administrators lolled around: two police officers, two Judges of the Peace, three tally clerks and a tea-boy. The black ballot box was in its doorway.

A number of men whom Richard had noticed in Mike Walsh's company, the evening of his Tammany initiation, waited in a line in front of the booth. Facing a large crowd, they were smiling to some of the voters and allowing them through. But they barred the way of others. Richard saw for the first time what 'shoulder-hitters' were. Other big, hefty men were mingling in the crowd. Pretending to be pushing their way through, they roughly jostled those who'd been turned away, forcing them from the area completely. If someone was protesting or fighting, the police officers on the truck simply turned their backs, nonchalantly lighting cigarettes or sipping tea and pretending not to notice.

Richard was surprised to see the gentleman who'd spoken up for him the day he'd been arrested at the wharf years before. Older and more feeble, he was still intent on being a good citizen. When the toughs barred his way, he challenged them:'This is preposterous treatment for taxpayers to receive from the authorities.'

He spoke as loudly as he could, but few were listening. Tammany repeaters began pushing at him and one was becoming extremely aggressive. It was Jack McHugh. Richard was becoming upset by the rough treatment of his former defender. But he remembered Mike Walsh's words and pretended not to notice.

'Now skedaddle, chappie,' McHugh told the infuriated old gentleman.

'How dare you, sir! Why, I am old enough to be your father. I will have you know I voted for the President eight times.'

McHugh laughed: 'That's nothin' Methusela, I voted eighty times before noon today.'

During this confrontation others were being prevented from voting. They began gathering in clusters, becoming more angry and vociferous. Then Richard spotted Oweney Geoghegan and some of his Gas House Gang trying to help those who'd been turned away. He could scarcely believe this. A Tammany Hall member assisting the opposition candidate! He remembered what Mike Walsh had said about people wanting to get him out rather than get the ward candidate in. At the same time he heard a whisper in his ear: 'Send your boys in and let's see how good you are.' It was Walsh. Still perplexed, Richard began questioning.

'But –'

He was silenced by a glare that flashed like tempered steel.

'Send your buzzards in and by Jeeze they'd better be good.' Walsh strode away. Richard blew his whistle. From among the crowd and from across the block beyond the booth, the answering shrill notes were echoing. Some voters began running away.

Oweney Geoghegan scowled at Richard and raised a clenched fist. Immediately, ten hoodlums gathered around him. He spoke to them and five dashed to the booth, upending two of Walsh's men. They began rocking the booth, tumbling the judges, police officers and assistants. The remainder of Walsh's roughs, however, seized the opportunity and began stuffing the fallen ballot box with prepared ballot sheets, all favouring their own candidate.

Oweney Geoghegan's other five did not even reach Richard. The Tin Whistle coterie of the Fourth Avenue Tunnel Gang set on them, viciously kicking and punching and ejecting them. In the street behind they hammered them more, before ordering them out of the ward. Richard was not even obliged to take part in routing the remainder. They fled with the Tin Whistle coterie in pursuit.

Richard's old defender was still protesting. He had witnessed the stuffing of the ballot box and he was challenging Jack McHugh again.

'I saw you and your Plug Uglies infringing the law. Casting innumerable ballots. I saw –'

'Listen, granddaddy, I'll infringe your rectum with my boot if you don't get to hell out of here.'

'Utterly disgraceful! Where are the police officers? They should be here. There were two in the booth a moment ago.'

'They are gone home to bed, where all washed-out old codgers should be. You, for instance.'

The old man raised his cane to deliver a further admonishment.

'Oh! So you are about to assault me! Well, I must act in self-defence then, mustn't I?' McHugh smashed his fist into the old man's face and felled him. Richard saw that the crowd would trample on him. He ran to help. Pushing McHugh aside, he caught the gentleman by the collar and set about dragging him from the mob. Hailing a passing carriage, he heaved his load into the back seat, stuffed five bucks into the driver's hand and told him to bring the passenger to the nearest casualty station. The ward courthouse clock was striking six when Richard returned to the polling area. It was deserted, save for the two policemen who had returned and were escorting the officials and their ballot boxes to a waiting van. Mike Walsh stood by, chatting to the presiding judge.

'How do you think your candidate got on?' Richard asked.

'I don't *think*. I know. We won. Four to one. Come over here.' He led Richard behind the booth.

'You and your boys did well.' He was speaking quietly.

'Thanks.'

'The old geezer. You went to his assistance out of gratitude – for that evening when you were arrested?'

'Yeah. He was gettin' it rough, the poor divil.'

Walsh's eyes said more to Richard than his following words. 'You'll have to learn that gratitude is okay in its place. Same as fightin'. Never fight till you are forced to. Never fight for fun. Know who you thumped?'

'One of your guys but –'

'But nothin', Dick. You hit Jackie the Mule. Nobody hits Jackie the Mule, Dick. I'll talk to him, but you'd better watch your ass.'

Richard felt like saying he could take care of himself, but did not. He was grateful that Mike Walsh still called him Dick.

SEVENTEEN

'DRESSING UP in my good suit to bring you to an art gallery. I can't believe it.' Richard was linking Elizabeth as they sat before a gigantic oil of a hunting scene in its enormous gilt frame.

'Keep looking at it for a while.'

He did.

'Cripes, you're right. I nearly feel part it. Come on! We'll have a geek at a few more.'

'Isn't she so life-like?' Elizabeth said, when studying the *Portrait of a lady in a 'Van Dyck' dress* that was part of a touring exhibition.

'And it only a bit of what? Charcoal?'

'And a little chalk.'

'Jeepers!' Richard could not believe this was exciting him.

'There are many good things to be enjoyed in life. Pictures, horses, and all with you, I hope.' Elizabeth squeezed his hand.

'And Tammany Hall, I suppose,' she added, resignedly.

'That place! William Marcy Tweed is now the Boss. The fellow that seemed to be okay at my initiation ceremony.'

'Has he changed?'

'He's a bit like a volcano – quiet, but likely to erupt. His vulgar language would put the hair standing on your head.'

'On mine, perhaps. Hardly on yours.' She laughed and looked beautiful. 'He frequents New York's high society, I believe.'

'He does. Knocks around with Vanderbilt, Astor and Ottendorfer. All fierce wealthy buggers.'

'Richard!'

'Beg pardon, Ma'am,' He made a mock curtsey and she giggled and held him closer.

When the visit was over and he had walked her to a spot near her home, he went to keep an appointment with Brian. Tweed was still on his mind.

'He's a bloody expert in manipulating municipal fraud,' Brian said. 'And is always paying close attention to his corrupt machine. His exploitation of New York's immigrants is barefaced. Those who settle in or are lured to his ward become the scapegoats of all wrongdoing.'

'But he's getting a grip on the city, Brian. No city services, be they police precincts, courts of justice or railroad authorities escape his grasp.'

'He's after bodies providing infrastructure on Manhattan Island too, Dick.'

'Do you know what they're calling Mayor Oakley Hall?'

'Yeah, I heard. Major Haul.'

'Him and his lackeys needs an overhaul.'

'But all the advantages Tweed enjoys could belong to someone else in the future. Someone who could give the public the appearance of having more integrity.'

'Sometime in the future! Begod, my father hinted as much to me.'

'Tammany needs a more honest face. Mike Walsh could never fit the bill.'

'Who, then?'

'It would be great if it was an Irishman but the "Know Nothing Party" would make that difficult.'

'The what?'

'The anti-Irish element in Tammany. They sprang from a secret anti-Irish, anti-Catholic society of scumbags called the Order of the Star Spangled Banner. When the cops or anybody else asked a member about his organization, the answer was always, "I know nothing".'

'A shut mouth gathers no flies! Malachi Hurley was right, begod!'

'Who?'

'Ah, a man back in Ireland.'

'Do you know, Dick, you are too young to become Boss now, but you could make it in the future.'

'And what about you?'

'No. Not me, sure the fellows around the leader always have the most power.' Brian laughed, then added, 'Ah, but I forgot. It can't be you.'

'And why not, my friend?' Richard feigned gravitas.

'You may look the part but a Chief Sachem needs to be punctual and dependable. You can't even turn up at parties when you're expected.'

'You'll never let me live that down. God, I'll have to meet that mother of yours soon.'

'Seriously, though, I'm not sure if being Mike Walsh's man is too helpful, Dick.'

'So do you think I should start putting my eggs in another basket?'

'I do.'

'But Jaysus, Brian, he saved me from jail and got me the job with Moses.'

'And proposed your initiation at Tammany. I know. Still, you could do worse than begin building up a relationship with Slippery Dick Connolly.'

'Tweed's comptroller? The bastard that's hiving off municipal rents for wharves, docks, markets, stalls and the divil knows what!'

'Sometimes you have to mix with bums to get what you want.'

They both knew that, with Connolly as its comptroller, New York's debt had risen by $70 million, while the 'Tweed Ring' had established its own Tenth National Bank to secure a resting-place for the cash it was raking off.

'A Harlem plasterer told me that he was getting $50,000 a day for small jobs on City Hall and that a friend in a printing business controlled by Tweed got $7,000,000 from a municipal department for work that he never carried out,' Brian told Richard. 'The plasterer duly delivered his co-workers' votes to Tammany candidates, of course. That's how it works, Dick, boy.'

'Connolly's a fair one at fund-raising for Tammany, too.'

'But he hasn't the right public face, Dick. It's now time for some other fellow – let him be a rogue as long as he's a likeable one and preferably Irish and Roman Catholic. Someone to get the votes of the huge influx from the Famine and their offspring.'

Brian kicked a rye-bread wrapper from the pavement while they were both walking, heads down, thinking.

'What about John Kelly? He's a son of Irish parents.'

'Not bad, Dick. Kelly might indeed give Tammany a respectable face, without giving its guts too much indigestion. And his age could mean that just a few years down the road, Tammany Hall might seem to have reformed – in the public mind, at least.'

'Rich for the picking by another Irishman.'

'Yes, Boss!' Brian slapped Richard on the back.

'Of course, you shouldn't part with Mike Walsh yet. Continue playing him along until it's convenient to dump him. Look, I'm hopping over to the Baxter Street rat-baiting for a while. Want to come?'

'Not now, thanks.'

They parted. Richard felt hungry and decided to drop into a steak-house for a meal. He settled his napkin carefully to protect his best suit and began pondering over his discussion with Brian and its possible implications.

'Your check, sir.'

While Richard was wondering had he ever been called 'sir' before, he realized that he had spent nearly two hours over his meal. He paid and, having slipped a gratuity under his plate, he left.

Swinging into Prince Street he saw Oweney Geoghegan and some of his gang loitering on the sidewalk. Instinctively, he reached for his whistle – but cursed himself on discovering he had left it behind him. He was about to re-trace his steps, when Geoghegan spotted him.

'Come on, guys. It's Pea-brain Croker out for his constitutional. All dandyish too. Let's take him.'

About five of the gang tumbled towards him. He felled the first one up with a right swing, but the others crashed into him and bowled him over. One kicked his groin and he doubled up, screaming in pain. Another bashed a studded sole on his neck and began pressing. He was gasping for breath and beginning to panic. Geoghegan stood over him, a nasty-looking knife in one hand, dramatically testing the blade's sharpness with the other. Richard tried to cough but could not. And his chest felt as if it was going to explode. Geoghegan was bending. A shaft of sun bounced off the steel blade, blind-ing Richard. He closed his eyes.

But suddenly the boot lifted from his neck.

Hurried footsteps running away.

Someone laughing.

He began uncoiling himself and looked up. Brian was beaming down at him, a police officer on either side.

'Where the hell did you re-appear from?'

'I was in the precinct headquarters looking for a licence for a new sport-ing gun. The office dealing with it backs on to this street and I spotted what was happening through the window. We almost got here ahead of them.'

Richard stood, brushing himself down and sighing relief. Swivelling his upper arm to make sure there was no serious injury, he thanked the officers and they left.

'Let's celebrate,' Brian said, excitedly. 'Do you know where I got the money to buy the gun?'

'Robbed a bank?'

'No! I won twenty-five dollars at the rat-baiting. In as many minutes. This great big elephant of a dog was odds on favourite and I bet on a whip-pet that had less meat on it than you'd see on a mousetrap. Fifty-to-one I got from a Houston Street fireman. I bought the gun and the licence but I have ten bucks left. Where will we go to spend it?'

'I know, we'll go to a concert saloon.'

'Ah, Brian. I was at an art gallery already today, I don't feel like sitting through a recital.'

'No, Dick. A concert saloon is a bar with entertainment. Or should I say "assorted entertainments". The Germans call it a *Stube*.'

'Sounds good. Maybe I'll get up and sing them an Irish song. Come on.'

Brian led the way down Seventh Avenue and into Vandam Street. Approaching the Hudson River, he turned into a lane that was so narrow they had to start walking in single file.

Clothing fluttered from windows above and sultry women in bright dresses sat around in windows and on steps. Those who bothered to notice them passing were gaping vacantly. There was a strange, sweet smell that was new to Richard.

They came to an iron gate and a flight of steps that dropped to a cellar.

'It's narrow in here. Follow me.'

Brian led Richard through a door at the bottom. This brought them into a dark passage that smelt of ordure and decay. Only a spitting gaslight ahead was guiding them. Stone flags were glistening with wet silt and Richard guessed that water covered them when the tide was high on the river. After reaching the light and turning left into another flight of stone stairs, the damp odour became a stench.

Richard thought he heard water trickling and began to feel scared. Then, from somewhere ahead, he heard the music: a slow, melancholic, twelve-bar sequence, every second set of four the same as the first; syncopated, melodic lines with a primeval attraction. Brass dominated and regularly, between the major and minor interval, a trombone began tearing a note out of tune. The result was stunning. Then a woman's voice – high pitched, shrill – trilled an improvisation on phrases in a stirring upper register. It had the mournful quality of keening that Richard vaguely remembered hearing once coming from a wake-house in Clonakilty. But it was more emotive; a music for the soul rather than the ear, with each note hanging for a moment between heaven and hell. Richard found himself wanting to hurry.

'It's from the plantations in the deep South,' Brian explained. 'Anybody can come here, but the opium is optional.'

'Opium?' Richard was stunned.

'Don't worry. I never smoked any. I thought of trying it. Was tempted to take a woman too. Some of them are cute. But they say an odd one slips in from a brothel down the alley and that they are riddled with syphilis. The hostess here is Barbara, the dance-cellar queen. She will dance with you for a dime, talk with you for two and do the divil knows what for a quarter. That's what they say, but I'm not so sure about the last bit.'

They pushed open a black steel door and Richard recoiled from the reek. A flat blue disk of smoke lazed between the gaslight and the dancers. When the draught from the open door reached it, a slender ribbon began trailing off towards the ceiling.

Richard had never seen women so lithe. Dancing on a low platform in the middle of the room, their satin-clad Oriental bodies were like transfers on their escorts' chests. Large male hands were encasing their buttocks and massaging them slowly to the throb of repetitive notes. One couple began to kiss, the woman grinding against her partner. Others sprawled on benches beside the band, knotting themselves in embraces.

Most of them smoked long dark cigarillos or clay pipes that were less cumbersome than the one he remembered Malachi Hurley using; they had narrow bowls and long, bent shanks. The rising wisps were green-blue from the dried milky juices of opium poppy seeds.

'Opium smoking helps oppressed people across the world to overcome their depression,' Brian explained. 'But some become dependent on it. It numbs the pain of the body and helps them sleep and have pleasant dreams.'

'I think I'll pass on it, Brian.'

'Don't drink the swipes. Cheaper, but dynamite.' Brian's warning was superfluous. Richard had not taken a drink since his initiation night and he had no intention of starting in a joint like this.

'What are swipes, anyway?' he asked, surprised at Brian's familiarity.

'A costermonger runs this place. He has a gang of urchins who go around the saloons each morning, swiping the counter and work areas of slops; all into buckets. That's what he sells mostly. Because it's cheap and the poor people you see drinking here can't afford to buy anything else. Right around this room there is a network of passages like the one we came down. They connect up a warren of cellars, all inhabited. The conditions are dreadful. They reek with fever, dysentery and venereal diseases of all types. Some of the people you see here never come up onto the streets at all.'

Richard was appalled. 'Like the sewer rats! What the hell did you bring me here for?'

'To meet Barbara. She's not here yet.'

A group sat around a table and lit candles of different colours.

'They're practising Feng Shui. It's supposed to date back 4000 years,' Brian said.

'The red candle represents fire. It smells of eucalyptus, cedarwood, geranium and spices, and is supposed to bring luck. The white is for purity.'

'What the hell's it doing in here, so?' Richard was pleased with his joke.

'My mother still lights candles. She would have told you about it if you'd come to her party.'

'I'm sorry about that, Brian. I did mix up the date. Honest! And I'll visit her soon. Promise. But back to them candles. What about the blue?' Richard nudged Brian over towards the table.

'Water and sky. The scent is from hyacinths. Simplicity and Peace. But you should be going for the green, Dick.'

'For Ireland?' Heady fragrances he had never experienced before were making Richard feel good.

'For wealth! The greenery of plants receiving energy from the sun. Sandlewood and assorted herbs go into the making and there's a strong-smelling stuff called patchouli. The whole practice is based on opposites. Yin is negative but Yang is positive. Speaking of which, here comes Barbara.'

Brian was nodding in the direction of a tall, beautiful, red-head nonchalantly strolling towards the musicians. Reaching them, she elbowed the pianist away from the piano and sat. Her right foot began beating time on the floor, freeing a long, shapely leg through a hip-high slit in her clinging blue-satin dress. Richard had never seen a woman's limb in fishnet stockings before. He felt his groin jitter. Barbara was flicking long, white fingers along the keyboard, tormenting an animated arpeggio.

Only the clarinet player was accompanying her. Smiling broadly, the other bandsmen began clapping to the energetic beat of her stride chords.

The crowd was clapping too.

Slowly.

Rhythmically.

Abandoning their kissing and embracing in corners, more and more of the clients were responding.

Humming.

Eyes closed.

Hands in the air or on hips.

All but a stubborn few still clasping parts of partners' bodies.

Richard pulled at his tie. The heat was stifling and his eyes smarted. Barbara reached a crescendo and the brass took up the melody.

Bold.

Harsh.

Intense.

Overpowering.

Rupturing every emotion until the crowd was swaying together in a great wave of feeling. Richard moved closer to the piano.

Her leg.

Red garter flashing on black fishnet.

Standing over her swaying shoulders.

The deep cleavage.

Christ, he could see her nipples.

Tomato ripe.

Hard. Like the music.

Beating.

Throbbing.

He moved to her. Could not control his hand. It rested on her breast.

Erect!

Barbara kept playing, but arching her back and parting her lips to meet his kiss as she began standing. Arms at full stretch, one hand moving up two octaves, but not before she pulled him between her and the keys. One leg, beating time, flayed his thigh; the other curled around his and drew him in there. A roar from the crowd. One voice louder than the rest.

'Have no mercy on the kid, Barbara.'

'Yeah girl. Give it to him now.'

The trumpeter blared a long B Flat. The trombonist took it up and teased it. A siren shriek from an early epoch that had been handed down; demanding a response to its torturing throb.

The clapping eased, dropping to the padding of a hundred tigers. In counterpoint, a low chant arose and quickened.

'Bar-bra. Bar-bra. Bar-bra.'

Then louder. 'Bar-bra. Bar-bra. Bar-bra.'

Now screaming to shaking heads, hands and bodies. 'Bar-bra. Bar-bra. Bar-bra.'

And Barbara was laughing and playing and beating time with her bare leg, lashing her body against Richard's groin, hopelessly responsive.

And the crowd was shrieking in triumph, 'Another lad made a man!'

Brian pondered. He did not join in the banter.

EIGHTEEN

THE DEMOCRATIC PARTY was in disarray after the Civil War but its quarrelling factions began coming together, even if tentatively, under Tweed. Whatever they thought of him, he had forced the legislature to back a charter giving the New York City authorities more autonomy and virtual self-rule. With Tammany Hall's influence, this opened up opportunities for personal gain in a burgeoning metropolis. Contractors for new sewers, water mains or sidewalks were offering remuneration in return for profitable agreements, for hiking land prices, for protection. As their wealth increased, the lot of dwellers in the dark slums kept deteriorating. Richard worked enthusiastically, trying to improve their position. He operated mainly in the docks ward and Brian O'Connell in an adjacent one.

'Jeeze, the poor Irish are living in tenements where you wouldn't house a skunk,' Fay reported to him one evening.

'I know, Fay, no water and primitive sewage.'

'Poopin' in the drains, most of them. One week of sunshine has them coughin' and spittin' like a pit of snakes.'

'Brian, I saw nine or ten sick people crammed into one room and others trying to sleep on stairs and balconies.'

'I know, Mother. But my friend Richard is trying to work on it. There's a man named Kelly beginning to get a bit of power at Tammany Hall. Richard gets on well with him. Things will change. You will see.'

'And so will the weather.' Fay was pessimistic.

'An' the stench, Brian. Ugh!' Nellie was, too.

'Italian quarter same,' Rosa said.

None of the three women had any cash to dispense but they scrubbed and cleaned, attended to the sick and offered good cheer and consolation. They gave one old woman particular attention. She was doubled up with arthritis and sat out on the sidewalk of a small street all day. At night, she had permission from an ice-vendor to sleep in a corridor over one of his stores. Even in high summer, it was cold and damp there. Nellie or Fay regularly washed her, took away her clothes for laundering and brought her fresh ones. Rosa cooked her some food each day until Jack McHugh caught her sneaking it out of The Sleeve and slapped her face. After that, Fay and Nellie took it in turns to bring her some sustenance. One day the old woman said, 'You are my Three Angels.' On the way home, Fay laughed and said 'Three Angels! Two with rings over their heads and one with a ring somewhere lower.'

Richard heard about their good work and made an unexpected visit to the arthritic woman one day. Fay and Rosa were with her at the time. He got on well with them but he was disappointed that Nellie was not there.

'There's some jinx on me getting to know that fine mother of yours, but I will yet,' he told Brian when he met him.

Neither Richard nor Brian sought anything in return for what they and the women were doing. They had enough faith in human nature to believe that they would get the support of these people when they needed it most – at election time. What they achieved humanely, Tweed did coercively. Either way, dependence on Tammany Hall was developing and increasing support for Democrats at the polls.

The press took notice and began to hound Tweed. Eventually he received a number of criminal indictments and was convicted, with a judgment of six million dollars made against him. Mayor Oakley Hall escaped censure; he had so many matters to deal with, he pleaded, that he could not examine closely every demand or note placed before him.

Tweed's home was under surveillance, but he managed to escape to New Jersey. Convicted in his absence, he fled, via Florida, to Spain, where he thought there was no extradition agreement with America. He was wrong, and the Spanish authorities eventually returned him to spend two years in Ludlow Street Jail.

In 1868 the House of Representatives impeached President Andrew Johnson. The Republican candidate, Ulysses S. Grant, became President. That year Richard Croker became an alderman. Three years on, 'Honest' John Kelly became Boss of Tammany Hall, with Richard as his henchman.

'In a good position coming into the straight,' he grinned to the horse-racing friends with whom he was beginning to mix, some of whom were pronouncing Tammany Hall dead.

'Kelly will roll back the stone and Dick will make it rise again,' Brian assured his mother. 'This city has a great future.'

'But the slums are still a dreadful sight.'

'I know, Mother. More and more people are pouring in. Your work and

Fay's and Rosa's is more important than ever.'

'There's Poles and Russian Jews in the ward now. I wouldn't mind bringing my poor father over. He'll soon be getting too old to work.'

'You might be able yet, Mother. John Kelly is a practising Catholic and will help the Irish and Italians, particularly. For his own good, mind you.'

Richard was also taking note of Kelly's popularity with Catholics. And he had another reason to consider converting to the old faith.

'I gave Elizabeth Fraser the ring,' he told Brian.

'I don't believe it. Hard man Croker engaged? To a toff at that.'

'She's not showin' it to her parents yet. They'll never let us marry if I don't become a Catholic. How would I go about doing that?'

'Well, you'll have to see a priest and you'll have to tell him about things such as rat-baiting, your display at Barbara's concert saloon, what you had for breakfast – little things like that.'

'Get away out of that, you rogue. But tell me something, Brian. Does the costermonger that owns Barbara's place sleep with her?'

'Never! Barbara loves life and lives it to the full, but she is not even spoken for.'

'Alright! I only asked.' Richard wondered had Brian felt offended, especially when he added, 'In any event, the costermonger is gone.'

'Gone? Where?'

'Nobody knows. Some say Barbara bought him out.'

'And then kicked him out, eh? Whatever way she done him, he's no bloody loss,' Richard pronounced.

'Barbara is a lady behind all her brashness, Dick.'

'You know, I think you have a rag on the bush for her, Brian,' Richard teased.

'I have a soft spot for all women who work hard to make a living.'

'But Barbara enjoys it, Brian.' Richard was curious about Brian's apparent righteousness.

'Barbara is different. But I hate seeing Fay and the rest of the women at Jack's having to prostitute themselves. Many of them are doing it to earn enough for a bite to eat, or to help them rear a kid. Thank God, my mother escaped it.' Brian did not tell Richard how much it disturbed him that she was playing a part, however unimportant, in the seedy situation.

'She wouldn't be found within a mile of Jack's joint, if it wasn't for having me to rear.'

'But you're standing on your own feet now.'

'Yes, but she's still trapped. God, as soon as I have the money, I'll buy her a fit place to live. Maybe bring over her father, too. She misses him. She has endured The Sleeve for long enough.'

'It has a bad name, The Sleeve.'

'Well deserved, Dick.'

'Is there any prostitution in Barbara's?'

'I suppose prostitutes use it to get business. But it's more illicit drinking and smoking of opium. But the customers are good-hearted, hard-working people.'

'I have no interest in them things but I like going there with you. I enjoy the fun. Barbara is powerful gas.'

'And you love the Feng Shui,' Brian joked.

'Well, I wasn't brought up like you – lighting blessed candles in St Patrick's.'

'I suppose it's hard to fully understand the attraction of Barbara's, Dick. Many of the customers are demoralized, depressed or destitute. There, at least they can find someone ready to have a chat with them.'

'Maybe they could tell us a bit about where extra support for Tammany might be available.'

'Indeed, yes. And some of them could tell you about activities of the city's gangs. Very useful stuff. Why don't we have a night out there to celebrate your engagement?'

'Oh, Jaysus will you stop! Her pious parents would have a fit.'

'But aren't you taking her to other places, without them knowing?'

'Ah, I wouldn't want to be challenging their principles, no matter how dull they are.'

'I suppose. So when are you off to see the priest about becoming Holy and Roman?'

'Tomorrow. Oh, Lord!'

NINETEEN

GEORGE WASHINGTON PLUNKITT had been brought up in similar circumstances to John Kelly and in the same area. He owned a butcher shop and was a bank director and building contractor, in addition to being an alderman and magistrate. A bootblack stand in New York County Courthouse served as a pulpit for his frequent expoundings on Democratic Party affairs. Mainly through his construction connections, he amassed wealth by what he called 'Honest Graft'. After one Tammany meeting, he called Richard over.

'Good to see you getting on well with Boss Kelly, Dick. No use carrying the sack of flour around if you don't know who the baker is.'

'So you've often told me, Mr Plunkitt.'

'It's George, Dick. Call me George. A man shouldn't use the respect due to age for keeping smart folk at a distance. I'll give you a bit of advice: keep watching out for your opportunities and snatching them before others.'

'That's good counsel, sir.'

'No "sir" either, boy. Listen! The Democrats are back in power in this city now. Just when it is undergoing major expansion and improvement. Right?' Plunkitt was not waiting for any answer; he was in full spate.

'OK, now! Supposin' there's a big park goin' to be laid out in the city and I hear about it. What do I do?' This time, a pause invited an answer, and Richard obliged.

'You buy some of the land in the area.'

'You're darned right, I do. As soon as I hear about the project. Then, when the plans for the park are announced, every varmint with a wallet will be after that plot, so I'll sell at double or treble the price I paid. That's an example of Honest Graft, Dick.'

'You done the same thing when they built New York Central Railroad, didn't you?'

'Yep. You sure do your homework, kid. I like that in a guy. Now I didn't buy Manhattan, mind you, but I purchased all the land where approaches had to be constructed before they started building. I don't call that dishonest. Do you?'

'I suppose it's a bit like investing in stocks.'

'Or in coffee or cotton. Sure thing.'

Richard was enjoying the discussion. And Plunkitt had more to say.

'I made a killin' at the waterworks, too. Got a peep at the municipal plans for the route the mains would be taking from the watershed. I bought in time. Would I be tellin' you all this if I was not convinced what I was doin' was not dishonest? You're darned right I wouldn't.' Richard wondered had Plunkitt some reason for giving away so much information.

'An' even when I get municipal contracts through knowing someone on the inside, what sin is there in that? I do the job well. I get paid – no more than the goin' rate. Not a buck stolen from the Treasury. The books always balance. The city is satisfied. I'm satisfied.'

'Are you not scared of the reformers?'

'Reformers? What reformers? No such thing as reform, lad. Just replacement. Let the so-called reformers take over and, in two shakes of a skunk's tail, they'll be at the same thing.'

'But they may carry out inquiries.'

'So what, Dick? What will they find? That friends looked after George Washington Plunkitt and he in turn looked after them. In your private life you give things to your pals. Why should it be any different in public life?'

'I suppose you're right. It would also follow, I suppose, that if you don't treat your friends well, you'll not remain in public life too long.'

'Especially if your enemy can vote more times than your friend.' Plunkitt was laughing, but not for long. His eyes began narrowing and he was leaning into Richard's face.

'You've served a good apprenticeship in Tammany, Dick. Some young men think the only thing of importance in politics is bein' a good orator. Piffle and nonsense. The less you say in this game, the better. You're a man who does things and shuts up. People respect that. They value it. Keep it up and you'll be okay.'

'Especially if I get good at the Honest Graft,' Richard smiled.

'No "especially" about it lad. You're involved in the Harlem Railroad, ain't you? And in machinery? Ever stop to think how rail transport is goin' to develop – in the city and elsewhere? There's a heck of a lot of country lyin' beyond New Jersey and Connecticut, boy.'

'But where would I get money to buy land?'

'Who said anything about you buyin?'

'You mean ...?'

'I told you you was a good apprentice. Let me know what the railroad company's plans are and come and talk to me.'

'I don't know their plans.'

'But you work in the goddamn place. Documents get left lyin' around, don't they? You can sell information the same way as you sell land, Dick. And it's often an expensive commodity.'

'Like how much?'

'Let's just say Plunkitt's honesty stretches to paying a decent wage, then shut up.'

Now Richard knew why Plunkitt had confided in him. Just then he slapped Richard's back and left him, saying, 'I must hob-nob with the elite of Tammany – merciful Jesus!'

Richard sat sipping water as the drinking and smoking began. He was studying all the smiling, back-slapping and jostling that went on among those trying to get closer to the new Boss. Brian sat beside him and whispered, 'They're like tendrils of convolvulus, weaving their way towards the tallest shrub.'

'Jesus, you're getting horrid poetic. Would you not say a flock of drones trying to get at a queen bee? Then the commoners like me would understand.'

'It's not how you say it, Dick –'

'It's how you do it. Right!'

'Dead on, friend. Christ! Will you look at them.'

'If he excreted, they'd take it home for meat pie.'

'You dirty divil. Hold it Dick. Trouble comin'.'

'Oh, shit!' Richard saw Jimmy O'Brien bearing down on them. He was wriggling like an eel through the crowd, heaving around the bar, dodging under arms and waving to the bartenders for service.

'Should we leave?'

'Too late.'

'He'll start trouble, Dick.'

'Bet he won't. He just wants to find out what I was discussing with Plunkitt.'

'Do you know my uncle died at the graveside when Plunkitt's grandfather was being buried?' O'Brien said, as he drew up a stool.

'That must have cast a gloom on the occasion,' Richard answered before winking to Brian and whispering in his ear, 'What did I tell you?'

Undaunted, O'Brien tried again. 'His wife is so gracious. And so slim! She says she can still get into the petticoats she wore before she married Plunkitt.'

'And I suppose you wish you could.'

O'Brien was tempted to repeat this joke to Plunkitt, but he suspected George would enjoy it. So he changed tack.

'Isn't this camaraderie great? Every young man should be a member of the Democratic Party. It's a party for energetic guys.'

'I burst my gut for the organization in the '65 election; you know that,' Richard said, nudging Brian.

'And I know you voted fourteen times for Bill Lyman in Greenpoint that year.'

'Sure, you know. It was you who told the newspapers.' Richard was testy now.

'Were the newspapers right?' Brian ventured.

'Sure they were right,' O'Brien tutted.

'They were not right,' Richard shouted and a few frowning faces turned from the bar, Plunkitt's among them. O'Brien noticed and saw a chance of ingratiating himself with the Sachems. If he could only taunt Richard into causing a scene!

'I had six witnesses.'

'Well, they were six cursed liars.'

'They were not.' O'Brien's voice was low, but teasing.

'I say they were.' Richard's was raised.

'Sshh!' Brian tried to silence them.

'I say I can get any one of them to swear that you voted fourteen times for William H. Lyman.'

'And I say that is a lie. I voted seventeen goddamn times for the bum.' And six times six faces turned from the bar on hearing the loud, earthy guffaw of Alderman Richard Croker.

The night progressed and, as usual, heavy drinking began sabotaging conviviality. Soon one drinker would cause offence to another. Sachems would take sides and supporters would join them. There would be awkward scuffles, not good, honest fighting. Glasses, perhaps furniture would be broken, and what should have been a hearty night of celebration would become a messy brawl.

Richard nudged Brian again and suddenly said to O'Brien, 'Bejaysus, Jimmy, I think I see John Kelly nodding for you to go over and join him.'

O'Brien responded like a scalded cat, bounding from his chair and darting towards Kelly.

'Cripes, he scooted over like a cow with a wasp on its teat. Come on!' Richard dragged Brian by the arm and they hurried out of The Wigwam.

'The younger Tammany captains will celebrate at Barbara's,' Brian called out. Richard bet Brian he would beat him in a race to the concert saloon. He was leading when they arrived, but he skidded on the wet passage and fell. Brian was waiting at the door with a beaming face, shouting with delight.

'First at last! I was always behind before.'

Richard pulled the stake from his pocket and handed it over.

'Spoken like a namesake of the great Liberator,' he laughed, and placed his arm around his friend's shoulder. 'Come on in and let's get down to enjoying ourselves, for chrissake. I've had to lie in more muck tonight than a copulating sow.'

Barbara's eyes sparkled when she greeted them.

'The concert saloon is honoured to have educated the protégé of John Kelly.' To Brian, she said, 'Thanks for introducing him to the delights of our humble premises.' Then she ran from them, leaped onto the bandstand and called for order. An Italian youth groaned reluctantly and pulled his face from between his partner's breasts. An older *uomo* drew long on his pipe, inhaling the opium he hoped might carry him through whatever was to come. A dancing couple had not even noticed that the music had stopped. The girl's slim body gyrated slowly, until there was a harsh call from Barbara.

'You there gropin'! Get the hell outa here if you wanna make a goddamn baby.' They stopped and she began her speech.

'We have pleasure in announcing the arrival of a distinguished member of Tammany Hall –'

'Oh, no!' Richard groaned.

Someone at the table where the candles were burning began hissing. Barbara's glare throttled any further expression of contempt. She reiterated:

'An *influential* member of Tammany Hall –' She paused, as if daring further interruption. 'Richard Croker, a close associate of Boss Kelly from Hester Street.'

A wag began reciting a popular city slogan:

> Walk on Hester Street
> And you'll have festered feet…

'And you'll have a festered ass if you don't shut up,' Barbara screamed. When someone began applauding, she took a mock bow.

'We are honoured that a young man, with so bright a future at Tammany, has torn himself away from The Wigwam to enjoy, with his friend Brian O'Connell –'

'Good old Brian Boru. Ya bate the shit outa the Danes and you'll bate it out of the Gas House Gang –'

Barbara shot a concerned glance towards the drunken heckler. From experience, she knew that provocative words about gangs could lead to a riot. She had a scar on her right buttock to prove it.

'You! Big mouth! Yes, you! Up here!' A slim finger pointed.

'Who? Me?'

'Who the hell do you think.' A member of the Gas House Gang saw his chance and went to drag the offender to the stage.

'Not you, leatherhead.'

Two women closed in on the drunken Brian Boru supporter and steered him to the bandstand.

'Sit there.' Barbara indicated a point on the stage directly in front of her feet. The man flopped. Barbara spread her legs and continued her speech. She embarrassed Richard by predicting that it would not be long before the leader of Tammany Hall would be visiting the concert saloon.

'And that man will be Dick Croker.' She finished to cheering and shouting, as a swaying group descended on Richard, toasting his praises, his country and his friends.

Barbara never stirred. She knew that, as long as the drunk on the bandstand was looking up at her knickers, he would remain quiet.

'A woman can be confident at times,' she joked with Brian and Richard afterwards when the three were alone. It was late and Brian was wondering why Richard was lingering, strangling the final dark hour before dawn, just talking and smoking an occasional cigar.

Richard knew well. A woman with authority like Barbara could be more than just good company. She, her staff and customers could command votes. Many, many votes.

TWENTY

MAYOR HAVEMEYER made Richard a City Marshal and Commissioner of Street Openings. The sinecures were in Slippery Dick Connolly's department. Connolly had little option but to approve, because Richard had recently obliged him by bidding on his behalf for Washington Market and by taking control of Connolly's secret 21st Ward organization, St Patrick's Alliance.

In that ward on the evening of Monday, 5 September 1871, a man was standing at the corner of Twenty-first Street and Third Avenue. It was about nine o'clock when Richard and Brian passed by, on their way to Barbara's place. While they were still within earshot, the man called after them.

'Tunnel Gang whoremasters off for their blueberry pie.'

The pair looked back and their antagonist was starting to run towards Lexington. They took off after him, knocked him on the sidewalk and began kicking him. Richard thought he recognized one of the Gas House Gang.

'I seen you with that no good Geoghegan swine, didn't I?' There was no reply and Richard took out his slung-shot. Its leather thong whirred as he swung the metal around and around his head, threatening.

'Answer me! Didn't I?'

'Don't use it, Dick. You could kill the bastard.'

'I'll drive a hole into his head and you won't know it from the Grand Canyon, bechrist. Are you with Geoghegan?'

'No.'

'What's your name?'

'James Moore.'

Hoping to take the tenseness out of the situation, Brian laughed and started teasing.

'Sure, that explains it, Dick.'

'Explains what?'

'Why he called us whoremasters. He knows all about these things. Remember the rhyme we heard in Barbara's?

> *Jimmy Moore, bedded a whore*
> *Woke up with his balls in a skewer*
> *Took it out, stuck it in his snout*
> *And a dirty lump of clabber fell out.'*

'A right lump of muck we have here. I still think he's one of them Geoghegan whelps. I should of wrote down all their names the day we hammered them.'

Brian's ploy was partly successful in appeasing Richard; the shot had almost stopped spinning when it hit Moore's rump.

The incident was reported in the *New York Times* next day. It was a Saturday afternoon. Elizabeth's mother liked to be seen helping charitable organizations and had sent her with some clothes to the orphanage at Park Place Lodge, where homeless newsboys slept. Five or six of the ragamuffins, waiting for the late editions, were loitering. They were barefoot, thin, dirty and small. They frightened Elizabeth as they started gathering around her and pulling at the parcel of clothes. One was poking a dirty finger through the paper and pulling out a cotton shirt. Another was tugging at the cord. She wanted to slap their hands away but was afraid. Reaching the house, she rapped on a huge black knocker in the shape of a fist clutching a ball. Before the echo fully retreated, a pale long-faced woman opened up, took the clothes and slammed the door. All without saying a word. Not even a greeting or an expression of thanks.

A wagon trundled down the cobbled street and the newsboys descended on it. They grabbed their papers and fanned out to meet customers in their respective areas. A boy dropped one copy and did not notice. Elizabeth read the headline: TAMMANY HALL MEMBERS IN FRACAS.

She did not pick up the newspaper; just placed her toe on it and read the first few lines of the report. She was furious. Unluckily for Richard, she happened to meet him on her way home.

'You are a disgrace. I was just about to tell my parents about my going out with you. But now my Daddy will have read about you in the paper and I cannot dream of doing so. I only hope he will not remember when, and if, I ask him eventually.' She emphasised the 'if'.

'I'm sorry, Elizabeth.'

'And apart from that. I didn't know you were a hoodlum. I thought you were considerate towards others.'

'He called me names.'

'Names! And you had to hit him with a slung-shot for calling you names!'

There was silence for a moment. Elizabeth flounced a few steps away and began tipping a greyed orange peel along the pavement with her pointed shoe. Richard's thick bottom lip slid under the other, while he tried to think of some way to stop her being cross with him. She turned again to him.

'What did he call you anyway?'

'I can't tell you.'

'Why can't you?'

'It's ... it's a bad word.'

'I have heard a few bad words in my time. I doubt if it would shock me.'

'Reading about me on the paper shocked you and sure that was nothing.'

'Richard, are you seriously telling me that you consider a bad word more serious that almost killing a man?'

'I didn't almost kill him. A pity I didn't.'

'Richard!'

'Sorry!'

He moved to place his arm about her.

'Honestly, I am sorry.' She pulled away.

'You ... Richard Croker, I am absolutely disgusted with you. I ... You ... Maybe I should have ... Oh, I really don't know what to say.'

'Say you love your darlin' Irish *garsún* and give us a kiss.'

'Richard, will you be serious, for God's sake! What did he call you?'

'An Irish gentleman who should have swam back to the auld sod years ago instead of trying to figure out you Americans. What the hell is so serious about the fight? Sure, it's not the end of the world?'

'It could be the end of our friendship if you don't tell me what the poor victim called you that provoked such an attack.'

'Right, Missie! But don't give out the pay to me if you don't like hearing it. I was with my butty, Brian O'Connell –'

'Who's he?'

'Look, do you want me to tell you the story or don't you?'

'How dare you speak to me like that, you ...you ... whoremaster.'

Richard's black eyebrows began gathering around the node of flesh above his nose. His mouth was forming a broad smile that quickly became a chuckle, before erupting into an uncontrollable fit of chortling. He began pummelling his left palm with his right fist, and spinning around on one leg. Elizabeth was trying to remain stern but his antics became too much. She knew part of this man's attraction was his rugged frankness. The society in which she moved was often such a sham. She liked its good manners, its refinement, its regard for the arts and for aestheticism. But straightforwardness did not always complement these characteristics. Too many of her parents' friends forgot that they had started off their lives as destitute children. It was true that they had all worked hard to achieve what they had, but they had been blessed with luck, too. Many, who had been just as industrious were still living in penury. It disgusted Elizabeth to see the successful ones maltreating others.

Richard was coarse, uneducated, tough, a fighter. Yet he was like a breath of fresh air to her. But now she was wondering why he was laughing so much. Was it at the word she had used?

'I never in all my life heard anything as funny. A whoooore ... mas ... ter ... I don't believe it!'

Then Elizabeth remembered that she had not the faintest idea of what the word meant. From the balcony outside her boudoir one day, she heard the gardener call the dog a whoremaster. He was always trying to climb up on the bitch's back and that day it was happening in the rose bushes.

Supposing –? She composed herself as best she could and asked:

'Richard, what's a whoremaster?'

'I'm one. You have just said so.' When he tried to continue, his lips just kept flapping about, trying to utter words that his jollity was strangling.

'Richard, will you control yourself and tell me?'

'It's a breed of dog. An Alsatian,' he lied.

She kissed him then, and they both went to look at the horses trotting in Columbus Park. Later that evening, Elizabeth told her prim mother that she was taking the whoremaster for a walk.

TWENTY-ONE

TWO YEARS into Kelly's leadership, Richard converted to Roman Catholicism. Reluctantly, Elizabeth's parents agreed to a marriage.

Brian was to be best man. He felt honoured because more and more Tammany members were tipping Richard for further advancement in the pantheon of New York municipal affairs. Yet he was apprehensive about the assignment. While Richard had often spoken about his mother and father and of his younger sister Eliza, he had seldom mentioned the older girls and had never, as far as he could remember, alluded to his brothers. Except to say three of them were older than he was, had been brought up in some place near Mallow in County Cork, and had come out to America in their early adulthood. Still, in the normal course of events, one of the brothers ought to have been chosen as best man. Brian asked Richard about it. His answer was, as usual, blunt.

'First, I hardly know those geeks. Second, you have shown me the ropes in this city and I respect a close friend more than any relative. Third, you're a handsome fella' and the Frasers will appreciate that. Fourth, the Crokers are a rough bunch at a gathering, while you know how to behave yourself.'

'You mean to say you are not even inviting them to the wedding?'

'That's right.'

'Your own brothers?'

'Nope. My father, sure, if you promise to keep an eye on him for me. My sisters, yes. And Mother, if she is able. I can spend a few bucks on good dresses for them and they will be well behaved and will impress the elite. I won't be drinking and you will be able to make sure I take up the right knife and fork and that. I guarantee you, though, Brian – if I allowed Elizabeth to invite Henry, George and John, the older fellows would cut loose at all the free drink that will be available in the Fraser household and my wedding day would finish up like the Battle of the bloody Bull Run. My father is still a mess after the war; cantankerous and a nuisance when he's drinking, but I'll have to chance bringing him and rely on you to control him.'

'God, I can't understand you, Dick. I have only one relative, my mother. I would love to have brothers and sisters. I often thought how nice it would be to go strolling along the harbour or across Manhattan with a blood relation. You are the closest I have ever come to having a brother.'

'Indeed and that's a fact anyways. Why, I don't know,' Richard grinned.

'You're right. In many ways we are direct opposites.' Brian remembered the strange urge he felt that day in the doctor's surgery. Something had driven him to help Richard. He had formed friendships with others along the way but never one as close as this. Dick Croker was becoming his idol. There were times when he thought it advisable to do something about this; to strike out on his own in politics, to make his own decisions and plan his own actions. But something always drew him back to Dick. As if he were needed. He had felt the same way when he had changed his route and happened upon Dick and Elizabeth escaping the riots.

When Brian told his mother that he was to be best man at Richard Croker's wedding, he thought she went a little pale.

'Are you feeling all right, Mother?' he asked.

'Richard Croker, did you say?'

'Yes, Mother.'

'You never mentioned him before.'

'Don't you remember I was to have brought him to meet you at the party Fay arranged?'

'You never said.'

'Oh, Jeepers, I didn't. You're right. I meant it to be a surprise.'

'Where is he from, this Croker fellow?'

'From Cork. Like yourself. That's why I was bringing him to meet you.' Nellie reached for a chair and sat.

'Are you okay, Mother?'

'Oh, I'll be fine, Brian,' she replied, trying as best she could to hide the shock and excitement sparring inside her. The following day, she was as elated as if Brian himself were getting married. She helped him choose a suit, shirt and gloves and kept prattling on about how he was to give every support and encouragement to the groom.

The Frasers spared no expense and St Patrick's Cathedral was garlanded with flowers for wealthy guests arriving on the morning of the ceremony. The mother of the bride was a statue of liberticide in pink. Tall and angular, she refused to meet Richard before the wedding. Also, she had objected to the expensive reception and had vowed not to attend the ceremony. Father O'Brien had pleaded with her; saying the bishop was extremely pleased at the reception of Richard Croker into the Roman Catholic Church and that His Lordship was convinced that Croker would, one day, be a powerful figure in New York. Mrs Fraser glanced across at the man who was to marry her daughter. Squat, bull-necked, uncouth-looking, she told herself. Richard considered how he would have to turn towards the woman when he stepped into the aisle to take Elizabeth's hand and lead her to the altar.

'Jayze, will she damn-well hurry up?' he whispered to Brian O'Connell.

At the door of the cathedral, Samuel Fraser looked at his gold Hunter and tut-tutted his annoyance at his daughter's tardiness. Then he saw the carriage, the white plumes of the black horses bobbing and the gold-leafed door and window supports glistening in the morning sun. He moved to the edge of the sidewalk and helped Elizabeth down. He did not whisper the words of encouragement for which she longed. Just a gruff reprimand and a heartbreaking rebuff:

'You're late. There is still time to call this off, you know.'

Richard was stunned by the elegance of his bride. Golden ringlets rolled on her shoulders and formed a gilt frame for flushed cheeks and pale red lips. He kissed those lips. Gently. It was like brushing moonlight. But then he saw the storm clouds gathering in the eyes that glared at him across the aisle. For a moment their stares locked, until Mrs Fraser found the Pieta to the right of the high altar more interesting.

Richard and Brian were smartly suited and, like Samuel Fraser, each of them had a watch-chain hanging from his vest pocket. A soft shaft of sunlight eased through a rose in a stained-glass window settling on Elizabeth's face before spilling onto Richard's.

From a side aisle behind the wedding party an old woman worrying her beads was watching. With great difficulty, holding the backs of pews for support, she tottered across. A wooden crucifix on her Rosary tapped out her progress. Her frail hand was a wickerwork of ridged veins in mouse-flesh. It rested on Mrs Fraser's shoulder. She recoiled, but the old lady whispered:

'Don't be thinking ill of the craythurs. Put everything in God's hands. Ask Him anything when the Host is raised and you will be looked after.'

Mrs Fraser was a staunch Roman Catholic and knew she could never ask God for what she wanted at that moment. Because her daughter was saying 'I do!' and Father O'Brien was pronouncing Elizabeth Fraser and Richard Croker man and wife.

A prayer came stealing from the old woman's heart to the blue-clad Virgin, whose statue was gleaming above its carpet of candlelight. She had watched marriage ceremonies in St Patrick's for years and could always tell, by the faces of the two families, when the newly weds needed a few Hail Marys.

Nobody had noticed the woman who entered the church after the ceremony had begun. Nellie wore a hat with a heavy black veil that covered her upper face. She moved to the end of a pew at the back of the nave and smiled feebly. She had thought Richard might be like his father in appearance and was pleased that there was little resemblance. Her biggest shock came with the realization that, for some years, she had been admiring Richard without knowing who he was. He was the well-dressed man with a gold watch on a chain that she had often seen standing on the steps of Tammany Hall when she was passing. Her eyes became steely when they sought out Eyre. Old and decrepit! A vulture dropped from a black cloud of the past. She shuddered.

The Consecration bell rang.

'Thanks, God, for allowing me to see Richard again. Now bring Tim to me. Please, God!' she whispered. Then, she wept a little and began praying for the bride and groom.

Would she herself ever find joy, she wondered. She was now in her early forties and approaching the end of her fertile years. Even if she and Tim met, could they possibly recapture the magic of those few moments on the *Henry Clay*? She had to admit it was unlikely. Was she foolish not to have heeded Rosa and Fay when they had urged her to find another man?

Thinking of her friends made her smile. More prayers came stealing from her heart to the Holy Mother of Jesus.

'May Rosa and Butch find a way of enjoying their love. And help Fay in her attempts to give up prostitution and hard drinking.'

Brian! How handsome he looks all dressed up. And so manly looking among all those dandyish nobs!

She left before the end of Mass, and on her way home felt good knowing her son was such a close friend of the bridegroom.

'He will save Richard from the curse of the guinea-fowl,' she whispered to the smoky city. It did not reply, but its dark walls would soon test her confidence.

Had the old woman with the beads been at the reception afterwards, she would have prayed a Rosary instead of a Hail Mary. The Fraser women ignored Richard's mother and sisters completely. Those who had laid the tables had received instructions to avoid the customary mixing of families. So, with Richard and Brian in the bridal group, Eyre, Frances, Mary and Eliza huddled at the end of the long table, almost hidden by a gigantic floral table-ornament fashioned into the Fraser coat of arms.

'I suppose the wine bottles are the Croker arms,' Eliza giggled to Mary.

There were short speeches. Father O'Brien hoped the couple would have as long and as happy a marriage as the Frasers. Mrs Fraser told herself that

Father O'Brien had no idea of the hell she had lived through on account of this repulsive sex thing. Her husband wished he could tell the priest that the rules of his religion destroyed any chance of marriages being successful. Samuel Fraser proposed a perfunctory toast. Brian's was sincere, but he felt only cold stares from the Fraser guests.

As soon as the wedding breakfast ended, Eyre Coote Croker whispered his excuses to his son and disappeared to get drunk in a saloon, on a block far from the dismal function. Richard told him he wished he could join him.

A large orchestra played in the ballroom but nobody went to dance. A few of the younger people sat around drinking Vichy but by one o'clock in the afternoon, the Croker and Fraser women had left. By three, most of the guests had followed them. Richard lied to Elizabeth, saying it had been a lovely day. There was nobody to whom she could toss her bouquet so she gave it to a waitress. A sorrow-drowning party was beginning back at the Fraser home.

Elizabeth was a little hurt by her family's behaviour. 'They could have put up a better front for my big day,' she said to Richard.

'Ah, sure, what about it? Aren't we together now?'

By the time they had reached Bear Mountain, forty miles upstate, Richard had revived her spirits and she clapped excitedly when she saw the quaint clapboard lodge in glorious woodland isolation, overlooking the Hudson River. There was a charming little hamlet called Highland Falls close by and she and Richard spent many hours in its small tea-rooms, frequented by students from West Point, the military academy founded by Thomas Jefferson in 1802. Richard remembered his father telling him that the President did not simply want to provide technical education for officers; he wished to make a standing army more acceptable by training its officers as engineers who would perform public works.

The young newly weds enjoyed wandering along the banks of the Hudson and its tributaries upstate, but exploration of the physical side of marriage was fraught. Like many women reared in a strict Roman Catholic environment, and like her mother before her, Elizabeth was apprehensive. It seemed an unwritten rule that Richard would go to their bedroom first and be in bed before she returned from the bathroom, undressed behind a screen, put on a long nightdress and approached her husband. The kisses and willing embraces that had promised so much during courtship began to lose their urgency, as her refined upbringing found the carnality of coupling distasteful. Richard's eagerness did little to help. He responded too quickly to his passion, unaware of his new wife's need for gentle assurance.

Wistfully, Elizabeth recalled the day of their visit to Barnum's Museum when Richard had protected her from the Draft rioters. Her all-consuming physical longing then, and on other occasions, now eluded her. Like other well-brought-up Catholic girls, she had learned nothing from her mother, her teachers or clergy about what to expect within marriage. Enjoyment and fulfillment proved not just elusive but unattainable.

They cut their honeymoon short and returned to a fine home purchased for Elizabeth by Samuel Fraser. Richard's name did not appear on its deeds. 'Maybe I won't use it that much, anyway,' he told Brian, who considered the statement ominous.

Richard was glad to be back on his political sod that now covered all the Eighteenth Gas House District of Lower East Manhattan. Wholesaling and retailing 'honest graft' there began appealing to him more than his marriage bed. 'Honest' John Kelly had arranged a pleasant surprise, too.

'I have set wheels in motion and I can guarantee that you will be City Coroner, within a year.' The Boss was grinning broadly. 'The office commands annual fees amounting to $15,000.'

'Be the Lord! Thanks John.'

'Your thanks will be your loyalty, Dick ...'

'A Croker never done a friend wrong.'

'We'll be testing that soon,' Kelly said. 'O'Brien is running for Congress.'

Jimmy O'Brien was probably the only man who could aggravate Richard into forgetting his rule of keeping peace with political enemies. The bitterness festered. But Richard knew he would be hard to beat.

'What about running Abraham S. Hewitt against him?'

'Think it's a good idea, Dick?'

'It will be hard to bring off, but we can do it.'

Richard had never canvassed with such vigour. He used every contact in the Railroad, at Barbara's and among Moses Kohn's customers, to garner votes against O'Brien. Working just as hard on O'Brien's behalf, were his two brothers, Steve and Larry, an Irish-American named John McKenna and another old enemy of Richard's, Oweney Geoghegan.

Tammany Hall's young men sweated at hand-operated printing presses, churning out hundreds of election posters. They combed the city for volunteers to paste them up. And for others to tear down O'Brien's. Women seldom participated in electioneering, but Nellie, Fay and Rosa set up a booth on the corner of Baxter Street and prevailed on passers-by to take handbills from them. They also kept a kerosene burner going and provided hot chocolate, coffee, tea and bagels for weary canvassers.

'Little do they know I could offer them lots more,' Fay laughed and Nellie patted her on the back.

'Keep it up, Fay.'

'About all I manage to keep up nowadays, goddamnit!'

On the morning of Election Day, Brian came dashing into The Wigwam where Richard was marshalling repeaters for the afternoon's polling.

'Get the Tin Whistlers quick; Geoghegan and O'Brien's brothers are wrecking booths and hustling every Hewitt supporter in the ward,' he said.

Most of the Whistlers were present, so Richard began ushering them out. 'Stick together and don't be gentle,' he ordered as they raced down towards Second Avenue.

On the corner of Thirty-fourth Street they found some of O'Brien's supporters. One of them, Bill Borst, was from a West Side district.

'What are you doing in this ward?' Richard challenged.

'It's none of your bloody business,' Borst replied.

'I know whose business it will be if you don't get to hell back to where you belong.' Richard was menacing, his craggy face inches from Borst's.

At that moment the three O'Brien's came around the corner. Jimmy called out: 'Hey, Bill, don't take any notice of that loafer. Move on and do what I bid.'

'Who's a loafer, O'Brien?' Richard's question crushed across gravel.

'You are! A loafer, a repeater and the scum of Tammany Hall.'

'Take that back, O'Brien.'

'I'll take nothing back.'

'No more than you ever give anything back, you thief.'

'Who are you calling a thief, Croker?'

'You, scumbag! Want to make anything of it?' A crowd was gathering and each man knew he had gone beyond the point of return. Any softening would invoke censure, ridicule and accusations of cowardice. O'Brien was squaring up, raising his fists and growling.

'You're nothing but a low-down cur, Croker. Maybe you don't know that I helped to drag you up from the gutter where I should have left you to rot –'

'You! How could you do that when you *are* the gutter? No, I'm wrong. You're the sewer. Full of the swill and shit of Manhattan.'

'I say it again. I put you where you are. Helped your association with Mick Walsh.'

'You did like –'

'Aye! And then you dropped Walsh and began licking Kelly's arse.'

'You –'

'Yes! Licking Kelly's arse. And backing Hewitt against me. I suppose it's because he's wealthy and you are part of his elite now, after marrying into it.'

John McKenna rushed over to support O'Brien. Richard's left hand was in his pocket. He swung his right fist but fell on the pavement because Brian O'Connell had deliberately charged into him. The sharp report of a gun elicited gasps of horror from the crowd, now dispersing quickly. John

McKenna toppled into a grotesque heap, blood pouring from a gap left by a piece of his skull that spattered the white limestone wall. Unintelligible gibberish accompanied a gush of greenish-red from his mouth.

Richard wanted to call an ambulance, but Brian hustled him away. A police officer crouched close to McKenna. It was Frank Randall, who had suffered ridicule the day of the arrest of young Richard Croker and Elizabeth Fraser, many years before. He was only with the victim for a few moments when an ambulance arrived and took McKenna away. He died on the way to Bellvue Hospital. Police Sergeant Randall called to the Coroner's office the next day and arrested Richard Croker on a charge of murder.

'You must want your head examined, officer. As long as I can use my fists, I will never, never carry a pistol.'

'McKenna named you before he passed away,' the sergeant replied icily.

Brian told Nellie that he had pushed Richard to save him and claimed he had seen the stranger who had fired. Nellie was not sure her son was telling the truth, but she said nothing. She did not wish to show too much concern for Richard. Not until she was free from The Sleeve and could tell Brian his real name and many other things – like how well he had looked at the wedding in St Patrick's Cathedral the day he was best man for his half-brother.

Next day, a District Coroner's Court formally charged the City Coroner, Richard Croker. 'Honest' John Kelly and Abe Hewitt were present to put up the agreed bail. Richard returned to his distraught wife, who was pregnant. As he was trying to explain the situation, there was a knock on the door. Sergeant Randall was back.

'I have a warrant for your detention.'

'You imprison me and those chevrons of yours will be in the river.' A flash of memory, and Richard was recalling Mike Walsh's threats on the wharf long ago. But Walsh had got results that he was failing to achieve.

'How can you arrest him? He is on bail,' Elizabeth shrieked. 'Oh, what will my father and mother think? Please officer, don't take him away. It would kill them.'

'You and your parents. You don't care a rat's shit about me. Right you be, Sergeant Randall. Haul me away. But, by Christ, you'll be sorry for doing it.'

Randall took him away in a police wagon and incarcerated him in The Tombs to await trial.

He was only an hour in his cell when he heard a key rattling in the lock and saw the door opening. It was Eyre. Although nervous and sickly-looking, he was forcing a smile.

'Don't let it beat you, lad. You wouldn't be the first Croker in trouble.'

'But the only one caught, Father.'

'Oh, I don't know about that. Is there anything I can do?'

'No. Thanks for offering.'

There was an awkward pause. Father's and son's eyes met and Richard said, 'You were good to come.'

'Whatever its trickle, Croker blood runs in the one stream.'

Another silence.

'Is the Hall working on it, Richard?'

'I hope so.'

'They'll solve it. You'll see.'

The third break lasted longest. Eyre fiddled with his coat button and Richard cracked his knuckles. Eyre looked up.

'Did you do it, Richard?'

Richard drew a long breath. Keys rattled. The door opened again.

'All right, Mr Croker. Time's up, I'm afraid, sir.'

'But –'

'Sorry, sir! It's the rules. The first night there should really be no visitors.'

Eyre nodded resignedly.

'Goodbye so, Richard. And good luck.'

'Thanks, Father.'

Fay, Rosa and Brian came to visit him next day. They chatted, the women trying to cheer him up and Brian assuring him that Tammany Hall would do everything to assist. Richard was not so sure.

'I have enemies, there, Brian. Many enemies. Any one of them would be glad to see me swing.'

'Jumpin' Jesus!' The prospect had never crossed Fay's mind.

Brian had told the women that he would need a short while on his own with Richard so, after a little banter, they said their goodbyes early and left.

'The Hall is trying its best, Dick.'

'Listen, Brian. Three years ago, John Kelly quietly paid for Harry Clinton to help prosecute Tweed. He is the city's best lawyer. He succeeded against all the odds. Tell Kelly I want Clinton on my case.'

'Jeeze! He's expensive, Dick. I can help a little and I might be able to get the doctor I stay with to give me a loan but –'

'We're not talking costs here, Brian. Thanks for the offer but the Tammany Treasurer won't be found wanting. Nor a few tubbies in this town that I have feathered nests for. Now tell Kelly to get moving.'

'OK, I'll ask him.'

'I said "tell", Brian.'

'Anything you need in here, Dick?'

'Yes. Freedom.'

Late that night, Brian called on Kelly. Within an hour he was talking to Harry Clinton.

'You will get plenty of municipal business in the future if you secure Croker's release,' Kelly promised.

'I already have a busy practice, Mr Kelly.'

'Indeed! Operating from a building on a site that just might be required for a new waterworks.'

Clinton understood the raised eyebrow.

'Tomorrow, I'll see if I can rearrange things so that I can take on the case.'

'You won't see tomorrow, Mr Clinton. You'll be busy sending an estimate of your fee to my office. Good night, sir.'

Brian was allowed to visit Richard on the morning of the trial.

'You're lucky to get Clinton, Dick. John Kelly told me that when he was younger and less wealthy, a friend to whom he had given large sums of money refused to help him pay for a good lawyer to defend him.'

'Never give a man money, Brian. Lend it to him. That way, you have him under your finger. And always try to have any so-and-so you need on the wrong side of the law. That's like pulpin' sugar beet. Brings sweet returns always.'

'I don't know, Richard. I haven't much regard for the police at all.'

'Well find it, Brian. Them officers is the steppin' stones of politics. If you hold on to them, you'll stay on top.'

'They took you in, Dick.'

'One did. Just one. Because he held a grudge about something that I hadn't hand, act or part in. It was Mike Walsh that done him wrong and he took it out on me. But one cop is not enough to send Dick Croker down. You just wait and see.'

'I'll be there to see. Best of luck!'

'Thanks, pal.'

They took him to the same courtroom where he had appeared as a lad. He looked around to see if Elizabeth, his mother, father or sisters were present. They were not, and it hurt. Then he saw Brian giving him a slight wave. Good, loyal Brian!

The proceedings opened with Sergeant Randall's evidence.

'The defendant shot Mr McKenna at point blank range, your Honour.'

'And you saw him do so, Sergeant?'

'Yes, your Honour.'

'Have you got the weapon as an exhibit, Sergeant?'

'No, your Honour. The defendant escaped from the scene.'

'Any questions, Mr Clinton?'

The lawyer tugged his lapels and stood. He paced before the witness box, hands wringing each other behind his back. Unnerving Randall. Making

Richard edgy too. Jaysus, he was thinking, is he trying to make up something to say? Brian was on the edge of his seat.

'You say you saw the weapon being fired, Sergeant?'

'Yes, sir.'

'Other witnesses have said they saw no gun in the defendant's hand. That he had one hand in his pocket.'

'Well, maybe. Yes, sir. He struck John McKenna with one hand and fired the gun from his pocket.'

'I see.' Clinton was pacing again. This time, the judge had to urge him to continue.

'Certainly, your Honour.' He walked calmly to his desk. Agonizingly slowly, he took a parcel from under it and began opening it.

'Will you please hurry, Mr Clinton.'

'Yes, your Honour. Now Sergeant, two prosecution witnesses yesterday confirmed that this was the coat the defendant was wearing when he was fighting with John McKenna. Was it?'

'Yes, sir. That was the coat.'

'And you say the defendant fired from the pocket?'

Randall saw the trap but could not think of a way of avoiding it. He paled. Brian almost squealed with excitement. Richard grinned. A ripple of whispered conversation ran through the courtroom.

'Order!' The judge struck his gavel on the bench while Clinton began walking around before him, the coat held high, and one of Clinton's hands in each of its two pockets. He did not have to say, 'No, holes, your Honour.'

'But the deceased whispered the defendant's name before he passed away, your Honour.'

'What name did he whisper, Sergeant?' When Clinton asked the question, the audience became hushed again.

'Richard Croker, your Honour.' Another gasp.

Richard glanced over at his friend's steely features. Brian was not betraying the turmoil he was suffering. There had been stories about another death – a drowning in the East River, when Richard was said to have tripped over a ring-bolt and knocked a sailor into the water. Brian was disturbed about that and about the present affair. He was not even sure why he had knocked Richard over during the melee. Did some urge drive him to do it? Had he sensed that somebody was going to fire on Richard? Maybe somebody did and hit McKenna instead? Or did he think it was the only way to stop him fighting with McKenna, giving the remainder of O'Brien's mob an excuse to hammer Richard? Brian knew one thing: he would never be certain that his friend had not fired the shot. He could have done it. Might have, even. Too much had happened too quickly to notice everything. He noted too that the defence lawyer had Richard's coat all wrapped up and ready. So, Tammany Hall was powerful enough to discover the prosecution's evidence and pass it on to Clinton.

Most puzzling of all, Brian had decided at the outset of the trial, that if Richard were convicted, he'd protest and claim that he, Brian O'Connell, had shot John McKenna.

Why the hell should I do a crazy thing like that, he wondered. His mother would have known the answer.

As he was testifying to seeing the accused pull a pistol, Jimmy O'Brien was leering sinisterly at Richard. Billy Borst corroborated, and scowled.

The defence paraded four eyewitnesses. These well-paid men had no problem swearing that Richard was flaking away with both fists during the fight and could not have fired the fatal shot.

When the jury was about to retire, Mr Clinton asked permission to re-call the prosecution witness, Sergeant Randall, for one further question.

'Objection!' the district attorney called, but the judge overrode it saying, 'Well, it's unusual, but there's a man's life at stake.'

'And your next promotion,' Richard mumbled into the chubby fist held to his mouth, while Randall took the stand again.

'Sergeant Randall, you stated earlier that, before he passed away, John McKenna told you his murderer's name.'

'I did, sir.'

'And you said that name was Richard Croker, is that right?'

'That's correct sir. "Richard Croker" was his words.'

Clinton turned to face the courtroom. His hand swept around all those who had testified before he spoke.

'Sergeant Randall! Not one of these witnesses, for the prosecution or for the defence has referred to the defendant as Richard Croker. Among his peers and on the street and in Tam ... in every place he frequents, except perhaps in his own and his parents' home, he is known as Dick Croker. Thank you, your Honour, for allowing me to ask the question.'

'You may step down, Sergeant. The jury will retire.' The judge yawned and looked glad to hurry to his chambers.

When they brought Richard to the courtroom waiting-cell, his father was sitting there. Looking more tired and almost broken.

'I came down but could not bear to enter the courtroom. I'm sorry.'

'Don't be looking so serious, Father. I understand. You didn't want to hear what muck was on the bottom of that stream you were talking about.'

'This kind warder allowed me in here.'

'So you can say you were as good as me!' Richard laughed to Eyre and thanked the warder: 'If I get out of this, look me up in Tammany Hall.'

Eyre looked on sadly when they led his son to the prison van.

The jury deliberated for seventeen hours and it was well into the afternoon of the following day when a huge crowd assembled to hear its verdict. Rosa and Fay sat at the back, whispering.

'Rosa, do you think Nellie acted strangely when we asked her to come?'

'Very strange. Say she want for to say Rosary for defendant.'

'A Rosary would be no good to him. It's the Pope of Rome and St Patrick's jock he needs. Jeeze! Here they come.'

When the foreman was filing into the box, Brian was chewing his fingernails. Harry Clinton kept tapping an index finger on his bench. The judge began yawning and looking at his watch. Richard remained impassive.

The twelve men, six Republicans and six Democrats, could not agree. It was a split decision. Judge George C. Barrett was pleased to be able to acquit. After all, Richard might have considerable influence at Tammany Hall when his re-appointment came up in a few years' time; even promotion, perhaps. In the meantime he could surely influence the granting of contracts for the new Brooklyn Bridge, something dear to the judge's heart.

TWENTY-TWO

THE NEWSPAPERS are calling "Honest" John Kelly the "Bismark of New York", and noting how alike in appearance he is to his protégé, Richard Croker,' Brian said to Richard who was sitting behind Kelly's desk at Tammany Hall.

The city was buzzing with the news that Kelly might move aside for Croker. Little wonder, since Richard was now arranging all appointments, development permissions and licences for Tammany district leaders without even consulting Kelly. Since his prison release, although keeping a comparatively low profile, he had worked harder than ever securing lucrative contracts for friends. Particularly as the city's elevated rail line, affectionately called the 'El', stretched along Second, Third, Sixth and Ninth Avenues and was pushing on towards Brooklyn, Queens and the Bronx. City folk were beginning to overlook Richard's imprisonment; they had little option, because he seemed to have a hand in every pie they wished to bake. Richard's trial judge, George C. Barrett, saw his dream come true in a cloud of handsome legal contracts. Brooklyn Bridge opened amid great jubilation with a ceremony on 24 May 1883. President Chester A. Arthur attended. Richard was there, but the Irish who had worked on the structure and had seen some of their comrades die in its construction, stayed away. The boycott occurred because the date selected was Queen Victoria's sixty-fourth birthday.

'Congratulations on being re-elected, Dick.'

'Thanks, Brian. Fair play to Kelly. He tested the water, put his head down like a puck goat and nominated me. Friends is what men needs in this life.'

'True for you.'

'But I'm not taking the job.'

'Why not?' Brian was aghast.

'Mayor Edson is after making me New York Fire Commissioner, and I can't be alderman and commissioner at the same time, that's why. Edson knows there's an election coming. He doesn't know I am nominating Abe Hewitt for Mayor.'

'You what! I don't believe you. After Edson giving you that plum job!'

'All's fair in love and Tammany, Brian. Giving the power to Hewitt under these circumstances is like making myself Mayor.'

'Mike Walsh said he would leave the city if Hewitt became Mayor.'

'He's already gone. Retired to a farm somewhere in Connecticut.'

'We should have given him a send-off.'

'I offered him one but he refused it. Ah, he fell foul of the wrong people, Brian.'

'Or had you no more use for him, you blackguard?'

Brian was unable to interpret Richard's grin. There was silence but for his fingers tapping on Richard's desk. Then he walked to the door and back again.

'Jaysus, you're like a hen on a hot griddle. What's up with you?'

'Dick, I'm a bit embarrassed asking you, but my mother would love to meet you.'

'Cripes, yes. You told me that before. I'm a selfish bastard to forget, and she from my part of the world and all.'

'I know you're busy, but –'

'It would be a bad day that a Croker wouldn't have time to meet a good friend's mother. Bring her up here anytime, can't you?'

'Eh …'

'You're still humming and hawing.'

'She's outside now, Dick. I'm sorry but she –'

'For chrissake, don't leave the woman out there. Bring her in.' Richard tossed a pencil on his desk, tugged at his tie and settled its diamond pin. 'I must be tidy for my overdue meeting with the West Cork mother of my distinguished colleague,' he quipped, as Brian was leaving.

Brian wanted to accompany Nellie, but she insisted on entering the office alone. After closing the door behind her, she stood still. At the wedding, she had not been close enough; now she was tilting her face either way, searching for remembered features. Some were there. The eyes, definitely. Others slipped dull signals through creases of middle age.

At first he did not recognize her but when she smiled and began walking towards him, shock gave way to incredulity.

Four outstretched hands spanned miles and decades. A young face in a pasture in Balliva pulsed through a foaming swell around the *Henry Clay*: an image that had haunted him in his darkest moments. Her erect, slim body seemed to have changed little, nor her eyes, despite the tears now brimming. Carefully groomed hair framed her elegant features and Richard abandoned all that sitting at the Boss's desk stood for, as the wheeling and dealing of power politics dissolved before a potent past deep in his soul.

They embraced.

Fiercely.

Her fingers were gouging his arms and his back and he was whispering, 'Nellie Hurley' into her hair.

She held him at arm's length then and saw in his eyes green, Irish fields backing the inset of a glowing hearth in a large flagged kitchen.

'Not many cows to milk here, Richard!' Her giggle was as damp as his tiny hands had been.

'Jaysus, I still don't believe it. Nellie Hurley! Well, I'll be damned. I thought you were drownded. Christ, why didn't I call on you when Brian asked me?'

They clung again, until he broke the embrace suddenly.

'So that explains it. Brian told me his mother was from the Balliva area and I couldn't place you. You married an O'Connell, then?'

Her perfect mouth silenced his. It was a hard, hungry kiss, yet not carnal. Not even erotic, but banishing ghosts and emotions of years.

'Have you still got the mole on your groin, Richard?' she laughed when she released him.

'I can't see any more, girl. Middle-age spread! Nellie Hurley! Well, holy Jaysus! Give us another hug!'

They held each other again and, for one glorious moment, Richard was wishing to be that innocent child again. He let her go and studied her. 'Here, wait till I get Brian. How much did the blackguard know about all this?'

She grabbed his arm.

'A minute, please, Richard. Brian must know nothing about my name being Hurley.'

'What?'

'Please, Richard. Not until you do something for me first.'

'I won't ask why and I won't argue, Nellie, but if I can do anything, and I mean *anything*, you just spit it out. You look like a woman who knows what she wants and gets it.'

'I've known for a long time, Richard. Today I have got part of it.'

Thinking he understood, he asked:

'You lost your husband?'

'I never had one, Richard.'

'Brian then? And O'Connell?'

For a brief moment she considered telling him that Brian was his halfbrother. She knew he would understand. But she would have to tell Brian first. And that meant she would have to be free of The Sleeve.

'I'll explain another time, Richard. Look, Brian would kill me for asking but the truth is, I could do with a decent job.'

'Couldn't have asked at a better time. I am nominating Abe Hewitt for Mayor and I need an election secretary immediately.'

'But I ... well, I suppose I have done a type of secretarial work.'

'In Jackie the Mule's.'

'Oh, good God! How did you know that? I told Brian never to tell any-body.'

'And he didn't. But I knew his mother, Mrs O'Connell, was receptionist there, and better looking than any of the, eh, products on sale. And, eh ... I meet Jack McHugh an odd time.' He noticed her shock and quickly added, 'On business, of course.'

Nellie was not sure what he meant, but forgot about the statement when he continued:

'Now, when Hewitt is elected – and I didn't say if – he will find a per-manent place for you on his City Hall staff.'

'How do you know he will have me?'

Richard guffawed and said, 'Ask your son why I am so sure.'

'Oh, thank you, Richard.' She hugged him again.

'Think nothing of it. It's the least I could do after you cleaning my back-side when I was a babby. Oh, by the way. There will be a nice little house with the job.'

Nellie was dumbfounded.

'No, Richard, I couldn't.'

'Sorry. Rules is rules. The Mayor's secretary must live in accommodation close to City Hall.'

Nellie could not believe it. All that she had longed for settled in a few minutes – well almost all. If only Tim could be with her – making a home out of the house!

'Why don't you and Brian and myself go on the town tonight?'

'Thanks, Richard, but I'm working.'

'I didn't give you your hours yet.'

'When do I start?'

'You've began.' Richard was heading for the door. She almost corrected his grammar. Like she had done when he was lisping infant phrases in Balliva.

'Hey, Brian Hurl ... O'Connell! Come in here.' He closed the door for an instant and whispered, 'Don't worry. He didn't notice the slip.'

She would have loved to tell Brian there and then. After all, she was prac-tically finished at The Sleeve. But she would wait until they were alone.

'Brian, I am moving to a new job and into a new house, courtesy of your friend.'

Brian glanced apologetically at Richard. 'Mother, you shou –'

'Shut up, O'Connell. Let's just say your mother and me got on horrid well.' Not a flicker of an eyelid and, all over again, Nellie was adoring a little child for his goodness. They did not kiss or embrace before she left. Just shook hands.

'Thank you so much, Richard.'

'You're welcome, girl.'

When she had gone, Richard thanked Brian for bringing her. 'She'll be a breath of fresh air in that stuffy crowd above at City Hall.'

The telephone rang. 'Good old Alexander Graham Bell. A great invention, this talking machine.' Richard reached for the receiver. Brian watched his face darkening. Heard the curt 'Yes', 'No' and 'Sure, I'll be there.'

'That was Mary. It's Mother! She's dead. Will you come with me?'

'Of course I will, Dick. God, I'm sorry, pal.'

'I know. Thanks. Come on. Let's face it.' Somehow, Richard would not have dreamed of facing his mother's dead body without Brian by his side.

'And I asked Nellie to go on the town to celebrate. I have to disappoint her again. Will you explain and say I'm sorry?'

'Of course I will, Dick.'

━━

Elizabeth was the only member of the Fraser family at the funeral.

The burial was over and Richard and his father were going through Frances's few personal belongings. Richard asked for a locket that had his own picture as a boy opposite that of Eyre.

'You may have it, son. It's yours by right. Did you know she almost died having you? A bad haemorrhage while I was celebrating your arrival with the staff in Balliva. Fear was making her problem worse. One of the Hurleys, I think it was the little girl, had told Sarah Donnelly, another member of the staff, that she had heard the guinea-fowl cry and that it meant the newborn would grow up to kill or be killed before his time. Sarah blabbed it to Frances, of course.'

'So I was destined to plug someone or die early?'

'What's early, Richard? Plugging someone wouldn't be your way of doing things, would it?' Although Eyre was laughing, Richard did not like his father's sardonic smile. A dream he had had the night before Frances died came to mind. In it, Brian O'Connell turned into a guinea-fowl and picked the eyes out of a stevedore who was attacking Richard down at the harbour.

A month later, Eyre took ill with cancer. Richard visited him every night in hospital and watched his body waste away until it was a parchment for features scribbled in charcoal. On the night before he died, he reached up to hold Richard, who was sitting on the bed. Richard did not see. He was look-ing out the window, thinking of the happy times he'd had with Eyre in Cincinnati; visiting the place he worked and handling the horses.

'I think, Father, I might throw up all this dirty politics business and buy a racehorse or two.'

Now Richard was thinking of the shipwreck of the *Henry Clay*, with Eyre's death rattle a capstan chain whipping itself loose, his groan a creak-ing timber. When he eventually looked around, his father was dead.

This time, no member of the Fraser family attended the funeral. Not even Elizabeth. Brian wanted to accompany Richard but Richard would not let him.

'Sit in my office till I get back. There's more rats snooping around that Hall in the mornings nor you'd find in the city dump. Hewitt has turned out to be a bad choice.'

It was a dark, wet morning. Ideal for Nellie. Her umbrella would help hide her. When Brian told her he would not be attending, she felt an urge to be there. A compulsion she could not explain. But she did not want Richard to know. He would want to introduce her to his wife and family and she could not face that.

Why did she want to go to the interment? Maybe to be sure he's gone down, she joked to herself. In the cemetery she stood beneath a tall cypress. An unobserved observer. Just like she was at Richard's wedding, she thought. She found it difficult to say a prayer for the soul of her defiler. For his eternal salvation. If he went to heaven would she want to be there when she died? Her church taught that she should pray for those that persecuted her. So she tried, but each rapid thud of earth on the coffin was a loathsome thrust into her innocence on a Balliva couch. She began saying the Our Fa-ther, but stalled and could not utter the words 'forgive us our trespasses as we forgive those who trespass against us'.

The grave was filling, making the sound of falling clay duller. She closed her eyes and saw the face of Brian. Only then did she find it possible to com-plete the prayer. And she thanked God that she was now free of The Sleeve, that she could tell Brian everything and give herself and her son back their surname. She looked over at the crowd and saw a raindrop clinging to Rich-ard's nose. His wet hand holding his silver-handled umbrella reminded her of when it was tiny and milky, clutching hers. She crossed herself and left.

At the family gathering after the obsequies, Richard's brothers and sisters announced that they were returning to Ireland. Richard did not care. He had the friendship and support of Brian and his mother. He would survive the infighting and the brutality of the city and its political life. He would beat the Frasers at their own game, by becoming wealthy without etiquette or niceties, with no family background to support him. Just a dogged Irishman against the rest. But with a savage hunger to win.

He would leave the horses until later.

Richard grieved for his parents more than he thought he would. Brian had trouble shaking him out of some periods of deep depression.

'I never told either of them that I loved them, Brian,' Richard said one day when they were out walking.

'Bet they knew it, all the same, Dick.'

'Elizabeth is seeing less and less of me and not caring. Obeying her … our Church and giving me what it calls "conjugal rights". Jaysus! As much passion as a frog on an iceberg! Even the sound of the word disgusts her.'

Brian assumed that mere obedience to precepts accounted for the Croker offspring, arriving one each year since the marriage. As if reading his thoughts, Richard continued:

'She lavishes all the love she once had for me on the children. I wish I had more time to play with the little divils. They're great gas. Especially Frank and Herbert and Flossie. She's my favourite.'

Richard indeed had great affection for the children. But Elizabeth's constant care and comfort meant more to them and, as they grew up, they began to notice how much he was absent and how neglectful of Elizabeth he was. They clung to their mother. She then began drifting back to her parents' home and sleeping there, often for weeks at a time. Richard hardly noticed. His work-load was growing. He took no time for relaxation; not even to visit Barbara's. He knew that the more people he obliged, the more influence he would build up for himself.

One of those he had facilitated did not fall into line, however. Mayor Hewitt. The man was wealthy, a friend of Elizabeth's father, and was becoming a nuisance. He also insulted the Irish by becoming the first Mayor in thirty-seven years to refuse to review the St Patrick's Day Parade.

'He'll have to go,' Richard told Brian.

TWENTY-THREE

THE SACHEMS never appointed Richard Croker Boss at Tammany. They accepted that he would succeed Kelly. By the time 'Honest John' died in 1885, Richard managed all the affairs of The Wigwam and was wielding more power and pulling more strokes than Boss Tweed had ever done. His technique was different, however, always doing his best to avoid clashes. He forbade any formal installation ceremony and this tendency towards common sense started to appeal to more and more Tammany members. His boisterous bonhomie made him popular too.

Contributions rolled in from friends who received municipal appointments and from investors in companies that Tammany was steering towards lucrative contracts. Money was Richard's main weapon against opposition.

'An honest man is a man who, once bought, remains bought,' he told Brian in Barbara's one night. After a decent lapse of time since Kelly's death, they were celebrating its implications for Richard. No banners flew, no announcement came from Barbara, yet there was a palpable excitement. At the end of the evening Barbara led Richard to the centre of the floor and they began dancing to a waltz from 'Willow Tit-Willow', the Gilbert and Sullivan musical still drawing crowds to the Fifth Avenue Theatre. Richard was not a good dancer, but Barbara's dexterity and strong left arm were keeping him on a steady course. Brian led the company in applause.

When the dance ended, Richard thanked Barbara and asked her if she could bring him to a private room.

'Jeeze, I've been waiting for that invitation for a long time. This way, honey,' she jested, knowing Richard wanted a different measure of privacy.

He looked around the room and said, ''Twill do!', then threw a fistful of banknotes on the table. 'I'm hiring it for meetings every Monday night. I won't be here, but a few Irish acquaintances will. All males. Including Brian, at times.'

Barbara counted the notes. 'One thousand bucks! Jesus! Do they all want free liquor and opium? Who are these anyway? The Tunnel Gang?'

'They call themselves Clan na Gael, Barbara. Look after them.'

He came back to the table and said to Brian, 'I have did my bit for old Ireland. Drop into the Clan meetings an odd time.'

'I knew you were a great patriot, Dick,' Brian laughed.

'Old Ireland might be able to do something for me too,' Richard grinned. 'The Clan can muster a good few votes.'

'You're giving Hewitt the bum's rush, then?'

'Aye.'

'Who will you run to replace him, Dick?'

'Hugh Grant.'

'Flossie's godfather!'

'Aye, my favourite girleen.'

The Clan's votes made a significant addition to the hundreds cast by a few repeaters. Grant enjoyed spectacular success at the polls and he assured Richard of first call on many more profitable contracts. He delivered on his promise and Richard established new companies to handle them. Grant also appointed Richard City Chamberlain. The annual remuneration for the sinecure was $25,000. In turn, Richard demanded an increase in salary for Nellie Hurley and a complete refurbishment of her house.

There was another celebration at Barbara's. This time, Fay came along with Nellie, Rosa and Butch Maguire. They joined Richard and Brian, who introduced them all to Barbara. Richard announced loudly:

'This night out is overdue. I promised it to Nellie a while ago and it had better be a good one. All the drinks are on me. Nobody puts a hand in his pocket.'

'For money anyway!' Fay could not resist the quip and it helped break the ice.

'Brian, we must to get that *Mamma* of yours muzzed,' Rosa said, adding, 'She need forget about her *Henry Clay amico*, too.'

'Did she ever tell either of you much about my father, this Tim O'Connell?' Brian asked.

Nellie flinched.

'Only that she love him so much,' Rosa ventured.

'I wish she would talk to me about him,' said Brian.

'Some day I will explain everything,' said Nellie.

'Could you find her a decent man, Barbara?' Fay asked.

'Not many of them in my place, Fay, I'm afraid.'

'I object to that,' Butch Maguire interrupted.

'Fine one you to talk 'bout being decent *uomo*.'

'Yez are all terrible worried about Nellie. Sure, maybe herself and myself will settle down.' Richard hugged Nellie playfully. 'Do you know Nellie, you're a great woman altogether.'

'Everyone love Nellie.'

'I barely remember her as a child,' Richard said. 'Nellie was the loveliest little girl you could imagine. She came with our family to America and we thought for years she was lost in the *Henry Clay* shipwreck. God, I can still see her skipping around the fields with me. I had a pet robin, would you believe, and we used to talk to it.'

'Dick Croker with a pet robin!' Fay laughed.

'And Macha! Don't forget Macha, Richard.'

'Cripes, yes. The loveliest horse you ever laid eyes on. You used to hold me on his back, remember?'

'You're very quiet, sweetheart.' Barbara nudged Brian.

'Sweetheart, I ask you! Begod, Brian, Barbara must have got working on you at the piano like she did on my first visit here.'

Brian was indeed quiet. But he was listening. And cogitating.

'When these immigrants start talking about home, it's no use butting in.'

'Do you hear him? And he only a wet day in America when he was borned. Barbara, can I buy a few cigars, please?'

'A loaded one?' Barbara slapped his back and laughed.

'Butch Maguire has a great one, hasn't he, Rosa?' Fay croaked coarsely.

'Shut up!' Butch was embarrassed.

'I'm afraid what I stock wouldn't be expensive enough for you, Dick. But I'll give you a present of a few that will see you through the night.'

'Bring us all another drink too, Barbara,' Fay called.

'Vichy for me, Barbara. And it's not Fay's round. On me, I said. Remember?' Richard called after their hostess.

'Water! Imagine an Irishman buying water,' Fay remarked. 'A bit like Jack McHugh paying for slit. Jeeze, but there's more smoke in this place than came from that locomotive you're always boasting about building, Dick. And all those coloured candles!'

'Be like chapel shrines on St Patrick's Day,' Rosa giggled.

'The music is good, though,' Brian was swaying his shoulders.

'Very not like chapel on St Patrick's Day.' Now Rosa was laughing and pulling Butch Maguire's arm around her.

Barbara came back with the drinks. They raised glasses and she proposed a toast.

'To Dick Croker!'

'And to all who flail with him!' Fay laughed.

'And to his success,' Butch looked at Richard.

'That you and many like you helped along, Butch.' Richard winked.

'Help or no help, just how the hell did you do it all, Dick?' Butch asked.

'I seen my opportunities, Butch, and I took them. I am working for my own pocket and I admit it.'

'Like us all,' Fay grinned.

'There's them that condemn what I do, Fay, who does the very same but won't admit it. I still has my principles.'

'And your friends,' Barbara added.

'All five of us,' Brian teased.

'Youze are good friends too. I would rather if one of youze stole money out of my pocket than be disloyal. Do you know that? Honest! Same with my employees. I am a partner in a firm of realtors, in an auctioneers and in a bonding company. I take a lot of money from them outfits, but I look after the employees. Them's the best-paid workers in New York. But they give me loyalty.'

'You're the sort of an old fox that commands allegiance,' Brian said, admiring his friend brushing a fleck of dust off his impeccably tailored jacket. His gigantic diamond stick-pin was sparkling as he leaned back to light one of the cigars Barbara had brought.

'You use bigger words nor my father used to, O'Connell.'

'God rest him,' Butch said.

'Amen,' Brian added.

'You be having other monies, you not speak about, Dick.'

Rosa was matter-of-fact, but the others sensed suppressed grievance.

'I have begod and I know well what you're getting at, Rosa. Now, forgive me for saying it because you're a decent woman but your husband or separated brethren or whatever his present status is; he deserves no better nor what he's forced to do.'

'I not like what he do, but he have to pay so much to Tammany Hall, Dick.'

'And isn't it worth every penny to him? Don't we keep the police away from The Sleeve? And there's more nor Jackie the Mule stumping up. Every brothel in this city is doing the same. And I admit it, a little commission comes my way from it.'

'Same as does from gambling houses, rat and dog pits, saloon-keepers.'

Was Rosa grumbling? It was hard to tell.

'I don't mind taking bucks from bad bums, Rosa.'

'And why should you?' Brian tried to sound convinced, but he was not.

'I'll tell you another thing, Brian. I have lists of clients of every fleabag and whore-house in this city. And a lot of them are wealthy. So I get rewarded for keeping my gob shut. See? Not money, mind you, but information.'

'Like?'

'I'll tell you like what, Brian. Like as your man Plunkitt said, it's as valuable as gold. The right bonds, the right lands, the right properties to buy. And when I take my pick I can get my palm crossed passing the rest on.'

'What did you pay for the latest real estate, Dick?' Barbara ventured.

'That Fifth Avenue home cost $80,000 and my stud farm was $250,000.'

'Whew!' More than Barbara gasped.

'You came a long way from the Moses Kohn's greengrocery, Dick.'

'I did, Brian, and so did you. And I will help you go farther. And all of the rest of you too, if you're prepared to remain loyal to Dick Croker.'

'To Boss Croker,' Brian corrected. 'Make that another toast.'

They raised their glasses and cheered. A Chinese man looked up from his partner's breast and peered.

'Another drink? On the house.' Barbara was standing.

'Good girl Barbara,' Brian said slapping her backside.

'Rosa, I hope I didn't offend you – talking about Jack the way I did.'

'No offend, Dick. Butch now my *uomo*. But maybe you try to make less what Jack pay. For me.'

'What do you mean, "For me"?'

'You do, then I tell Jack that he pay less to Tammany Hall if he give me divorce.'

'Bejaysus, but you're learning quick, Rosa.' Richard lifted his glass of Vichy to her and winked.

TWENTY-FOUR

BRIAN, I HAVE something to tell you.' Nellie had invited her son out to a restaurant in Baxter Street. After a fine meal, they were sipping coffee together. She was looking radiant in a trim black business suit and broad white-collared blouse, and was glowing at being able to afford the treat. Brian feared she was going to embarrass him again by asking him to accept some money. She had not allowed him to buy even a leg of lamb since he had moved from the doctor's premises into her new home. Yet, since clearing off all her bills, she had been offering him cash for all sorts of things. With a refusal ready, he watched her chasing a pea around the plate-rim with her fork. Slowly then, she looked up. Brian noticed her eyebrows puckering in apprehension.

'What is it, Mother?'

She spoke slowly and deliberately. 'Brian, you must promise not to let what I tell you affect how you feel about me; not to be harsh on me for hiding it from you. Believe me, I wanted to tell you dozens of times. I ached to confide in you, but I had made a vow never to do so until the shame of being involved in Jack McHugh's brothel was past.'

'Come to the point.'

God, he sounds so like his late father at times, she thought. It made her nervous.

'There is no easy way of saying this, Brian. You are a half-brother of Richard Croker's. Your name is not O'Connell. Nor is mine. It is Hurley. I gave you a false surname out of family pride. My parents were good-living people and I felt so ashamed at being in The Sleeve.'

The suddenness of her statement was overwhelming. It drained his face of colour. Then he looked down and began fingering a napkin, slowly smoothing it, curling its end over, studying its folds.

Nellie was watching fearfully, but could detect no anger in his face. Nor in his eyes, at first, when they met hers.

'That doesn't matter, Mother. I mean about the name. But Dick! You mean his father and you?' Now the stares were gentle and sad, defiant and angry, but only for an instant, as they fused and softened in understanding.

'He took you by force. Eyre Coote Croker.' Brian was not questioning. He was asserting emphatically.

'Yes. But do not let it affect your friendship with Richard. Please, Brian.'

'Does Dick know this?'

'When you brought me to his office I told him about our name but not his father. I wanted to tell you then, but I felt obliged to keep my stupid vow.'

'It was not stupid, Mother. Well, maybe it was at that point, but otherwise it was admirable.'

'Thank you, son.' Like lovers, they sought each other's hands across the table. Her eyes brightened and the candles stole some of their sparkle. Although still trying to assess the full implication of her information, Brian was pleased to see how great a burden had been lifted from his mother.

'What do I call myself now? I mean, I can't go around explaining.'

'You must, Brian. The Hurley name is a proud one. I committed no sin and the result of Eyre's violation of me has given me great joy. I love you, my son.'

'I know, Mother. That has always been obvious. But tell me, why did you never marry? I don't mean the scoundrel Croker, of course. But surely, you were … are so beautiful –'

'Oh, Brian!'

'You know you are.'

'Somebody else thought so, too.' And there, as other customers were finishing meals and leaving, and the night was becoming smokier and greyer and the candle-grease was sculpting sprite stalactites, she told the full story to her son. All of it. Omitting no tiny detail. He did not interrupt.

'This Tim O'Mahoney. Where was he from?'

'Tipperary.'

'About what age would he be now?'

'I don't know. A couple of years older than me, I suppose. Lord, I almost forgot that.'

'He must be close enough to sixty, Mother. Cripes! Are you sure you want to meet him?'

'If he were ninety, I would still want it.'

Long before their discussion ended, they were alone. Waiters emerging from the kitchen looked at their fob watches but neither Brian nor Nellie noticed. Then the men began turning chairs up on tables, while a cleaning woman swept and mopped the hardwood floor before turning off the lights.

Even the candle-butt on the table began spluttering a complaint. The room was almost in total darkness, but when Nellie Hurley's story ended it was alive with warmth. Because her son had said he was happy for her and that there was nothing whatsoever to forgive. And that he loved her.

They stood, and he held out her coat. As she slid gracefully into it, he laughed loudly and startled a prying cat that had slunk in from the kitchen.

'Sssh! What's so funny?' Nellie asked.

'I can't get over it. Dick Croker, my blood-brother!'

They linked arms and went out into the night. Passing Tammany Hall they noticed a light in Richard's office.

'Come on up and tell him, Mother.'

'Are women not barred from there?'

'Ah, who'll know at this time of the night.'

She held his arm tighter and dragged him along the sidewalk. 'No, Brian. I would rather if you would tell him. Would you mind?'

'Not in the least. Begod, he'll have to look after me better now that I'm his half-brother.'

'He would have done that anyhow. He told me so.'

'When you had that hugger-mugger in Barbara's, I suppose.'

Brian left Nellie boiling the kettle for tea and ran back to Tammany Hall. When he told Richard, his face went ashen.

'The cur! The bloody pig-shit. Of all the people to have his way with, Nellie Hurley. Was it on the *Henry Clay* it happened?'

'No. Back in Balliva, she says.'

'Christ! And she only a child. Oh, Jaysus, will you ever forgive me, Brian?'

'What do you mean "forgive"? He was our father, remember.'

'Our father – who art in heaven. I doubt it, says Croker.' Richard recalled Nellie in Balliva; her beauty and that haunting odour.

'It's better not to say more about it. Now, or ever again, Brian.

> *Shake hands, brother.*
> *You're a rogue and I'm another.*
> *You stole ten sheep*
> *And I stole another.*

Nellie taught me that as a child.'

They shook hands, grinned and embraced.

'Here, give her this for a present. There's a photo of me as a *garsún* in it.' He gave Brian Frances's locket from which he had removed the photograph of Eyre. 'There's a spare space in it. She can put you or that Tim fellow into it, but tell her Croker has to stay.'

TWENTY-FIVE

I N THE ROOM hired from Barbara by Richard, the Clan leader John Devoy was guest speaker.

'We must get a firm grip on Irish-American opinion and spread anti-English propaganda. Any spare cash we can lay hands on, we must send it to those backing the cause of freedom in Ireland. We are entering the last decade of the century. Let the nineties belong to Ireland.'

There was a cheer and one tall, greying man, stood and clapped as Devoy left the meeting accompanied by Dick Croker. The others joined in the standing ovation. Brian turned to the man and asked: 'Wasn't it Devoy that organized the rescue of the six Fenian prisoners from an Australian jail? How long ago was that?'

'Fourteen years. He was one of a committee that planned it. We all came back on a whaler named *Catalpa*.'

'You mean you were one of them?'

'No! I was one of the crew.'

'God! Pleased to meet you. It's an honour. I'm Brian O'Connell – I mean Brian Hurley.' Brian was still not used to using his proper name.

'Tim O'Mahoney.'

It took a while to sink in. Brian was flabbergasted. Could it be? He seemed to be around the right age. The appearance his mother had described after their meal in the restaurant? Yes, allowing for the years.

'Tim O'Mahoney!' Brian whispered the name again while they shook hands. He held the hand, trying to decide what way to ask the question.

'By any chance, were you shipwrecked back in '47. A ship called –'

'The *Henry Clay*. Indeed and I was.'

Like in his mother's accent, traces of a modulating lilt were discernable. Anxiety exaggerated them. 'You said Hurley and O'Connell. Which is it?'

'It's a bit involved. My mother could explain it better.'

'By any chance, did she ever say that she was on the *Henry Clay*? Your mother?'

'Indeed, she did. Never stops talking about it. And she never stops thinking about a Tim O'Mahoney she met on the ship.'

'Nellie Hurley! This is incredible! After all these years!'

'She never had anything to do with another man, would you believe?'

'But I am puzzled, Brian. Did she marry an O'Connell, or what?'

'No. She never married. She searched around for you, making enquiries at ticket offices and in all sorts of places for years. Then she gave up looking. But she was always waiting. She seemed to have a conviction that she would meet you again. Jeeze, she'll be over the moon.' Brian was bashing fist into palm with delight.

'But what about you, then? Hurley or O'Connell?' Tim was frowning.

'Look, Tim, it's a long story and as I said, I think my mother would prefer to tell you herself.'

'Well, whatever it's all about I am sure of one thing. It's a bit late in life, but I would marry Nellie Hurley in the morning if she'd have me.'

'I might have some say in that. I am particular about who I would have as my stepfather! Although my mother says you would make a great one.' Brian laughed. 'Listen, why don't you come and meet my mother. I'll arrange it as a surprise. Tomorrow?'

'Could we not go now?'

'God, I'm sorry. I have to go to another meeting now. In Tammany Hall. Look, I'll meet you in O'Malley's saloon tomorrow at two o'clock. How is that?'

'Fine by me. I'll bring along the biggest bouquet of flowers in New York.'

'Bring yourself along. That's all she needs.'

On their way out, Brian noticed Richard sitting at a table talking to John Devoy and Barbara. He thought of joining them to ask Richard about something on the Tammany agenda, but Richard nodded towards the door. Brian understood and kept walking. When they were at the door, Barbara tripped up behind them.

'Mr O'Mahoney! Mr Devoy wants a word with you, please.'

Tim was about to apologize to Brian but he was already opening the door.

'See you tomorrow so, Tim.'

At half past one the next day, Brian was arguing gently with his mother in her elegantly decorated parlour.

'Please let me go with you, Brian.' Nellie was as excited as on a distant day when she sat on the back of the bogey and trailed her tiny toes along the dusty road in Balliva. Then she had enjoyed listening to her father whistling on the other side of the haycock, and interrupting 'The Minstrel Boy' with encouraging 'Hups' to the old mare. Now Brian was settling his tie and singing a popular song from *The Bohemian Girl*:

> *Come with the Gipsy bride,*
> *And repair to the fair,*
> *Where the mazy dance*
> *Will the hours entrance!*

He ran to Nellie and danced her around.

> *Come with the Gipsy bride,*
> *Where souls as light preside!*
> *Life can give nothing beyond*
> *One heart you know to be fond,*
> *Wealth with its hoards cannot buy*
> *The peace content can supply,*
> *And rank in its halls cannot find*
> *The calm of a happy mind.*

'Boy, is right, Brian. Tim could be over sixty now. And I'm not a whole lot younger. I suppose I should have more sense.'

'Love never grows old, Mother. You know that. Besides, since I told you the news, you have become ten years younger looking.'

'God! You're a right flatterer.'

Nellie was worried about their ages. Would the sweet fleeting moments experienced on the *Henry Clay* be retrievable in their late years? She had never had any physical relationship since the episode with Fay. Nellie recalled the years gone by, when she was forever wondering if she was being foolish by waiting in the hope of meeting Tim again. Yet, as time passed and the wondering had changed to worry about such forfeiture of youthful fulfilment, she still could not develop any interest in a relationship with another man. Tim was always in her heart, beckoning and reassuring, and waiting for him seemed perfectly normal.

Her youthful experience with Fay had made the years of longing all the more difficult. So much so that she had been tempted to have other encounters with Fay. She had resisted, believing that reality would replace fantasy some day. Now her body would not have the same fire, would it?

And what about Tim?

Somehow, she had always taken it for granted that he would have lived a similar life – waiting for their reunion. Now, as the time of their meeting approached, that conviction was beginning to lack credibility.

'Right, Mother, I'll be off. I will lead Tim O'Mahoney back to the door and I will knock four times. Then I will skedaddle and you can have the house to yourselves all evening.'

From the moment he left, Nellie kept pacing up and down her kitchen. She made herself a cup of tea but did not drink it. Every time she went into the hall to check her hemline in a long mirror, she tugged nervously at her collar and at her belt. Each minute brought a new anxiety, a fresh fluttering inside her. She spread her fingers as wide as possible and slowly brought her two hands together.

Once.

Twice.

Three times.

She tried saying a Hail Mary to the Blessed Virgin but a truant pigeon from Central Park perched on the windowsill and she succumbed to its pleading eye and pulsating breast. She turned the lever and tossed out a bread crust. This frightened the bird into a whirring escape, but it returned almost immediately and pecked at the offering. Nellie smiled and looked at the clock.

Five minutes past the time Brian said he would be back!

More tea. Three sips this time.

More pacing.

Another dress check.

After an hour that became a century, Brian slowly opened the back door. When he told her, Nellie felt foolish.

'All dressed up and nowhere to go!' she joked weakly.

'Dick will know where he is, I bet. He was with him when I left him last night. God! If I had only come then as he suggested instead of attending that bloody meeting.'

'What's that you said, Brian?'

'The meeting. I had to deputize for Dick chairing one at Tammany.'

'No, before that. You said Tim suggested coming. Did he?'

'He did, Mother. I swear. Shit! Why did I not – Sorry, Mother!'

'Then he'll find me, like I always thought.' Nellie's calmness was as remarkable as her confidence. 'Nothing has happened to him. It couldn't, after all this waiting.'

Brian had expected an outburst and could not comprehend Nellie's philosophical acceptance of the news.

'I will go and visit Rosa.'

'Yes, Mother. That would be good for you.'

Brian did not know that, as soon as she was in the street Nellie could compose herself no longer. She wept bitterly.

Two hundred miles away, there was no calmness in Tim O'Mahoney's reaction to events. In his dingy hotel-room in Boston, he was fuming and mumbling to himself, while pacing the room.

'I should be with her now. A full day here and still no instructions. Jesus! Just when I was about to meet her.'

He thought of the one or two women he'd been out with over the years and how they'd meant nothing to him. And of the jeers from numerous whaler crews because he'd shunned women. Of the drudgery of loneliness, whether sailing out of Halifax, Battle Harbour or, more recently, Boston.

'Blast it. If I hadn't got to know Boston so well, I wouldn't have got this damned assignment from Devoy. "Dynamiters" my foot,' he muttered to the bedpost. 'I'd put a stick of it under Devoy's rump this minute if I had him here.'

Then he began visualizing what Nellie might look like now. As he had done so often before.

'Nellie with a fine adult son! Cripes! He could have been ours. Oh, shit!'

He stood and kicked a shoe across the room and it rattled against a tin rubbish receptacle. Devoy's curt instructions were now etched in his mind forever. He went to the mottled mirror in its frame pocked with woodworm and began imitating the leader of the Clan.

'Now Tim, I have a job for you and I don't want you to ask any questions about it. Some of the Clan members are causing problems. They are calling themselves "The Dynamiters" and are carrying out acts of terrorism. They have to be stopped and I am sending you to Boston tonight to help do just that. Mr Croker here is helping with the arrangements. You will leave here right now. Two men will meet you outside. They will guide you. You are to take nothing with you. Everything you need for a short stay will be provided, and if the job takes longer, we will take care of everything. Tell nobody where your are going or why. Do not contact anyone before I get in touch with you. A man named McGarrity will meet you at your hotel in Boston. He will issue instructions.'

Tim spat at the mirror.

'Blast! Damn! Shit!'

He recalled the exhilaration he'd felt in anticipation of meeting Nellie and how it had condensed into an impermeable fog of depression. He had wanted to protest, but the determined look on Devoy's face made it clear that any objection would have fallen on deaf ears and would receive a curt reminder about his oath to the Clan.

He began pacing the room again.

'Blast Devoy! Christ, if I get back, I don't even know where Brian and Nellie live.'

Five more paces. A sudden halt.

'But wait now! I'd be able to find Boss Croker! Everyone knows Boss Croker.'

At that moment Boss Croker was talking to Jack McHugh and sipping from the mug of strong coffee Rosa had made for him.

'Of course Fay has to quit the game. Should have done ten years ago. Jaysus, it must be horrid on the poor wretch to be still at it. But you're not going to throw her out on the street, Jack. I'll damn well close you down if you attempt to.'

'You have been swine, Jack McHugh, but Dick right. You cannot do this. Fay have destroyed body for your gain. Her soul too. Even her life, *Mamma mia*! You treat her worse than you treat me. Like scumbag. Have some pity for Fay now that she spent.'

'Well let Tammany pay for her keep. Not many of them come here now.'

Rosa had no particular wish to see Fay stay on in the sordid room across the courtyard. And, even though Rosa would be leaving Jack soon, she was glad to see him showing some backbone, so she added her say to Richard's.

'This place is not good enough for them pawta crappa once they begin to scoot up ladder,' she scolded.

'Now Rosa!' Richard's reprimand was devilling through bushy eyebrows rather than from the words and Rosa remembered the deal they had made in Barbara's. Richard softened immediately and decided to have a little fun. Without taking his eyes from Rosa's, he said, 'I think I know a couple might take Fay into their home. A childless couple, and likely to remain so.'

'Oh, good!' Jack thought the stand he had made was already beginning to get results. But Richard whipped his head around and glowered.

'Jackie the Mule will kick in the few bucks for board and lodging, of course. A sort of pension, like.' He could hardly keep from bursting out laughing at the startled change in Jack's countenance.

There was a hurried knock on the kitchen door. Nellie entered, her eyes red from crying.

'Nellie! You look beautiful, all dressed up. But what wrong?'

When Rosa hugged her tightly, Nellie's tears began flowing again.

'Can I help, Nellie?' Richard asked, softly and awkwardly.

'Naw! This be women's talk.' Rosa's pudgy hand behind Nellie's back flicked three times and the two men knew they would have to continue their conversation outside, in the grocery store.

'What the trouble, Nellie? Tell your *amica*, Rosa.'

'Oh, Rosa! Brian met Tim O'Mahoney last night.'

'What? Your long lost *uomo*? I not believe! But why you cry, then?'

'Brian was to meet him again today and bring him to me. But Tim didn't turn up.' Nellie's body shuddered and her tears trickled into Rosa's ear.

'There now! There now! He will come soon. At least you know he lives.' Comforting words, skilled touches and caresses, gentle kisses. 'Brian and Richard will discover him. You'll see.'

'He wanted to come immediately but Brian had to go to Tammany Hall. But he must have changed his mind. He mustn't want to meet me. And if he doesn't, then I do not want anybody to force him to come to me. Nellie Hurley only welcomes those who want her welcome.'

'He want you, Nellie. Now, you just go back to being way you were. Certain that you and Tim will meet.'

Rosa's experience of women's concern for others' problems convinced her that Fay's predicament would bring Nellie back to being herself again so she told Nellie about it. She was right. Nellie responded immediately.

'I'll take her. I have a spare room.'

'I don't think City Hall like that. Retired hooker in official *casa*?'

'Retired crooks, and active ones too, infest their premises, Rosa.'

'And Brian be with you.'

'Yes, but I would still have room, if Tim doesn't –'

Then Rosa knew that Nellie's dream had been cracked but not shattered and she smiled. Before Nellie could cry again, she joked.

'Then there be Fay's rust for you. Don't forget that.'

'Rust, Rosa? Oh, you mean lust, not rust.'

'Maybe rust now, eh!' Rosa's wheezing whoop shook her hearty flesh, and distracted Nellie. They held hands and looked into each other's eyes, smiled and hugged again.

'We will look after Fay somehow. Between us.'

'Good idea, Nellie. I could make Jack leave her in room, but Fay deserve to spend fall of life in someplace good, eh?'

'Someplace very good, Rosa.'

Outside, Boss Croker and Jackie the Mule had come to an arrangement. About Fay, and many other things.

TWENTY-SIX

RICHARD TOOK over Tammany at a time when the organization had lost considerable influence. He had applied his energies to pursuing a policy of reconciliation towards opponents, a ploy that began showing immediate results. It overcame the County Democracy's opposition and eradicated the rise of conservative business elements in the leadership of the Democratic Party. He retained a few activists at a lower level, men he considered useful for arranging bribes or for regulating cash flow towards Tammany's coffers. As he continued initiating more and more amenities and infrastructural schemes in the city, he was creating employment for supportive workers, especially the Irish, and ruthlessly routing all who opposed Tammany. He was building his own empire too, not all of it savoury. The police were openly protecting rackets in which he was involved.

'I'm a sleeping partner in many concerns,' he explained to Brian. 'But I walk in my sleep and I have full control of profits.'

'But what if the police investigate? Or if that Reverend Parkhurst sticks his nose in?'

Richard grinned.

'Listen, Brian. The police are protecting my interests and they get well paid for doing so. As for Reformer Parkhurst, if he sticks his nose in, as you say, he'll get a bad smell that will stuff it. But we'll find something to block up his gob too. Every man has his price.'

Although vice pervaded the city, its raw testimony to spirit and energy, and the commercial channelling thereof, became Richard's substitute for matrimonial fulfilment. Elizabeth increasingly ignored him and her lack of affection made him lose confidence in himself. But he seldom let it show. He tried to win her back by erecting a mansion for them in fashionable Mount Morris Avenue, which gave him the satisfaction of quitting a house provided by Samuel Fraser.

Elizabeth, however, had had about all she could take of Richard and of Tammany Hall, and was seeing a lawyer with a view to legal separation.

The 'Gay Nineties' started by swinging along at a tempo that suited Richard's bonhomie. While its beat changed his fortunes spectacularly for the better, the Republican Party was becoming impatient at the blatant corruption in the city perpetrated by Tammany Hall. In 1890 it instituted what became known as the Fasset Investigation, which exposed Richard's influence on the municipal authorities of New York and implied he had received a large sum of money from the mayor, in cash, delivered through his young daughter, Flossie, the mayor's godchild.

Newspaper cartoonists gleefully depicted a blissful domestic scene with Flossie bearing envelopes packed with banknotes to her mother and gurgling, 'Nice Goo!' while a benign father and benevolent godfather looked on.

Reporters asked Richard why he purchased real estate for his daughter rather than putting the money in a bank account for her. He told them, 'I have always had peculiar notions about putting money in banks and I have always kept my money around the house. We never kept a bank account.'

The man with the ready cash was to be far away from New York when he read the Fasset Committee's report.

One of the chief witnesses for the prosecution was Elizabeth's brother-in-law, Patrick McCann. Richard could condone many slights, but his wife's passing of information about his affairs to this man was more hurtful than all the rebuffs she had given him in their marriage bed. He remembered what Eyre had said about the Frasers the day they were out walking and met Elizabeth and her mother: 'Be careful, because they'll smile and be polite to you even when they're pulling knives from the pockets of their frock-coats.'

Richard believed that a man and wife should be able to share secrets in the knowledge that one would never divulge anything that might harm the other. He had seen too much infidelity and lack of integrity in his father's marriage and had vowed never to let a wife of his suffer as Frances had done. But his outlook had changed with Elizabeth's continuing apathy towards his attempts to save their marriage. This latest division was the final blow.

He hoped that his life with Elizabeth might improve when she returned from her Grand Tour of Europe. She had taken Ethyl and Flossie with her. But he was horrified when she came back without the girls. Each of them had been swept away by whirlwind romances. They had already announced their engagements, Ethyl to a riding master in Frankfurt, Flossie to an Italian count from Milan. Unfairly, Richard blamed Elizabeth.

'You left poor Flossie! She's too young to be over there on her own, woman,' he ranted.

'She is as well off away from you and your influence,' Elizabeth replied.

'You had no right for to leave her.'

'She has found a man who is cultured and well-mannered; she will be happy,' came the caustic reply.

'Begod, if you think good manners will make a couple happy, you haven't learned much.'

'At least I don't consider the bedroom the be-all and end-all of marriage.'

'Oh, I know right well that's how you think, Elizabeth. You promised great things before we were married. Put me to the pin of my collar to … to … to respect you. But when we married and it came to the real thing, you had more bloody headaches than a field of cabbage in a heatwave.'

'Why, you … you … Oh, I detest you.'

Elizabeth flounced away. It was probably the moment that their marriage finally sank beneath a dark, depressing wave. The huge four-poster bed in each of their rooms seemed to emphasize the hopelessness of their situation. All dark mahogany, old-fashioned brocade and faded pelmets. Dull! Dreary! Lifeless!

Still awaiting the legal separation, Elizabeth eventually returned to the Fraser home permanently. She and Richard seldom met and when they did they spoke in clipped, cold phrases. Sometimes he made an attempt at humouring her but when there was no response, he would just leave her and try to find solace among his horses and bulldogs.

He began travelling more around Europe, enjoying the life of a wealthy man in spa resorts like Wiesbaden in Germany. While there, he loved visiting factories that manufactured metal goods, and savouring all the comforts of the fine, airy Hotel Victoria. Visiting Lisbon and Madeira was a pleasure too. Their climate brought comfort to his increasingly painful rheumatic condition. He took delight in the comfort of fine cabins on cruise ships and the honour of dining at captains' tables.

Slowly, he was discovering that being wealthy was of little use unless a man could enjoy himself. If he were to keep his nose to the grindstone of Tammany Hall politics for much longer, he would be too old to do that.

The trips also helped him to forget about Elizabeth. They were of benefit to her, too. Without him, she began renewing old friendships and fostering new ones among the social class she had enjoyed before marriage. She was able to enjoy entertaining them, free from the fear of being embarrassed at an intrusion by her unrefined husband.

Richard began delegating more and more of his Tammany affairs to Brian and allotting various business concerns to his family. He established his sons, Frank and Richard Junior, in some of them, giving Richard Junior powers of attorney over many interests, and selling off others.

As Richard's zeal for politics waned, his passion for racing, gambling and bulldogs grew. He finally decided to set up a horseracing establishment in Europe and opted for the classic turf of the English countryside. He found a suitable estate at Wantage on the Berkshire-Oxford border, and within weeks had settled comfortably at Antwicks Manor, far from the seedy joints and baiting dens of his previous life. It took a while to get used to the leisurely pace of rural England, and he never felt at home among its people.

In the local tavern, he tried to chat to neighbours but they gave him the cold shoulder, especially when he praised Prime Minister Gladstone's passing of the Irish Home Rule Bill.

'That's only the Commons, my man. The Lords will block it,' an individual in plus-fours snorted through his handlebar moustache.

'You Irish are never satisfied. I wish you were left to fend for yourselves; then you would know jolly soon how much you rely on Britain.'

'Don't ate me. Sure, Jaysus, I was only borned in Ireland.'

'By all accounts, your conduct in the United States left a lot to be desired,' the adversary jeered.

'What I did in New York is my own business, sir.'

'Oh, get away from us and drink in the snug. Can't you see you are not wanted here?'

He went to Mass one Sunday and the clergyman, following the example of the parson, was meeting his parishioners as they entered the church. As Richard approached, he stepped past him to greet a stud-farm owner who lived near Richard. When this man passed Richard, he sneered: 'Persona non grata with the clergy too, eh?'

Richard did not understand but the tone was derisive and he was deeply hurt. He regretted missing a proper education too.

One incident after another underlined resentment towards him: a fence broken; a valuable mare wandering and falling into an overgrown quarry; a rick of hay for fodder burned; one of his bulldogs bruised and beaten. Even traders, despite wanting his custom, were cold and aloof. Where he'd expected some degree of camaraderie – among the horse-breeding and racing fraternity – a claustrophobic, unwelcoming attitude persisted.

Only his stubbornness made him stay. He could ignore the slights, but he needed companionship. He missed the loyalty of Brian, Nellie, Rosa, Barbara and Fay. And their fun.

On impulse one day, he cabled Elizabeth, describing the place and asking her to join him and to give their marriage one more try. To his surprise, she agreed, and arrived within the week. He met her at the small railway station. After giving her a welcoming kiss he realized he'd made a mistake. It was like embracing cold granite.

Her main reason for coming was to experience English social life. She had heard about polite ladies of good breeding having afternoon tea and genteel soirées and she thought she would find the lifestyle agreeable.

Richard was disappointed, but tried not to show it. In spite of the continuing rebuffs and rudeness he encountered when among the male members of that class, he encouraged her to go out and enjoy herself. So he was alone again. Often.

Whenever he felt depressed, he put on impeccable riding gear, mounted his favourite American horse, Dobbins, and cantered through the local countryside. The chalk downs south of the Vale of the White Horse provided splendid gallops and equal solace. The old world market town of Wantage and its rural hinterland was agreeable, except for its inhabitants. Even his new trainer, Charlie Morton, proved patronizing at times.

As Richard remarked good-humouredly to Elizabeth one day: 'Alfred the Great was born here and Croker the Greatest will die here. Of heartbreak!'

She fingered *The London Illustrated News*, Elizabeth announced, 'I'm expecting a few lady-friends over. Have you anything to do in the stables?' Richard bit his tongue while she continued: 'We're meeting before going over to Lord Wantage's. And I do hope you'll behave yourself at his reception. He and his wife are so impeccably behaved.'

'I've no mind for going. Not one of them who'll be there gives a tinker's damn about us.'

'I can't say I blame them where you're concerned, but we're expected to attend. You are, after all, one of the racing fraternity. It's pity you don't try to behave like them.'

'Listen, Elizabeth. I've been through a lot during my life. There's things I done that maybe I shouldn't have. But I never touched the forelock to anyone. I behaved the way I felt and even if you think I was ignorant from time to time, at least I wasn't putting on a show for anyone. I was my own man.'

'You were that, indeed. I will be ready by half past six. It's evening wear.'

'I've dressed up for all sorts of affairs, even for dinner in my own house, before I ever came over to this bloody place and I don't need you to remind me what to wear.'

He took a Havana cigar from one of the new boxes that had had just arrived, each one flashing a 'Boss' monogram on its gold band. He lit it, puffed blue smoke towards the candelabra and said, 'Elizabeth, I loved you for a long time. Very much. No matter what I was like, I don't think I deserved the treatment you gave me. I will go to the bloody Wantage's with you, but don't blame me for what might happen there.'

He strode out, slamming the door behind him. In a closet, he donned his rainwear. He began to leave, but noticed a new crop of cornflowers in a vase on the hall table. He grabbed a few and stuck them through his top button-hole. On his way outside he muttered, 'I'm damned if I'll let her grind me down.' He saw Elizabeth's friends arrive and lifted his hat to them.

'How are yez, ladies?'

There was no reply.

While approaching the farmyard, the heady scent of gorse after rain helped to atone for twilight's glumness. He began walking briskly. Strong wellington boots left imprints for scurrying mud to puddle up. Passing a pig run, Richard began chuckling impishly, calling its inhabitants by the names he had given them: Slasher, Tweed, O'Brien, Hewitt.

His revived spirits were because of an expected guest, Charles Lynham, a Berkshire horse trainer from whom he'd leased stables at Moat House in Letcombe Regis. Lynham was coming to discuss selling the property and Richard was optimistic about becoming its outright owner.

'He's anxious to sell, but he's worried about what his colleagues will think,' Charlie Morton called. Richard had not heard his trainer approach-ing from the stables.

'At a fancy price, I suppose?'

'Unfortunately. The word is out that you are a wealthy man.'

'By the time the missus and a few more New York parasites is finished, my money will be easy counted. Them and my cash is woeful great with each other,' Richard replied.

'I'm not so sure you should buy at all if you keep insisting on importing American horses, Richard. They won't make any running on our tracks here.' Morton had been giving the same advice since becoming Richard's trainer, but his employer kept refusing to heed it.

'Don't worry, Charlie, boy. Time and patience brought the snail to Amer-ica and it learned how to sprint there.' Richard walked away from Morton and began singing, hopelessly out of tune:

> She's a little horse you could put your shirt on
> Watch her jump when she puts a spurt on
> Point to Point or anywhere
> It's ten to one on Hennessy's mare.

Richard went to the stable-yard and began yoking Dobbins to the rub-ber-tyred sulky. A gypsy appeared at the farmyard gate, leading a donkey.

'Find out how much he's askin' for it, Charles.'

'Are you going to run it along with your Yankee nags? It might do as well.' Morton went to the gate, came back and said, 'Forget it. He wants nine pounds. Nine shillings would be nearer its value.'

'Right, me man!' Richard called. 'Tie the beast to the gate there.' He handed Morton a ten-pound note.

'Leave him the change or keep it yourself.' Morton had difficulty concealing his contempt for what Richard regarded as simple bonhomie.

Richard noticed, but asked, 'Are you goin' to th'auld party in Lord Wantage's?'

'Yes. His receptions are always enjoyable.' He emphasized the word receptions. 'Will you be there?'

'I've no mind for it, but herself insists. Says it's expected of us. As if I cared about them crowd of nobs.'

'Or about their views concerning English thoroughbreds!' Morton could not resist the jibe.

'What's keeping Lynham?' Richard asked the trotter more than Morton.

'Perhaps he is at the house. Shall we drive up?'

'Herself is entertaining his wife and a few other hens for tea. Maybe he came too. He'd fit in well with them. Hop on and we'll see.' Morton stood on the frame and held the seat. With a flick of the reins, Richard urged Dobbins to a trot and they began rattling across the cobblestones and along the drive until they reached the house. The ladies were sipping tea from china cups in the drawing-room. Elizabeth was talking about the fashions available in New York stores.

'Furs from Oklahoma are extremely popular this year,' she was saying when her husband strode into the room.

'How'yez, girls? Is Charlie Lynham hidin' up any of your shifts?' he asked genially. The silence might have chipped off Elizabeth's icy stare. A small, thin woman recovered from shock to stammer, 'Chawl's will be here presently. I instructed him to meet you in the piggery.'

'Back to the shit, then,' he grinned and, puffing another cigar plume towards the group, he withdrew.

Morton stepped onto the sulky again as Richard was leaping into the seat. While they headed back towards the yard they met Lynham's car speeding around a bend. Its driver swerved in the same direction as Richard was pulling Dobbins and a disastrous collision was averted when Morton leaped off, grabbed the bridle and dragged the horse's neck to the right. The sulky tilted. One wheel mounted the car's bonnet, rolled along the windshield to the roof, tossing Richard into a prickly shrub.

'Jaysus! There's thorns the size of six-inch-nails in my buttocks,' he screamed, as the effeminate and frightened Charles Lynham was alighting.

'You, you, you ignorant cad,' Lynham stammered.

'The damned cheek of you. You were coming around that corner like shit through a goose!'

'Why, you're abominable!'

'And your mother was one too.'

There was no sale of Moat House that evening, but, when Lynham calmed down, Richard bought a bulldog from him and swore, 'I'll make it win every dog-show from the Oxfordshire County Championship to Crufts.'

He was making the same extravagant forecasts at Lord Wantage's reception. His expensive frock-coat was becoming flecked with cigar ash and ladies were coughing politely when each nimbus of rich Havana smoke surrounded them. Richard was trying to make small talk but the men snubbed him while the ladies turned their backs. Eventually, he called to the butler for his silk hat and cloak. Dressed in these, he walked up to where Elizabeth was chatting to a cluster of expensively dressed women and said, 'I will send over the chauffeur for ye. I'm going creosotin' a fence while I'm dressed for the job. Not many of them ones' fellas could do that because their ass-covers is probably hired.'

And he went home and began creosoting a fence in formal wear, occasionally murmuring to himself, 'I'll show them stuck-up gets!' Although it was dark, he went to his room when he'd finished and undressed, pulled on his swimming-togs, ran down the drive and jumped into the millrace. As he lay afloat on his back, his cigar above water, he felt reasonably at peace with the world.

Leading the campaign of persecution against Richard was archrival Colonel E.W. Baird, whose hobby was playing percussion in an amateur orchestra. Baird was passionate about artistic pursuits and found Richard's unpolished behaviour loathsome. He generated opposition to the Boss among the Newmarket trainers and frowned on his fondness for bulldogs. Richard paid £800 for a fierce-looking brute officially called Rodney Stone that, privately, he renamed Goofy Baird. He trained it and groomed it and took it to shows all over England. The dog won a number of prestigious events, rewarding its owner handsomely. Richard was less successful with the American horses he still persisted in purchasing.

'Valuable horses never acclimatize adequately for racing when transported thousands of miles. Breeding is possible,' Charles Morton explained, 'but even then there are dozens of instances of the progeny's failure on the track. Conditions here just do not suit American horses. They cannot match the English thoroughbred on its own turf.'

'English thoroughbreds, my tail end! I suppose your great God-almighty Baird told you that crap,' Richard grunted and added, 'That cur may beat his bloody drums, but he won't beat me. And you just see that he doesn't.'

Morton lifted his trilby and scratched his head, perplexed at his employer's robust stubbornness, a legacy of days at Tammany when he commanded and was obeyed, when he voiced opinions and was seldom questioned. He realized that this was not a satisfactory owner-trainer relationship.

Instead of being tactful Richard increasingly antagonized his adversaries. He was coming under fire back in New York, too. During its hot, humid summers, ice was an essential and The Tammany Hall Ice Trust saw to it that profits from the commodity went in its direction. 'Hold That Tiger' was still a Tammany supporters' call. At election time repeaters paid voters to call out, 'Put a tiger in your tank and a dollar in your pocket and whatever you like on the ballot paper, as long as the top name is a Tammany one.'

A municipal election loomed and citizens calling themselves the Fusion Party were expressing outrage at Richard's regime. Mark Twain, the popular author of *Tom Sawyer* and *Huckleberry Finn*, supported the movement's hard core, known as the Order of Acorns. Richard scoffed and shrugged off Twain's charges: 'Great yokes from little popcorns grow.' New York, however, was beginning to emerge from its forest of fear.

Brian had become prominent in Tammany affairs too. He'd studied Richard's ways and been a good pupil. He had a steady lady-friend and was thinking of getting married. If he did decide to wed, he wanted very much to invite Dick to the celebrations. It would be a nice surprise for his old friend. Yet, he was inclined to think it might be wiser to undergo the formalities in a registry office and keep the whole thing quiet. He feared hurting the feelings of some to whom he would be looking for patronage. The sort of instinct Richard used to have. Coincidentally, at that moment he took up a copy of *Harper's Magazine* and read that, over a period, Dick had invested $250,000 in Wantage, $130,000 in race horses and $80,000 in another Fifth-Avenue mansion. Salaries to stud-farm hands and jockeys came to $20,000 and his chauffeur-driven car was costing fifty dollars a day.

I might indeed replace Dick, Brian thought, but as I grow older I think I would prefer a more conservative way of making a living.

Elizabeth went to her local presbytery and asked to see a priest. 'It's near his lunch-time so don't keep him long,' a brusque, suspicious housekeeper warned. Five minutes later a young man bounced into the parlour, making Elizabeth feel foolish and wonder how on earth an inexperienced child like this could offer her advice.

'Hello. I'm Father Jim Murphy from Mallow, County Cork. How can I help you?' he said, but did not extend his hand in friendship. Elizabeth did not ask him if he had ever heard of her husband's grandfather or uncle from Quartertown. He looked the sort of lad that would not have bothered about local history. Furthermore, she was not at all proud of her connection with the family. Or sure any more that she wanted to discuss her problem here.

'Well, what can I do for you, my good woman? I always think women have a hard life – raising children, seeing them growing up and getting into God knows what divilment. And looking after husbands, of course.'

Elizabeth remembered the housekeeper's warning. This young man should not be kept late for lunch! Yet here he was palavering her about female hardships. Well, she would not delay him. Or discuss her problems. She reached into her handbag, withdrew a purse and took out a note.

'I'd like you to say a Mass for me,' she whispered. Then she added, 'And for my husband.'

'Oh, but this is too much. Honestly!' But Elizabeth was already walking out the door, saying, 'I'll let myself out, Father Murphy. Thank you.'

Deeply upset, she walked down the drive from the presbytery and turned into the road leading to the town. Scattered houses, then – a semblance of a street but instead of continuing on she turned into a small lane she had never noticed before. Hurdy-gurdy music was coming from somewhere and getting louder. A fairground! She remembered Barnum's and the Hall of Mirrors and the fun she'd enjoyed with Richard that day. Her step quickened. A rank smell of trodden grass, a red and yellow metropolis of canvas and timber and there she was throwing darts at balloons, trying to get a ring around a tilted block, laughing at a Three-Card-Trick man calling:

> Too late, too late will be the cry
> Billy Fair Play with the money has passed you by.

Another, spinning a roulette wheel whose pointer was a corset stay tried to shout Billy down:

> Have another go, with your old pal, Joe.
> Your mother won't know, and I won't tell her.

For a few moments Elizabeth was back in her carefree youth. Those who did not know her wondered why a fashionably dressed, wealthy looking woman was here alone, playing the fun-fair games like ordinary folk. Those who did whispered that the poor woman must have been going a little mad.

Elizabeth won a stuffed bear at the Hoopla stall and gave it to a passing child. The boy said, 'Thank you,' politely before his mother tugged him along, giving Elizabeth a strange look. Elizabeth did not mind. These simple recreations were giving her temporary relaxation, at least. She sighed and headed for the exit gate.

'Madam Zaritia', said a rickety sign above a light canvas tent that had strange symbols daubed in red on its panels. Elizabeth thought again of the young priest and of her despair when she was leaving him. She remembered that her Church forbade 'superstitious observance of omens and actions' as being sinful yet, answering some urge, she entered. A gnarled old woman sat at a table where a red lamp's rays danced on a crystal ball. There was a smell of some exotic oil and something like the incense the priests burned at Benediction.

'Sit, please and pass silver,' the woman bid, solemnly.

'How much?'

'Just silver.' Elizabeth took out all the silver coins she had and gave them over to Madam Zaritia. They began talking and, as if the fun of the fair had rid her of inhibitions, she was soon telling this complete stranger all her problems. How she had found trying to be a wife distasteful, how her husband's bawdy ways disgusted her, how his way of life appalled her. She was on the verge of legal separation but was concerned about her Church's views on this. She had visited a priest but could not confide in him. He was too young. While her outpouring was becoming incoherent she was beginning to suspect that Madam Zaritia was not heeding a word she was saying. So she stopped talking.

'Tell me about your children, Mrs Croker.'

Elizabeth was almost annoyed at herself for obeying. She told all about the dreaded frequency of her childbirth. About their growing up and missing the parental care of their father so much. She told how her husband seemed to detest the boy named after him but did care for the other boys and the girls – especially Flossie. She even told how upset with herself she had been when she and the child became involved in the Fasset Committee's investigation. Then she backtracked and elaborated on the trouble between the two Richards. In passing, she mentioned the names Frank and Howard. Madam Zaritia suddenly became impatient and told her to stop talking. She peered into the crystal and kept repeating the names over and over.

'Frank! Howard! Frank! Howard!' until she was only whispering; until every muscle in her body seemed to be frozen and two black stones were staring from her eye-sockets. Elizabeth did not know what the woman meant when she told her, 'You will be far away when it happens, Mrs Croker.' She thought of questioning her, but something in Madam Zaritia's demeanour compelled her to remain silent.

On her way back to Antwicks Manor she pondered her dilemma, disappointed that neither religion nor superstition had helped her. She'd just have to sit down, weigh up all the pros and cons, and decide for herself whether to leave Richard or not. She was almost certain what that decision would be.

TWENTY-SEVEN

'Everybody is talking about reform, Fay.' Nellie was pouring her friend a cup of tea in her kitchen.

'Everybody except Fay Clark!' When Fay tried to laugh, a cough creaked from smoke-clotted lungs.

'The Reformers think they'll have the city cleaned up before the twentieth century dawns.'

'If Boss Croker comes back, he'll fix them, Nellie.'

'I bet he will return. He's too energetic for the English countryside.'

'And he won't like a Republican Mayor trying to link Queens, Staten Island and Brooklyn with Manhattan.'

'I never realized you knew so much about politics.'

'Well, I formed enough policies for them in my day, didn't I?' Fay's coughing laugh made Nellie wince.

The women were right. The Democrats' power was tottering, but in September 1897, unannounced and without a welcoming party, Richard disembarked and took a cab to Tammany Hall. He intended re-introducing the Croker stamp on the city.

'Jesus! The return from Elba,' Brian shouted from the landing outside the Boss's vacant office. Then he flamboyantly opened the door, signalling entry. Richard bounced in, sat at his desk and began spitting orders, calling for officials and asking Brian for an up-date on events.

'Did your mother meet that fellow of hers yet?'

'Tim? No.'

'Did you talk to Devoy?'

'No! He has been touring the states and nobody seems to be able to get word to him.'

'Bechrist, I'll get to him. Is Nellie still in the Mayor's office?'

'She is, and loving every minute of her work.'

'Then, get her to hell over here to see me, you half-breed half-brother,' he ordered. Richard reached for the phone.

'Hello. Croker here. Is Devoy there?'

'Where, then?'

'I don't give a shit. Tell him to get back to me straight away.'

Brian smiled and left.

Nellie arrived within an hour. Richard kissed her and said, 'My Balliva beauty, you are going to have a new boss come the next mayoral election.'

'Who?' Brian asked.

'Many Sachems want to put Grant forward again, but not me. Judge Robert C. Van Wyck is my man.'

Brian was astonished. 'A little lack-lustre, isn't he, Dick?'

'If that means he's a bit of an old coot, yes. But he has a name for being decent. That will clog up the Reform machine,' Richard promised.

'But he is a terrible prude, Dick. He won't go along with our ways.'

'He will, Brian. Under pressure, Van Wyck will do what he's told. Just you wait and see.'

—⁓—

Despite cringing at Tammany's slogan – 'Well, well, well; Reform has gone to hell' – Richard became reinvigorated, swinging his old machine back into action and enlisting new and energetic recruits. Brian had recommended his godfather as chief organizer and brought Butch to Richard's office.

'You've helped me before, Butch, but I'm now giving you the whole harbour area and West Manhattan to fix for us. By the way, eh, how is your personal life? When you're not looking after this whelp's spiritual welfare,' Richard gurgled and slapped Brian's back.

'I am now living happily with a divorcée in my harbour home, Boss.' Butch smiled and Richard had not the heart to tell him how Rosa had got her divorce.

'She will help the campaign too,' Butch assured Richard.

And she did. Wading in with enthusiasm even though it meant meeting her former husband on occasion, when a lively and good-humoured Rosa would stick out her tongue at Jackie the Mule and shout, 'Bastardo!'

Butch's influence among fisherfolk, seafarers and dealers was bringing thousands of new voters into Richard's grasp and on election day Van Wyck swept to victory. Butch was an honoured guest at 'Croker's Hoolie', held at the fashionable Murray Hill Hotel on Park Avenue.

'Be best party since little Brian's christening!' Rosa swore.

The women looked stylish in expensive clothes bought for them by a doting son, Jack McHugh's 'pension' and an adoring husband.

'Maguire woo me for so long with Irish blarney, I give in,' Rosa joked.

Butch kissed her and was smiling when he said, 'If Nellie O'Connell – sorry, Hurley – had not met me after she landed in New York, you would still be unsatisfied, Rosa.'

'Oh, now. Jack McHugh not all that bad in bed,' Rosa teased. 'Our age good time for love. Not as urgent. Nice and slow.'

They regretted their banter when they noticed Nellie's gaiety collapse. Looking down, fondling a tassel on her gown and trying to stem melancholy with stiffened lips. Rosa touched her hand. Their eyes met.

—▴—

Richard began spending most of his time in the plush new Democratic Club on Fifth Avenue. Wielding all his former power, and wearing formal attire, he was interviewing clients seeking favours and granting as many as he could. Wealthy callers craving discretion would cringe at his ostentatious behaviour.

'I don't do it out of grandeur; only to get their goats,' he told Brian with almost childish delight. 'And what did I tell you?' he added, 'Mayor Van Wyck is like putty in my paws.'

'I have a bit of information that you might appreciate, Dick.'

'Spit it out, then.'

'Since you left, it has become fashionable for rich people to own winter homes in a coastal area of Florida where land is going cheap.'

'Go on!' Richard was indeed interested.

'Twenty years ago a cargo of coconuts from a shipwreck took root, propagated and formed a lovely palm-shaded Atlantic beach. Jeaga and Tequesta Indians once had settlements in the area, so it has historic appeal too. It's fierce isolated but Henry Flagler is about to extend his Florida East Coast Railway to it.'

'Wheew!' Richard whistled. 'Isn't Flagler a partner of John D. Rockerfeller's in the Standard Oil Company?'

'He is.'

'Get to a realtor quick, Brian. Don't tell him who you're bidding for or the price will jump.'

Within an hour, Richard was owner of a secluded lot of shoreline. It covered over two miles and was overrun with sandspurs and weeds. Over the following weeks, in a clearing among the woods facing on to the ocean, he built a large two-storey residence of cypress shingle. It had nine windows upstairs and six below, three on either side of a stout door. A teak balustrade enclosed a terrace that ran the length of the façade. He employed a local gardener who planted morning glory vine and yellow creeper. Carefully tended borders contained wild vinca, nicknamed periwinkles, and cacti. Proudly, to underline his power at Tammany, Richard called his summer home The Wigwam.

During his first stay, he angled for blue fish and mackerel. Great rollers prevented him casting his bait for sharks one day, so he became bored, stripped off and began swimming with the sharks instead. He explained to his horrified house guests, Fay, Rosa and Butch, 'If you keep moving in the water, no shark will bite you.'

'Maybe it helps to have Irish blood in you,' Fay hollered.

'No clothes on keep sharks away too!' Rosa added.

'Jeeze, Rosa, I never found that to be so,' Fay laughed.

In the evenings Richard liked watching the shoreline to the north of the pineapple fields through a telescope. He could spot bootleggers unloading their straw-jacketed flagons from rowboats or deep-sea fishermen heading home with their catch. He was pleased to see black people swimming there with his permission, the first blacks in Florida to receive such a concession. Locals called the place 'Croker's Beach'.

He smiled with smug satisfaction when Flagler, E.F. Hutton and others followed his example, building winter homes and exclusive hotels in Palm Beach, thereby increasing the value of his property enormously.

On Labour Day Richard hosted a Democratic Club dinner at the Metropolitan Opera House. Its staff removed the seats from the auditorium and erected temporary kitchens on the sidewalks. Guests in formal dress were standing at their tables, while another few hundred people looked down from balconies and boxes. A military band played a selection from the hit Morton-Kerker musical, *Yanky Doodle Dandy*, but it changed suddenly and began a rousing interpretation of 'Hail to the Chief'. Everybody turned towards the door and began clapping Boss Croker. He was ambling up the aisle, leading Mayor Van Wyck and his small party of personal friends to a table on the stage. The clapping changed to cheering and some ladies took to jumping up and down in adulation, shouting, 'Bravo Boss' and 'Croker is King!'

Brian excused himself to Mrs Van Wyck and whispered to Nellie, 'I knew you would finish up on the stage, Mother. Maybe we'll dance "The Irish Washerwoman" after the dinner!' The re-echo of an echo of fiddle and flute and *bodhrán* in Malachi's kitchen in Balliva stirred.

Richard's largesse was as obvious as his playful ostentation. The day after a particularly stirring welcome-back ceremony, Butch Maguire received a call to the office of New York's Harbour Master. There he sat through a mock trial, on a charge of sailing an unseaworthy vessel, before the Harbour

Master collapsed in gleeful paroxysms and handed Butch an important-looking document.

'Here's your Master's Certificate for your new long-haul cargo-ship. Courtesy of Boss Croker. You are to hold a launching ceremony on Friday and he will do the honours.'

Butch was staggered. He had scrimped and saved to buy the old craft he plied, often perilously. It was fit only for short haul runs along the east coast. It was in such poor condition that he was ashamed to point it out to Rosa when they went walking by the docks in the evenings.

'Why you not show me your vessel, my darling?' she had asked once.

'Because it is like your colander when you make your *cannelloni*, Rosa. It leaks and is smelly.'

'How dare you! If you not meet me, you die knowing nothing better food but Irish stew.'

'Rosa! There is nothing better than Irish stew. And if I ate your *cannelloni*, I would die.'

Butch thought of that incident when he was rushing home to tell Rosa the good news. She was hugging him with delight when he added, 'And the better news is, Rosa, you can make pounds of *cannelloni*. Because we are going to have a big party on board. But only if you feel like it. Boss Croker has given me authority to hire caterers and stock up wine and booze for a right good shindig.'

'Be careful, Butch. What he want in return?'

'Nothing, Rosa. I swear! Except the honour of launching and naming it.'

'What you going to call it?'

'Isn't that what I'm telling you? Croker wants to name it.'

'Oh! What he name it? Jackie the Mule?' She placed her laughing face against his and ordered him to come to bed.

'Here's one old bark you are not to replace,' she teased.

Friday was a bright day. Brian told Nellie to dress up in her best clothes and reflect the glory of the weather.

'Why should I dress up to go walking with you?'

'Because the sun is shining and I feel good and I want to stride out with the most beautiful woman in Manhattan.'

'You and your blarney!' She kissed her son before agreeing.

Brian thought she was having a little trouble climbing the stairs. Nothing precise, but an uneasiness that he had not noticed before. Concern disappeared, however, when she reappeared in a few minutes. He looked, gasping at her elegance. She had merely changed her dress and brushed up her hair, still rich and dark, yet Brian pondered on how, if he met Nellie in Barbara's without knowing her, he would ask her to dance. She must have been a very young child when Eyre Coote Croker raped her. What a waste her life had been! For her and for Tim O'Mahoney.

Whatever her true age, it was not showing as they went striding along by the wharf. She was taking on a robust gait, and breezes playing around stacked bales began whispering to her tresses and brushing colour into her cheeks. Clearing the commercial area and facing into the open harbour, her bearing became almost regal. At the far end of Pier Four, a new ship was flying bunting and a band was playing on its deck. It was the unmistakable 'Semper Fidelis', the new march composed by John Philip Sousa. Nellie held back her shoulders, linked Brian and tripped along as sprightly as a military recruit. They were nearing the ship when she spotted the musicians' uniforms.

'Brian! It's the Unites States Marine Band. I saw them marching on Columbus Day. I know it. So the leader must be – Yes! It's Sousa himself!'

Now she was almost running, but about a hundred yards from the ship, she halted abruptly.

'There's some sort of a private celebration going on, Brian. Maybe we should turn back.'

'Not at all. Come on and we'll have a look.'

'That would be rude. No, we'll go away.' Brian eased his arm under hers and urged her on to where she could see a familiar squat figure in evening clothes and tall hat standing at the top of the gangplank welcoming guests.

'That's Richard. It is some official reception. It would be bad manners to go on,' Nellie persisted.

'Ah, Miss Hurley! Upon my soul, you look ravishing! Pray, come on up.' Richard was being playfully gentlemanly.

Nellie was turning to go back but Brian wheeled her around. When she looked down to catch up her skirt, Richard winked at Brian and whispered, 'Devoy can't be contacted, my ass!'

Shyly, Nellie held the handrail, all festooned with ribbons and garlands and Richard kissed her and clasped her hand warmly. He signalled to Sousa and the bandleader smoothly led his musicians into a romantic waltz.

'Allow me to introduce you to the captain of this ship, Miss Hurley,' Richard announced grandly.

He guided Nellie to the companion-way. Butch Maguire, impeccably attired in naval jacket and cap was standing with Rosa beside him. Sweeping his cap to the deck in a formal bow, he said, 'Welcome on board, my Queen of Manhattan.'

Suddenly the band began playing a fanfare and Mayor Van Wyke appeared to announce that Mr Croker had a ceremony to perform.

Richard waddled forward and began: 'My good friends, most ships are launched from the shore but them that does be doing it that way hasn't the right idea at all. Today, I have the pleasure of launching Butch Maguire's boat the Tammany Hall way: it's all done from the inside!'

There was an outburst of cheering and Richard signalled for quietness. When he received it, he continued.

'Today, I have all my good friends around me. Not my family, but people who have supported me a whole lot of ways over many years. I could go on all night about them, but them all has other things to be doing – like eating and drinking. So, if yez all lean over the gunwale here – well maybe just a few of yez, we don't want to turn the bloody thing over – I will lift this piece of canvas from the nameplate. It will remind some people of when a certain ship did turn over.'

With a sharp wrench he whipped away the cover and a sun sinking through smoky city clouds sent a spotlight to bounce off the sparkling brass. Nellie read *Henry Clay II*. She was cupping her nose and mouth in her palms, but Richard Croker and Butch peeled them away and led her towards the stern area. She found herself behind a suspended sail. There was a small table with a bottle of champagne – opened – two glasses and a small key. Nellie looked back to question, but both men had gone. She was moving to sit down and figure out what was going on, when he stepped from behind the large capstan. For a moment he stood looking at her, then she held out her hands. She felt his strong arms around her and his face next to hers; warm and comforting, ending years of pain.

⁓

In a large quayside saloon Barbara was pirouetting to John Philip Sousa's music as part of the entertainment for Boss Croker and his friends. She ended her dance by taking the trombone from a bandsman and playing it brilliantly. Its sly notes rose lazily to ricochet around the rafters, even after she left the stage to wild whoops and cheers.

A dusky young Indian then regaled the company by trotting across the stage and around the aisles dressed in full tribal regalia. Sitting backwards astride a black stallion, she sang 'The Star-Spangled Banner' in her native Cherokee. After the performance, she approached Richard.

'My name, sir, is Bula Edmondson. I am an Indian princess. I have studied music and singing and am interested in fostering a better understanding of my native culture.'

'You're a good woman on a horse,' Richard said, a little shyly.

'My Indian name is Keetaw Kaiantuckt. I am a direct descendant of Sequoyah, the Cherokee chief who invented my tribe's alphabet.'

'We should have you in The Wigwam,' Richard joked.

Back on Butch Maguire's new ship, Tim was smiling and asking, 'Would you like some of my lobscouse, Nellie?'

They laughed.

'The key?' she questioned.

'The captain's cabin! Your son is an old romantic. Dick Croker too.'

'Maybe they only left it for us in case it rains,' Nellie laughed.

TWENTY-EIGHT

'S O THAT'S MY STORY, Tim. Raped before my sixteenth birthday by Brian's father. And another attempt after we parted that day on the *Henry Clay.*' They had been talking frankly for an hour, and coldness was seeping in from the sea.

'The cur! I would have torn him to strips if I had met him. But here! Leave the past behind and let's make up for lost time.' Tim was filling the glasses with champagne.

Nellie took hers and touched Tim's, but just as on the evening of Richard's birth, she did not drink. The couple left down the glasses and leaned over the gunwale. Nellie was fondling the key and peering at it.

'You'll understand, then, why I could never make love in a ship's cabin, Tim. I'm sorry.'

'Barbara's concert saloon then,' he invited. 'She is renting a room to me until I get fixed up permanently.'

'No, Tim. Please.'

'Butch and Rosa's house? They'd give us a room for a while.'

'You got to know all these friends of mine very quickly!'

'In a couple of days. Dick Croker's work.'

'Tim, I remained a strict Roman Catholic.'

'Then marry me, Nellie,' he said matter-of-factly.

'Of course I will.' She kissed him.

'When?'

'As soon as the banns are read. Or maybe Richard might arrange that we could wed without them.' She laughed and held him tight.

While they waited for clerical permission, she began worrying. Was it credible that Tim had been travelling to Canada and some of the northern states without knowing or making love to any woman? Impossible as it seemed, her heart reassured her. Then she began recalling her innocence when she had come to New York and experienced her single wild passion with Fay. Could any similar physical release be achieved with Tim now?

It was another quiet ceremony in the oratory where Brian's christening had taken place. She'd wanted to celebrate afterwards in the same saloon but Richard had insisted on the Plaza Hotel. It was a lively evening of dancing and singing.

Fay remained sober. 'I'll not spoil your big day, darling,' she assured her.

Rosa and Butch danced like young lovers. Closely. They came over to where their friends were sitting and Butch whispered in Nellie's ear, 'Take note and take heart. Did you never hear it said around Balliva, "The oldest fiddle plays the sweetest tune"?'

'Who's old? Speak for yourself, whaler man.' Nellie's retort frisked through a bold smile.

'Will we dance like we did at the party, Mother?' Brian asked.

'If you get an oil-can for my knees,' she joked.

'Yez should have gone on a cruise for your honeymoon,' Richard said.

'Don't mention any sort of a craft to us,' Tim answered, suddenly serious.

'Except craft of love!' Rosa was smiling and hugging Nellie. Butch placed his palm on Tim's shoulder and said, 'You'll be great for each other. I know it. Best of luck, fella'.' And he and Rosa danced away.

Nellie did not follow the custom of throwing her bouquet before leaving. Instead, she handed it to Fay, kissed her and hugged her warmly.

Brian smiled, before saying, 'By the way, Mother. I won't be back in your house for a fortnight and then only to collect my things.'

'But why, Brian?'

'Now, Mother! Go home and turn the picture of the Sacred Heart and the Holy Mother to the wall. I am taking over Tim's temporary accommodation at Barbara's on a permanent basis.'

Richard slid an inquisitive look at Brian, who just winked.

The newly weds retired late that night to Nellie's house.

Barbara had quickly taught Tim about the Feng Shui fragrances and so he lit yellow candles on the mantelpiece. Their sweet aromas mixed with wisps of errant smoke from a log fire smouldering in the grate.

They sipped wine, mulled by plunging a red-hot poker in the glass – a method Nellie had learned in Balliva. It was her first taste of alcohol. Her eyes became heavy and they lay together on a settee.

Barbara had also told Tim about the antidepressant and aphrodisiac effects of oils from rose, jasmine, sandalwood and ylang ylang. She'd blended a mixture of these for him.

He slid down the top of Nellie's dress and began rubbing the soothing concoction into her neck and shoulders. Infinitesimal body-hairs glistened in fair-tipped dampness and mirrored the stray flickers of revived firelight leaping from the ashes.

Deeply inhaling the heady mix of oils, the fire and the candles, Nellie began to relax. Tim was touching and stroking with the merest suggestion of contact. To her surprise, streams of bliss began coursing through her. He stopped to take off his shirt and she asked, 'It doesn't matter terribly, Tim, but I have to know. You must have been with other women, down all those years. Were you?'

'Yes, Nellie my love. Just twice and just a few kisses. I swear. I admit that loneliness made me want to fall in love. I could never explain why our short meeting could have stopped me, but it did. There just seemed to be no question about it and no sacrifice in it. That's the God's truth, Nellie. I swear it.'

'And I believe you, Tim.'

He lay beside her. 'Let us try making magic, Nellie, *mo stór*.'

And as the fire's embers absorbed the vestigial scents of oil and candle, leaving spent air charged with a lingering sorcery, they did.

━━

Richard conducted the final years of his Tammany stewardship by cable, supplemented by occasional visits to New York, where he was also involved in a number of complex deals involving the planning and construction of a new subway for the city.

He spent more time in Palm Beach and in Wantage and this absentee rule was again taking its toll, reflected in dwindling support. His standing at Tammany waned more when he insisted on nominating Mayor Van Wyck's brother Gus to run for Governorship of New York State.

The Republicans had a popular hero of the Spanish-American war, Theodore Roosevelt, as candidate. Richard worked harder than he had ever done and almost succeeded, but Roosevelt won, by only 17,000 votes.

Jack McHugh was running The Sleeve alone, daily cursing Butch Maguire for taking away his wife. Divorce proceedings had eaten into his savings and he was forced to sell ownership of the brothel and become its paid manager. A false name appeared on the transfer papers. The true owner was Boss Croker. After his father's death, Richard had begun to get involved in the business and now he was paying Jack a handsome wage to run the joint on his behalf.

Throughout the city, resentment of rackets and vice rings was growing to such an extent that Dr Charles Parkhurst, the pastor of Madison Square Presbyterian Church, decided to see with his own eyes how gay the nineties really were.

Togged out in a ragged mackintosh over chequered black and white breeches topped off by a jaunty grey trilby, the reverend gentleman dismounted from a buggy spider in the harbour area one evening. Walking along the pavement, his guide urged him to respond when Jackie the Mule began issuing his usual sidewalk solicitation.

Richard had received a late tip-off about Parkhurst's visit but had not had time to get in touch with McHugh. He knew Parkhurst would either accept Jack's invitation or enter the store to buy produce and discover the entrance to The Sleeve. In desperation, he contacted Nellie, told her to find Rosa and Fay and drop in to The Sleeve.

'The confectionery and vegetable shop won't fool that guy but try to convince him there's only a refreshment room inside.'

They were late and the reverend gentleman and his companion were already in the reception area when they arrived. Nellie slid in behind her old desk. Fay and Rosa took Parkhurst's coat and invited him to have a drink. They did the same with his friend.

'You are such a handsome gentleman; full of refinement,' Fay was assuring this man while Rosa chatted to his Reverence. Nellie served the two men bourbon. She offered some to Fay and Rosa but winked.

'Oh dear, no thank you, my girl. Never allow a drop to pass my lips,' Fay lied gleefully.

'Only occasional drop of *vino* I like.' Rosa's eyes were sparkling with delight, enjoying the game they were playing.

Nellie's ploy was to get the two men so drunk that they would have to be carried out of the place. She hoped Jack McHugh would stay outside soliciting until she succeeded.

Parkhurst was hesitant. Vintage wine was his normal tipple, but he thought he would arouse suspicion if he demurred. He finished his first drink too quickly, smacking his lips.

'May I have another of those, please, my lady?'

Nellie obliged and he drank the second libation faster. This time he did not have to ask Nellie. She was pouring as he was listening to Fay, who was enjoying playing her part.

'The two of you are the nicest folk ever came into this establishment to look at our vegetables. We might arrange a little presentation pack of them before you go.'

'So kind of you, my dear!'

'She a very refined and good lady.' Rosa was having a good time too.

'Oh, real quality, Padre! Fay Clark came on this earth to give a good example.' Fay's eyes fluttered like an angel's and Rosa and Nellie all but collapsed.

'Leh ... Let's get on with our in ... inspection,' the escort was stammering.

'Take your time, my dear man. These ladies are exhilarating. True virgins of Christ. Witty and generous.'

'Witty anyway,' Rosa whispered to Fay.

'And very generous, Padre.' Fay placed a hand on the parson's thigh.

'Come! Let's dance! A polka!' Parkhurst leaped to his feet, grabbed Fay and began prancing about. While he was doing so, Nellie filled his glass again. Rosa told his accomplice to look at the fine plasterwork on the ceiling and while the man was telling her he could see none, Nellie was topping up his glass too.

'Richard doesn't realize how good a team he engaged,' she whispered to Rosa.

Fay whirled Parkhurst about, making his head swim. But when they were passing Nellie, he swiped the bottle from her and began slugging its contents. Fay had no option but to forget about dancing and try keeping him on his feet.

Singing, swaying and waving his long arms then, he swept Fay aside and began marching into The Sleeve. But not before his accomplice took the bottle from him, slumped on a chair and began slugging.

In consternation, Nellie and Rosa tried to grab Parkhurst's coat tails, but he stumbled on, booming in his best preacher's voice.

'Who said God doesn't love the whores and lechers of this earth?'

He pulled aside the curtains of the first cubicle at an inopportune moment for its inhabitants. His eyes began bulging and his neck flaming around an Adam's apple that started flipping up and down. Then he pulled himself to his full six feet five, sprang to attention and saluted the couple. Smarter than he had ever done during his former naval career.

'Permission to leave ship, sir,' he called, before dashing back out and whipping the drapes together again.

Unfortunately, he turned the wrong way and began tottering into other cubicles. Fay, Nellie and Rosa were trying to restrain him but The Sleeve was erupting in screams of female dismay and the angry shouts of partners' protests. Fay dashed back into the street, pressed a few dimes into a ragamuffin's palm and told him to go and find Dick Croker at Tammany Hall.

'Tell him to hurry over here,' she ordered.

She returned to the screams of one of the prostitutes.

'When he told me to "repent or die," I got an unexpected orgasm and injured my client.'

The client was running towards the exit, doubled up and screaming, 'I'll demand compensation from Jackie the Mule. I didn't pay for a shit-kicking contortionist.'

'Shut up and cover your disgrace with your clothes,' Fay called to him, while Nellie gave him some advice.

'Boss Croker of Tammany will be here in a minute and you can make your complaint in person.'

That ended the matter. The client dressed quickly and left.

Reverend Parkhurst, meanwhile, was in what Jack always called the 'auditorium'. It was a long room at the end of The Sleeve, where men who found it difficult to perform in the cubicles gathered before trying again. Six naked lovelies performed an erotic Dance of the Goddesses of Nature there each hour while a piano-player trickled out a sensuous jazz number. The session always ended with the more unresponsive men bounding over the girls in leapfrog fashion. They were at this stage when Parkhurst blustered in.

'Great fun. I loved this game in my childhood,' he cheered while he stood back to take a run.

'God help us, his tiller is at a slant,' Fay giggled while she, Rosa and Nellie held him and tried to guide him along.

The parson didn't really leap. Most of the girls squatted and his three guides helped him over. He was coming face to end with the third girl when his innate respectability got the better of the alcohol. Dropping to his knees and bowing his head, he began praying. Unfortunately, his joined hands and walrus moustache touched the wrong places and the girl whipped around, kicking him smartly in the ankle. He stood and hopped in agony before reeling backwards into Fay and onto the ground under the second girl. She was standing astride him and he started screaming at what he saw.

While all this was going on Richard arrived. On the pavement outside, he challenged Jack.

'Do you not know Parkhurst is inside inspecting The Sleeve, you lug?'

'I saw no dog collar,' Jack said, with great concern.

'I trust the good women I sent along done their job. Come on,' Richard spat. As as they entered the store, they heard pandemonium in the 'auditorium'. When they reached it Richard could do nothing but laugh. Looking down at Parkhurst, he pointed the silver knob of his cane at his crotch and mocked, 'Begod, I never knew you'd such spirit, Reverend. I hope you write what you've seen into your report. And don't forget to use your red pencil.'

By then Reverend Parkhurst's escort had struggled down the corridor. Richard and the girls dragged him and the reeling cleric back to the kitchen, and kept pouring thick black coffee into them until they were fit to return to the night, but not to their crusade.

'Now, remember how much you depended on us,' Fay said to Jack before leaving. Rosa just sniffed as she walked past him. Nellie gave Richard a peck on the cheek and said, 'Thanks for making me just a visitor here.'

Parkhurst was unable to write a report on The Sleeve but he vowed to nail Jack McHugh and Boss Croker some other way. He discovered that Tammany Hall was receiving income for favours granted to wealthy businessmen incarcerated in Ludlow Street Jail. Richard's enormous spending came under scrutiny too.

When he had his information compiled, Parkhurst joined with a willing Republican, Thomas C. Platt, to initiate two investigations. Richard was disappointed by Platt's action because, despite being in opposing camps, the pair had colluded on a number of deals over the years and Richard despised turncoats. Volumes of evidence were piling up against both the Mayor and the man behind his chair, Boss Croker. The Mazet Committee and a Lexow Commission each reported adversely but Richard scoffed at their accusations: 'Every man in New York is working for his own pocket.'

When the interrogations ended, Richard nonchalantly boarded a liner and sailed to England. In his cabin he pinned up a satirical verse that *The New York World* had published. He smiled at its reference to Thomas C. Platt, his accuser. It read:

> *Those Mazet people make me smile,*
> *Inquiring how we made our pile*
> *And why we own Manhattan Isle –*
> *Myself – and me.*
>
> *They'd pry into our bonding scheme*
> *And find out how we skim the cream.*
> *Of all the business, that's no dream –*
> *Myself – and Platt.*
>
> *They've had us on the witness rack;*
> *Now we'll seek pleasures at the track,*
> *And if we lose, we'll still come back –*
> *Myself – and me.*

For the mayoral election of 1901, Richard returned once more to his Tammany office. All his old gusto went into the task ahead. Tim O'Mahoney and Nellie, enraptured by their reunion, helped him enthusiastically. Fay and Rosa too. And, of course, Brian. As well as fighting the election, however, Richard was taking on enemies within Tammany: enemies who resented his autocratic methods and his abrupt orders, which all too often came from abroad. Comparative upstarts questioned his decisions openly and this was making him bad-tempered.

The halo on the Boss's crown was tilting sharply and he was canny enough to realize this. Never one to go down without a fight, he responded by rising early and pacing the halls of The Wigwam long before the cleaners had left. Ordering, chastising, nit-picking, his behaviour was that of a man under great stress. Unused to failure, he was devastated when the anti-Tammany candidate, Seth Low, became Mayor, under the slogan:

> Tammany's waste makes New York's want
> But Croker's Wantage makes New York's wastage.

Open letters to newspaper editors, snide asides at meetings, more and more accusations of bribery and corruption were all taking their toll. Eventually Brian Hurley advised his long time friend and half-brother:

'You've done a good job, Dick. Maybe it's time you took it easy. Enjoy yourself with the horses and the bulldogs.'

The Boss was laughing more heartily than he had done for months when he answered, 'After winning fifteen victories and only two defeats during my seventeen years as Chief Sachem of Tammany Hall, you are the only bugger in New York that has the guts to tell Boss Croker he is washed up. You done the right thing by telling me, brother. God bless you for it and to hell with the begrudgers.'

Despite the apparent bravado, the hurt was obvious. Hoping to ease it a little, Brian arranged to mark Richard's retirement with an elaborate send-off. To a farewell dinner in the Democratic Club, he invited former Mayors and Tammany celebrities, newspaper editors, senators and members of the judiciary. Nellie was there and two of Richard's sons. The inimitable and ageless Barbara sang and danced with the outgoing Boss. The band played a slow jazz number and she dragged Richard over to the piano and began playing. Brian saw that she was giving Boss Croker the same treatment she had tried on him many years before. And the old guy was loving every minute of it. She had trouble hauling his squat bulk between her legs while she stood to continue hammering out the throbbing tune. He kissed her neck gently and whispered, 'The old spark is well quenched, girl, but you're a lady.'

Brian noticed his sadness and clapped his hands for attention.

'I want to thank Barbara for her usual brilliant entertainment –'

'You should know,' Fay heckled, but the remainder of the guests whispered a disapproving 'Shhh!'

Brian continued, 'On your behalf I want to offer Dick Croker a token of your appreciation for what he has done for New York and for its people.'

There was a cheer and some people stood and clapped loudly.

'In making this gift, we represent two generations of New Yorkers who have benefited from Boss Croker's zeal,' he said. 'There are many who revile this man. Some say he has made millions out of Tammany Hall and the Democratic Party. But I have been close to Dick Croker for a long time and I say that poor people, particularly the Irish immigrant poor, would still be living in atrocious conditions but for the energy and enterprise of our departing chief. God save Ireland and God look kindly on Dick Croker.'

'Bless you, my friend.'

The half-brothers met in a brief bear-hug before everybody began cheering wildly. Richard wiped a damp eye as he accepted a giant mahogany chest of solid silver cutlery. Then, holding up its ivory-handled carving knife and fork, he said, 'I should of had them things a few months ago, to cut strips off the curs that done me.'

The party lasted all night, and when Richard arrived at the quayside to embark next day, Sousa's band was performing and a small group again cheered him on his way – those close friends who had done so before. He pretended not to care.

'Begod, Barbara, you didn't hammer the keys on the old piano hard enough to get a tune out of me,' he tried to quip, but he swallowed the final phrase. Fay rushed to him and kissed his rugged cheek. Nellie's lips found his mouth. Rosa turned away. She did not want him to see her tears.

As he walked up the gangway, a larger crowd gathered behind him and began hurling ticker tape and rice. While the ship was pulling away Boss Croker stood at its rail, a lonely, grey figure waving and blowing kisses. Did he know that Sousa was playing a number from the new Broadway musical *The Billionaire*?

TWENTY-NINE

W HEN RICHARD ARRIVED in Wantage, black flags were fluttering from windows. Queen Victoria had died after almost sixty-four years on the throne. Richard began settling back by renaming two of his pigs Platt and Parkhurst. Then he paid the purchase price demanded by Charles Wynham for Moat House. In September of the same year Theodore Roosevelt became President of the United States.

'And to think I had him nearly beat one time,' Richard remarked to Charlie Morton.

'You might have won in politics, Richard, but if you remain stubborn, you'll do no good on the racetrack. I keep telling you, you'll have no success with American horses here.'

'And I tell you I will, Charlie.'

'Well if that's your attitude, I think we had better part company.'

'Suit yourself, Charlie boy.'

Morton did suit himself – and the local racing community. He would have stuck it out with Richard and ignored their criticism if his boss had only cooperated. When he and Richard parted company an Australian trainer, J.E. Brewer, took over and, idiosyncratically, Richard purchased three good English-bred fillies. Yet, just like his predecessor, Brewer found Boss Croker reluctant to accept the possibility that others might know more than he did about English racing.

Richard was still loyal to his friends, however. He invited Nellie and Tim over to Wantage to celebrate their fifth wedding anniversary and paid for their passage.

'Youze won't damage the bed, I hope,' he joked coarsely when he welcomed them. He showed them to an expensively furnished suite overlooking the broad downs where his horses were grazing or exercising.

In the evenings, they strolled through country lanes and woods, listening to shepherds whistling and dogs barking in the distance. On these occasions, the hardships of two lifetimes receded and Nellie would remember playing with Richard and little Peter O'Donovan in the green fields around Balliva. Once, in the slant of a weakening evening sun, they sat on a tree-stump. Tim found a straw and twirled it idly.

She saw, and whispered, 'Remember the pile of nets on the *Henry Clay*?'

'Would you believe, I was just thinking of that, Nellie.'

'You touched my face with a straw.'

'And I knew I had fallen in love.'

They both agreed that a Wantage woodland was a thousand times more idyllic than a creaking ship's stern. It was dinnertime before they reached the manor.

When she came into the dining-room Nellie sensed that Elizabeth had been crying. She was saying little and was just sitting graciously and behaving with impeccable manners, passing condiments and inquiring after their needs. Richard, on the other hand, was in a jovial mood. Dressed as usual in formal clothes, he told stories about his horses and claimed that some of the snobs in the area were jealous of his wealth.

'You wouldn't mind only half of them would have no backsides in their pants if it wasn't for their bank managers.'

He began discussing the cost of living and asking Tim and Nellie how they were faring out in New York.

'I'm no longer in the Mayor's office, but I have a nice part-time secretarial post with Brian. Tim works with him, too.'

'Brian, the scallywag! What is he doing?'

'Contract gardening, and I am his head gardener,' Tim informed.

'Tim is good at looking after old shrubs.' Nellie's eyes were teasing her husband.

'I just take the orders!' Tim knew what she meant. He too was grinning.

Elizabeth noticed, and remembered with bitterness the coldness of her own fifth anniversary. Taking a tiny lace handkerchief from her bosom, she began dabbing her eyes.

Richard enquired roughly, 'Another bloody cold, is it?'

There was an embarrassing silence.

'Honey dissolved in hot water with a squirt of lemon is good for a cold, Elizabeth,' Nellie ventured, to break the tension.

'Too sweet, Nellie. Too sweet.' Richard's five words implied a million statements, all of them heartbreaking. Thoughts on the failure of his marriage chased a realization that he was the only Croker of his generation still living. Slurping soup, he promised his conscience that he would visit all the family graves soon.

248

Then he recovered abruptly and asked loudly: 'Where the hell are there gardens to make a living from in New York?'

'On top of the new multi-storey buildings they call skyscrapers.'

'Gardens on the roofs! Now, why didn't I think of that?'

'Don't mind him, Richard. Brian's biggest contracts are at the three big luxury hotels in Coney Island,' Nellie informed.

'That kip! Fleabag saloons, filthy brothels and race tracks you wouldn't run a mongrel terrier around.' Between comments, Richard was tearing bread rolls apart.

'Oh, it's not that way now, Richard,' Nellie said. 'The Oriental, Brighton Beach and Manhattan hotels are very posh. Huge long wooden buildings with balconies and verandahs facing the sea. And they've acres of lawns and gardens with lobelia, hollyhocks, snapdragons and geraniums of all sorts.'

'Jaysus, Nellie, you're getting horrid bloody romantic.'

Croker took up the gold-handled knife. He began sharpening its blade vigorously on steel before carving thick wedges from the roast lamb and wild boar that a butler had placed before him. An imperceptible wrinkling of a nostril betrayed the servant's distaste on hearing the bad language.

'You really should watch your tongue,' Elizabeth chastised icily, when the servant withdrew. Tim and Nellie were discomfited again. Richard was undismayed.

'Ah, him and me are no great butties. Haven't seen eye to ass since I came here,' Richard laughed. Elizabeth's nose quivered.

Richard enjoyed the meal. He had felt lost since arriving in Wantage, missing the hubbub of Tammany Hall and the commercial bustle of New York. Playing the life of an English country squire was not all he'd hoped. He'd resurrected his mother's maiden name, Welstead, to impress. Richard Welstead Croker sounded grand but the gentry continued to shun him.

Elizabeth still got pleasure from entertaining the local ladies of quality but Richard needed some ordinary folk like Tim and Nellie around him all the time. On an impulse, he asked, 'Why don't you become my head gardener, Tim? Then Nellie could look after all the damned paperwork I need done for the horseracing.'

Elizabeth was horrified. Here was another indication of his disregard for her, a further display of his growing contempt for their marriage. With two close friends living in the same estate, perhaps under the same roof, her place in his life would be further diminished.

I wouldn't put it past him to bring over that prostitute Fay too, she mused.

When his shock subsided, Tim found the idea appealing. But would he be too old to look after Richard's huge gardens, he wondered.

Nellie had no doubt whatsoever. Gardening in Wantage would be far more leisurely than in New York. And healthier. Furthermore, she was able to recognize the promise of a hundred woodland walks. 'What a glorious idea, Dick,' she enthused.

Richard's trouble with the racing authorities and his lack of success on the track rankled. He blamed his trainer, jockeys, opponents – everyone and everything but his own stubborn ways. When he applied to the Stewards of the Jockey Club to have his new string of fillies trained at Newmarket, they refused a licence and he blamed a rival, Colonel E.W. Baird, for the snub. Furious, he began selling off most of his livestock. Enmity with the racing world ensured a huge loss; nobody would pay him a decent price. Later, when some of them started winning races for their new owners, he was outraged, and took a trip to Germany to cool off.

A few years later, when he heard of King Edward VII visiting Ireland, Richard began thinking again about his heritage and about the number of his relatives who had passed away in the land of his forefathers. Regretting that he had only visited the country once since he had left it as a boy of six, he started thinking seriously about moving there.

Acting on an impulse, he made a trip to Dublin, booking into the Shelbourne Hotel on St Stephen's Green. He contacted some racing acquaintances and, within a few hours, he was sitting down talking to them in the hotel's restaurant. One man began telling Richard about an establishment that was coming on the market near Sandyford, in South County Dublin. It had belonged to Judge Murphy, who was celebrated for convicting members of a Fenian splinter group, The Invincibles, for the 1882 Cavendish and Burke murders in the Phoenix Park. The group kept talking late into the night but Richard was up early next morning to present himself at the office of the auctioneers handling the sale. By afternoon he was the owner of Glencairn House.

'We're moving to Dublin,' he curtly informed Elizabeth.

'What!'

'I've found a lovely place –'

'I don't care how lovely it is, I am not going. You didn't even discuss the proposition with me.'

'I just thought of it out of the blue.'

'Without a thought for me. Well, that's the final blow as far as I'm concerned. Damn you, damn your horses and bulldogs! I'm going home.'

She flounced away.

Richard left her his opulent New York dwelling and arranged an income that would provide for her comfort. He struck her off his many New York business interests, however, and added to the powers of attorney that he had already given Richard Junior. There were no further recriminations, only cold farewells, when the woman with whom he had fallen in love in his youth and had cherished and adored before marriage finally departed.

Richard would miss many things, particularly the peace of the Berkshire countryside, though not its people. As he left, he also vowed to return to England to avenge his humiliation by winning the greatest race of all, the Epsom Derby.

THIRTY

RICHARD SPENT a considerable sum of money converting his new acquisition into a mock-Scottish baronial castle. While Glencairn's gaunt new façade was bereft of architectural appeal, inside he refurbished it with more taste, and at great expense. A dramatic mahogany staircase wound beneath stained-glass windows to dominate the vestibule hall. The same wood blended with the polished oak floors in the Grand Hall, Oriental Room, study, billiard and drawing-rooms.

While renovations were under way, his American stallion, Americus, and brood mare, Rhoda B., were in the care of J.J. Parkinson at French Lodge on the edge of the broad Curragh plains, thirty miles inland. Rhoda B. was sired in Wantage by an English stallion, Orme, and Richard called her foal Orby.

'R.B.! D'yez get it?' he asked his trainer.

'What do you mean by R.B., Richard?'

'R.B. That stands for Richard, Boss.' Richard laughed heartily at his childlike ingenuity.

Parkinson began getting winners for his client, but Orby failed in its first race for two-year-olds.

On its second outing in the Railway Stakes at the Curragh, the horse came third to another Croker entry, Electric Rose. Richard had backed Orby. He had a furious row with Parkinson and when the Glencairn stables were ready, the Boss transferred his horses there, installing Colonel F.F. McCabe, who had been having success with a small string, as his private trainer.

Richard had paid the expenses for Tim and Nellie to return to New York and wind up their affairs there. They visited Fay.

'We'll have a place of our own on the Glencairn estate and you are welcome to join us,' Nellie promised.

'Jeeze! Live in the countryside? Not on your life. But thanks, Nellie. No, I'll end my days a dirty old woman in this dirty old town.'

'You have more quality in you than most of its sham aristocracy, Fay.'

'Like the Frasers. God! The way that lot treated poor old Boss Croker.'

Fay and Brian and Barbara came to see them off. Each of them held Nellie tightly, not saying a word but conveying bruised emotions with every tightening grip. They clutched Tim too and Fay said, 'Take care of her. She's a jewel.'

'Don't I know it, Fay. I'm a lucky man.' Then, in afterthought, 'Thanks for the bed, Barbara.'

'Shit, don't let Nellie hear you saying that.' Fay's attempt at making the situation less maudlin failed. She took Barbara and Tim in each arm and moved away. 'Now leave Brian and his mother for a minute.'

Nellie went behind a ticket booth. 'Never take that gospel I gave you from off your neck, son. Promise me.'

'I promise, Mother.'

And Nellie Hurley was back behind a similar shack by the pier in Cove, suffering the first of ten thousand painful episodes. She said a silent prayer to her father.

'Your grandfather, who must be a long time in Heaven, will mind you, Brian. Along with my prayers.'

'I will come over to Ireland and visit, Mother. Honest!'

When Tim and Nellie stood by the rail and the three figures on the wharf became smaller, Nellie cried and whispered into his heavy coat, 'They looked after me, Tim. When I was so far down.'

'You'll never be that way again, Nellie. I'll mind you now.'

The night after they settled into the gardener's house in Glencairn, Richard invited all his staff and their relatives to a party in his new 'American Bar'. Hewn from solid oak, the counter was shaped like a horseshoe and a silver footrest ran its full length. Upholstery on the high stools was of regal purple and gold, a theme continued in the expensive fabric wallpaper. Spittoons placed around the walls were golden, too. Richard had never imbibed since the night of his Tammany initiation. That night Nellie noticed him take the occasional sip of Jack Daniel's. Most of the time, however, he stood behind the counter pulling a gold-trimmed ivory pump to dispense draught Guinness for all who wanted it. He did not bother using the silver measures when he was serving Irish whiskey or bourbon, fine wines, brandy or champagne. He discarded his expensive cigar for a humble Wild Woodbine 'coffin nail' cigarette. Music blared from a phonograph and coloured lights played on the first ballroom crystal sphere ever installed in Ireland. After a lavish buffet, he brought neighbours on a tour of his elaborately furnished reception rooms and bedrooms, billiard hall and library, stocked with a bizarre mixture of comic cuts, algebra texts and detective novels. He pointed to a pair of elephant's tusks on the wall and remarked, 'Did yez ever see anything like them yokes? Them's the biggest tusks outside Africa.'

Late that night when the crowd had departed, Richard switched off the music and the lights. All but a single red spot on the slow revolving ball. The three began talking of New York and, later on, Nellie sang 'Danny Boy'. Each time the beam came around and picked out her features, Richard saw a young girl holding his hand on a long wagon and turning his head into her strange-smelling body for comfort when they were passing a pile of corpses.

Tim was looking from a capstan, marvelling at her beauty, responding to her dulcet invitation.

> *But come you back, when spring is in the meadow,*
> *And when the valley's hushed and white as snow.*
> *'Tis I'll be here, in sunshine or in shadow*
> *Oh Danny Boy, Oh Danny Boy, I love you so.*

The O'Mahoneys settled into Glencairn and were marvellously comfortable. Their house was beside a magnificent conservatory that sprouted a long greenhouse; both built to Richard's own specifications. Tim spent hours attending to flowers and plants inside, and to shrubs and fruit-trees in the orchard garden and around the magnificent lawns and sheltered paddocks. At weekends he cut or picked all surplus produce and, on Richard's instructions, brought them to patients in Blanchardstown and to other hospitals in South County Dublin.

One Sunday, Nellie accompanied him while he was hanging the tenth Station of the Cross, donated by Richard, in pretty Glencullen Church.

'It would take Croker to select the tenth station – the stripping of the garments,' he laughed.

'He picked the right man to hang it too,' Nellie countered.

While Tim was hammering in the nail, Nellie wandered around near the altar. With her bonnet firmly in place, so as not to offend the Lord, she lit a candle, knelt and gave thanks to Him for granting her lifelong wish. She said she was sorry for missing Mass many times and for earning a living abetting the sinful practices of others. Then, she asked advice about adopting a child, if her age did not prevent the authorities from allowing her. One of the chambermaids at Glencairn had conceived out of wedlock and, terrified of her parents, had confided in Nellie. The unfortunate girl had asked Nellie to help find somebody to take the baby when it was born. Nellie had not asked who the father was, but remembered an awful incident in Balliva and wondered could history possibly have repeated itself.

'Will I ask Tim about it, Lord?'

As if in answer, Tim tiptoed up behind her and knelt beside her.

'Penny for your thoughts,' he whispered.

'It's a bargain. Light a candle there and come for a walk.'

They took a long stroll, down towards Kilternan and up a narrow, un-metalled lane whose furze border was brushed grey with dust. Off this, they trod where shepherds, farmers, hikers, ramblers and lovers had, over centuries, worn the earth to an unyielding crust while winding their way towards The Scalp. Where mountain calmed and meadow became moor, they disturbed a grouse and its bulleting escape signalled an eruptive urgency in the calm afternoon. They approached a deep, natural chasm through a defile of shelving granite and weaved through dislodged rocks that squatted or perched according to the whim of the contour on which they'd tumbled in aeons past. The black-streaked clouds seemed to cool the air. Nellie shivered, tugging her cardigan close with folded arms. Ahead, the Great Sugar Loaf challenged any exit, but when they passed through the narrowest cleft, warmth greeted their step on to a lightly grassed plateau. A glorious scene surrounded them.

Off hillside, sea, city and Bray Head, hues of colour and light splashed and danced. Clouds crossing the sun conjured shadows of waves and warriors, fantasy beasts and phantom birds over field and village, heather and house. Exhilarated, they sat beside a craggy rise and stared. Then they made the place their Wantage woodland, and talked about fostering a child, but reached no firm decision.

Late in the evening the sun that had so thrilled them was dimming as the couple returned to Glencairn. Tim and Nellie noticed their Master standing under the verandah, looking pale and shattered.

'It's Frank. There's been an accident.' Richard shook his head wildly and wrought a weird whimper of suppressed sobbing before falling on Nellie's shoulder, saying, 'The son who stuck with me at all times, and didn't side with the others when Elizabeth and me split up! Dead! Crashed his sports car in Palm Beach. I have to go, Nellie.'

Nellie patted his back gently and wondered why the toughest of men found it most difficult to grieve. She knew at that moment that she would adopt the chambermaid's child. And that she would call it Frances or Frank.

———

Richard was just coming to grips with his heartbreaking loss when, within months, tragedy struck again. His second son, Howard, died of narcotic poisoning in a Santa Fé train. When he returned from the funeral he converted an upstairs room at Glencairn into an oratory. Stained-glass windows depicted the four seasons. He prayed and meditated there regularly, and had a priest from Sandyford parish perform evening devotions on Sundays. Tim and Nellie always joined him on these occasions. His old ebullience died and he would often spend long periods leaning morosely on wooden fences, staring at his horses. He began visiting the graves of his relatives, lingering longest while praying for his Aunt Elizabeth, whom he remembered as kind and affectionate. Strange that he had married a girl called Elizabeth, he thought.

His remaining son, Richard, visited regularly, but the old Boss always had the feeling that his reasons for calling had more to do with checking up on things than with filial bonding.

Colonel McCabe helped rescue him from his lethargy by bringing Orby to peak fitness. The colt won his first race as a three-year-old, the Earl of Sefton's Plate at Liverpool, by an impressive margin. McCabe knew of Richard's ambition to win the Derby and had entered the colt, but to his amazement Richard ordered his withdrawal.

'Me and you has different ideas about horseflesh,' Richard raged when McCabe insisted. He began champing on his cigar, however, and McCabe learned that this was a sign of uncertainty in the Boss. So he persisted and, after a minor argument, owner and trainer reached a compromise.

'Win the Baldoyle Plate with him and he stays in the Derby.' McCabe turned away and chuckled to himself. After taking a few steps across the stable yard, he turned to Richard and laughed, 'The Newmarket crowd might have stopped you, but not me.' Richard reached down for a hard knob of horse-dung and flung it at his trainer. Tim O' Mahoney, wheeling a barrow of manure from a stable to spread on his roses, witnessed the incident and was glad that Richard seemed to be returning to his old form.

McCabe was right. Orby won easily at Baldoyle. Richard immediately engaged Johnny Reiff, an American jockey who lived in France, to ride for him at Epsom on the 5 June 1907.

An Irish-trained horse had never won the Derby and few gave Boss Croker's rangy chestnut colt a chance, particularly against the top-class Slieve Gallion, winner of the Craven Stakes and the Two Thousand Guineas and owned by Captain Greer. It was a colonel's horse that Richard most wanted to beat, however. Jockey Otto Madden was to ride Wool Winder, owned by old Newmarket adversary, Colonel E.W. Baird. Newspaper reporters claimed that 'no Irish trainer knows enough to even dare to compete for the greatest race in the world'.

Unusual in length from hip to hock, lacking in muscle development and ill-groomed, Orby was receiving little attention as Tim paraded him in the paddock. Nellie was standing by the rails with Richard. Dressed in a cerise straw bonnet and long white crochet coat, she looked elegant, even calm.

'You're still a fine-looking woman, Nellie,' Richard said.

'I'm shaking in my shoes and I've promised St Anthony a pound from my winnings if Orby wins.'

'Ah, can't you give the poor old bugger two?' Richard laughed, while lighting a cigar. 'He'll have a fair job, with the poor old nag a sixty-six to one outsider. A win would be nice, but as long as he beats that bastard Baird's nag, I don't care. If he does, I'll give you and Tim back what you lose. How's that?'

Nellie, grabbed his arm and placed her cheek against his.

'I'm going to pretend it's Macha galloping around the Red Strand!'

'As long as you mind the thistles, Nellie.'

St Anthony's intercession must have begun immediately, because Orby's odds kept dropping until they reached ten to one. Now, Nellie was feeling almost sick with terror, because she and Tim had bet most of their savings on the horse.

The start was perfect and at the one-mile post the favourite, Slieve Gallion, went to the front. After another four furlongs, he was two lengths clear of Bezonian and Galvani. Orby, Earlston and Wool Winder were well positioned, too. In the stand, looking through binoculars with solid silver eyepieces, Richard almost bit his Havana through when Wool Winder sped down the hill. But Otto Madden almost had to pull the horse up after a collision with a cluster of runners and he fell back to last place. Tim had joined the others and all three were wringing their race-cards and trembling with growing hope.

Entering the straight, the English crowd cheered Slieve Gallion on; he was well in the lead. Three Irish people ground their teeth and murmured ejaculations – profane and sacred – willing on the Glencairn entry. Nellie dropped her card and began fingering her Rosary. A palpable silence fell on the crowd as the favourite began sprawling slightly and veering away to the right, letting Orby through. A great Irish roar began to reverberate around the grandstand and the tip of Richard's cigar was becoming a gob of pulp on his tongue. The rest was gone – bitten right through. Tim admired the sparkle of excitement in Nellie's eyes but as the Hibernian clamour began waning he looked back down the track to see Orby changing legs and hanging badly to the right, just as Slieve Gallion had done earlier. Hurtling along to take him was Wool Winder, now fully recovered from the mistake.

'Shit!' Richard spat tobacco stew onto the astrakhan collar in front.

The majority of punters were screaming, 'Come on, Slieve Gallion,' as the favourite began making another run.

'Me auld sagosha,' the Irish punters roared, because Orby was making a recovery. He was laying back his ears and Johnny Reiff was hunched over the horse's mane flicking a whip to extract a final, mighty effort. The colt responded and stretched its lead to two lengths. Thundering hooves and soaring Irish clamour seemed to propel Orby past the post to win a couple of lengths ahead of Wool Winder. Slieve Gallion was just a half-length behind, in third place. The jubilation among the Irish following was unbridled. They battered down the tall hats of sedate Englishmen and swore that they would spend a month in celebration.

When Richard went to the winner's enclosure to congratulate and thank Johnny Reiff, a chant of 'Boss Croker', 'Boss Croker', 'Boss Croker' rose and spread across Epsom downs. There was a mere whisper in reply, but it gave Richard the greatest satisfaction of his life. Passing Colonel Baird, he leaned over and said, 'Now you know what to do with your training permission!'

Inside in the owners' lounge, he gave the barman a five-pound note to send a telegram back to the steward at Glencairn. It read:

ORBY WON. GIVE EVERY STAFF MEMBER £3 AND A COCK OF HAY

Further instructions followed. The American and Irish flags were to fly over Glencairn. Colonel McCabe sent a telegram to his old regiment ordering an issue of champagne to all ranks.

It was the custom that all owners of Derby entries should dine with the King, but although the Prince of Wales and the Duke of Connaught left the Royal Enclosure to shake Richard's hand, King Edward VII did not extend the usual invitation.

Word of the win spread like wildfire around Ireland. An old woman ran down the Sandyford village shouting, 'Thank God, I lived to see a Catholic horse winning the Derby.' The staff at Glencairn had bet heavily and all were jubilant. They strung bunting along the iron railings around the ornamental entrance gates, then hung it along treetops until Murphystown Road was a multicoloured carnival land. The Kilternan Brass and Reed Band hired a bus and toured the villages giving recitals. In case anybody was unaware of the mighty victory, a bonfire burned on the summit of The Scalp and a bigger one on Three Rock Mountain cracking knuckles of amber fingers to lift its flame skyward. Around every fire, jubilant supporters of Orby and people who were never at a race meeting in their lives danced and sang. They hugged each other and clasped bottles of stout. The customers of The Gallops Bar poured into the street in a long line chanting:

> *Orby! Orby, ran, ran, ran,*
> *The bold Boss Croker is a great old man.*

The proprietor of the pub ordered drinks on the house and sold kegs of porter at cost price and a crowd of cheering men and women rolled them up the hill to the biggest bonfire.

'Will yez look at the newspaper headlines,' Richard said to Nellie and Tim at breakfast the next morning. He poked one after another at them.

AN IRISH DERBY. BOOKIES, PRESS, JOCKEY CLUB BAFFLED

DID THE KING REFUSE TO MEET MR CROKER?

ORBY WINS THE BLUE RIBAND

BOSS OF THE TURF

SANDYFORD GOES STONE MAD

WINNER TAKES ALL!

'They are all hot under their oxters about the King giving you the cold shoulder,' Tim laughed.

'That's because I told them that th'oul King and me is no enemies. I said, "He's welcome to drop in to Glencairn for a cup of tea any time he visits Ireland."'

It was a lively breakfast, with Richard relishing the nods towards him that the other hotel guests were making.

'Begod, I showed that Newmarket Jockey Club where to get off,' he whispered to Nellie.

'And that Colonel Baird!'

'Hey, listen to this,' Tim said later, reading from the *Freeman's Journal* on the boat that they took home. 'It says, "If the truth were known, the Jockey Club was under sedation and England's racing experts had faces redder than the *Sacred Heart Messenger* at the success of the racehorse trained on Boss Croker's Gallops under the Dublin Mountains."'

'The *Sacred Heart Messenger*!' Richard laughed and his face too was becoming as red as the Catholic pamphlet's cover.

A huge crowd gathered to greet the winning party. When the boat docked, Richard led Orby down the gangplank to loud cheering and cries of 'Good old Boss Croker' and 'Orby the Wonder Horse'. A stout woman grabbed the nearest man to her and began swinging around, singing:

> *Says auld Richard Croker, the Boss*
> *I tauld yez I knew a good horse.*
> *I'm telling you this, son,*
> *If you'd backed mine at Epsom*
> *You wouldn't ha' been at a loss.*

'Yeow!' her partner yelled, and a thousand throats roared an echo.

Grooms put Orby in an open horsebox and hitched it to a small truck decorated with banners in the Croker colours bearing legends like 'Good old Boss' and 'Welcome Home, Orby'. The Glencairn staff sat behind, all waving tricolours and flinging streamers. Next came the open Packard motor car that Richard had imported from America. Tim and Nellie were in the back with him. A cavalcade of motor cars followed, honking horns and revving engines.

Mobs of cheering onlookers crammed the roads and footpaths on the way through Dublin's suburbs, holding glasses high and drinking toasts to Orby and to Boss Croker as they ran along the footpaths. Richard waved at them, delighted.

'Here, Tim, give us some of that champagne from the "dickie".'

Tim leaned back and pulled out a bottle. He handed it to Richard.

'Ah, for chrissake, where do you think you're going with one lousy bottle? Bring out another dozen. Here, Nellie, you help me opening them.'

Corks popped and the bubbly spouted. Those who had been proposing toasts a moment before, gulped back their drinks and their pint and half-pint glasses were soon overflowing.

After about two hours the cavalcade passed Foxrock Railway Station. The stationmaster stood on the road, raised his hand and halted the Packard.

'Now, Mr Croker, if you'll follow me, please,' he said, smiling.

'I think I know what's coming,' Richard whispered to Nellie before he stepped out.

Since arriving in Glencairn he'd often taken the train, but had found the wooden seats in the waiting-room too hard. Somehow or other he had acquired the throne chair of the Lord Mayor of Cork and had had it installed. He had become so fond of using this that he often sat for hours, just watching passengers come and go and forgetting completely about boarding the train. Once or twice, he had fallen asleep.

At the stationmaster's request, a groom took Orby from his box. The stationmaster then took the reins and led the animal gingerly onto the platform and into the waiting room.

The 'throne' was festooned with garlands and a porter led Richard to it, sat him down and handed him the reins. Then the stationmaster unrolled a parchment and read with mock formality.

'Foxrock Railway Station is proud to welcome home the Chief whose throne stands in our humble premises. On its plush upholstery, Boss Croker has often rested his weary form and we never knew that he was plotting a scheme that would bring honour to his country, to Glencairn and to all places associated with him. So, on behalf of the staff of this station, I now place this garland on this magnificent horse.'

Orby sidled nervously and tossed his head when flowers encircled his neck, but he settled. The stationmaster then presented Richard with a miniature railway sleeper.

'This, sir, is just one more little nap you'll have had in Foxrock Station.'
Richard thanked the official for his touching and humorous gestures.
'I'm the happiest railway sleeper the station ever had.'

The American Bar in Glencairn was packed with staff and friends again that night. More champagne flowed. And it was to flow in racing establishments and households throughout Ireland and as far away as South Africa, where the Commanding Officer of the South Irish Horse authorized its issue to all ranks.

THIRTY-ONE

HROUGHOUT THE YEAR 1914, troubles festered in the Balkan states and in Europe. After the assassination of its Archduke Francis Ferdinand in Sarajevo, Austria allied with Germany to declare war on Serbia. A day later Russia mobilized along the Austrian and German borders. During the first days of August Germany opened hostilities with Russia and France, and invaded Belgium. Britain declared war on Germany on 4 August. World War One had begun.

John Devoy cabled Richard. 'A young fellow will be arriving over from England next week. I would like you to meet him in Vaughan's Hotel. He will be carrying a copy of *Dubliners*, by an author called James Joyce. He is an official in the British Post Office and he hails from near your old home in Cork. His name is Michael Collins.'

'The damned cheek of Devoy, after I hiring Barbara's place for his bloody Clan. Vaughan's Hotel, my ass! Let him make an appointment for this Collins fellow to see me here if he wants to. After all, I'm a Freeman of Dublin now,' Richard told Nellie.

'The Squire of Glencairn' was popular locally. Behind his aggressiveness, penetrating stare and wide chest, his employees found him humane and personable. He payed handsome wages. When Orby's dam, Rhoda B., died in 1913 Richard held a lavish wake for her in the stables, with porter and whiskey laid on. He and his staff then buried the mare in the East Lawn and a surround and headstone was ordered from a Sandyford stonemason.

Richard liked to entertain famous people such as the raconteur surgeon and author, Oliver St John Gogarty, and the politician, Arthur Griffith. Griffith had supported the landing of arms by Irish volunteers in July 1914 and his paper *Sinn Féin* was suppressed when it called upon Irishmen to reject John Redmond's call for recruitment to the British army. This pleased Richard and, remembering how they had treated him in Wantage, he enjoyed listening long into the night in his library while Griffith outlined plans for a Dublin rebellion against the British.

Michael Collins eventually came by and Richard found him intriguing.

'Collins would be a good fellow to head up a movement. But he's not very tactful. He wouldn't last a week in Tammany,' he told Tim.

'Why do you think that?'

'Well, he was beating around the bush looking for money to buy arms and you'd see what he was after a mile away.'

One night after a meal, tenor John McCormack sang 'Macushla' in Glencairn's American bar and Nellie cried. Tim held her hand and gently brushed his lips across her neck. Richard Croker slapped McCormack on the back, took his own cornflower spray from its lapel to put in the singer's, saying, 'Jaysus, John, you get a great auld lift under it, so you do.'

When McCormack obliged with 'Mother Macree' as an encore, a tear dampened the corner of Richard's eye.

'I have a soft spot for mothers,' he explained unnecessarily to Nellie. Then he added, 'But fathers doesn't be bad old sorts either, isn't that a fact?'

Nellie wondered if she had discovered why Boss Croker had purchased a staff plot at Kilgobbin Cemetery to bury the chambermaid, who had died from diphtheria not long after giving birth to her foster-son, Frank. She searched Richard's face for a confirmatory sign, but got none.

～

As news reports told of Serbs throwing back Austria's original offensive, Richard, now suffering from severe rheumatic fever and other ailments, received a telegram that his estranged wife, Elizabeth, had died in the Austrian Tyrol.

'She is to be buried in New York. I'll have to go to the funeral,' the ageing Boss told Nellie.

'I'll go with you, Richard,' Nellie said, throwing her arms around him.

'I wish you were able, Nellie, but you couldn't at your age, girl.'

Nellie had never really faced up to her years and the statement quietened her. Since her marriage, nobody had ever reminded her and the long postponed love between Tim and herself seemed to have kept them feeling young. Little Frank had helped in this respect; both of them loved playing with him around Glencairn's roaming paddocks or across their beloved foothills of Stepaside and Glencree.

All this had sped them through the autumn and deep into the winter of life without fully realizing it.

Richard noticed Nellie's reaction.

'We're all into extra time, Nellie my darling! Maybe it's all we done in our lives that makes us want to hold on.'

His big hand took hers and squeezed it; then he kissed her on the mouth. Nellie was surprised at the force, and a little shocked. But she could not bring herself to chastise him. 'I'll get your things ready,' she offered.

The voyage across the Atlantic felt longer than ever. Brian met the liner and gave him a warm welcome, but the obsequies were wearying. When they were over, Richard was sitting in the foyer of the Waldorf-Astoria Hotel chatting with some of his family. Brian was regaling him with details of recent developments in New York.

'Barbara and myself are hitched. But don't tell mother yet. It was a registry office job.'

'You're right. Poor Nellie wouldn't approve of that.'

'We'll have a church ceremony soon. Would you all come over? It would be great if you could.'

'I think we're all a bit on the old side for travelling, Brian. This trip nearly did for me. But you'd never know. How is Fay?'

Brian's face darkened. 'We cabled but you had left. We buried her two days ago.'

'Poor whore,' Richard said, without the least irony.

A page-boy passed calling, 'Mr Richard Boss Croker to the check-in desk, please.'

Richard was pleased that a New York bellhop still called him 'Boss' and his step became lighter when he responded. A beautiful young woman was leaning against the desk. He could recognize her features but could not recall from where or when. She extended her slim, graceful arms and drew him to her.

'My darling!' she said, and Richard was embarrassed.

'You remember me, Richard? Bula!'

'Bula? I don't –'

'Bula Edmondson! I performed for you after the launch of the *Henry Clay II*. Well, I only danced, really.' She smiled, a dazzling lantern of white in dusky flesh.

'Oh Jaysus, the young Indian one that sang "The Star-Spangled Banner" in Cherokee!'

'I sang it in Irish for you later.'

'And you dancing a hornpipe at the same time! Indeed and I do remember. Well, well! Isn't it a small world?'

'We kissed too. Remember? Like this.' He wondered if he was really seventy-three years old. Embarrassed, he began muttering coarsely about his old totem pole.

Bula took Richard's hand and led him to a small, concealed alcove off the foyer that had a lone settee. She sat him down and began kissing him more vigorously. Looking in his eyes then, she told him how she had been forever admiring him and his methods when he was Boss at Tammany.

'I read every report and studied every election result. I so love a man to be decisive and vigorous,' she said as her delicate fingers trailed down his shirtfront to rest gently on his thigh tantalizing him with their straying caresses. Then she giggled and started tickling him under the chin.

Richard stared at her, bewildered. Holding his rugged jaws in both hands and fixing her sultry eyes on his, she told him huskily, 'You are a real man, Boss Croker.' Her final words spilled into his gaping mouth, to which she gave her undivided attention.

When he had been missing for about forty minutes, Brian became a little concerned. Richard Junior and his sister Ethel were worried too. They decided to investigate. The receptionist told them that a young woman had made the paging call and that she seemed to have been a close friend of the elderly man who responded.

Brian remembered mentioning to Barbara that he was arranging to meet Richard, and he began thinking she might have discovered where they were; she was still able to make herself up to look astonishingly youthful. The Crokers were less worried about the caller than about their father's health. His rheumatic pains had got worse and they had noticed a significant deterioration in his physical condition since they had all been together in Palm Beach, the previous spring. Doctors had told them that his condition could lead to chronic heart disease. So they were more than a little astonished when they rounded a corner and discovered Bula, urging their father along as if she were astride one of her Cherokee tribe's war steeds.

And when Bula spotted them, she knew that Richard's children would remember this encounter for a long time and would use it if the plan she had begun forming the night of the launching of the *Henry Clay II* appeared to be succeeding.

For that reason especially, she decided to act fast.

THIRTY-TWO

BULA EDMONDSON had guessed correctly that Richard would respond to her advances. She'd done her research well, estimating her position in true Indian fashion and coming up with a course of action. She needed money to finance her passion for preserving Indian culture. Ideas for museums and places of learning, libraries and repositories, all devoted to her subject, kept jostling among her plans. If Richard's wealth and generosity could bring even some of them to fruition, it would give her great satisfaction. Judging by the way he had enjoyed himself the evening he launched Butch's boat, he too would get pleasure from his largesse, she surmised.

The plan was proceeding well. Perhaps too well, because she found herself drawn to Richard in a way she'd not expected. As if a call from some of her ancestors was willing her to give him some solace in his late and lonely years. And she felt attracted to his unpolished ways that seemed to come from the earth, like many of her Indian emotions. She chose a good time to make her move – a time when Richard was disturbed; when he was brooding over an unhappy marriage and enduring difficult discussions with his children, a period in which he was regretting that physical joy was probably unattainable. She had no trouble persuading him that a spell of reflection with her in his Palm Beach home, absorbing her Indian methods of dealing with age and loss, would be comforting.

'The old territory of the Jeaga and Tequesta Indians will be bracing for us both,' she assured him.

On the journey south Richard pondered the likelihood that Bula was after his money, but by the time they arrived at The Wigwam, he was not concerned. Here was a remarkable young woman; beautiful and exciting, showing an interest and opening up new horizons for him. Why else would a man of his age be sitting calmly in Palm Beach, listening to her crooning voice tell so many stories of her beloved Cherokee race?

The sun was sinking behind the clapboard out-office and he watched it through the French window of his living-room. He was relaxing in the couch with its huge velvet cushions that Bula had propped behind his back. She was kneeling beside him, stroking the back of his neck. Although enjoying it immensely, he wished he was years younger.

She was telling him some of her tribe's folklore and lulling him into satisfied peacefulness by the soothing tone of her narration.

'The chief Sequoyah was an ancestor of mine,' she claimed. 'He spent hours working on documents about the Cherokee tribe. One day, he left his wife Utoyu to go hunting and she seized the opportunity to terminate her husband's mad fancy that had been taking up time he should have been devoting to her. She took the parchments from a hollowed out log – yellowing scraps, all scrawls and diagrams – spat on them and threw them into the flames. She did not realize that she'd destroyed twelve years of mental torture and that the original version of the Cherokee alphabet was burned.'

'Papooses couldn't learn their ABC any more,' Richard chuckled.

'But that act meant that an Indian squaw would never again be jealous,' Bula laughed, nudging Richard playfully.

'Well, to continue my story – Sequoyah was devastated when he returned and learned what had happened. And Utoyu was quite furious next day, when he started compiling and note-taking even more diligently than before. Within twelve months he had the alphabet reconstructed. But by that time, Utoyu had had enough; she had left and had gone in search of another husband.'

'Be the hokey!'

Was Richard's comment a response to her story or to what she was doing just then, Bula wondered.

'The alphabet does not represent letters and phonetics but divisions of syllables.'

'Cripes, girl, you're making it sound very hard to talk.'

'Sequoyah wrote its first word on a slab of stone. It was *tasa-qui-li.*'

'*Tasa-qui-li,* be Janey! What does that mean?'

'It means a horse, Richard and the second word means a cow; it's *wa-ku.*'

'Well, fair play to the man. Putting a horse first was good thinking. Then a cow! Meat! Not a bad one for second place, at all. I suppose he put a woman third!'

Bula smiled and Richard was pleased that she liked his joke.

'I used that alphabet in my Oklahoma school of Tahlequah, Richard,' she said proudly. 'There, I gave music recitals and lectured on Cherokees, their dress and traditions.'

'What's this you told me your original name was?'

'Keetaw Kaiantuckt.'

'Not many of them around Sandyford.'

Richard was rocking in his chair. The sun had disappeared but its red glow was still pencilling edges on wisps of cloud to the west. A great wave of contentment was palpable, and Bula felt a part of it. She began singing softly:

> O'er Sequoyah's lonely grave
> The tall oaks their branches wave
> Not e'en a stone to mark the place
> Where rests the Cadmus of his race.

She thought he was asleep, but he whispered, 'You really love your Cherokee tribe, don't you, Bula?'

'Almost as much as I love you, Daddy.'

'Don't call me that, Bula. Please.'

'But I want you to mind me. Like a Daddy, Richard. And I want my Daddy to bring me looking for pirates' treasure.'

'I have all the treasure I want in you, my little Indian princess, and in what Tammany – another Indian, remember – made for me.'

Richard listened to her with a dubious expression as she told of a Miracle Strip and pirate treasure in the area around Choctawhatchee Bay on the other side of Florida.

'Richard, I believe I have a map that shows the spot. I have used it before and failed to find anything but I would like to try again. Tradition tells that hunting treasure should take place when you are in love. I was not in love when I searched previously.'

Richard believed she was in the land of the fairies but he liked hearing her say that she was in love. Nor could he resist her appealing eyes when she asked him to bring her across the isthmus to search for the treasure next day.

Driving across the state in its seductive sunshine, Bula told him about a particular treasure trove buried by a pirate named Billy Bowlegs, and Richard said it would be a good name for himself, now that he was walking with a bit of a wobble. She opened up a large chart.

'Cripes, woman, I'm trying to drive the car,' he protested as she poked the heavy-smelling parchment under his nose.

'Phew! That stinks like a goat's groin. Put it away.'

She did not. She was certain that they were going to find treasure. Now that she was in love!

'I think you're a dingbat, do you know that?' Richard grinned, but she ignored him.

She prattled away about huge amounts of gold and silver ingots from Mexican and Peruvian mines; about a chest of minted coins – all part of Bowlegs' booty. 'Seventy million dollars worth, Richard! And jewels!'

'I'd prefer mine in real estate, Bula, but I admire your faith.'

By the time they reached their destination at Fort Walton Beach, it was late afternoon. Richard wanted to book into a hotel and begin the search in the morning but she insisted that dying sunlight on a calm evening was an ideal environment for the senses to sniff out buried treasure.

'Jaysus, wouldn't a dog be better, Bula,' he said sarcastically but she did not notice. She directed him from a map to a place called Elliott's Point, where she said Bowlegs had lived.

'The door of his wattle shack faced into the setting sun and he could see where his treasure was buried,' she said.

'So, all we have to do is find the site of an eighteenth-century shack and walk as far into the sunset as a pirate's eye can see. Didn't them fellows have big long telescopes? It could be on any one of them other islands out there.'

'No, Daddy! It's on this one. It's exactly as it appeared in my dream.'

'You dreamt all this! Jaysus Bula, you make me drive you over here to see if a dream can come true!'

'No, Richard, no! I have the spot clearly marked, but I dreamt about it too. On midsummer day, when Indians are close to Mother Earth and she divulges her secrets.'

'Like where she has an old ulcer caused by lumps of gold in among her gallstones!'

'Ah, Daddy. Please be serious.'

'One more *Daddy* out of you and I'm going back to Palm Beach.'

'All right – Daddy!' She laughed and ran along the shore splashing up water and drenching herself until he could see the outline of her body. He tried to trot after her but soon realized that he was too old. When she came back to him he could see her flesh through the wet clothes and he cursed his age. They reached the copse and she sat on a sandy dune. She explained that if she could find trees with brass markers hammered into them, they would lead her to the treasure.

'I have found eight of the trees on previous searches. The brass markers had disappeared inside the bark, of course, but their outline remained. If I could only find the other two!'

Richard stayed in the car reading a newspaper while Bula searched for her last two trees. He reflected on her youthful passion the previous night and of how frustrated it had made him. Would such an age gap bring more torment than happiness? Was it worth incurring the wrath of his family?

The sun beat down and he adjusted his Panama hat to ward off its rays.

The sea and sand were shimmering when Bula appeared through the heat-mist, all dark and beautiful. When she came closer, he could see that she was dejected.

'I found where the chart says they were. The measurements were so accurate! But they have been cut down.'

'Stumped, girl!' Immediately, he was annoyed with himself for making the pun, so he put his arm around her. 'Come on and we'll go home, child!'

Bula was far from stumped in her true ambition. She allowed him to cheer her up in a thousand ways and responded in a million others. Few of them were old Indian customs but they worked as well. In Palm Beach that evening, Richard Boss Croker proposed to Princess Keetaw Kaiantuckt Sequoyah, alias Bula Edmonston.

Not one of his family attended the wedding that Brian arranged in the home of a wealthy friend and supporter, Nathan Straus, former State Senator and proprietor of the celebrated Macy's store. Straus was also a best man. Richard had asked Brian to be the leading best man but he had said it would be more beneficial to invite the current Secretary of Tammany Hall, Thomas F. Smith, to do the honours. Another Tammany personality and businessman, Andrew Freedman, was groomsman. On the way into the house, reporters asked Richard if his bride would continue to work on behalf of Indians.

'If she does, it will be by herself,' he answered gruffly.

'You're not interested in Indians, then, Mr Croker?'

'I'm interested in Bula and I like hearing about the others,' he said.

In the beautifully decorated grand ballroom, where the ceremony took place, Richard was stunned when Bula appeared, her hair arranged in an Indian style and her lithe body wrapped in her tribe's silk.

'I have been inspired by the example of Pocahontas, who did so much to make the white man understand our race,' she whispered and he joked that he had no trouble understanding her at all. Which was more or less a lie. Most times he could not make head nor tail of her.

Afterwards, she was in her element talking to reporters.

'The "Indian Bird Woman", who piloted the Lewis and Clark expedition guided me in choosing Richard. She and Talahina, the Cherokee maiden who helped Sam Houston to free Texas.'

Flamboyantly, she tossed her bouquet to them on leaving and said, 'It is the dearest ambition of every Indian girl to win a chief and I have won the chief of men.'

THIRTY-THREE

WHAT WILL THE BOSS do for his young squaw?' a customer at the Gallops Bar in Sandyford asked. Nobody ventured to reply, and all guffawed when he spluttered, 'He'll keep her little wig wa'm!'

Word about 'The Indian Princess' had reached Glencairn long before Richard stepped off the White Star liner at Queenstown, formerly Cove, with his exotic young bride. He'd arranged for his chauffeur to collect them.

'I'm only twenty-three,' Bula teased, when he asked if she would like to visit the place where he was born.

'What has that to do with it?' Richard asked, puzzled.

'The spirits of your forefathers might object.'

'Not half as much as some of the smart set around Glencairn, when they see you arriving,' Richard laughed. 'Come on!'

They went to Balliva. Richard knocked on the door of the house, but there was no answer. He took Bula's hand and they went strolling through the orchard. They looked down on a stretch of clear blue sea, towards which the low green hills of land once farmed by his father funnelled. Skirting the orchard, they began walking through meadows. After leaving the shelter of the gentle hills, they arrived at the Red Strand. Richard was tired, so they stretched on a patch of rough grass overhanging the shore. Bula tried kissing him gently first, then tantalizingly. She took off her Persian paw coat and flat felt hat with its weave of miniature pearls. He watched her black satin dress flashing the lines of her limbs. With narrowed eyes, he peered a little suspiciously. She wondered was it because of the sinking sun or because of what she was saying.

'I love you dearly, Daddy. And your father approves. I see him and some older military man on the craggy cliff yonder, each nodding approval.'

'Jaysus, are you a brick short in the hod?' Richard laughed nervously.

An old man then passed by and Richard wondered could he be Peter

271

O'Donovan, his childhood playmate. He considered asking him, but thought the better of it. 'No use raking up the past when we're moving on,' he muttered, pulling himself to his feet.

Continuing on to Quartertown, they viewed the mills there. After an overnight stop at Cashel, they visited its rock as a young morning's sun was whetting its rays off stone as old as time. Bula went clambering over walls, pressing her hands against the ancient structures and chanting words that Richard could not understand. It was crazy, he knew, but this young woman and her mysterious ways were exhilarating to an elderly man who had given all his adult life to the rough and tumble of New York politics. Bula was a daffy bird, he thought, but what harm when she was bringing some spright-liness to an old cock-sparrow? But Bula shuddered within that imposing ed-ifice as she received energies terrifying in their power.

It was late when they neared the narrow lanes skirting the Leopardstown foothills that would bring them home to the entrance of Glencairn. A lanky, red-faced woman emerged from the gate-lodge and admitted them. She looked as if she had been crying and was unsure about approaching. Richard opened the window of the car and tossed out a parcel as they passed.

'A present from America, Mrs Quinn,' he shouted after her.

Bula was unable to admire the turreted edifice that was to become her residence. Her premonitions were confirmed as the car pulled up alongside the massive front door and Nellie emerged. Her face was almost transpar-ent; her eyelids rested on its pallor like faded purple tulip petals, even to their yellow-green tapers. Here was profound grief, magnified in its projection against the cold opulence of Glencairn.

Richard was first out.

'It's Tim, Richard. An accident while he was out walking on Fern Hill. Shot dead by a grouse hunter. Oh, Dick!'

Nellie did not speak the words. They stole from a nightmare and loitered on the dulled twilight. Richard could not believe that the woman who had been so vibrant was, now, just an icon of an existence without further rea-son, a mere human diagram, drained of spirit. A stricken shadow on Glen-cairn's threshold, she extended a hand and welcomed the new Mistress. But only just, for Richard was wrapping her in a bulky embrace and crying on her shoulder.

Such tragedy on the day he brought his new bride to Glencairn was bru-tal and Richard buckled suddenly and noticeably. Bula tried to console him.

'I will tell you an Indian method for coping with sorrow, Richard. It will help you enormously.'

'Will you for God's sake have sense, child,' he snapped, resisting her con-dolences and sinking into despair.

They buried Tim O'Mahoney in Kilgobbin. Nellie continued grieving, and ten weeks later wept more after reading a letter of sympathy from Butch and Rosa Maguire. Brian had brought it over. It was his first visit.

Richard called his chauffeur and took them all to Kingstown. They had tea in the Pavilion and then lingered awhile, watching the bowlers padding canvassed white feet on lush greens. Hand in hand, the four began walking down the pier. Groups of khaki-clad soldiers with kitbags were hanging around waiting for troopships to carry them away to the Great War that was developing in Europe.

Brian and Bula were shocked at how quickly Richard and Nellie tired. Richard invited them to a fine meal in the Royal Marine Hotel, but Brian noticed that Bula signed the cheque for payment.

———

'Richard has given us the use of it for the day,' Nellie told Brian when they were getting into the car the next morning.

'Bring us to Glencullen church, please, Joe,' she asked the chauffeur. 'We will walk the Stations of the Cross. For Tim's soul,' she whispered to Brian.

When they did, they dwelt a while at the tenth station, praying for the man who was its donor; the ageing colossus who had been so much a part of their lives.

Then they drove as far as they could along the lane that led to The Scalp. They stopped, and Nellie pointed to a rock half-way to its summit. 'That's the rock of heaven,' she said and Brian knew by her eyes and by the gentle pressure on his hand that he should not question her. They stood there looking up. Allowing the silence to wash their souls.

'And what's your wife like, Brian?' Nellie asked.

'You'd like her, Mother.'

'I'm sure I would, son. How long are you married now?'

'I was hitched a couple of months after you left for Ireland. I didn't want to drag you back on another long sea journey so soon.'

'I wouldn't have gone. I was shipwrecked the first time I went that direction.'

They watched a hawk hovering overhead, its wings purring. Brian wondered why his mother was not questioning him more. She always liked knowing about everything he did. The hawk was diving on its prey when she spoke softly:

'You left it late in life, like myself.'

'The Hurleys must be slow movers, Ma.'

'Well, I suppose it took a fine woman like Barbara to make you move.'

'Mother! You knew! Did Dick tell you?'

'Indeed and he didn't. Your own eyes told me. Long before I left New York.'

'And I not saying a word, thinking you would not approve.'

'Not approve? Of Barbara? She may have been running a concert saloon but it's what a woman holds inside that counts and Barbara binds herself around nothing but the best.'

'You're right about that, Mother. Behind all her brashness, she's a jewel.'

'Well, now I can pass away in peace, knowing my son has a good woman.' Nellie breathed a sigh of contentment.

'Barbara's place is very plush and stylish now. We are joint proprietors.'

'Be joint proprietors of your love too, son. Take care of her and she will keep you a good man.'

Before they got back into the car they sat on a boulder holding hands, looking into each other's eyes. A score of incidents and a hundred memories dwelt in the contact, not one recalling anything but love and consideration, for each other and for friends that they cherished.

The chauffeur had to cough nervously to remind them that the evening was drawing in fast. Before they took heed, Nellie whispered to the stillness, 'God rest your soul, Tim.'

As they were winding back down the narrow road, Brian was studying her. He had noticed her decline since Tim's death, but now it had suddenly become startling. It was almost as if she had left the will to live back there in the foothills near The Scalp. His heart pitched, then melted when she said, 'I'm like the autumn leaves on the old chestnut tree behind the barn in Balliva.' He hugged her tenderly.

When Richard visited her the next day he too noticed, with horror, that a change had taken place. Shuddering a hand free from beneath the bedclothes, she took his and whispered, 'You have lived to a great age too, Richard. At least I beat off the curse of the guinea-fowl.'

He thought she was rambling until she began to talk of the past. They chatted gently for about an hour. About New York, about Tammany Hall, about Fay and Rosa and about Brian. Mostly about Brian. He pleased her when he said, 'Nellie Hurley, my father was a blackguard, but he gave you one hell of a son and gave me a bloody great half-brother and friend.'

'A strange bunch, the Crokers.'

'Strange, but worth knowing. Most of them.' She was trying to smile, but it was more a crinkling of white paper.

Eyes deeply sunk in nothing saw Richard wavering and becoming a small child in a bright green field, clutching the rim of her milking pail. The bucket was filling up and he was tottering to the bank. Now the imp was coming back to her, with a posy of cowslips and primroses. Giggling, he was offering them to her, 'For you, because I love Nellie.'

Small feet running on ahead. Not to the house, but to the Red Strand. Walking into the waves and beckoning her.

'Come on, Nellie. It's lovely.'

Nellie was leaving down the bucket and following him. The water was warm and soothing and, as she moved forward and it was becoming deeper, the boy began to grow. Just like the waves, that suddenly were becoming mountainous and lashing. Now the lad was a man, but tall, fair and handsome, and it was Tim's hand that reached from the swirling surf to touch hers. This time, they held. Fast.

Richard saw the frightening alteration of her features. Overcome with emotion, he could barely utter words that he knew were going to be his farewell.

'Thanks for all you done, Nellie.' He took a corner of the patchwork quilt and pulled it up around her breasts. 'Keep yourself warm, child. Let you be knowing that two men in your life – one good, one a codger – loved you. Loved you very much, Nellie.'

She wanted to wave to somebody she was leaving behind, but feared losing Tim's hand again.

Richard knew he must leave her then. To get to the house as fast as possible and ask Bula to help. He was holding the iron railings that stretched down from her door. Half way to the car, he stumbled and the chauffeur ran to catch him. Richard was trying to straighten up, but it was difficult. The chauffeur helped him into the car. He slumped into the seat and the chauffeur heard him muttering.

'Maybe you and Brian saved me from the guinea-fowl, Nellie. Maybe! Who's to tell? But you forgot to watch out for the buzzards.'

The day before Brian was to return to New York, Nellie died from a wretched, broken heart.

They buried her in Kilgobbin, too. Beside Tim.

'They'll enjoy theirselves, lying there together,' Richard whispered to Brian at the graveside, both men trying to hold back tears.

After Brian's return to New York, Richard withdrew to his oratory while Bula set about trying to lift his black depression.

'A house party would be a good idea, Richard.'

'A sort of advanced wake, woman?'

'You mustn't be so down in yourself, Richard. Your deceased friends can be there. I keep telling you that if you would only become interested in spiritualism and begin meditating with me, you could continue enjoying Nellie's company and Tim's wit.'

'Aye, and my aunt can have balls.'

'What does that mean, Richard?'

'Forget it.'

But he had the party.

Bula decorated the great staircase with Indian and Irish motifs and laid out tables, with dishes and drinks from both cultures. Michael Collins was among the guests. He brought his fiancée, Kitty Kiernan, and the two women got on well. Until Bula tried some gentle flirting with Collins and invited him into the library to show him some books on Indian culture.

'In Ireland, women look after their own men and Michael has enough half-baked Indians of his own to deal with, without studying the habits of real ones,' Kitty informed her. Collins went to the library later – with Richard. But the Boss told the Big Fellow that he refused even to consider joining a secret organization like the Irish Republican Brotherhood.

During the following week Richard and Bula attended the Dublin Horse Show. She had no comment to make on the agricultural displays in the grounds of Leinster House. The Royal Dublin Society was developing its jumping arena in Ballsbridge, so they went there. She watched some of the events but was critical of the standards.

'I could ride better than anybody in that ring. And bareback too.'

'Backways, singing 'Molly Malone',' Richard agreed.

A group of women from Sandyford saw her pass by and nodded.

'She dresses beautifully,' one said so that Bula would hear and be pleased. But as soon as she was out of earshot, they began to disparage her.

'She seems to be a perfect wife but she could be pulling the wool over everyone's eyes until you know what!'

'Until poor Boss dies and leaves her everything? I wouldn't be surprised.'

'I wonder why he brought that Nellie one over from New York.'

'And why she never appeared in the village until Francie was born.'

'Poor Francie! Or Frank as they prefer to call him. But Mrs Quinn is looking after him well in the gate-lodge.'

'Certainly that Bula lady doesn't seem to care much about him.'

'She might have her reasons.' There was a cackle of laughter.

Coincidentally, Frank was on Richard's mind when they got home that evening and were having an alfresco snack. They were sitting in the gazebo, looking over the lawn and nibbling sandwiches from a silver salver.

'You don't seem to be too fond of childer, Bula.' Richard took his young wife by surprise. She knew he was referring to little Frank and that he was right. The busybodies of her spirit world were whispering things to her. They were also encouraging her to move away from Glencairn.

'I said, you don't seem to be too fond of childer.'

'Oh, I'm sorry Daddy. I was deep in thought. Eh, I suppose it's because I want to give all my time to you.' Her argument was weak and both of them knew it. She tried to make light of the topic. 'Of course, if we had a child of our own, I'd get to love it.'

'Jaysus! Fat chance of that. You'd want to get that Sequoyah ancestor of yours to work a miracle.'

'I was thinking of you, Richard. It can happen with older men, you know. Especially among Indians.'

'You are an Indian, Bula, but I'm only a retired Tammany Hall Sachem. Maybe you should try that Collins fellow or some of our other handsome guests.'

Bula peered at him. She did not wish him to dwell on their age difference and above all she wanted him to be sure of her faithfulness. She might flirt mildly at parties but would never betray him. That night, she consulted her spirits and came to a conclusion. She would ask Richard to take her away for a long spell to Palm Beach.

He agreed and they spent much of the next four years there. She went on one more treasure hunt to Choctawhatchee Bay. Alone. Richard was finding it difficult to walk in the heat and, besides, he told her he had some business to do while she was away. Even before she came into the living-room that evening, he could smell her rose-scented perfume and cornflower corsage that so appealed to him.

'Well, is the dickie of the car weighed down with gold?'

'Not yet, Daddy. But I discovered the ninth tree.'

'What are you talking about? Didn't you find its stump the last time?' His mind was as agile as ever.

Then he grinned and said: 'There's an envelope for you in the hall.' She went out and he playfully crept to the door to listen. He heard the envelope tearing and the susurration of parchment. When she squealed in delight and ran in, his arms were open, awaiting her embrace.

'Oh, thank you; thank you; thank you, my love. The deeds of the land around Choctawhatchee Bay! Oh, you are so kind and thoughtful!' She kissed him all over and thanked him profusely again before he got a chance to speak.

'Now you can look for your treasure sometime in the future but spend the rest of my days with me.'

She was a little shocked and saddened and, when she kissed him again, it was not out of greed.

For Richard's sake only, she still accompanied him on a number of extended breaks in Glencairn. She disliked the place intensely and claimed that her spirits behaved badly there. Gradually, she prevailed on him to return to playing host to his old friends. She entertained effortlessly, making everyone feel at ease. After dinner, she would play the piano or sing in Cherokee, English or Irish as the mood demanded.

One cold February evening, Richard was reading a newspaper by the fire. Normally, he confined himself to the racing pages but he noticed something in the news section.

'Begod, I'll be doing no travelling to Europe for a while.' He began reading aloud, finding some words difficult to pronounce.

'It says here that the Germans have attacked Verdun and that it will force France into an a … ttrition … al, def … en … sive battle on the Somme that could last months.'

'Men! Wars! Will they never learn? I hope the comings and goings of those characters to your library have nothing to do with war. In the village, they tell me about some rising or other that may take place in the city.'

'I'm a bit on the grey side for fighting, Bula. My wars are of the heart.'

'That's almost poetic, Daddy.'

'There will be a right scrap if you don't stop that Daddy business. I'm telling you. But you're right. They are training for a fight. They practice up around Hell's Kitchen. Did you never hear the shots?'

'Hell's Kitchen? What a name! Where, or what, on earth is it?'

Richard had picked up a little local history from members of his staff and he was able to explain.

'The Hellfire Club used to meet there. Some fellow called Conolly, who was related to the Speaker of the Irish House of Commons, built a hunting lodge on Mount Pelier, above the way. When the builders were clearing the site they removed a cromlech – that's a sort of old Irish tombstone or memorial or something – and the pagan gods connected with it brought bad luck to anyone who lived in the house. It later became a centre of activities for Dublin's bucks.'

'Bucks?'

'Aye, wealthy young blades, like them bloody Frasers. Only these were up to all sorts of divilment and debauchery. One of them was a namesake of my own. Richard Chappell Whaley, a descendant of Oliver Cromwell. He was known as "Burn-Chapel" because he hated all religions, especially Catholicism. On Sundays, he would mount his horse and go skiting around the Dublin Mountains with a torch, lighting the thatch of churches.'

'But tell me more about this Hell's Kitchen, Daddy.'

'Shut up with your Daddy or I won't.'

'Richard, then. Please continue.'

'I don't know much more, except that they held orgies and everything there. And Black Masses, some says. They toasted Satan, saying, "Damnation to the Church and its prelates". One night they poured hot whiskey over a cat and set its fur alight. It lepped screaming through the window and ran flaming around the mountainside.'

'My, oh my! This is marvellous.' Bula's eyes were sparkling with delight. Relishing her enthusiasm, Richard embellished his story.

'Since that night, many's the time the old cat with its tail blazing has been seen darting through the furze and heather.'

Overjoyed by this information, Bula climbed Mount Pelier the following morning. She found the old ruin and placed her palms against its rugged stone.

'I feel evil here,' she whispered to the wind. Then, following the Indian custom of facing each cardinal point with eyes closed and hands outstretched, she began meditating. Occasionally, she would bend and place her hands on the earth. 'There is sombre energy here,' she told a furze bush.

When she returned to Glencairn, Richard was concerned about the change that had come about in her.

'What's up?'

'Oh, Richard! You were right about that Hell's Kitchen place. There is great iniquity up there.'

'There's what?'

'Badness. And it is about to spread across the countryside. It will begin at Easter. The fight of which you spoke will take place then. It will die down but executions will take place and the country will rise up. But the real evil will follow. Brother will fight brother and father will fight son.'

As she'd predicted, a rebellion began in Dublin on Easter Monday, 1916. When the British forces quelled it and executed its leaders, the country began sliding towards a people's war. Bula suspected that Richard was assisting Michael Collins in bringing arms from New York, and was confused by the fact that some Irishmen were fighting against British Crown forces at home, while others fought with them in the horrifying Great War.

Forces were gathering for a domestic war, too. Since their shock discovery on the day of their mother's funeral, the Croker children, Flossie excepted, grew increasingly angry. They considered Bula to be a gold-digger. They also suspected that their father was sending money, through this man Collins, to Clan na Gael in New York for the purchase of weapons. Quarrels were becoming frequent.

'Them crowd thinks of nothing but money,' Richard complained to Bula.

'Poor Daddy, are they annoying you?'

'And not one of them ever done a decent day's work to earn what I gave them.'

'Tut, tut! How awful. My poor dear!'

'I looked after them well, giving them valuable property and paying them for every bit of work they done for any of my businesses.'

'I suppose you cannot be too hard on them, Daddy. They are bound to be suspicious of my intentions.'

Bula did not add how obvious it was that the Croker children were furious at an attractive and vivacious young woman seducing an old man into acting rashly.

'Write to your eldest son, Daddy. Get everything off your chest and perhaps things will turn for the better.'

Richard took her advice. He wrote to his son, accusing him of not telling the truth about their business affairs in New York and of not handling other financial affairs as he had instructed.

'I am tired and bloody sick of this kind of thing,' he wrote.

THIRTY-FOUR

IN NOVEMBER 1917, while in Palm Beach, Richard conveyed The Wigwam and his entire estate there to Bula. Richard Junior was furious. In his home on East Forty-fifth Street, he began studying notes and documents that he had collected during visits to State archives and municipal records offices. Armed with what he considered evidence, he eventually travelled to Palm Beach and confronted his father.

'Your new wife is sucking you for all she's worth, Father.'

'Your stepmother.'

'You might care to know she is still lawfully married to another man.'

'You muck-raker. You were never any good for anything but rooting out scandal.' Richard Senior's face reddened and his neck bulged.

'Here's the evidence.' Richard Junior thrust a document at his father, who snatched it and tore it in flitters.

'That's okay, Dad, I have plenty more copies.'

'I'll bet you have.'

'They all say that Bula lived as a lawful wife with a man called Guy Marone at Northampton in Massachussets and at Moncton, New Brunwick.'

'If you don't show some respect to me and your stepmother, Richard, I will take everything off you. The warehouses, stocks, shares – the lot. You'll be finished and it will serve you right.'

'And if you as much as try to do that, Father, I will drag you through every court in this land. You are a simple old man who has been taken for a ride by a tart. Indian princess, indeed! She has as much royal blood in her as a Tennessee turnip.'

Richard Junior stomped out of the room, slamming the door behind him. His father heard the front door banging too. Overcome with fury, he began to stagger and grabbed at an oak dining-table for support. His fingernails whitened as his hand began slipping towards a finely-tasselled damask centrepiece. His eyes were burning; his brain pounding and his hand kept sliding. The room's rich furnishings, sculptures and paintings swept around in a crimson pond and his legs weakened into raffia. Years of fighting for survival must have taken control as he tried to prevent himself from falling by digging his nails deeper. But they were only scratching and dragging and, when he collapsed, they pulled away the centrepiece and its fine Waterford Crystal vase tumbled to the edge before smashing close to Richard's head. He crawled on all fours to the French window that opened onto the front drive, scowling thunderously at his son, who was opening his automobile door. Like one of the heavy-set bulldogs he admired so much, the old, shattered father barked his banishment.

'Consider it done. Nothing, will I leave you! Not a goddamn cent!'

'Just you try it and I'll tell the world the great Boss God-almighty Croker was duped by a scheming slut.'

A clunk of slamming metal drowned the Boss's parting shot.

'May the hair of your fat arse turn into drumsticks and beat the shit out of you, you cur! Go, and don't ever come back here. She is the only person who ever done anything for me and only her and Flossie care a damn about me, you ungrateful whelp.'

A son roared his car engine to life, scattering gravel and an old man's dignity.

A broken father took a silk handkerchief from his jacket and wept unfulfilled dreams into it.

He dragged himself from The Wigwam and walked slowly to his rock-perch on his beloved beach. Every wave that broke seemed to carry part of him away in its ebb. He thought of how his filial relationship with Eyre had developed in adulthood, of advice and encouragement exchanged in difficult times. He did not wish to die bearing animosity towards his son, but screaming gulls and flirting beach birds were telling him what to do. His step was sprightlier when he returned to his house and began drafting a letter to his lawyer. A few months later, they had arranged conveyance and transfer to Bula of all Richard's estate and interest in the house and lands at Glencairn and surrounds. The following August, they transferred the furniture, fittings, plate, horses and stock to her. The couple began living on a modest current bank account.

Richard Junior disputed his father's ownership of the remaining property, including the valuable warehouse concern in New York City. When he suggested litigation, Ethel, settled as Mrs White in Long Island, agreed with her brother, but Florence wanted no part in it.

Richard was back in Glencairn in 1918, when Orby died and received an equestrian state funeral. Stable lads loaded the animal's corpse onto a low cart and covered it with a blanket on which was embroidered the horse's name and the legends, 'Triple Derby Winner', 'Baldoyle', 'Epsom' and 'Curragh'; laurel wreaths lay alongside and black ribbons fluttered from the shafts of the cart. An old bridle and saddle rested beside the corpse.

Richard dressed in his formal attire and led a cortege from the stable yard. The complete staff and a number of villagers walked behind. They circled the grounds before arriving to where a grave was opened beside Rhoda B.'s. The strongest men lowered Orby with ropes and Richard addressed those present.

'We all came to love Orby and during his time in Glencairn he gave us all a great old run for our money, every time we brought him onto the track. He will always be remembered as the first Irish nag that won the Epsom Derby and showed them stuck-up English trainers, jockeys and breeders that Irish horseflesh is as good as you'll get.'

He took a cornflower corsage from his lapel and tossed it into the grave.

'That St Peter may mount you and win a Derby against Beelzebub, old friend.' A nod to the gravediggers and they began filling in the clay.

'Let yez all come back to the American Bar and drink the poor old bugger's health.' His Irish bull escaped Richard, but nobody escaped his hospitality as evening wore into night. Next day the Sandyford mason was called again to rebuild the surround and add the granite slab that said simply, 'Orby'.

At the eleventh hour of the eleventh day of the eleventh month in 1918, an armistice marked the termination of the Great War. Croker family hostilities continued, however, and eleven months later Boss Croker signed a one-page document, written in his own hand. A Grafton Street solicitor and a friend in Monkstown witnessed it. It revoked all previous wills, left everything to Bula and made her executor.

In the name of Richard's son, Howard, the children challenged his legal right to transfer power of attorney to Bula.

The two Richards had not met since the bitter row at The Wigwam. They avoided eye-contact when the trial opened in Palm Beach on 18 May. Every deposition given by either side hurt Richard more than the fists of Oweney Geoghegan long ago.

'Family feuds is woeful,' he told Bula when he arrived home to The Wigwam, a drained and unsteady wreck. She wrapped him in a warm embrace.

'Don't worry, Daddy – I mean Richard.' Her amendment was wise. The poor man had enough torment in his heart.

She led him to the dining-room and served him a sumptuous meal that she had spent the day preparing. Although disappointed when he merely nibbled at it, she went to the back of his chair, put her arms around him and kissed the nape of his neck. Into grey bristles she whispered, 'You do not have to go through this for me, my love.' Did she know that her words would reinforce his determination?

After three days there were no more lavish meals. Richard's assets were frozen for the duration of the trial and he and Bula were forced to live frugally. The trial dragged on and became a punishing experience for the old man.

Bula dressed in her Indian regalia for the final day on 10 June. On their way to the courthouse she clung to Richard's arm and whispered, 'I stole from our bed and went to the beach last night. The full moon was making my spirits extremely responsive. They told me that you will win the case.'

To his surprise, Richard was encouraged by her words. She was full of joy when he laughed for the first time in weeks and said, 'Begod, I turned the few coins I had in my pocket when I saw the full moon last night. Between Irish *piseógs* and Indian spirits, I feel like a leprechaun in a feathered hat. Come on, child, and we'll get this over with.'

Their giggling before proceedings began infuriated Richard Junior. He looked at his father for the first time during the trial, with black animosity. And as if it were at Sarah Donnelly in Balliva, Boss Croker impishly stuck out his tongue at his son. He whispered to Bula, 'Jaysus, them spirits of yours is better nor bourbon.'

They stood for the judge's arrival. Bula squeezed his hand.

'I find in favour of Richard Croker Senior, on all counts.'

There were gasps from Richard's children and their legal team, and the Clerk of the Court had to chastise Richard Senior when he called to the departing judge, 'Me auld sagosha!'

Outside the courtroom, Bula hugged him and kissed him hard on the mouth. 'Let's go and celebrate,' she invited.

'How the hell can we? Do you know how much money the billionaire Boss Croker has on him?'

'How much?'

'Two bucks and five nickles.'

She snuggled her head to his. 'There are other ways of celebrating.'

After attempting to right his financial affairs, Richard and Bula returned to Glencairn. It was 1920. On the morning after their arrival, Bula climbed to Hell's Kitchen and repeated her ritual. The furze bush had no blossom when she told it the worst evil was to befall the country still.

'And two giants of men will fall in the same year,' she whispered.

Richard became weak and more melancholy. Yet he still directed what charitable bequests should be made and he arranged services for his dead sons. He began compiling instructions about his own funeral arrangements and organizing the building of a mausoleum near the artificial lake to receive his remains. When it was completed, he drove down on his sulky and supervised the work of sinking a metal casket into the granite tomb.

'It must have a small glass window at the head, so that I can view your embalmed body,' Bula instructed.

'I'll be a grand-looking sight,' Richard mumbled.

Every day, he attended morning Mass and Evening Devotions in his oratory.

He settled $250,000 on Bula for the upkeep of Glencairn during her lifetime and called her into the library one day and gave her a sealed envelope. 'For Flossie,' he said. 'A draft for $10,000 when my assets are realized. It is a sad thing that an old man must die loving only one daughter and two dead sons.'

'But don't you love me too, Daddy?'

He peered at her disturbingly. Then he leaned his left hand on the sideboard, stooped and drew out a sherry bottle.

'I was never a man for the booze, Bula, but I want to drink to your health and to my death.'

After pouring two glasses, he handed one to his wife and stood erect. The amber liquid began swirling in his shaking hand as it raised the glass.

'Richard, why are you looking at me like that? Please, stop.'

'A final toast to us, my love! I done things my own auld way and if the next world is half as good, I'll be happy evermore.'

'It will be good, Richard.'

A bent, frail man took a sip, held the glass high again and echoed the words of an ancestor.

'I doubt it,' said Croker.

The same evening, Richard struggled to the stable-yard, dragged himself up on his sulky and allowed old Dobbins to amble slowly to the main gate of Glencairn. Whenever a wheel slipped into a rut and jerked him, he winced. Only his doctor and he fully realized the extent of his ailments. As well as the admitted rheumatic fever, he was suffering from jaundice, gallstones and valvular disease of the heart. A long life filled with stress and tough political and family battles had worn him down. Where once it jutted challengingly, his jaw now sagged. It took him some time to dismount and deliver an envelope to Mrs Quinn with the words, 'Do an old man a favour, Missus. Keep this safe and don't let anyone open it until after I snuff it.'

Mrs Quinn looked after him as he returned along the drive. The last few leaves of the beeches and chestnuts were dropping slowly. One or two landed on his stooped shoulders. He looked so frail that she began thinking how they might almost hurt him. She went inside and lifted a floorboard near the window. She drew out a square Oxo tin and placed the envelope inside with a few dog-eared, yellowed documents. Replacing the lid, she lowered her hand and returned her personal safe to its hiding place.

Next day, Bula called the doctor. Richard had a fever. The doctor ordered him to bed and, after a week of occasional raving, semi-consciousness, loud laughing and wretched sobbing, he received the rites of the Roman Catholic Church and died on 29 April 1922.

Bula regretted his not allowing her to hold a Cherokee ritual at his sickbed. A Sandyford farmer who kept guinea-fowl wondered why they were kicking up such a dreadful row.

A truce in the Irish War of Independence had came into effect on 11 July 1921. After long negotiations, a Treaty was signed on 6 December. Atrocities against nationalists began in Northern Ireland and Michael Collins protested to Sir James Craig, its first Prime Minister. Collins also learned that anti-Treaty activists had robbed £750,000 from branches of the Bank of Ireland. He told Arthur Griffith that civil war was a real possibility.

'I am meeting Dev today and can't go to Boss Croker's funeral. Will you give the wife my sympathies and tell her the Boss was a generous man?'

'I will,' Griffith answered and began to walk away. Then he turned and added, 'Hey Mick! Maybe we should have practised some of Croker's "Honest Graft".'

'There will come plenty after us who will be doing that,' Collins growled.

Francie was busy sticking a buff oval label bearing the proprietor's name on each bottle of Guinness, stacking the shelves and attending to fires in the bar at The Gallops.

He completed the work quickly, because he was in a hurry. After finally dusting away a fog of ashes that had lodged on the counter, he ran home to Glencairn's gate-lodge, got into his best Sunday suit and set off with Mrs Quinn.

Arthur Griffith and Oliver St John Gogarty attended. Richard had given them cash, contacts and encouragement when they were needed. The least they could do was to make an appearance and help carry the coffin.

Gogarty told Bula that, after James Joyce, Croker was the best company he had ever enjoyed. 'Without a drink in his hand,' he said, 'he could light up a party and you always felt you were living on the edge of danger; that he was liable to cut loose and shock or insult someone at any minute. He rescued many a dull evening for me by doing just that and there are bores and snobs in this city that never got their comeuppance until Boss Croker came to Glencairn.'

When Griffith conveyed Collins's condolences to Bula, she stared at him strangely.

'The first great man has fallen,' she whispered.

Griffith and Gogarty helped lower the open coffin into the crypt. The corpse was dressed in evening clothes. When they placed the windowed lid on it, they saw it was covered in fresh violets. A tiny card said, 'To Daddy, from Bula'.

Francie broke away from Mrs Quinn and laid a posy of cornflowers under the nameplate that read Richard 'Boss' Croker 1841–1922.

EPILOGUE

I T WAS EARLY EVENING and The Gallops Bar had only two customers. The barman had slipped into the kitchen for a cup of tea.

'The British ambassador's wife said in the *Herald* that the place is an arc ... an arc –'

'Architectural?'

'The very thing; an architectural eyesore.'

'Glencairn?'

'Yes.'

'The cheek of her.'

'"A cross between a castle and a villa but amounting to neither," she said.'

'And isn't that good enough for her? What more does she want?'

'I wonder what ever became of the Boss's childer.'

'Didn't young Richard help Aubrey Brabazon with the horses?'

'Bedad, but I think you're right.'

'He did. Somewhere up in Meath first and then on the Curragh.'

'Jaysus, wasn't Aubrey a great jockey?'

'I hear Richard Junior took the court case shockin' bad.'

'Ah, sure, why wouldn't he? That Bula one got everything.'

'God it went on for days in the papers.'

'Eleven of them. And all that dirty linen washed in public! '

'They said that she was already married to a fellow called Guy Marone who was still living in Canada or somewhere.'

'Sure I have the bit of the paper here. It says that the auld Boss was ... wait till I see ... that he was "fascinated by as young, attractive and clever a woman as had ever appeared in any court. The result was that he lost control of his affairs and although the hand that wrote the will was the hand of Croker, the real hand and voice were those of Bula Edmondson".'

'When the poor auld Boss was gone, she started saying he was giving her instructions from the grave. She was supposed to offer the place in Florida to Tammany Hall because his spirit instructed her.'

'Jaysus, did ye ever hear such balderdash?'

'No. Will we have one more?'

'I think we've had enough.'

'Francie is doing powerful well at the business.'

'I wonder where he got the money to start it.'

'Oh, I heard it wasn't a teddy-bear that was in the box under the floorboards.'

'Dollars or cash?'

'Maybe old Mrs Quinn left it to him.'

' "I doubt it," said Croker!'

They nudged each other.

'Just one more, so.'

BOSS CROKER CHRONOLOGY

1626	Tradition states that Delaware chief (Saint) Tammany sells Manhattan to the Dutch for $24 (see 1682, below).
c. 1640	Branches of the Devon Crokers spread to Raleighstown and Ballinagarde, Co. Limerick, and to Quartertown, Mallow, Co. Cork.
1682	Tradition states that Tammany sells Philadelphia to the English.
1789	The Society of Saint Tammany emerges in New York. The building in which they meet is called Tammany Hall. The Society's dinner toast is 'May the industry of the Beaver, the frugality of the Ant and the constancy of the Dove perpetually distinguish the Sons of Saint Tammany.'
1800	Eyre Coote Croker, fifth son of Major Henry Croker, Quartertown, Mallow, Co. Cork, Ireland, is born on 1 May.
1827	Eyre Coote Croker marries Frances, fourth daughter of John Welste(a)d, Ballywalter, Co. Cork.
1832	On 21 January, Eyre Coote Croker purchases a house and 69 acres at Balliva, on the road from Clonakilty, Co. Cork, to the Red Strand.
1841	Richard Croker is born at Balliva on 23 November.
1845–52	Great Irish Famine.
1846	Croker family emigrates to the USA on board the *Henry Clay*. They move from New York to Cincinnati, Ohio. Eyre Coote Croker is employed in veterinary medicine.
1848	Eyre Coote Croker's property at Balliva is sold to Hugh Smith Barry on 27 June.
1852	The Crokers move back to the Third Avenue, Twenty-third Street district of Manhattan. Richard Croker goes to school and becomes a 'Late Monitor'. He fights a youth named Patrick Kelly in a liquor saloon; Kelly loses an ear.

1853	Richard changes to the Lafayette Olney Grammar School, East Twenty-seventh Street. He fights and seriously injures a professional prizefighter, Dick Lynch.
1857	Richard leaves school, becoming a machinist in Harlem where, allegedly, he builds a locomotive.
1858	Richard engages in politics, joins Tammany Hall and soon becomes an alderman.
1860	Richard takes over the leadership of the 'Fourth Avenue Tunnel' gang.
1861–65	American Civil War.
1863	Draft riots in New York.
1864	Richard works for Tammany Hall on Election Day. He votes for the first time.
1865	Richard votes seventeen times for William H. Lyman, Democratic candidate for Constable in Greenpoint.
1868	Impeachment, trial and acquittal of President Andrew Johnson (1808-75). Croker's gang seriously injures Christopher Pullman, a Republican activist.
1871	'Honest' John Kelly replaces the notorious William Marcy Tweed as 'Boss' of Tammany Hall. Richard Croker is his willing lieutenant. Mayor Havemeyer appoints Richard a city marshal.
1873	Richard converts to Catholicism in order to marry Elizabeth Fraser on 1 November. 'Honest' John Kelly appoints Richard City Coroner.
1874	Election Day row. Richard is involved in a shooting incident in which a man is killed. He is charged with the murder of an anti-Kelly, pro-John O'Brien supporter named McKenna. Richard is arrested and denies involvement saying, 'I never carried a pistol in my life and never will as long as I can use my fists.' $2,500 bail is posted but he is later taken into custody and lodged in The Tombs to await trial. A jury of six Democrats and six Republicans divides six-six and he is acquitted. Allegedly, a friend, George Hickey, was in court ready to confess guilt had Richard been convicted. Many commentators suggest Hickey was the guilty party.
1874–79	While Richard takes a back seat in public affairs, the 'martyrdom' of his trial enhances his position in Tammany Hall.
1876	America celebrates 100 years of Independence.
1878	William Marcy Boss Tweed (1823-78) of the notorious 'Tweed Ring' in Tammany Hall dies after two years in Ludlow St Jail.
1879	Richard is re-appointed for a second term as Coroner.

1883	To test public reaction, Kelly nominates Richard for alderman. Elected, he does not assume office because Mayor Edson then appoints him Fire Commissioner of New York.
1885	'Honest' John Kelly dies. Richard moves into his office.
1886	Richard succeeds 'Honest' John Kelly as Tammany leader. He is therefore Boss Croker, the most powerful politician in New York. He nominates, campaigns for and ensures the election of Abram S. Hewitt who assisted him during his murder charge. Hewitt reappoints him Fire Commissioner. Allegedly, he is quite poor at this time (see 1893).
1888	Mayor Hewitt refuses to review the St Patrick's Day parade in New York. Richard, therefore, nominates Hugh J. Grant and has him elected Mayor. Grant appoints Richard to the $25,000 p.a. sinecure of City Chamberlain.
1890	*A Senate Committee on Cities Pursuant to Resolution Adopted 20 January 1890* (The Fasset Investigation) begins investigating corruption in municipal appointments, contracting, police bribing, etc. Patrick McCann gives damning evidence against Richard, who is his brother-in-law. Richard tells the Investigation that he never kept a bank account.
1892	The moral clergyman, Dr Charles H. Parkhurst, shocks New York with a sermon he delivers at his Madison Square Church. Taking 'Ye are the Salt of the Earth' as his text he says, 'There is not a form under which the devil disguises himself that so perplexes us in our efforts, or so bewilders us in the devising of our schemes, as the polluted harpies that, under the pretence of governing this city, are feeding day and night on its quivering vitals. They are a lying, perjured, rum-soaked and libidinous lot.'
1893	Since 1886, Richard has invested $353,000 in racing property and horses and $80,000 in a Fifth Avenue home. He owns Park Row properties and draws high rents for municipal department offices. He pays generous fees to managers, trainers and jockeys and travels in an expensive car. Richard moves to Wantage, England and semi-retirement. But he tries to control Tammany Hall as an absentee Chief Sachem.
1894	The power of Tammany Hall is exposed in the findings of the Lexnow Investigation, inspired by Republican chief of New York State, Thomas C. Platt, and Dr Charles H. Parkhurst (see 1892, above), whose pulpit outbursts against vice perpetrated by Tammany had become vitriolic. A sixteen-year-old prostitute gives evidence of 'tight houses' (where women wear tights), brothels

and certain concert saloons where girls as young as thirteen are employed.

1897   Richard and Elizabeth enter into a separation decree. Richard returns to Tammany Hall, amid rumours that he was to run for the office to become the first Mayor of Greater New York. In the event, he secures the nomination of a subservient Robert A. Van Wyck, who is elected. Every office in the gift of the appointment goes to a Croker nomination. Richard receives adulation and attends prestigious social functions.

1898   Richard purchases a racing establishment at Wantage, England and a summer home, 'The Wigwam', in Palm Beach.

1899   The Mazet Investigation into patronage accuses Boss Croker. One of its findings claims that Richard and Tammany Hall wrecked the Third Avenue Railroad Company and sent it into receivership.

1901   Alfred Henry Lewis writes two books on Croker. *The Boss* is a novel, based on his life. *Richard Croker* is a hagiography in which the author places Richard alongside Napoleon in greatness. Croker tosses the book into the sea en route for Wantage in England, where he moves permanently with his fortune. Elizabeth seems to have spent a short time there but they then separate permanently. The English racing fraternity snubs Richard as the Jockey Club refuses him permission to train on Newmarket Heath.

1904-05   Richard purchases Glencairn, Co. Dublin, from Judge Murphy. He carries out extensive refurbishment in the baronial and American Colonial styles, amasses art treasures and is generous to his staff.

1905   Richard's son, Frank, dies after a car accident in Palm Beach. A few months later another son, Herbert, is found dead in a railway carriage between Emporia and Newton, Kansas. The Coroner's jury attribute death to narcotic poisoning caused by opium smoking.

1907   Orby wins England's Epsom Derby at odds of 100 to 9 against. The Irish Turf Club refuse Richard admission.

1908   Richard is presented with the Freedom of Dublin.

1914   Richard's wife, Elizabeth, dies. In the same year, on 26 November, at seventy-three years of age, he marries Bula Benton Edmondson, allegedly an Indian princess.

1915   The funeral of Jeremiah O'Donovan Rossa (1831-1915) arouses national sentiments. There are suggestions that Croker assisted the Irish struggle financially.

1916	Easter Week Rising in Dublin, leading to the War of Independence (1919-21).
1919	Richard and Bula move to Palm Beach. Three of Croker's children take an action against their father concerning ownership of stocks, shares and Palm Beach property. Claiming their father is senile, they attempt to prevent him leaving his fortune to Bula. Boss Croker wins the case but it takes its toll on his health. He pays his last visit to Tammany Hall, 'a very old man, but still amazingly sharp', according to Judge Edward McCullen, Secretary of the Tammany Society. On 12 October, Richard bequeaths 'all [his] property real or personal' to Bula.
1922-3	Irish Civil War.
1922	On 29 April, Richard Boss Croker dies in Glencairn with his wife by his bedside. He receives the rites of the Roman Catholic Church. The funeral Mass is celebrated in his Glencairn oratory. His pallbearers include Oliver St John Gogarty, 'Alfie' Byrne and Arthur Griffith. Covered with a blanket of violets and a card with the inscription 'To Daddy from Bula', the casket is interred in a vault in the grounds of Glencairn by the lake. Later, it is reinterred in Kilgobbin Cemetery, Sandyford. A headstone also bears the name of Croker's housekeeper, Stella Bowman (d. 1914).
1923	Richard Croker Junior is plaintiff in a case against the late Boss Croker's widow, Bula, that opens at the Law Courts, Dublin Castle (due to the previous year's bombing of the Four Courts) on 31 May. The plaintiff seeks to have his father's will condemned. Boss Croker's daughter, Edith, testifies that Bula was the 'reputed wife' of Guy Marone, an Italian tailor living in Canada when she married Boss Croker. After twelve days the special jury finds in Bula's favour on all counts, with Richard Junior liable for costs. The Lord Chief Justice condemns the outburst of applause that greets his announcement of the verdict.
1963	On 27 June, in the Roll of the Freemen of Dublin, a name is engraved alongside Richard Croker's. It is John Fitzgerald Kennedy.

ACKNOWLEDGMENTS

This book belongs to Tim Walsh, who commissioned it and whose inspiration, dynamic enterprise and generous support made it possible. While researching and writing it, I enjoyed the hospitality and company of Tim and his charming wife Maxine. Their thoughtfulness, during a minor health setback restored my faith in human nature. I thank them sincerely. Tim also had the gallant support and encouragement of Howard Davies in pursuing the project.

I thank Donn, Susan and Kelli Barrett of Portland, Oregon, for helping with research and for performing miracles by hunting down rare books and documents. Eithne Sax, despite pending surgery, carried out valuable research for me in New York, as did Ray Ginnell, who discovered a rare pamphlet I was seeking.

Chancellor Hannon assisted with Palm Beach research. Although blind, he painted from memory a fine picture of the Croker residence there. Richard and Gay Brabazon galloped me around an unfamiliar horse-racing world in Ireland.

Ireland's librarians again gave tremendous assistance, notably Dr Máire Kennedy and her excellent staff at Dublin Corporation's Gilbert Library; Tim Cadogan of Cork County Library; Mary, Tony, Carmel, Ita and Greta of Westmeath County Library and the staff of the National Library of Ireland. The staff of the National Archives gave every assistance, as did the staff of the Smithsonian Institute, Washington, and Cincinnati Museum in the USA, and Wantage Museum in England.

The British Ambassador, Her Excellency Veronica Sutherland, kindly permitted access to Glencairn, where Bridget Coffey showed me her superb archive and Jane Atkin conducted an informative tour of the grounds.

I thank Antony Farrell of Sitric Books for his encouragement and Sarah Deegan and Frieda Donohue for their editorial expertise, patience and diligence. Thanks, too, to Maureen for reading the manuscript, pointing out problems and later carrying out painstaking proof-reading. She gave me tremendous encouragement and took countless phone messages and faxes. Aisling and Niamh helped with word-processing, and reading, too. Sir Mort Clark, Professor Emeritus at the State University of New York, Valhalla, read the MS from a New York perspective. He also offered useful comment. Compute-IT, Mullingar came to my rescue when needed at short notice.

Finally, I also thank Liam Collins and the *Sunday Independent*, Brigadier General Jimmy Flynn, Christy and Marie Davis, Carmel Henry, Patrick Cronin, Tony Hartnett, Emer Mortell, Pat Nolan of Hamilton Osborne King and others who helped in tracking down photographs.

Above: Quartertown House, Mallow, Co. Cork, home of Eyre Coote Croker's father. (Tim Walsh)

Left: Balliva House, near Clonakilty, Co. Cork, birthplace of Richard Croker. (Tim Walsh)

Below: Emigrants on the quay at Cork. (*Illustrated London News,* 10 May 1851)

Irish squatters in Central Park, New York, c. 1869. (*An Illustrated History of the Irish People* by Kenneth Neill, Gill & Macmillan, Dublin 1979)

Statue of Saint Tammany
above an early Tammany Hall
location. (*Richard Croker* by
Alfred Henry Lewis, Life
Publishing Company, New
York 1901)

Tammany Hall. (As above)

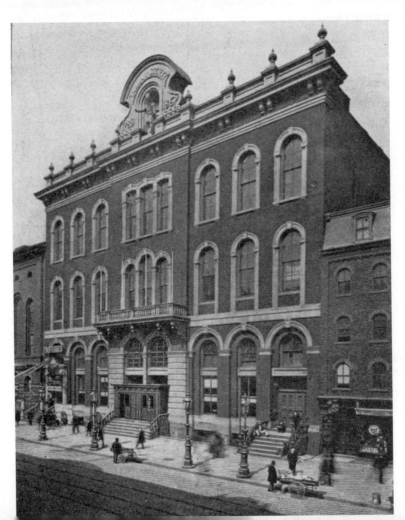

Richard Boss Croker. (The S.S. McClure Company, 1901)

His office at Tammany Hall. (*Richard Croker* by Alfred Henry Lewis, Life Publishing Company, New York 1901)

New York Harbour with Brooklyn Bridge in foreground. (*New York Journal,* 3 May 1896)

Wantage Cartoon. (*Tammany Hall* by M. R. Werner, Garden City Publishing Company, New York 1928)

Antwicks Manor, Berkshire, England. (Gerald Gadney, Vale and Downland Museum, Wantage)

Glencairn, Co. Dublin. (Hamilton Osborne King, Dublin)

Boss Croker's Orby, winner of the Epsom Derby, 1907. (Thoroughbred Bloodlines, Canada)

Richard Croker. (Sutherland Glencairn Archives)

Bula Edmondson. (Sutherland Glencairn Archives)

Richard and Bula at Palm Beach. (Sutherland Glencairn Archives)

THE HIGH COURT OF JUSTICE.

KING'S BENCH DIVISION (PROBATE).

Telephone 10 *Dundrum*
Telegrams Sandyford
Station Stillorgan.

Glencairn
Sandyford
Co Dublin

I Richard Croker of Glencairn Sandyford Co Dublin declare this to be my last Will. I hereby revoke all previous Wills made by me. I hereby bequeath & devise to my dear wife Bula Croker all the property real & personal which I may die possessed of or over which I may have any power of appointment absolutely. I hereby appoint my said wife Bula Croker to be the sole Executor of this my Will. In witness whereof I have hereunto signed my name this 12th day of October 1919

Richard Croker

Witness
John J McDonald
Solr
116 Grafton St. Dublin
Thomas J Fleming
13 Longford Terrace
Monkstown.

MR. CROKER'S ESTATE.

WILL CHALLENGED BY CHILDREN.

BIG LAWSUIT OPENED.

At the Law Courts, Dublin Castle, yesterday, before the Lord Chief Justice and a city special jury, the hearing opened of the case Croker v. Croker. The action relates to the will of the late Richard Croker, of Glencairn, Stillorgan, County Dublin, the plaintiff being Richard Croker, of New York, U.S.A., eldest son of the testator, and the defendant Mrs. Bula E. Croker, of Glencairn, widow of the testator. The plaintiff seeks to have condemned the will of the late Richard Croker dated 12th October, 1919.

Mrs. Edith White, a daughter of the testator, appeared as an intervenient, and, by permission of the Court, pleaded that the will had been obtained by fraud on the part of the defendant, the fraud alleged being that the defendant, Bula E. Croker, was the lawful wife of Guy R. Marone, to whom she had been previously married, and with whom she had lived as his reputed wife in Northampton, Mass., between September, 1911, and September, 1912, and in 1913 at Moncton, New Brunswick, Canada, and at other places.

Mr. Serjeant Sullivan, Mr. J. C. R. Lardner, K.C., and Mr. Kenneth Dockrell (instructed by Messrs. Montgomery and Chaytor) appeared for the plaintiff.

Mr. Jellett, K.C., and Mr. Hubert Hamilton (instructed by Mr. Valentine Miley) appeared for Mrs. Ethel White, the intervenient.

Mr. Serjeant Hanna, Mr. Patrick Lynch, K.C.; Mr. Sullivan, K.C., and Mr. Costello (instructed by Mr. H. B. O'Hanlon) appeared for Mrs. Bula Croker.

A copy of Richard Croker's last will. (National Archives of Ireland)
The Irish Times headline of 1 June 1923, reporting on the opening day of the lawsuit. (Gilbert Library, Dublin)